Praise for Muriel Jensen

"The very talented Muriel Jensen
has a definite skill for penning heartwarming
humorous tales destined to remain favorites...."
—*Romantic Times*

"Ms. Jensen has written an engaging tale
that draws the audience into caring what happens
to those citizens of Maple Hill."
—Harriet Klausner on *Man with a Mission*

"Muriel Jensen offers richly drawn romance
awash with energy and compelling conflict."
—*Romantic Times*

Dear Reader,

The editors at Harlequin and Silhouette are thrilled to be able to bring you a brand-new featured author program beginning in 2005! Signature Select aims to single out outstanding stories, contemporary themes and oft-requested classics by some of your favorite series authors and present them to you in a variety of formats bound by truly striking covers.

We plan to provide several different types of reading experiences in the new Signature Select program. The Spotlight books will offer a single "big read" by a talented series author, the Collections will present three novellas on a selected theme in one volume, the Sagas will contain sprawling, sometimes multi-generational family tales (often related to a favorite family first introduced in series) and the Miniseries will feature requested, previously published books, with two or, occasionally, three complete stories in one volume. The Signature Select program will offer one book in each of these categories per month, and fans of limited continuity series will also find these continuing stories under the Signature Select umbrella.

In addition, these volumes will bring you bonus features...different in every single book! You may learn more about the author in an extended interview, more about the setting or inspiration for the book, more about subjects related to the theme and, often, a bonus short read will be included.

Watch for new stories from Janelle Denison, Donna Kauffman, Leslie Kelly, Marie Ferrarella, Suzanne Forster, Stephanie Bond, Christine Rimmer and scores more of the brightest talents in romance fiction!

We have an exciting year ahead!

Warm wishes for happy reading,

Marsha Zinberg

Marsha Zinberg
Executive Editor
The Signature Select Program

MINISERIES

MURIEL JENSEN

THE MEN OF MAPLE HILL

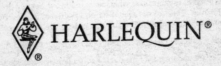

HARLEQUIN®

TORONTO • NEW YORK • LONDON
AMSTERDAM • PARIS • SYDNEY • HAMBURG
STOCKHOLM • ATHENS • TOKYO • MILAN • MADRID
PRAGUE • WARSAW • BUDAPEST • AUCKLAND

ISBN 0-373-21760-9

THE MEN OF MAPLE HILL

Copyright © 2005 by Harlequin Books S.A.

The publisher acknowledges the copyright holder
of the individual works as follows:

MAN WITH A MISSION
Copyright © 2002 by Muriel Jensen

MAN WITH A MESSAGE
Copyright © 2002 by Muriel Jensen

www.eHarlequin.com

Printed in U.S.A.

CONTENTS

Muriel Jensen is the award-winning author of over eighty books that tug at readers' hearts. She has won a Reviewer's Choice Award and a Career Achievement Award from *Romantic Times* magazine, as well as a sales award from Waldenbooks. Muriel is best loved for her books about family, a subject she knows well, as she has three children and eight grandchildren. A native of Massachusetts, Muriel now lives with her husband in Oregon.

MAN WITH A MISSION

CHAPTER ONE

HANK WHITCOMB STARTED backwards down the stairs in his office building, supporting one end of a heavy oak table that served as his desk. Bart Megrath, his brother-in-law, carried the other end.

"Whose idea was it to move your office anyway?" Bart asked. "And why is everything oak? Don't you believe in light, easy-to-clean plastic?"

"The move was my idea." Haley Megrath, Hank's sister, brought up the rear with an old oak chair. "If he's going to bid on City Hall jobs, he may as well conduct business from one of their new rental spaces in the basement instead of in this derelict old mill a mile outside of town."

Hank was counting. Twelve steps—eight to go. "It was my own idea," Hank insisted. Thirteen. Fourteen. "You just agreed that it was a good one."

"I'm the one who told you the City had decided to rent spaces."

"And when you told me, I told *you* that Evelyn Bisset had already called me about it."

"So, the suggestion had more punch coming from Jackie's secretary." Haley's voice took on a deceptively casual but suggestive note. He refused to bite. He would not discuss Jackie Bourgeois. He'd neither forgotten nor forgiven her. It was unfortunate that she was mayor at this point in time, but she was. Still, there was little chance they'd have to deal with each other. The city manager handled the bids on City Hall repairs, so Hank would be doing business with him.

"Hey," Bart said with a grunt. "Let Haley take the credit. Electrical power comes and goes in that ancient building, and the roof leaks. When the time comes that you regret moving Whitcomb's Wonders out of Chandler's Mill and into City Hall, you can blame your little sister."

"Hey!" Haley complained. "How'd you like an oak chair upside your head?"

Hank had reached the bottom of the stairs, but the hallway was too narrow for him to put the table down so they could catch their breath. He turned the bulky piece of furniture onto its side and aimed himself carefully out the door, angling the table so that Bart could follow with the legs at his end.

Snow flurried from a leaden sky, and Hank was instantly assailed by the cold of a western Massachusetts March afternoon, its harshness blunted by the delicious freshness of the air. Old snow crunched underfoot as he headed for the dark green van he'd bought to start his new life.

"Is this going to fit in there?" Bart asked, their pace considerably quickened now that they were outside.

"I measured it." A former engineer for NASA, Hank checked and rechecked even the smallest detail of any project he undertook. He put down his end, climbed into the van, then reached out to pull the table in. He'd removed all the van's seats to make room and now backed his way toward the driver's seat as Bart lifted up on his end and pushed the table under the hatch door.

It was a snug fit. Bart took the chair from Haley and slipped it sideways between the table legs.

"Is this it?" Bart asked. "We've got a little room under the table. What about those files you had in boxes on the floor?"

Hank climbed over the front seat and let himself out the passenger door. Bart and Haley came around the side. "No, I'll take those tomorrow. I've got to clean them out tonight. You guys go back to work and I'll meet you for dinner at seven at the Yankee Inn."

"I told you you don't have to take us out to dinner," Haley protested.

Bart had an arm around her and his thumb, Hank noticed, was unconsciously stroking the curve of her shoulder. In jeans and a fleece sweatshirt, her dark hair in one long braid and her cheeks pink from four hours of helping haul his office furniture up and down stairs, Haley looked about fourteen.

Bart had been good for her, Hank thought, though when he'd sent his friend to get her out of jail last August after a crisis on a space mission prevented Hank from leaving, he'd never imagined that his best friend and his little sister would fall in love. Haley still had the fearlessness that had encouraged her to challenge a crooked mayor and end up behind bars.

The sweetness she'd lost that fateful night five years ago when she and her fiancé had been attacked by thugs and he'd broken free and run, abandoning her to her fate, was finally back. Thanks to the timely arrival on the scene of an off-duty policeman, she'd been rescued, though not before she'd lost her faith in men. But Bart had restored it. Hank saw implicit trust in her eyes when she looked into Bart's face—as well as a hot, almost embarrassing passion that made Hank green with envy.

The lack of a personal life was part of the reason Hank had decided to come home to Maple Hill. NASA had hired him right out of the University of Southern California, and he'd spent the next fourteen years devoted to assisting in the exploration of space. One day six months ago, after he'd been up seventy hours when one of their space missions encountered a control problem, then finally landed safely, he realized he had no one to celebrate with. There were co-workers who understood the engineering problem and could share his happiness and relief that the astronauts were safely home. But there was no one who really knew what was in his heart.

He had girlfriends, party friends, who shared the intimacies of a bed without really caring about his thoughts and feelings.

He'd once believed that was freedom. Now he knew it was simply loneliness.

There was no one who knew about the warnings that filled his head—"You're not as good as you think you are. You'll fail just like the rest of us. But your high and mighty attitude will make you fall so far, you'll dig a hole when you land." No one who understood that every day was a struggle to live down the sound of his father's words. No one who grasped the depths of his relief every time he proved the voice wrong.

Fortunately, an interest in electricity, which he'd probably inherited from his father, led him to a summer job working with an electrician in high school, and apprenticeship summers while he was in college. When he'd decided to change careers, getting licensed had been a simple thing, and his hobby turned into his livelihood.

"I want to take you out," he insisted. "I couldn't have managed all this in one day without you. Make sure you bring Mike."

Mike McGee was a fifteen-year-old boy who helped Haley at the *Maple Hill Mirror,* the weekly newspaper she published. She and Bart had acquired custody of him when his mother went to jail.

"He's got an overnight with some friends from the basketball team. The kids are going to have a booth during the Spring Festival. The coach and his wife are hosting them this weekend so they can plan their strategy. Eleven fifteen-year-old boys. Can you imagine?"

He couldn't. Kids in general were not his forte. He liked them fine, he just thought every child deserved more tolerance and understanding than he felt capable of. They were mysterious little beggars, and he'd been an engineer. Specific rules applied to specific situations for specific results.

Even now that he was an electrician, the approach was the same. There was little mystery involved. If you held on to 120 volts, you fried. It was as simple as that.

"How are you going to unload this when you get to City Hall?" Bart asked, pointing to the table.

"Mom's there, straightening things up for him," Haley said with a grin. "She'll just order the table to get inside on its own power."

Bart laughed. "I can see that happening. But on the chance that doesn't work…"

"Trent promised to stop by and help me," Hank said, pushing the passenger door closed.

"Trent?" Haley asked.

"The plumber I hired yesterday. Seems like an all-right guy."

"And what's his story? Why is he joining your troupe of part-time tradesmen?"

"He's getting his MBA from Amherst, but wants to work part-time. Says school's too cerebral. He needs the hands-on work to stay grounded."

"You're sure you don't want me to do a story on Whitcomb's Wonders?" Haley asked for the fourth or fifth time. "It'd be good for business, and the public would love to know about a service that can fill any need out there at a moment's notice. How many men do you have now?"

"Seven." He didn't have to stop to think. He was surprised himself by how good his part-time help idea was. He'd started the business at the end of September, and by Christmas had employed five men who were surprised and pleased by the notion of working part-time while they pursued other careers, cared for their children, went to school. Evan Braga, a house-painter, signed on in January, and now Cameron Trent rounded out a pretty impressive roster. "We can do wiring, plumbing, landscaping and gardening, furnace repair, janitorial work, insulation and house painting. But I doubt that any of my guys is anxious for publicity."

Haley grinned. "It might get them girls," she cajoled.

He rolled his eyes at Bart. "Why is it they think we have nothing else on our minds?"

"Maybe because trying to guess what they want," Bart replied, "takes so much of our time and concentration."

Haley punched Bart playfully in the stomach. "I've told you over and over. Full-time attention and expensive jewelry."

Her wedding ring of pavé diamonds flashed as she punched him, and Hank concluded that Bart must have gotten the message. Or else he loved her so much that what he couldn't say with words, he spoke with diamonds.

"Thanks for the offer, sis," Hank said, walking around to the driver's side. Bart and Haley followed him. "I'll buy an ad instead to announce the opening of my new office."

"Oh, all right, I'll *give* you the ad." She hugged him tightly. "A good half page in the TV section so it'll be seen every day. Think about what you want in it. A photo of all of you would be good. We don't have to go into details, just let the town see you have a competent force."

"Okay. That sounds like a good idea. I'll see how the men feel about it." Hank shook hands with Bart, then climbed into the van. "See you at dinner. You're sure you wouldn't rather eat at the Old Post Road Inn? The menu's a little more elegant than the Yankee."

Bart opened his mouth, but before he could speak, Haley said, "The Yankee's great. I'm in the mood for their pot roast."

Bart sent him a subtle smirk over her head. She was as transparent as cling wrap. The Yankee Inn had been in Jackie Bourgeois's family for generations. Her father had retired two years ago, leaving her in charge. Haley wanted them to bump into each other.

"The Yankee it is," he said with a cheerful smile, pretending he had no idea what she had in mind. He'd studiously avoided Jackie for the six months he'd been home, afraid she'd see the feelings he couldn't control, even though she'd broken his heart all those years ago. He didn't want to care and never intended to do anything about it. He just couldn't help that he did.

He'd run into her by surprise on only two occasions—once in the dentist's office when he'd been walking out and she'd been walking in with two very grim-looking little girls in tow. He knew they were her daughters. Erica was ten, his mother had told him. And Rachel was six.

The second time was at the grade school when he'd been called in to replace a faulty light switch in the cafeteria. She'd been chatting cheerfully with other mothers who'd gathered there with classroom treats. He'd looked up at the sound of her laughter, startled and weirdly affected by the fact that though everything else about her had matured in the seventeen years since they'd been high-school sweethearts, that hadn't. It was still high-pitched and infectiously youthful.

He'd also noticed her pregnancy. Her stomach was bulbous, her cheeks a little plumper than he remembered. But her strawberry-blond hair had looked like Black Hills gold, her complexion porcelain with a touch of rose.

The moment her eyes had met his, she'd disappeared into the pantry area, the swift turn of her back coldly adult.

She had no use for him. Which was fine with him. He had no feelings left for the woman who had loved him as though he was her whole world one moment, then refused to share her life with him the next. If she was at the Yankee Inn tonight, he was sure she'd be as eager to avoid him as he was to stay clear of her.

Comforted by that thought, he turned the key in the ignition, waved at Haley and Bart, and headed off toward downtown Maple Hill.

He was amazed by how comfortable he'd felt coming home to this quiet little Connecticut River valley after being away for so long. If Jackie Bourgeois didn't live here, he thought, it'd be perfect.

Judging by outward appearances, very little had changed in Maple Hill in over two hundred years. Realizing that its cozy, colonial ambience was its stock-in-trade when tourists visited, the local merchants' association with the aid of City Hall had done everything possible to maintain the flavor.

The road to town was lined with old homes in the classic saltbox and Georgian revival styles and set back on spacious lawns, their trees now naked against the sky. Old barns housed businesses, and old inns had been refurbished.

Houses were built closer to the street as Hank drew nearer to town. Some of the cobblestones were still visible, and the streetlights looked like something out of Old London.

Maple Hill Common, the town square and the heart of commercial downtown, boasted a bronze statue of a Minuteman and a woman in eighteenth-century dress, surrounded by a low stone wall. Around the square were shops that looked much as they had in the 1700s. A 50-star flag and an old colonial flag with its thirteen stars in a circle flew from a pole on the green.

The sight never failed to move him. He felt connected to a historic past here, while bound to a town looking toward the future. You could buy a mochaccino, high-tech software and designer clothing, or sniff oxygen in a bar if you so desired. Maple Hill was quaint, but there was nothing backward about it.

Hank pulled into a parking spot on the City Hall lot, pleasantly surprised that it hadn't already been claimed. The spot next to his held a red Astro van and a sign that read, THE MAYOR PARKS HERE.

He turned off the engine and retrieved his key, annoyed that thoughts of Jackie interrupted his pleasant musings on the good life he lived here. But he'd better get used to it, he thought philosophically. He might not have to deal with her, but he was bound to run into her more often with his office in City Hall.

SUICIDE HAD SO MUCH APPEAL, Jackie Bourgeois thought as she put a hand to the rampaging baby in her womb. She would do it with a dozen Dulce de Leche Häagen-Dazs bars, pots of *caffeinated* coffee and several bottles of Perrier-Jouët champagne—all the things she hadn't been able to touch since she'd found out she was pregnant.

She'd have to wait until the baby was in college, of course. Responsible women simply didn't walk away from their problems. The Yankee ethic wouldn't allow it.

By the time the baby was eighteen, Erica and Rachel would be married and able to provide for him when he came home on school breaks. They wouldn't even miss her. They were all convinced her sole purpose in life was to make them miserable anyway.

Her father loved her, but he'd made his life without her and the girls since her mother died several years ago. He'd bought a place in Miami and often forgot to check in with his family as he embarked on new adventures.

And two of the city councilmen wouldn't miss her, except as someone to accuse of feminine ignorance or heartless female highhandedness, depending upon which complaint best suited their current disagreement. At the moment she was a harpy for renting space in the basement, a capitalist venture they considered beneath the dignity of city government.

Holding on to the railing, Jackie made her way carefully down the basement steps, checking on the city's two new tenants as a way of avoiding the councilmen blustering upstairs.

City Hall was housed in an old colonial mansion that had been built after the Revolutionary War by Robert Bourgeois, an ancestor of Jackie's late husband. City offices were on the first floor, the mayor's office and meeting rooms were upstairs, and local events were hosted in the old ballroom. The basement had been cleaned out and redecorated after a hurricane last summer left it water damaged, and Jackie and Will Dancer, the city planner, had come up with a plan to rent office space there to help support the aging building's many repairs. Will's office had handled the actual rental of space and Jackie had been too busy with other city affairs to find out who'd secured them.

She peered into the first office and found it chaotic, a sort of examining bed, an odd-looking chair, a file cabinet painted lavender and several pieces of brocade furniture clumped in the middle of the room. There were boxes on the floor filled with what was probably the contents of the file cabinet, and several framed landscapes leaned against the wall.

"Hi!"

Jackie almost jumped out of her skin at the high-pitched greeting. She turned to find a tall, slender woman perhaps a few years older than she, dressed in lavender leggings and flats and a long-sleeved lavender T-shirt. A wide purple band circled her carroty hair and was caught above her left ear in an exaggeratedly large bow.

"Mrs. Mayor!" the woman said breathlessly, offering her hand from under a large box she'd apparently just brought in from the side entrance. "How nice to meet you. I'm Parker Peterson."

"Hi." Jackie shook her hand and wanted to try to help her ease the box to the floor, but her pregnancy allowed very little bending at this stage. The woman seemed to have no trouble handling it on her own, a taut line of arm and shoulder muscles revealed by her snug shirt.

She straightened and put one hand on her hip and the other up to fluff her bow. "What a good idea this is! I'll be right in the thick of the stress and strain of business life. These poor nine-to-fivers are my client base, you know."

Jackie looked a little worriedly at the curious couch, the odd chair and Parker Peterson's flamboyant style of dress. She was almost afraid to ask. "What is it you do, Ms. Peterson?"

Parker gave the odd little chair a pat. "I'm a massage therapist. Here. Sit down and put your head right here." She fluffed the small cushion on the funny arm sticking out in front of the chair. "You straddle it like a horse."

Jackie patted her stomach. "We're not very athletic these days."

"It doesn't really take much effort. Here, I'll help you." She steadied Jackie's arm as she spoke and encouraged her to lift her foot to the other side of the stool-like chair.

Jackie would have continued to resist, except that Parker had put her hand to the small of Jackie's back as she spoke and rubbed her fingertips at the base of her spine where the pressure of five or six pounds of baby and fifteen or so pounds of "support" sat twenty-four hours a day. The relief was instant and melted her protests.

"We need to loosen up your back muscles," Parker said. "That's it. Feel that? Gotta prevent that tension or you'll be miserable until you deliver. A couple of weeks?"

"About a month and a half," Jackie replied, unable to believe she was a pile of jelly in this woman's hands after two minutes' acquaintance. She was usually very much aware of her dignity as mayor—not because she was pretentious, but because her council was always looking for something about her to criticize.

And she had to pretend to the town that though her husband had died in the arms of a cocktail waitress after promising Jackie he was rededicating himself to their marriage and their two children, he hadn't humiliated *her*, but embarrassed his own memory. And she liked to think that the pregnancy that had resulted from that promise was a testament to her trust.

The baby stirred as though also appreciating the massage.

Parker's hands went up Jackie's spine and down again with gentle force.

"You have to stop," Jackie said weakly, her voice altered by her cheek squashed against the pillow and the total relaxation of her now considerable body weight. "I have a meeting in fifteen minutes. You'll have to roll me in on the chair."

Parker laughed as her fingertips worked across Jackie's shoulders. "You'll have to come and see me when you need a break. I'm good, I'm reasonable and I'll give special rates to anyone who works in the building. I'll be here from eight to six."

Parker stopped working and helped Jackie to her feet. "Isn't that better?"

Jackie did feel as though ten pounds had been removed from her stomach.

"Watch that posture," Parker advised. "And drink your milk. You have a husband to give you foot rubs?"

"I wish," Jackie replied, then realized that she didn't really. Foot rubs would be nice, but hardly worth the anguish a husband could inflict otherwise.

"Me, too. So, you're having this baby alone?"

Jackie concluded that Parker had to be new in town. "I was widowed right after I got pregnant. But this is my third, so I kind of know what I'm doing."

"That's nice," Parker said wistfully. "I know all about pregnancies—what to eat, how to exercise, how to massage to relieve strain and pressure. But I've never had the experience. Two husbands but no baby."

"I'm sorry." Men weren't always worth the time devoted to a marriage, but children were. "I'll bring mine by to meet you," Jackie said with a grin. "Then you might think you've had a lucky escape."

Parker walked her to the door of her office.

"My purse is in my…" Jackie began, pointing upstairs.

"That was free of charge," Parker insisted. "Just tell

your friends I'm here. I'm taking out an ad in the *Mirror*, but it won't come out until next Thursday."

"I will. And good luck. If you have trouble with heat or plumbing or anything, let us know."

Parker promised that she would, then waved as she went back to the side door, apparently to retrieve more boxes.

Jackie rotated her shoulders as she passed the two dark and empty spaces. She'd have to find a way to work a massage into her daily schedule.

She turned a corner and walked down a small hallway that led to the last office. The hallway was dark, she noted. She would have to see that a light was installed overhead.

She peered into the only office on this side of the building and was stunned to see a figure she knew well standing in the middle of the room and looking around with satisfaction at what appeared to be a well-organized office.

"Adeline!" Jackie exclaimed, walking into the office, her arms open. "What are you doing here?" Adeline Whitcomb was her best friend's mother and the girls' Sunday School teacher.

"Jackie!" The gray-haired woman with a short, stylish cut and bright blue eyes went right into Jackie's arms. "I didn't have a chance to tell you I was moving into City Hall."

Jackie looked around as they drew away from each other. There were file cabinets against the wall, a map of the city tacked up on one side, a large one of the county on the other. A small portable bar sat under the city map, with a coffeepot on it and a box from the bakery. A low table held a cordless phone atop a phone book. A quilt rack took up considerable space in one corner of the room.

"Are you going into business, Adeline?" Jackie asked, knowing that Addy's skills as a quilter were legendary. She'd made one for each of Jackie's girls when they were born. "Have you found a way to make quilting profitable?"

Adeline looked amused by that suggestion. "As if," she said, then lowered her eyes and looked away for a moment, as though uncomfortable holding Jackie's gaze.

Jackie had a horrible premonition. "This is Hank's office," she guessed.

Adeline smiled and sighed, as though she'd suddenly made up her mind about something. "It is. I'm tidying things up while he moves things in. And the quilt rack is here because I'll be his office staff and help organize all the men."

Jackie's horror was derailed for a moment. "*All* the men? Does he have partners?"

"No. I thought you knew he started Whitcomb's Wonders." Adeline went on to explain about the on-call service of tradesmen and craftsmen Hank had started. If anyone had told her, she hadn't listened. She automatically tuned out when his name was mentioned.

"You know, he's been back in Maple Hill for six months, Jackie," Addy went on. "It's time you two stopped pretending the other doesn't exist."

Great. The ten pounds Parker's massage had alleviated were now back with a vengeance and, against all anatomical good sense, sitting right in the middle of her shoulders. She started to back toward the door. She would never deliberately hurt Adeline, but she would avoid crossing paths with Hank at all costs.

"It's great that you'll be here," she said diplomatically. "Maybe you and I can have coffee or lunch."

"It's childish and nonproductive," Adeline said, ignoring Jackie's invitation. Exasperation was visible in her eyes. "You're going to be in the same building. You have to come to terms with this."

"We've come to terms with each other, Addy." Jackie put both hands to her back, the pressure there tightening at the very mention of Hank's name. "We like pretending the other doesn't exist. Then we don't have to remember the past or deal with each other in the present."

"You were children when all this happened," Adeline reminded her. "Certainly you can forgive each other for behaving like children."

Jackie closed her eyes tightly against the image her brain tried to form of that time. She didn't want to see it. There'd certainly been grave and very adult consequences for the actions Addy considered childish.

"Just wanted to welcome you to the building," Jackie said, stepping out into the hall and turning to force a smile for Addy. "If there are any problems with the space, please call."

Addy sighed dispiritedly. "I will, Jackie. Thank you."

Jackie headed back the way she'd come, eager now to get upstairs. With Hank Whitcomb occupying office space in the basement, this would no longer be the place to hide from her councilmen.

In the dark corridor before she made the turn, she collided with something large and hard in the shadows. She knew what it was even before firm hands grabbed her to steady her.

Could this day get any worse? She drew a breath and cloaked herself in mayoral dignity. "Hello, Hank," she said.

CHAPTER TWO

HANK KNEW HE'D COLLIDED with Jackie even before he heard the sound of her voice. Her scent was different, but she was using the same shampoo she'd used seventeen years ago. The collision brought her cap of red-blond hair right under his nose, and the peach and coconut fragrance filled his senses with memories he'd kept a lid on for most of his adult life.

He saw her slender and naked in his arms, her gray eyes looking into his as though he controlled the universe. He saw her laughing, her eyes alight. Then he saw her crying, her eyes drowning in a misery to which he'd hardened his heart.

Why had he done that? he wondered now, as though he'd never considered it before. Then he remembered. Because she'd taken all their dreams and thrown them away.

He felt a curious whisper of movement against his hipbone and suddenly all memories of her as a girl vanished as he realized that her rounded body was pressed against him. For an instant he entertained the thought that if things had gone according to plan all those years ago, this would be his baby.

But the intervening years had taught him not to look back.

Aware that he held her arms, he pushed her a step back from him, waited a moment to make sure she was steady, then lowered his hands.

She hadn't had this imperious manner then, he thought, looking down into her haughty expression.

"Jackie," he said with a quick smile. If she could behave like cool royalty to show him she didn't care about their past, he would be friendly, to prove that he held nothing against her, because it had never really mattered anyway. "How are you? I wanted to talk that day we met at the dentist, but you were in such a hurry."

She looked as though she didn't know what to do for a moment. He liked seeing her confusion. The day he'd left Maple Hill, she'd made him think *he* was wrong, and that had confused him for a long time. Payback was satisfying.

She folded her arms over her stomach, then apparently deciding that looked too domestic, dropped her arms and assumed a duchess-to-peasant stiffness.

"I'm well, thank you," she replied. "I just came to welcome you to City Hall."

"I appreciate that." He smiled again, taking her arm and trying to lead her back toward the office. "Mom's in…"

She yanked her arm away, her duchess demeanor abandoned in a spark of temper. She caught herself and drew another breath. "We've already talked," she said politely. "I told her if you have any problems, to let us know."

"Shall I call you?" he asked, all effusive good nature.

Her eyes reflected distress at the thought, though she didn't bat an eyelash. "No, Will Dancer will be taking care of tenants. Extension 202."

He nodded. "We've been in touch a couple of times about updating the building's wiring with circuit breakers."

"We can't afford to do that," she said.

He shrugged a shoulder. "It'll reduce your insurance on the building. Dancer thinks it's a good idea. And I'm pretty reasonable."

He realized the opening he'd given her the moment the words were out of his mouth.

"Really," she said, old pain furrowing her brow. "That's not the way I remember it."

He didn't understand it. It had been all her fault. So why did the pain on her face hurt him?

She turned and started to walk away.

He followed, determined to maintain the I-don't-care-it-doesn't-matter pose. "I meant," he said calmly, "that I provide a good service at a reasonable price."

"Well, that's what the city would be looking for," she said, steaming around the corner, past the other offices and toward the stairs, "if we could afford to do such a thing. But Will Dancer notwithstanding, we can't."

She turned at the bottom of the stairs to look him in the eye. "I hope you didn't move your office here in the hope of securing City Hall business."

He liked this part. "I *have* City Hall business," he said, letting himself gloat just a little. "Dancer hired me to replace all the old swag lamps with lighted ceiling fans. He also invited me to submit a bid for rewiring."

She'd always hated to be thwarted. Curiously, he remembered that with more amusement than annoyance.

"Just stay out of my way," she said, all pretense dropped and her finger pointed at his face.

He thought that a curious threat coming from a rather

small pregnant woman. It suggested black eyes and broken kneecaps.

He rested a foot on the bottom step, his own temper stirred despite his pose of nonchalance. "I know it's probably difficult to grasp this," he said, "when you've been prom queen, Miss Maple Lake Festival and all-around darling of the community, but you don't control everything. I am free to move about, and if that happens to put me in your way, I'm sorry, but you'll have to deal with it."

Angry color filled her cheeks. "I do run this city hall." Her voice was breathless in her apparent attempt to keep the volume down. "And if you get in my way, I can get your bid ignored so fast you won't know what happened. And I can also see that no other city business comes your way *ever!*"

It was almost comfortable to fight with her again. This was familiar ground. "You're sounding just like the mayor you and my sister helped replace. The one who got too full of his own importance and eventually stole hundreds of thousands from the city and held the two of you at gunpoint? You remember? The one who's still doing *time.*"

She sighed and rolled her eyes. "You don't see me holding anyone at gunpoint, do you? And I don't need anyone else's money."

"You just threatened to arbitrarily deprive me of my livelihood. I'm sure Haley, as the city's watchdog, would have to look into such behavior."

She didn't seem worried. "Your sister is my best friend. I doubt very much that she'd come out on your side."

"She's a reporter before she's a friend, and I am her brother."

Her voice rose to a shout despite all her efforts. "Then keep your distance and don't give me any excuse to get rid of you!"

"You got rid of me," he reminded her, "seventeen years ago."

"Who left whom?" she demanded.

"We were *supposed* to leave together."

For an instant, emotion flashed in her eyes. He tried hard to read it but he was out of practice. Had it been…regret?

"Something unexpected…" she began, and for some reason those words blew the lid off his temper. Probably because they reminded him of what she'd begun to say the night he'd left—alone. *Hank, on second thought, it might be better if you went alone, and I…*

He hadn't let her finish. He remembered that he'd been so sure all along that such a thing would happen, that Jackie Fortin was never going to be his. He was sure she'd find that his father had been right all along and Hank was worthless.

"Yeah, you tried to tell me that then, too," he barked at her. "You expected me to fail, didn't you? And you didn't want to leave all your crowns and tiaras behind to take a chance with me."

IT WOULD BE SO SATISFYING to kick him in the shin, Jackie thought. But Parker and Addy had wandered out into the hallway at the sound of raised voices and now stood a short distance away, looking on worriedly. When Jackie finally did take her revenge on Hank, she didn't want witnesses.

Besides, much as she hated to admit it, even to herself, it hadn't been all his fault. She should have tried to make him listen, insisted that he understand, but she'd been frightened and hurt, too. And brokenhearted.

She was very tired suddenly and her back felt as though sandbags hung from it. "I think you have me confused with your father," she said softly, so that Addy wouldn't hear. "You wouldn't listen to my explanation then, so I doubt you'd want to hear it now. If you'll excuse me, I'll get out of *your* way."

But she couldn't climb the stairs until he moved.

He considered her a moment, his anger seeming to thin, then caught her arm and drew her up on the step beside him. "Come on," he said. "I'll walk you upstairs."

She wanted to tell him that she walked up and down stairs all day long. That was the price of occupying a building that had been constructed before elevators. But he looked as tired of their argument as she felt, so she kept quiet.

With his large hand wrapped around her upper arm, he led the way upstairs. The space was a little tight, but she did her best to ignore him. She didn't realize until they were almost at the top that she wasn't breathing. The baby, apparently convinced he was being strangled, gave her a swift kick in the ribs.

"Aah!" she gasped, stopping to give herself a moment to recover. This baby had Van Damme's skill at *Savate*.

"What?" Hank asked worriedly.

"Just a kick," she said breathlessly, rubbing where she'd felt it.

"Why don't you sit for a minute?" Without waiting for her compliance, he pushed her gently until she was sitting on the stair above them. "Are you sure you should be working in this condition?"

"It's pregnancy," she replied, a little unsettled by what appeared to be genuine, if grudging, concern, "not infirmity. I'm fine."

"You're pale."

"I can't help that," she retorted. "You're very annoying. Preventing myself from punching you is taking its toll."

A reluctant smile crossed his face as he studied hers. "It would be a lot for a woman who wasn't pregnant to run a hotel and a city while raising two children."

He used to do that when they were going together and she remembered that it made her feel very protected. In the middle of a dance or a drive or a game of tennis he would stop to look at her, and always gave her the impression that if he saw something wrong, he would remedy it.

Considering her embattled position as mayor, her ten-year-old having trouble in school, her six-year-old turning into a sometimes fun, but often worrisome wildchild, Jackie enjoyed the momentary fantasy of someone wanting to solve her problems, or at least being willing to help shoulder them.

She saw him note the brief lowering of her defenses and quickly raised them again. She caught the banister and pulled herself up—or tried to. The baby provided ballast that sometimes refused to move when she did.

Hank took her elbow in one hand and wrapped his other arm around her waist—or where her waist would have been if she'd had one.

"Steady," he cautioned. She felt the muscles of his

arm stiffen and was brought to her feet on the step. "Careful until you get turned around."

He held her securely until she faced the right direction, and kept his hold the rest of the way.

At the top of the stairs in a small hallway off the home's original kitchen, which was now the small but comfortable employee lounge, a tall man blocked the doorway and reached a hand down to help Jackie up the last step. He wore jeans and a blue down vest over a red sweatshirt. She'd never seen him before.

"Hi, Hank," he said as he nodded courteously to Jackie, then freed her hand. "I was just coming down to help you with the desk."

"Just in time." Hank cleared the stop of the stairs, and Jackie found herself sandwiched between the two men. "Jackie, I'd like you to meet Cameron Trent," he said. "The newest addition to my staff. He's a plumber. Cam, this is Her Honor, Mayor Bourgeois."

Cameron offered his hand and Jackie took it, liking his direct hazel gaze and his charming confusion. "What do I call you, ma'am?" he asked. "Your Honor? Mrs. Mayor?"

"Ms. Mayor seems to be the preferred greeting in the building. But Jackie will be fine outside. Are you new to Maple Hill?"

"I'm from San Francisco," he replied. "I came here to get my master's at Amherst and to see a little snow."

She laughed lightly. There'd been snow on the ground in Maple Hill since early December. "Are you tired of it yet?"

"No, I'm loving it."

"Good. Well, good luck with your degree." She

turned her attention to Hank, unsettled by their meeting and the knowledge that she could run into him at any moment from now on. "Hank," she said, unsure what to add to that. "Welcome to the building."

There was a wry twist to his mouth, as though he suspected she didn't mean that at all. "Thank you, Ms. Mayor. I'll see you around while trying very hard not to get in your way."

She gave him a brief glare, smiled at Cameron Trent, then turned and walked away.

"PRETTY LADY," Cameron said as he followed Hank down the stairs. "Shame about her husband."

When Hank turned at the bottom of the stairs, surprised that a newcomer knew about Ricky Bourgeois, Cameron nodded. "I came in July to find a place to live, and his death was in the paper with a story about how his family helped establish Maple Hill."

Hank remembered Haley sending him the clipping. She'd been discreet about how he'd died, just said that he'd been away on a business trip when he'd suffered a heart attack. He hadn't found out the truth until he'd moved back home.

"You'd think," Cameron went on, "that a man would value a classy lady like that."

Yeah, you would, Hank thought. Cussedness and arbitrary last-minute changes of her mind aside. He led the way out the back door to the parking area where he'd left his van.

"Nice rig," Cameron said. "I used to have one like it, but sold it to help pay my tuition." He pointed across the lot to a decrepit blue camper with a canopy. "That's mine."

"Whatever gets you there and back." Hank opened the rear door of the van. "Give me a minute to get around the side of this thing and push it out to you."

"Right."

They carried the table in without incident, Adeline directing them through the office door to a spot against the wall where she'd hung a map of the city. Hank introduced her to Cameron.

She shook his hand, studying him appraisingly. "Hank, if you're no longer interested in Jackie, maybe we can fix her up with Cameron."

Cameron smiled politely, but Hank saw the panicked glance he turned his way. "Thanks, but I'm a happy bachelor," he said.

"Nonsense," Adeline said. "How can a bachelor be happy?"

"No woman in his life," Hank replied intrepidly, knowing it would earn him retribution. "Yourself excluded, of course, but women just complicate a man's existence."

"Without a woman in your life, it is just that," she argued. "Existence, not life. Though some men never come to appreciate us."

"I like my simple life," Cameron insisted.

And Hank decided he really liked the man.

The telephone rang as Hank placed it on the desk.

"Hey!" he said, reaching for it. "They connected it while I was gone. Whitcomb's Wonders."

"This is the Old Post Road Inn," a panicked female voice said. "The top off one of the kitchen faucets just shot off and I've got water spewing everywhere. *Please* tell me that one of your wonders is a plumber!" Then she shouted to someone at her end of the line, "The cut-off valve! Under the stairs in the basement! The *hot* water one!"

Hank held the phone to his chest and raised an eyebrow at Cameron. "Do I have a plumber? You weren't supposed to start until Tuesday."

"An emergency?" Cameron asked, coming toward him.

"Sure sounds like it. At the Old Post Road Inn. In the kitchen. Top off a faucet, water everywhere."

Cameron headed for the door. "I'm on it."

"We've got a man on the way," Hank said into the phone.

The woman groaned. "I love you," she said, and hung up.

"All right." Hank turned off the phone and reached for the daily log hanging on a hook beside the map. "Business is picking up and we're not even completely moved in." He noted Cam's destination and checked his watch for the time. "Any other calls?" He hung the log back on its hook and turned to his mother.

She pushed a cup of coffee into his hand. "You should have gotten one," she said with an air of disgust. "But you didn't."

He knew the disappointed look meant he'd failed morally, somehow. But she was making some maternal point he wasn't quite getting. He knew he played right into her hands when he asked, "What call?"

"Your wake-up call!" she said emphatically. "What is *wrong* with you? How can you shout at a poor pregnant woman? And the mayor to boot! And the woman you once told me you loved more than your own life?"

He went across the room for his office chair and carried it one-handed to the desk. "She shouted first," he objected, realizing how absurd that sounded even as he said it. "And our love for each other died long ago. She married someone else, had his children…"

"And was miserable every moment."

"I can't help that." He didn't like to think about it, but it wasn't his fault. "She chose to stay."

"Maybe at the time," his mother said more quietly, "she thought she was being wise."

"She had an unhappy marriage." He rummaged through a box for his blotter and the family photos he kept on his desk. "And I had a successful career. Which one of us was right?"

"You can't always judge that by how things come out," she answered.

He looked up from the box to meet her gaze in disbelief. "How do you judge the right or wrong of an action if not by its result?"

"Maybe by the number of people hurt."

"Then her staying should go down as a disaster." The items located, he rose and carried them to the desk.

"Her parents were happy she stayed."

"How could they have been? She went to Boston for two years."

"Well, that wasn't California, where the two of you had planned to go. They had a hope of seeing her once in a while." She came to stand beside him while he centered the blotter on the desktop and placed the photos behind it. There was one of him and Haley and their parents on a trip to Disney World, all of them in Mickey Mouse ears. His father looked grim. He'd never had much of a sense of humor. Then there was Haley's graduation photo, and one of her and Bart on their wedding day. He was supposed to have moved home the day before, but he was still in Florida when the wedding took place, sick as a dog with the flu in an empty apartment. He'd insisted they not hold up the wedding.

"I just think you need to make peace with this," his mother said in the same voice she'd used to talk him out of his sulks when his father had been on him. "It happened. You both made your choices, and for better or worse, you've lived with them. Now you're going to be running into each other on a regular basis and it'll be easier in the long run if you just come to terms with it. And you could be a little nicer."

He remembered clearly how he'd felt that night when he'd had to leave without her. He'd been only eighteen, but there'd been nothing young about his love for her. It had been full and mature with roots she'd ripped right out of him.

"She cut my heart out with a trowel, Mom," he said, hating how theatrical the words sounded. But they did convey the feeling.

Adeline shook her head at him and reached for her coat. "Well, she must have, because you certainly don't seem to have one at the moment. I'm going out for scones."

"Thanks." He handed her a bill from a drawer on the coffee bar. It served as the petty cash safe. "Get one for Cameron in case he checks back in before going home."

She glowered at him and he added as an afterthought, "Please." When that didn't seem to appease her, he tried, "Thank you."

She sighed and walked to the door, turning to say

grimly, "Well, at least you learned 'please' and 'thank you.' I'll be right back."

If she were kidnapped by aliens, Lord, he prayed, falling into his chair to soak up the moment's respite, *friendly ones, you know, that play bingo and have ibuprofen and mentholated rubs readily available, I could deal with it. She'd be happy. I'd be happy. No, I know. No such luck. I have to learn to cope with her. And with seeing Jackie regularly, too, I suppose. Fine. But just wait until St. Anthony's needs a microphone for the Blessings Blow-Out auction. See what happens then.*

Hank opened the single drawer in the table to retrieve his Palm Pilot when the room fell into complete darkness.

He sat still, experiencing a sense of foreboding. Faulty ancient wiring, he wondered, or God responding to being threatened?

CHAPTER THREE

JACKIE INSERTED HER KEY in the lock on the front door of her home two blocks from downtown, grateful that her assistant manager had all the night shifts at the inn this week. She anticipated a cozy dinner with the girls and a peaceful evening. That did happen more often than not—at least, it used to—but she knew the moment she opened the door and heard screeching voices that it wasn't going to happen tonight.

She heard the baby-sitter's quiet efforts to calm the girls. They seemed to be having no effect.

With a wistful wish for a different life—any other life, at least for tonight—Jackie dropped her coat and purse on the nearest chair and hurried toward the kitchen, where the melee was taking place.

"I can't *believe* you did that!" Erica was shrieking at Rachel, who faced her down stubbornly, bony arms folded atop a flowered dress Jackie had never seen before. The fabric looked familiar, though. "It was *mine*!" she said, her voice high and shrill and almost hysterical.

Ricky had been a casual father at best, sometimes attentive but more often unaware of his children, caught up with the pressures of his work and his own needs. But the children, of course, had grieved his loss. Erica had turned from a happy, cheerful child to a moody one. Rachel seemed less affected personally, except that she wanted details about death and heaven and didn't seem to be satisfied with Jackie's explanation. "Mom bought it for *me!* You're such a selfish little brat! I *hate* you, *hate* you!" With that Erica flung herself at Rachel.

Jackie ran to intercept her just as Glory Anselmo caught Erica from behind and held her away. Glory was in her second year at Maple Hill Community College's computer classroom program. She played volleyball in her spare time and was built like a rock. A very pretty brunette rock.

"Erica Isabel!" Jackie said, pushing Rachel aside with one hand while catching one of Erica's flailing fists with the other. Erica was dark-featured, tall and slender, built like her father's side of the family. Rachel was petite like Jackie, and blond. Both seemed to have inherited personality traits from some long-lost connection to the Mongol hordes. "Take it back."

"I won't! Look at what she did to my pillowcase!"

"I made it beautiful!" Rachel extended her arms and did an end-of-the-runway turn. That was when Jackie realized she'd cut a hole for her head and two armholes in Erica's pillowcase, the one patterned with cabbage roses and violets, and was wearing it like a dress. She'd added a white silk cord that also looked familiar.

Jackie groaned. Glory, she could see, was having a little difficulty keeping a straight face. It *was* funny, Jackie had to admit to herself, if you weren't the one required to make peace.

Glory caught Jackie's expression and sobered, still holding on to Erica. "I'm sorry, Mrs. Bourgeois," she said. "I should have checked on Rachel. She was being really quiet."

Rachel, who had brains beyond her years and an almost scary sense of style in everything she did, said, "I was quiet 'cause I was…what's that word for when you get a really good idea and you just have to do it?"

"Inspired?" Jackie guessed.

Rachel smiled widely, delighted that she understood. "That's it!"

"Well, I think you should be inspired to give Erica *your* pillowcase," Jackie ruled. "It's fine to be inspired, but you don't try out your designs using someone else's things."

"Please." Erica clearly loathed the idea. "It has pigs and ducks on it. I think she should clean my room for a year!"

"No way!" Rachel shouted.

"Then she'll pay you the amount of the pillowcase out of her savings," Jackie arbitrated, "so you can buy a new one."

Rachel pouted. She was also frugal.

The tension eased somewhat, Glory freed Erica's arms.

"Now take back the 'I hate you,'" Jackie insisted.

Erica looked her mother in the eye. "But I do hate her."

That cold-blooded admission might have chilled someone who hadn't seen Erica defend Rachel from the neighborhood bully who'd tried to take Rachel's candy bar just two days ago. The fact that Erica had demanded half the candy bar in payment for her protection didn't really figure into it. Rachel understood commerce.

"No, you don't." Jackie touched Erica's hot cheeks. She was a very physical child and touch usually soothed her.

"You're just too young to understand the difference between frustration and hatred. What's our rule about hate?"

Erica gave her a dark look but repeated dutifully, "We can hate things, but not people."

"So?"

"So, I take it back," Erica conceded ungraciously, "but if she messes with my stuff again, even if I don't hate her, I'll…" She hesitated. Jackie also had rules against violence or threats of violence. "I'll let Frankie Morton take all her candy!" Frankie Morton was the bully.

Rachel ran upstairs in tears.

Jackie grinned over Erica's head at Glory. "Want to stay for dinner? Promises to be eventful."

Glory acknowledged the joke with a nod. "Thanks, but I'm meeting a friend."

"It's a guy friend," Erica informed Jackie. "They met at the library. But tonight he's taking her to dinner."

Jackie was happy to hear that. Glory worked so hard that she seldom had time for dating. "Anyone we know?"

"I don't think so," Glory replied, gathering up her things off one of the kitchen chairs. "His name's Jimmy Elliott. He works for Mr. Whitcomb. He's a fireman and fixes furnaces when he's off."

"Oh." The mention of Hank's name darkened her already precarious mood.

Glory, purse over her shoulder and books in her arms, asked worriedly, "Is that bad?"

"Of course not." Jackie walked her to the door. "He and I just don't get along very well."

"You and Jimmy Elliott?"

"Hank Whitcomb and I. He's just moved his office into City Hall."

"Oh. That's a relief. I really like Jimmy."

"Well, have a wonderful time."

Glory stopped in the doorway. "One more thing," she said, handing Jackie a folded piece of paper, her tone sympathetic. "This is from Erica's teacher. I didn't read it, but Erica says Mrs. Powell picks on her because she's having trouble paying attention."

A note from school completed the destruction of Jackie's flimsy attempt at a good mood.

She went back into the kitchen to ask Erica about it, but Rachel had just returned with her ceramic savings bank shaped like a castle with a blond princess in the tower. She knelt on a chair at the table, her eyes and the tip of her nose red from crying. "How much was the pillowcase, Mom?" she asked.

Jackie sat down opposite her, trying to remember. It had been part of the package with two sheets and the bedcover. Erica had been feeling blue, she remembered, and objecting to the childish decor of her room, done when she'd been about five. New bedclothes had seemed the simplest and quickest solution.

"It was on sale," Erica said, pulling silverware out of the drawer to set the table, her nightly chore. "The whole set was eighty dollars. I remember 'cause I thought it would be too much. But the lady said it was half price."

Encouraged by Erica's assistance, Jackie asked, "Then how much would you say one pillowcase would be?"

Erica came to the table and sat, the silverware in hand. "The bedspread would probably be half, don't you think?" she asked, her mood lightening fractionally.

"That sounds reasonable."

"So…" Erica closed her eyes, concentrating. "That

leaves twenty dollars, and the sheets would probably be three-fourths of that. So...that leaves five dollars for the pillowcases."

Rachel pulled the rubber stopper out of the bottom of her bank and reached in with little fingers to withdraw bills. Change tinkled to the tabletop. She counted four singles, then asked Erica, "Four quarters in a dollar, right?"

"It was two pillowcases for five dollars." Erica fell against the back of her chair in disgust. "You only wrecked one."

The disgust with her sister was a habit, Jackie knew. But this burgeoning willingness to be fair gave her hope after all.

"What's half of five?" Rachel asked, her expression also brightening somewhat.

"Two-fifty," Jackie replied. "Two dollars and two quarters."

Rachel handed over the money. "I'm sorry."

Erica snatched it from her. "Just leave my stuff alone."

"And?" Jackie encouraged.

"And I won't let Frankie Morton steal your candy."

Jackie's hope wavered. *"And?"* she repeated.

Erica looked at her perplexed, then asked uncertainly, "Thank you?"

"Yes!" Success at last. How often did a mother get to repair an argument and provide a lesson in math and morals all at the same time? "I'm proud of both of you. You fulfilled your responsibilities," she praised, hugging Rachel, "and *you...*" Erica tried to evade her embrace, but Jackie caught her and wrapped her in a fierce hug. "You were generous in victory and didn't gloat."

As Erica hugged back, the baby gave a strong kick.

Erica straightened away from her, brown eyes wide with awe. "It kicked us!" she said, putting a hand with purple fingernails to the spot.

"Probably just wanted in on the hug."

Rachel ran over to touch also, the three of them standing motionless and silent, waiting for another sign of life. It came with another strong kick. They looked up to share a smile.

Without warning, Erica's smile evaporated and she said with a sigh, "Pretty soon there'll be someone else to mess with my stuff."

Jackie refused to let Erica's change of mood dissolve her thrill of success over the pillowcase incident. She made a salad while microwaving spaghetti sauce from the freezer and boiling noodles, and chatted happily over dinner about nothing in particular.

While Rachel related a long and complicated story involving the lizard in the terrarium in her classroom and its shed tail, which someone had put in Mrs. Ferguson's purse, Erica caught Jackie's eye and smiled hesitantly.

Jackie smiled back, sure that before she knew it, Erica would be a teenager and they'd be at loggerheads all the time.

Or she could get lucky. Some mothers did. Evelyn, Jackie's secretary, had three daughters in their early teens, and they seemed to love not only each other, but their mother as well. With her own lively and interesting but contentious girls, Jackie envied Evelyn her family's closeness.

But Jackie was never lucky. She was blessed in many ways, but never lucky. Her victories were all hard-won.

Erica helped Jackie clear the table while Rachel took her bath.

"Are you gonna yell about the note?" Erica lined up three cups next to a stack of plates while Jackie sorted silverware into the dishwasher's basket. She went back to the table without waiting for an answer.

"Difficulty concentrating isn't exactly delinquent or disruptive behavior," Jackie replied, dropping the last spoon in. She didn't look up but felt Erica's glance of surprise. "But it's not very good for grades. Are you thinking about Daddy? It takes a long time to get over the death of someone you love."

Mrs. Powell's note had admitted as much but expressed concern that Erica's inability to concentrate seemed to be worsening rather than improving.

Erica put the butter and the fresh Parmesan in the refrigerator and went back to the table to collect their place mats and take them to the back porch to shake them out.

She returned and set them on the table. "I used to at first, but I don't much anymore." She came back and stood beside Jackie, leaning an elbow on the counter. "I mean, he kind of liked us, I guess, but he didn't really seem to miss us when he was gone, then it seemed like he was always anxious to be gone again after he came home. That's kind of weird for a dad, isn't it?"

"He loved you girls very much." Jackie kept working, afraid that if she stopped and made the discussion too important, Erica would withdraw. "Grandpa Bourgeois never showed Daddy much affection when he was little. The only time he spent with him was to show him around the mill and to teach him how the company worked. Some people have to be shown how to give love, and no one ever did that for him."

"You did," Erica said. "He didn't notice though, did he?"

Jackie was astonished by that perception. "No, I don't think he did." Now she couldn't help but stop, realizing this was important. "But when I came along, your father was an adult. Sometimes adults don't learn as well as children."

"Is that why he was with that lady in Boston when he had the heart attack?"

Erica asked the question so directly that she must have known the truth of her father's death for some time.

Jackie felt shocked, breathless.

"I heard Mrs. Powell and the principal talking about it when I brought in the permission slip so Glory could start picking us up from school."

"You mean…after I became mayor? You've known for that long?"

Erica nodded. "I think everybody knows. A lot of people look at us like something bad's happened. Not just Daddy dying, but something that isn't fair. Like they look at you when you're in a wheelchair. Like they don't want to hurt your feelings and they're pretending they don't notice, but you know they're really glad they're not you."

"You should have told me," Jackie said, touching Erica's arm, waiting for withdrawal and relieved when it didn't come.

"You couldn't fix it," she said sensibly. "He was gone. But why do you think he did it?"

Jackie struggled for the right answers. "I think," she began carefully, "that when someone doesn't love you when you're little, your heart is always empty and looking for love, and sometimes doesn't even recognize it when it gets it. So it keeps looking."

Erica shook her head. "Didn't that hurt you?"

"Well…" Jackie felt curiously embarrassed, as though Erica was judging why she'd stayed in a loveless marriage all those years. "It did hurt me, but maybe not as much as you'd think. Because I understood how he was. And being married to him gave me you and Rachel, and the two of you are absolutely everything to me."

Erica frowned. "And the baby."

The baby. Erica seemed to be ambivalent about the baby, excited over the feel of a kick one moment, then unhappy about its eventual arrival the next.

"What is it you don't like about the baby coming?" Jackie asked directly.

Erica looked guilty.

"You can tell me," Jackie encouraged. "Are you afraid the baby is more important to me than you are?"

Erica shifted her weight, looking down at the floor. "No," she said. It had a convincing sound.

"That it'll get more attention than you?"

"No."

"That it'll change everything?"

Erica heaved a ragged sigh then looked up, her eyes pooled with tears, her lips trembling. "Mom, what if *you* die?"

"What?" Jackie couldn't help the surprised outburst.

"Well, what if you do?" Erica demanded in a tearful rush. "Nobody expected Daddy to die and he did. And you're at risk!"

Jackie took Erica's hand and led her back to the table, where she pushed two chairs together and lowered her onto one. "What do you mean, 'at risk'? Where did you hear that?"

"Sarah Campbell's mom's a nurse. She was talking about it with Mrs. Powell at the Valentine's Day party at school. Mrs. Campbell brought treats." Erica drew an anxious breath. "All ladies over thirty are at risk of stuff going wrong when they have babies 'cause they're really too old. You should only have babies when you're young."

Caught between the need to calm her daughter and the personal affront at being considered "old" at thirty-four, Jackie focused on soothing Erica.

"Honey, that just means that they take special care of you if you're over thirty. Sometimes there's a problem, but most babies and mothers come through the delivery safe and sound. And I'm not old enough to be that much at risk anyway."

"Are you sure?" Erica looked worried. "You're not as old as Grandpa or Addy Whitcomb, but you're pretty old."

And feeling older by the moment, Jackie thought. She went to the counter for a tissue and brought it back to Erica. "My last checkup at the doctor's proved that the baby is growing perfectly, and I'm healthy as a horse. There is nothing to worry about."

Erica swiped at her eyes and dabbed at her nose. "We didn't know there was anything to worry about with Daddy."

"That was a heart attack. My heart's fine. My checkup was perfect, remember."

"What would happen to us if you died?"

Jackie accepted that as a legitimate question and was grateful she was prepared for it. "When Daddy died and I found out I was pregnant, I put it in my will that if anything happened to me, you and Rachel and the baby would go and live with Haley."

Erica brightened. Jackie tried not to be offended. "Really? And that's okay with her?"

"Yes. And her new husband, too. She talked about it with him when they got married."

"Wow."

"Yeah. So there's nothing to worry about. Now, you're not going to bump me off so you can go live with Haley, are you?"

Erica smiled—finally. "No. I was just worried. Brenda Harris's dad left when she was little, then her mom died in a car accident, and she's lived at a whole bunch of different places and hasn't liked any of them. All the houses have different rules and new people you don't know. I'd hate that."

"So would I." Jackie leaned forward to wrap her in a hug. "You don't have to worry. I've got everything looked after."

Jackie felt the strength of her daughter's return hug. "Okay. Thanks, Mom."

"Sure."

Erica went upstairs to do her homework and Rachel came down to report that she was bathed. She stood in footed pink pajamas patterned with black-and-white Dalmatian puppies.

"When I'm grown up," she said, dragging a stool over from the lunch bar that separated the kitchen from the dining room, "I'm going to wear one of those floaty nightgown things with the feathers around the neck and the bottom." She had a predilection for "floaty things" that was fed by Glory's love of old movies from the thirties and forties where the women wore glamorous nightclothes.

"I like those, too," Jackie admitted, closing the door on the dishwasher and setting it to run. "How was your day?" she asked, wiping off the counters.

"Pretty good. Things are kinda dull in first grade. How was your day?"

Jackie rinsed off the sponge, squeezed it dry and propped it up behind the faucet. "Well, things are never dull at City Hall. Some new tenants moved into the basement offices today. One of them is a man the city just hired to take care of our electrical repairs. And his mom is going to work in his office some of the time, and guess who she is?"

"Who?"

"Mrs. Whitcomb."

Rachel smiled. She loved Addy Whitcomb. "Does she do electric stuff?"

"No. She's just going to answer the phones, take messages."

"Erica's not so mad at me anymore," Rachel said, abruptly changing the subject.

"You shouldn't have cut up her pillowcase. But it was good that you paid her for it."

"I just didn't think pigs and ducks would make a neat dress like the roses. Your plain blue ones weren't very good either."

Jackie frowned at the knowledge that one of her pillowcases had been considered.

The chiming clock in the living room sounded seven, time for Rachel's favorite television show about castaway children on a tropical island. She leaped off the stool. "Gotta go, Mom. *Castaway Kids* is on!"

Jackie replaced the stool, looked around her tidy, quiet kitchen, and said a prayer of gratitude that though the evening had begun in crisis, they'd managed to turn it around. Another family miracle.

It was a fact of life, she thought, that raising two little girls was often more difficult than running a city of four thousand.

HANK DROVE HIS MOTHER HOME after dinner at the inn, grateful that Jackie hadn't been working tonight. Running into her once had been all his good humor could handle.

Fortunately the electrical problem he'd encountered at City Hall this afternoon had been simply a blown fuse caused when his massage-therapist neighbor plugged in a faulty microwave. Once he'd found his flashlight, then the fuse box, the problem had been easily solved.

"I've got a girl for you," Adeline said.

The problem of his mother was unfortunately less easily dealt with than electricity. Unlike other mothers, she didn't beat around the bush or try subterfuge to fix him up with a date. She'd once brought a pizza and the daughter of a friend of hers to his apartment and left them there.

"Doris McIntyre's niece is visiting for a couple of

weeks from New York," his mother said, "and she needs someone to show her around Maple Hill."

"Mom, she can see it in a two-hour walk. One hour if she doesn't go to the lake."

"Hank, don't be difficult." She folded her arms and looked pugnaciously out the window at the dark night as they drove down the two-lane road to the lake. "I'm not getting any younger and I have yet to have one grandchild. Not one. Everyone else in the Quincy Quilters has at least one, most of them several. Bedelia Jones has eleven. I have none. Zero. Zilch. Na—"

"I got it, Mom," he interrupted. "But I'm single. Shouldn't you be speaking to Haley and Bart about giving you grandchildren? They've been married six months. Let them give you something to brag about at your quilting sessions."

Adeline made a face. "They're *waiting*." She imbued the word with disappointment.

"For what?"

"They didn't say, I didn't ask."

"So I'm the only one you interrogate?"

"You're my firstborn."

"That means I inherit everything you've got. It doesn't mean you're allowed to harass me."

"Is wanting you to meet a good girl and settle down harassment?"

"No, but trying to pick her for me is."

"I'm not picking her for you," she insisted, apparently affronted that her good intentions were so misunderstood. "I'm helping you find some potential candidates. You don't seem to be working toward it at all."

"I'm building a business."

"I'm going to be seventy in ten years!"

He laughed outright. "Mom, that doesn't have any-thing to do with anything. Right now you've just turned sixty. And a youthful sixty. Relax. There's lots of time."

There was a moment's silence, then she asked gravely, "What if I told you I was dying?"

His heart thumped against his ribs and he swerved to the side of the road, screeching to a halt. "What?" he demanded.

"Well, I'm not," she said, tugging on her coat collar, clearly feeling guilty for having startled him, "but what if I was? Am I to go to my grave without ever holding a grandbaby in my arms?"

Hank put his left hand to his face and rested the wrist of the other atop the steering wheel. "Mom," he said, "I'm going to drive you to your grave myself if you ever do that to me again!"

"I was trying to make a point," she huffed.

"The point is you sometimes act like a lunatic!" He checked the side mirror and pulled out onto the road again, his pulse dribbling back to normal. "I'm trying to build a business, Mom. Relax about grandchildren, okay?"

"I'm thinking about you."

"I'm fine."

"You're alone."

"I like it that way."

He turned onto the short road that led to her drive-way, and drove up to the house. He pulled to a stop and turned off the engine. He always walked her up the steps and saw her inside.

"I thought you came home because you realized that

while you loved your work for NASA, you didn't have a life. It was all future and no present."

He jumped out of the van, walked around to pull out the step stool he kept for her in the back, then opened her door and placed the stool on the ground. He offered her his hand. "That's true. And I'm enjoying my life here. I just need a little time to get all the parts of it together. Be patient, Mom."

She stepped carefully onto the stool, then down to the driveway. After tossing the stool into the back of the van, he took her arm to walk her up the drive.

"You're not still trying to prove something to your father with the business, are you?" she asked. "I mean, you were an engineer at NASA. You don't have anything else to prove. You don't have to expand Whitcomb's Wonders until you have franchises all over the country and appear on the big board."

He opened his mouth to deny that he was trying to prove anything, but he knew that wouldn't be true. Every time he did anything, he could imagine his father watching him, finding fault.

"He always tried hard," she said, squeezing his arm, "and he did well, but everything was difficult for him. Then you came along, all brains and personality, and he couldn't help resenting that. I know I've told you that a million times, but I sometimes wonder if you really understand it. He loved you, he just resented that you were smarter than he was, that things would be easy for you."

"I worked liked a dog to end up at NASA."

"I know. But some people work hard all their lives and never get anywhere. He had dreams, too, but he never got out of that little appliance repair shop."

Hank remembered that his father had little rapport with his customers and slaved away in the back room, taking no pleasure in his work.

"Anyway," Adeline said, "sometimes old insecurities can come back to haunt us when we're trying something new, or reaching for something we're not sure we should have. You deserve to be happy, Hank. And if you won't reach for that happiness, I'm going to keep working on it for you. So, when can you see Laural McIntyre?"

Hank drew himself out of moody thoughts about his father to the present and the urgent need to get out of meeting the visitor from New York.

"Actually, I'm meeting Jackie on Saturday," he said, walking his mother up the porch steps.

She brightened instantly. He could see her smile in the porch light. "You are? Where?"

"Perk Avenue Tea Room."

She looked puzzled. "Where?"

"It's a new coffee bar, tearoom, desserty sort of place on the square." She didn't have to know that they'd be "meeting" because Jackie was cutting the ribbon for the grand opening, and he was helping with the wiring for the sign, which wasn't expected to arrive until late Friday night.

His mother studied him suspiciously. "You were fighting the last time I saw you together."

He nodded. "But you didn't see everything. I ran into her later, we talked, and…I'm seeing her next week." A slight rearrangement of the truth, but the truth all the same.

"Well, see now, that wasn't so hard." She gave him a quick hug. "Will you tell me all about it after?"

"The shop, yes," he said. "Jackie, no."

She shrugged, seemingly undisturbed. "I'll just ask the girls at Sunday School. Thanks for dinner, sweetie."

"Sure, Mom." He ran down the steps as she closed and locked the door.

Great. Jackie's girls were in his mother's Sunday School class. She'd mentioned that once, but he'd forgotten.

When he'd been a kid, she'd had spies everywhere. It had been impossible to see a girl, cruise downtown, or sneak a beer without someone reporting him to his mother.

It was annoying that he was thirty-five, and nothing had changed.

CHAPTER FOUR

HE MET HIS MOTHER'S SPIES on Saturday. He'd been working at Perk Avenue for several hours when the crowd began to gather out front for the ceremony. He'd turned the sign on and it glowed brightly, a tall cup of neon mocha complete with a swirl of whipped cream standing beside a fat teapot. Underneath, the name of the shop was written in elegant neon script. The whole sign appeared to sit atop a triangle of neon lace.

The two matrons who owned the shop applauded their approval then wrapped their arms around him.

Hank went back inside as several people in the gathering crowd came forward to congratulate the women. He was collecting his tools when the front door burst open and a little girl in a flared red coat and matching hat ran in. Long straight blond hair fell to her shoulders. In her gray eyes was a desperate look. He recognized her as Jackie's youngest. He studied her one brief moment, realizing that except for a slight difference in the shade of her hair, this was what Jackie had looked like as a child.

"Hi," he said finally, coiling a length of wire. "Lost your mom?"

She shook her head, looking left, then right.

He took another guess. "Bathroom?"

She nodded.

He pointed to the little alcove directly to the right of the door.

"Thank you!" she called as she ran off in that direction.

A moment later, a child he recognized as the little one's older sister walked in wearing a pink coat but no hat. She had thick dark hair caught at the side of her head in a ponytail. This child must take after her father. His mother had told him Jackie's girls were Erica and Rachel. He couldn't recall which was which.

She surveyed the room, then her dark eyes fell on him in concern. A child taught to be wary of strange men. Jackie was doing her job.

He pointed to the alcove behind her. "Your little sister's in the restroom," he said.

She started away, then turned to ask, "How did you know she was my sister?"

"I know your mom," Hank explained. "And I've seen the two of you with her."

"Are you her friend?"

"Ah...not exactly."

"You don't like her?"

Tricky question. "Actually, she doesn't like me very much."

"How come?"

She was beginning to remind him of her mother even if she did look like her father. She had a compulsion for detail.

How did one explain to a child about a bright love affair that had been halted abruptly by one lover's reluctance to follow the other? You didn't, of course.

"We had an argument a long time ago," he replied, "that we never really fixed."

She frowned at that. "Mom never lets me and Rachel fight without making up."

Aha. This was Erica.

"Adults probably get madder than children," he said. "So quarrels are harder to fix."

The little one ran out of the bathroom, hat slightly askew. Erica straightened it for her. "This is Rachel," she said.

He nodded. "And you're Erica."

She smiled and came forward to shake his hand.

"I'm Hank Whitcomb," he said, thinking her social skills were as polished as her appearance. He wiped his hands on a cloth out of his box before taking hers.

"Our mom's the mayor!" Rachel said with a wide smile, also offering her hand. "We're supposed to smile and be polite!"

Erica gave her a mildly impatient look. "He knows who we are. He's a friend of Mom's."

"I thought Mom just had friends who were other ladies."

WHILE THE WIDE WHITE RIBBON for the ceremony was still being stretched across the front of the shop, Jackie ran in search of her girls. She was sure they were fine, but bathroom runs never took this long. She'd thought a quick trip inside the shop would be the quickest solution to Rachel's second glass of milk that morning. After all, the café wasn't really open yet and there was no one inside. Erica had followed her sister in.

But a mother's trepidation filled her anyway as she

pushed the door open, knowing that safety should never be presumed, that it only took a moment for…

Her heart lurched in her chest at the sight of her girls in conversation with a large man in jeans and a chambray shirt. His clothes were streaked with dirt, his hair…

He looked up at that moment, blue eyes noting her presence. It was Hank. Sudden awareness of him took her by surprise.

She'd never seen him at work before. The other times she'd run into him, he'd been in street clothes. Even the day he'd moved his office into the City Hall basement, he'd worn a respectable sweater.

But he was a little grubby now, work clothes well-fitting but mussed, his dark hair disturbed from its usually neat side part and falling onto his forehead. A longing that was decidedly sexual curled around inside her and embarrassed her with its intensity.

To further confuse her, she saw enjoyment in his eyes, as though her daughters delighted him. That pleased and flattered her and, along with this sudden desire completely inappropriate to a woman in her eighth month of pregnancy, threw her completely off balance.

She was about to scold the girls for speaking to a stranger when Hank interceded.

"They did nothing wrong," he said gently, as though he understood and respected her concern. "Rachel ran in looking for the restroom and there was no one else around. I just told her where it was. Then when Erica came in, I told her where to find her sister."

"And he's not a stranger, Mom," Erica said, going to her. "He's your friend. Even though you guys never made up after the fight."

Jackie opened her mouth to reply to that, wondering just what he'd told them about their relationship, but decided it was all too entangled.

"There's a party here after the ribbon-cutting," Erica said to Hank. "You can sit at our table, so you and Mom can work it out."

Jackie turned to her in astonishment.

"You don't let me and Rachel stay mad," Erica insisted. "And let's face it, Mom. You don't have that many friends."

Jackie couldn't help the gasp of indignation. "I do, too." She ignored the childish sound of her own words. "I have lots of friends."

"But none of them are guys."

"I…" Jackie stopped abruptly when she noticed the amusement in Hank's eyes. "Anyway," she said in a more controlled tone, "Mr. Whitcomb's working. I'm sure he can't—"

"Bridget and Cecilia, the owners of the café, invited me," he interrupted with a slightly smug smile. "I'll be back after I've showered."

Rachel hooked her arm in his. "You can sit next to me if Mom's still mad at you. Are you, Mom?"

Rachel waited for an answer. Hank did, too, his smile expanding.

"I was never angry," she said a little stiffly, forgetting that the girls were listening and focusing only on him. "I was hurt. Crushed, actually."

His amusement vanished. She expected him to accuse her of the same, but apparently unwilling to do so in front of her children, he simply said feelingly, "I understand, believe me."

The front door opened and one of the councilmen stuck his head in. "Ms. Mayor?" he called.

She pushed thoughts of the past aside as she'd done so often throughout her life, and pulled herself together. "Thank you for helping the girls," she said to Hank with stiff courtesy. "We'll see you at the party, then."

It was the usual city function. Two councilmen spoke about the city plan to create a commercial and economic environment that would encourage new business in Maple Hill. The other two spoke about the need to preserve and maintain the area's natural beauty while doing so. The city council was evenly divided on almost every subject.

Jackie's speech centered around Cecilia Proctor and Bridget Malone, sisters-in-law in their early forties who enjoyed each other's company and, now that their children were married or off to college, wanted to spend time together in a profitable endeavor. Each had been involved in community service for many years, so Jackie had the opportunity to praise them for all the time they'd devoted to the city and wish them luck in their commercial venture.

The community college's band played a few rousing numbers, then Jackie cut the ribbon, her daughters on either side of her. There was loud applause and everyone streamed into Perk Avenue.

Bridget caught Jackie's arm and led her to the dessert buffet set up at what would eventually be a long service counter. Jackie turned to make sure the girls were behind her, but saw that they were talking to Haley. Haley shooed Jackie on. "I've got them. Go."

Bridget directed Jackie to the head of the line already reaching out the door.

"If you hadn't fought for us," Bridget said, giving Jackie's shoulders a squeeze, "Brockton would have insisted on holding this spot for 'something that would have put the location to optimum use.'" She was clearly quoting. "Like a chain store or a fast food franchise. So you get to eat first."

John Brockton, one of the councilmen who fought Jackie's every move, had stood at the head of the line until Bridget placed Jackie there. He was short and small and balding, with sharp dark eyes. He smiled continually, but that seemed to contribute to, rather than soften, his poisonous personality. Jackie happened to know that John's brother's Cha-Cha Chicken franchise deal fell through when he learned he'd have to locate it on the highway rather than on the Square, the lifeblood of Maple Hill business.

"You don't mind, do you, Mr. Brockton?" Bridget asked with feigned innocence, aware of the animosity between them.

"Of course not," he replied for all to hear, then added for Jackie's ears alone when Bridget wandered off, "Ms. Mayor is a privileged person around here and gets whatever she wants."

Jackie could have laughed aloud at that claim, but chose to ignore it instead.

"But we're going to change that." The threat was quietly spoken and chillingly sincere. "You wait and see."

Then Cecilia, who was serving up sampler plates of gooey desserts, handed her one and engaged her in conversation. Jackie was forced to dismiss thoughts of John's retribution and focus on her job as mayor and this event's cheerleader.

Plate in hand, a glass mug of decaf mocha topped with whipped cream in the other, Jackie stepped away from the buffet and looked around for her girls in the small sea of well-wishers.

Then she spotted Rachel, head and shoulders above the crowd—literally. She knew a moment's horror. It would be just like Rachel to stand on a table to find her. Then she realized the child stood too high to be on a table. Jackie headed straight for her.

As she drew closer, she saw that Rachel sat on Hank's shoulders, looking very much as though she owned the world.

"Here, Mom!" she called, waving. "We're here!"

Jackie kept moving toward them, trying to ignore the sexy appeal of the man who held her daughter. He'd changed from his work clothes into casual gray slacks and sweater. His dark hair had been shampooed and combed into order. He looked like the good-twin version of the dangerous-looking man she'd seen that morning.

As Jackie approached, he lifted Rachel off his shoulders and set her down on her feet in the U-shaped booth he'd reserved for them. Rachel nimbly scooted into the middle of the booth, patting the place beside her. "Come on, Mom."

Hank held Jackie's plate for her while she put her mocha down, then he stood aside to let her slide in. He sat at the end of the booth beside Jackie. "Erica's with Haley," he reported. "They told us to hold the booth, that they'll get our plates. But Rachel and I are beginning to wonder if that was wise. Who can be trusted with all this delicious stuff?" He pointed to her plate.

"I can," she said, pretending an ease she didn't feel at all. She offered her plate to Rachel, who chose a little square of cake with lots of cream.

"Yum!" Rachel anticipated her first bite with a gleam in her eye.

"Hank?" Jackie offered him the plate.

After a moment of surprise, he selected a plain tube of a cookie with chocolate inside. "Thank you," he said.

"You're welcome."

They studied each other warily for an instant, then seemed to reach the mutual decision that this moment was meant for peaceful celebration.

He snapped the cookie in half with his teeth and made a sound of approval, then popped the other half into his mouth.

Jackie dipped a plastic fork into a brownie-like concoction covered with a white chocolate mousse and took a bite.

"This is to die for," she said, putting the fork into it again and offering it to Rachel.

It earned another "Yum!"

She scooped up a bit of the mousse, determined to appear unaffected by his nearness. Intending to hand him the handle of the fork, she turned his way. "Bite?" she asked.

His closeness stole her breath. He simply sat beside her, but his large body seemed to block out everything behind him, his arm along the back of the booth hemming her in, tightening her space.

Curiously, it was not an altogether unpleasant sensation.

"Please," he replied without making a move to take

the fork. His eyes told her he didn't believe she had the courage to feed him the bite.

Flustered and challenged, she did it before she could think twice.

His strong teeth closed around the little fork as he slipped the morsel off, watching her with mingled surprise and reevaluation.

"Here we are!" Haley appeared with Erica, then stopped in the act of placing their plates on the table, her attention snagged by Jackie, still holding the empty fork to the edge of Hank's lips. She looked from one to the other, obviously confused.

Jackie lowered the fork and turned back to her plate. "All right, you two," she said to Rachel and Hank as though they'd wrested samples from her. "The rest is mine." She dropped the fork on her plate and lowered her hand to her knee, hoping to hide its trembling.

Haley finally distributed plates and slipped into the booth beside Rachel, Erica sitting on the end.

Bridget arrived with a tray bearing a large pot of tea and several cups. "Here we are," she said, handing out cups and a big-handled mug for Hank. She hesitated over Hank's mug as she poured. "Is this going to be all right for you, Hank, or would you prefer something else to drink?"

The aroma of orange and cloves wafted around them from the steaming tea.

"This is fine," he said. "Thank you, Bridget."

"Good. I'll bring tiramisu as soon as it comes out of the kitchen." She picked up her tray, returned a wave to Cecilia across the room and left.

"What is that?" Rachel asked.

Jackie was beginning to feel more like herself, in control again and steady. "It's a cake soaked in Kahlúa, I think, and topped with whipped cream."

"What's Clua?"

She should have guessed that was coming.

"It's Kah-lú-a," she enunciated. "That's a coffee-flavored liqueur. It's alcohol. Sometimes people put it in their coffee or make other drinks with it."

Jackie was not surprised to learn she hadn't answered all her questions.

"If it tastes like coffee," Rachel asked, "why do they put it *in* coffee? Isn't that a lot of coffee?"

"It doesn't seem to be," she replied. "It tastes wonderful." Before Rachel could ask another question, Jackie forestalled her by pointing to a round cookie covered in powdered sugar. "Try that one next," she encouraged. "You'll love it."

Distracted, Rachel was mercifully silent as she ate.

"I love it here, Mom!" Erica held up a macaroon drizzled with chocolate. "Is this one of those coconut cookies?"

At Jackie's nod, she took a careful bite, then apparently finding its taste satisfactory, took a bigger bite. She wriggled in her seat while she chewed, her eyes focused on her mother, obviously about to make a statement.

After finally swallowing, she said eagerly, "When it's my birthday, can we have my party here instead of at the pizza place? My friends and I can all dress up and have pots of tea. I'm going to be eleven, after all."

"That's coming up, isn't it?" Haley asked. "March something?"

"Twentieth," Erica said. "And instead of seeing a movie we could do something more grown-up."

"Like housework?" Jackie teased. "Or go to the library?"

Erica made a face at her. "Funny, Mom. I was thinking maybe go to Boston shopping. Grandpa always sends me money for my birthday. Rachel has that float dress for Easter, but I don't have anything." She made her case to Hank. "I've grown two inches since September."

"Sounds like that requires a shopping trip to me," he agreed. "But when's the baby due?"

"Tax day," Haley replied for Jackie. "April fifteenth." She gave Erica a rueful smile. "I'm afraid your mom's not going to feel like walking all over Boston by that time." Then she turned to Jackie, her eyes bright with an idea. "But I could take Erica and her friends shopping. We could start with a tea party here, then you can go back to bed and I can handle the trip."

"Yeah!" Erica said eagerly. "That would work, wouldn't it, Mom?"

"It would work," Jackie agreed, turning to Haley with a smile, "if you brought along a unit of commandos or Legionnaires. When you're in charge of eight ten-year-old girls, you..."

"I'll be eleven then," Erica corrected.

"Eleven-year-old girls," Jackie continued, "you should have seasoned veterans with you, skilled in hand-to-hand combat."

"She can take Bart along," Hank suggested.

"Excellent idea." Haley slapped her hand on the table. "That's settled."

The crockery shook and everyone reached out to steady their cups.

"Sis, come on," Hank chided. "Let's not break the crockery on their first day of business."

"Sorry." She looked guilty and embarrassed. "I was overcome with enthusiasm."

They finished their treats, went through a second pot of tea, then Haley shooed Erica out of the booth. "Okay, we're off. I'm taking the girls back to the paper with me," she said. "I have some inserts to fold for the next edition, and they can be a lot of help to me. Don't worry about their good clothes. I'll put them in aprons. Hank, can you get Jackie home? She and the girls rode in with me."

Jackie frowned at her. "I thought we were all going shopping and to lunch?"

Haley shook her head, gathering up her things. "I couldn't possibly eat now, I'm stuffed!"

"I'll get her home," Hank said.

"But…" Jackie tried to protest the sudden turn of events, sensing a set-up. It was Saturday. She always spent her weekends with the girls.

Hank slipped out of the booth and stood helplessly by while she squirmed her considerable bulk sideways toward the edge of the booth. He tried to offer her a hand, but she waved him aside. "It's slow work, but I can do it," she said, already weary from the effort. "It's like getting the first pickle out of the jar."

Once she reached the end, he caught her arm to help her laboriously to her feet.

She finally stood, the energy expended draining her. "When did you all decide this?" Jackie asked.

"While we were in line." Haley wrapped an arm around each of the girls.

Jackie couldn't dispel the notion that there was some sort of plot underway here.

"Erica told me that the two of you met here to patch up your old quarrel." Haley looked into Jackie's eyes as she spoke, but seemed to be carefully avoiding her brother's. "We're just going to get out of the way so that can happen. I'm sure it'll be healthier for both of you to put that behind you." Haley consulted her watch. "It's ten-thirty. I'll have the girls home by one. Can you reestablish productive communication in two and a half hours?"

Neither Jackie nor Hank answered.

"Good," Haley said. "See you then. Come on, girls."

The three went off giggling, apparently pleased with their collusion.

"Since your sister solved her own problems and found love," Jackie said to Hank, "she's almost intolerable."

Hank placed an arm around her shoulders as a new influx of patrons pushed past them, headed for the buffet line. "She's always been intolerable," he said. "It was just never directed at you before. There's Bridget. Let's say our goodbyes."

He led her across the room, shielding her with an occasional body block to prevent her being jostled by the cheerful group.

Bridget wrapped her in a hug, then embraced Hank. "Are you two seeing each other?" she asked, looking from one to the other with new interest. She had to shout over the crowd to be heard.

Jackie leaned closer. "We were in high school together."

"Oh!" She seemed to like that notion. "Sweethearts who've rediscovered each other. I love that!"

Jackie wished her luck, thanked her for the VIP treatment, and promised to be back.

"Please do," she said. "We have a special dessert for lovers. Comes on one plate and requires two forks. Have a great day, you two. Thanks for coming."

Hank got them through the crowd, then outside. Jackie drew in a deep gulp of air. Her breath was visible on the cold air.

"I hate to leave the aroma of that place behind," she said, turning up her collar. "But I'm grateful for a little room to breathe. If they're that busy every day, they should be able to retire next year."

Hank studied her, his eyes knowing, and she realized he wasn't going to be sidetracked from a discussion of their past by her business predictions.

HANK SAW THE RELUCTANCE in her eyes and wondered if reverse psychology would work on her. As he remembered, nothing ever really "worked" on Jackie. Either she was in agreement with what he wanted to do about something, or she wasn't. If she was, her help brightened and simplified any project or pursuit. If she wasn't, she could be coolly detached while he struggled on, or deliberately obstructive, depending on how strongly she felt about the issue.

But he'd always believed that risking nothing got you nothing. So he tried it.

"Shall I take you home?" he asked. "The fact that Haley and the girls set this all up doesn't mean we have to cooperate. It was our decision to spend the rest of our lives disliking each other. We're entitled to that."

Her eyes had been focused somewhere over his shoulder while he spoke, but suddenly met his with the force of a clang he swore he heard.

She frowned. "Dislike." She repeated the word, seeming to analyze it while she lifted her shoulders and stretched her back as though it hurt. "You dislike me?"

Score! he thought, careful not to appear satisfied. "So, you *do* want to talk about it?" he asked, keeping all urgency out of his voice.

"No," she admitted with a deepening of the frown. "But I live with two little busybodies who'll ask questions, and I never lie to them. I also try to practice what I preach, and I never let them quarrel without trying to make it up as soon as possible." She gave him a disapproving look. "This never would have happened if you hadn't told them we'd fought all those years ago."

He accepted that responsibility. "I'm sorry. Your daughter was interrogating me and I couldn't lie to her either. She asked me if I was your friend, and I didn't think you'd want me to say I was. So when I explained why I wasn't, I kept it simple by just saying we'd quarreled."

She gave him an understanding nod. "Nothing's simple with children. You want to come to my house?"

"Sure," he replied casually, leading her toward his van.

He hauled out the stool he used to help his mother.

"Thank you," she said in pleased surprise. "I wondered how I was going to do this."

Yeah, me, too, he thought, silently congratulating himself on his brilliant tactics.

He had to know more about the impulse that had

prompted her to feed him a bite of that brownie-white chocolate thing. He'd never thought of food as particularly erotic, but that moment had been electric. In the years they'd been apart, he'd thought of her often, even fantasized that she'd come looking for him one day. Then anger over how much she'd hurt him would set in and he'd put those thoughts aside.

But he'd seen sexual interest in her when she'd fed him the dessert. She'd spent all the time after that pretending it hadn't happened, but she didn't know the man he'd become.

In his days with NASA, he'd outwitted weather and gone head-to-head with the rules of science. He was going to find out what was brewing in Jackie Fortin's heart.

CHAPTER FIVE

JACKIE'S HOME LOOKED just as he'd imagined it would. She lived in an old Victorian just a couple of blocks from town. It was painted soft yellow with pale blue trim and dark blue accents—the insides of the window frames, the fancy shingles, the front door. It had a full front porch with window boxes filled with ornamental cabbage—the only green that survived the winter in this part of the country.

Inside, one formal room flowed into the other. A front room, a parlor, a dining room, a sort of study she seemed to be using as an office. Though the rooms were set up formally with tall windows, bay windows and fireplaces, the furnishings were covered in floral chintzes, with lace and fresh flowers everywhere. It was definitely feminine and like a throwback to another time, but he was curiously comfortable in it.

In the study she pointed him to a light blue brocade settee. She removed the dark green wool jacket she wore to reveal the round-necked, long-sleeved dress in the same shade.

She went to the chair that matched the settee, kicked off her shoes and sat down, propping her feet on the matching ottoman. She let both arms fall over the sides of the chair and expelled an "Ahhhh!" whose relief he could feel himself.

He sat on the settee and angled one foot on the other knee.

"No, I don't dislike you," he answered, as though fifteen minutes had not elapsed since she asked the question.

"You said we'd decided to spend the rest of our lives disliking each other," she reminded him.

"We had," he interrupted. "And I did for quite a while. But I don't anymore."

"Why not?" she asked candidly, a wry smile in place. "I still have dreams of murdering you."

He wasn't sure he could analyze that. When he'd spoken to her the day he'd moved his office into City Hall after not having exchanged a word with her in seventeen years, his anger had come right back—hot and resentful. But despite his anger, he knew that the old feelings had survived. He hadn't wanted them so alive then, but now he understood that love that enduring deserved a future. And he had an agenda.

"I guess," he finally replied, "because I realize that it was all so long ago and we were so young. In relation to all that's gone on since, it hardly matters. You've been married and had children, and I've spent all that time in the rarefied atmosphere of space research. We're not even the same people we were then."

"No. We're not." There was a note of sadness in her voice, as though she regretted that. It came as no surprise. She was now alone in the world with two children, a baby due in six weeks and the lingering scandal of her unfaithful husband.

"My mother's organizing a group of women at

church to help you for a couple of weeks when the baby comes." That was really none of his business, but he felt called upon to tell her something cheerful.

She smiled fondly. "I know. She's been wonderful to me. She's the girls' Sunday School teacher, you know."

He smiled, too. "I know. She intends to use them to spy on our conversations. I told her we were seeing each other today, even though we weren't intending to actually speak."

When she raised an eyebrow, he went on to explain. "She's always trying to set me up with someone. This time it's the niece of a friend."

She looked amusedly concerned. "You shouldn't give her hope that something will develop between us because then she won't leave either of us alone."

"Hey," he said, unrepentant. "If I have to suffer through this, so do you. You're the one who changed your mind."

He hadn't intended that to come out. The mild censure had begun lightheartedly, but apparently traces of anger lingered.

She bristled instantly, sitting up and swinging her feet to the floor. "And you're the one who wouldn't let me speak. Maybe I had a reason for changing my mind. But you wouldn't know that, would you, because you never heard it."

Anger sparked in her eyes and he felt the answering anger within himself. But he'd just claimed to have magnanimously put the past aside because they were both more mature now. This was going to take more than simple determination. He would have to be clever and patient.

He swallowed the anger and asked quietly, "Do you want to tell me now?"

Her anger seemed to have collapsed also. "It hardly matters anymore, does it?"

"We're supposed to be making things right," he reminded her. "Haley and your girls will question you. I hate to tell you what she might do to me if I don't make an effort here."

JACKIE GROPED for a reasonable response. She hadn't wanted this to happen. She hadn't wanted to try to mend fences, to become friends again. Because then she'd have to explain, and she couldn't. At least, not so he'd ever understand.

Still, she'd always felt connected to Hank in a way that couldn't be denied. Despite her sexual response to him, their relationship could never be romantic again, but she wanted to right the past. What happened after he left couldn't be fixed, but he didn't know about that. And this was now. Perhaps they could forgive each other for the way they'd parted and just move on. It would be such a relief not to feel panic every time she saw him.

So she had to make something up, because the reason she'd chosen to stay behind was connected to what had happened later, and he couldn't know that.

She tried desperately to think of a good excuse that wouldn't make her seem like the shallow, selfish person he'd thought wouldn't leave her comfortable surroundings.

But nothing came to mind, and he was already looking at her with puzzlement.

"You were absolutely right," she said, eager to be able to say something, anything. "My parents were indulgent, people knew my name, I'd been accepted to Boston College. Even though I thought I loved you, I couldn't see myself giving all that up. I told myself you had a better chance of fulfilling your dreams on your own, and I believe I meant that sincerely, but I know I was also thinking of myself."

She waited for the scorn, possibly even an explosion of anger.

Instead, he simply nodded, a tolerant smile in place. "And you were probably right. My college years were a struggle. A marriage might not have survived them. I've resented your choice all this time because as a kid, I interpreted it as a decision against me, rather than one of common sense. And it hurt so much that even as an adult it's taken me a long time to come to terms with it."

He stood, seeming to feel restless, and walked around the beautiful room with its floor-to-ceiling books, elegant but comfortable furnishings, long, lace-covered window looking out onto snow falling on a small yard and a bare hawthorn tree.

"Two years after I graduated, I could have bought you a mansion," he said, "but I couldn't have lived in it with you. I was at work day and night most of the time, and when I finally had free time, I spent it with other engineers and all we talked about was space anyway. You got your comfort and security. You did the right thing."

It was generous of him, she thought, to forgive that youthful attitude. Yet she couldn't help a niggle of annoyance that he'd been forced to live without her for all those years and could say in an even voice, "You did the right thing."

"You said a lot of nasty things then," she reminded him with mild pique, standing in her stockinged feet because his restlessness seemed to be catching.

He stopped his perusal of the room and turned to look at her.

"I know," he said. "I'm sorry."

"They hurt," she insisted, her annoyance building.

He hesitated a moment, a pleat forming between his eyebrows. But his voice remained calm. "I'm sure they did. I'm sorry."

"Yeah, well, that didn't help when you walked away without even listening to me." She went to the window, hearing herself in disbelief. He'd just forgiven her, and though her explanation was fictitious, he was generous to do so all the same. There could be peace now. They could meet each other without acrimony. His mother and his sister would be happy. Her girls would be happy.

So what was she doing?

"Pardon me," he said. There was an edge to his quiet voice now. "But didn't you just admit to shredding my heart out of pure selfishness? I'm willing to let all that go, and now you're going to batter me because I got angry about it at the time?"

She hadn't understood the strange tension building in her, until she remembered one of the details of her lie. The one detail in all she'd said that was true.

She padded toward him across the blue, burgundy and white Persian carpet, emotion that had been capped all this time bursting its way out of her.

"Well, I'm mad about it now!" she shouted at him. "I let you go so that you could live your dreams, so you would be free to have everything you wanted, and what did you do?"

He was looking at her as though she was a madwoman.

"What?" she demanded. "What did you do?"

She saw him scan his mind for an answer. "I accomplished my goals. I did live my dreams."

"Yeah," she said, as though that wasn't the point. "Then you came back! I was lonely and went through hell with a husband who could never find the real me, and look what you did—you gave up and came *back!* So my life was all for nothing?"

He folded his arms and stared at her, probably thinking that if he studied her long enough, he'd be able to make sense of what she was saying.

"I did not give up," he said reasonably. He had done that even when they'd been kids, she remembered—always grown calmer in the face of her irrational behavior. "I'd done everything I wanted to, then realized that I'd done nothing for myself personally. I thought I explained that. In no way does that equate to giving up. I'm simply starting over. And anyway, you just said that selfishness was at the heart of your decision. You stayed because you wanted to remain comfortable."

She put both hands to her face, baffled by her own logic. "Things would have been a lot easier for both of us if you'd started over somewhere else."

HANK HAD NO IDEA what was going on here, but he was beginning to believe that her distress was more related to the fact that she cared about him now than the fact that she'd been angry at him then. He could see it in her eyes, love overlaid with anger and frustration. And they weren't old feelings. This was something fresh and new, something that might have begun in the past but now had a very present identity. He was careful not to betray his satisfaction.

"I'm sorry I'm not making sense," she said, dropping her hands and slipping on her shoes. Her feet were puffy and she was having difficulty.

"Sit down," he said. "I'll help you."

She tried to fend him off but he pushed her gently back into the chair. The shoes slipped on with a little effort.

"At least you've escaped having to deal with an unglamorous and moody pregnant woman," she said.

"That seems to be what I'm doing," he countered, then added with an apologetic smile, "except for the unglamorous part, of course. You're very beautiful."

That stopped her cold. She looked at him as though he was insane, then stood. He got to his feet. She led the way to the door.

"What're you going to tell my mother and Haley and the girls?" he asked.

"Me?" She looked flustered.

"Just tell them we made up," she said, turning the knob.

He placed his hand over hers to hold the door closed. "They'll want proof."

She frowned. "What kind of proof?"

"You have to invite me to dinner or we have to make a date. Something definite to give them so they'll be satisfied and leave us alone." He wasn't leaving here without a plan in motion.

She didn't know what to make of that suggestion. Of course, she didn't know, either, that her eyes revealed the same lingering traces of love for him that had reignited within him for her. He'd botched it as a boy, but he'd grown into a smarter man.

She shook her head. "That's a bad idea."

He fell back on the old it-doesn't-really-matter tactic. "Okay. Just thought you might want to be prepared. I'll refer all questions about this discussion to you."

He pulled the door open, but she caught his arm before he could pass through. Beyond the porch, snow fell in silent beauty, making all the big old homes in the neighborhood look like a Christmas card.

"Okay. Next weekend? I have a really busy few days coming up."

He knew about that; everyone at City Hall was talking about it. The Massachusetts Board for the Homeless Foundation would be visiting all week. They were being escorted around western Massachusetts, and a tea and a reception were scheduled at City Hall.

"Next weekend is fine," he said.

She leaned against the door frame and rubbed her arms against the chill. "Thank you. I apologize for shouting at you. I was very upset all those years ago, and every time I think about it, it happens all over again. But you're right, of course. We're not even the same people who hurt each other, so we should just put it away."

He offered his hand. "I'm willing."

She took it. "Then, that's done. I'll see you next weekend."

"All right. Get back inside before you get chilled." He ran down the steps to his van without turning back.

He drove home while snow drifted down onto Maple Hill. Calls to Whitcomb's Wonders would be forwarded to his home over the weekend.

So she still cared, he thought as the pace of traffic slowed through town. She wouldn't get so angry if she didn't care. She wouldn't want to hurt him if it didn't matter.

Memories of the past created images of the two of them as kids. He saw himself holding her on a balmy night at the lake, astonished by the depth of his feelings for her, confused by and yet accepting of the soft puddle she'd created in the center of his being where—like the other guys his age—he'd been trying to grow rock.

She was beautiful, seductive, and smart, and she had a way of turning to him, of leaning into him, that made him feel as though he had potential even he wasn't aware of.

She made him feel invincible.

It was ironic, he thought, accelerating as the traffic began to move, that it had been the strength she'd given him that eventually made him leave Maple Hill even when she wouldn't follow.

He'd lived a challenging and exciting life, but in the quiet hours of night, he'd thought about her, wondered if she'd regretted her decision. He certainly did.

But there was no time for regrets now. He couldn't change the past, but he could certainly do something about the future—starting now.

He was going to get her back.

CHAPTER SIX

JACKIE FUSSED around the table set up in what used to be a ballroom but was now used to host various social events at City Hall. The Massachusetts Board for the Homeless Foundation, a group made up of government officials and representatives of contributing charities, was expected in an hour to celebrate the building of a shelter for the homeless on a piece of property donated by Alfred Warren, one of Maple Hill's prominent citizens.

Jackie had become mayor when the man who'd held office before her was found guilty of trying to abscond with the funds provided by the board. At the time, Jackie had been a junior councilwoman, but had lived in Maple Hill longer than the others. She'd been considered the person most likely to help the city recover from the embarrassing situation.

She wanted this reception to go without a hitch so that the board would be impressed with Maple Hill's rebound from near disaster, and more likely to contribute to their program in the future.

Half an hour into the proceedings, she realized she should have known better than to think anything would go the way she wanted it. She was talking to Jeremy Logan, who chaired the board, explaining that during the January blizzard that had paralyzed New England, Maple Hill had sheltered their homeless in its three churches. The two of them had been sipping coffee and eating fudge gateau catered by Perk Avenue when the lights flickered.

Jeremy looked up at the Hancock chandelier.

"Please don't worry," Jackie said with more confidence than she felt. "It happens all the time. The furnace probably kicked on and that makes everything else flicker. Old buildings, you know."

He nodded appreciatively. "This is quite a place." Then he returned to their discussion. "I didn't realize such a small town would have so many homeless."

"More families are homeless now than ever before," she said, wondering why he didn't know that as head of the board. "And our program is better than the surrounding cities, so their homeless come here."

"I see. I'm new to the position and still learning. Then how do you…?"

Before he could pose his question, the lights went out. They didn't flicker, they didn't dim, they went out, leaving the room black except for the faint glow from a streetlight beyond a corner window.

There was an instant of silence, then something crashed to the floor, followed by a shriek and the sound of excited voices.

Jackie knew she had to do something quickly.

"Do you have a lighter, Mr. Logan?" she asked.

She heard the rustle of fabric, then a small blue flame at the tip of the man's lighter pierced the darkness around them.

"May I borrow it, please?" she asked.

"Of course." He handed his cup and plate to the person beside him, then took her plate and passed her his lighter. The room fell silent.

Jackie pointed to her half-eaten gateau. "This better be the same size when I return, Mr. Logan," she teased.

The man smiled and there was a titter of laughter around them.

She went to the wall behind the buffet, the lighter guiding her way, people stepping back to let her pass. She lit the candles always kept in the sconces on either side of the fireplace.

There was an aah! of approval as that part of the room took on a golden glow. She lit two other sets of sconces in the room and was relieved that people could at least find the buffet table and see who they were speaking with.

"This is a disaster!" John Brockton whispered behind her as he followed her to the double doors that led to the corridor. "We should be investing money in this rattle-trap of a building rather than building something to shelter those who contribute nothing to this community."

"It makes it clear that we don't waste our money on opulent surroundings, doesn't it?" She pushed the door open. "Or is that what you'd prefer?"

"Don't get sanctimonious with me, Ms. Mayor. You know what I mean. There isn't that much money in Maple Hill that we can waste any of it on those who don't produce. And by the way, a lot of good having an electrician in the basement office is doing us."

She was speechless for a moment, astonished by his attitude. "Where did you learn that method of governing? *Mein Kampf*? Civilization is judged by how it treats its weakest members. And Hank isn't our maintenance man. He's been hired to replace the ugly old swags, that's all."

He made a scornful sound. "I'm not for mowing the homeless down, I just don't think they need a building. And Whitcomb says he's replacing the swags in order and my office is last. Me! A councilman!"

She sighed. "What did you do to him first, John? And we have the money for the building for the homeless already, so there's not much you can do about it. Why don't you do *your* job as a representative of the city and go keep our guests entertained. Get out of my way, please."

He moved away from the doors and she pushed them open, stepping out into the hall and closing them behind her.

Holding the lighter flame in front of her, she took her cell phone out of the small bag on her shoulder and punched number 13 on her speed dial. She prayed that Hank was still in his office, or at least within reach. She closed her eyes, wondering how to ask for his help when she'd been so adamant that he leave her alone.

"I'm on it, Jackie," he answered. "Lights are out on the main floor also. Caterers probably plugged in too many warmers or something. We've got fuses fried all over the place."

"Can you fix it?"

"Give me ten minutes."

There was silence on the line, then she added sincerely, "I'm grateful you were still here. I had visions of having to make torches out of the cattail arrangement in the gallery and leading people with them down the stairs to their cars."

He laughed. "Primitive but resourceful. Hang on. Lights will be on in a minute. Only one of the fuse boxes is beyond repair, but that's for the back stairs. Make sure nobody leaves that way later."

"Thanks, Hank."

"Sure."

Jackie went back to the ballroom, certain that Hank would do precisely as he'd promised.

"According to our new resident electrician," she told the crowd that turned her way, "the lights will be on in ten minutes."

"Who is it?" someone asked.

Before she could reply, someone else said, "Hank Whitcomb."

She heard a low rumble of relief. "They'll be on in five," another voice said.

And they were right. Jeremy Logan had just provided Jackie with a fresh piece of gateau and was telling her that he'd spent the last few minutes speaking to the editor of the *Maple Hill Mirror*, when the room was suddenly flooded with light.

There was laughter and applause directed at Jackie.

She took a modest bow, thinking guiltily that the restored light was all due to Hank at work in the basement after an already long day in his office.

"And what did she tell you?" Jackie asked.

"That you've accomplished a lot despite a divided council and animosity toward you personally. That you and she are the ones who caught the old mayor who tried to abscond with our money."

"We did."

He nodded thoughtfully. "You know," he said finally.

"I have a friend on the Historic Buildings Restoration Board. You should hit them up for funds."

"We did last year." She shrugged regretfully. "We didn't qualify, mostly, I think, because our mayor was already under investigation for the money for the homeless shelter."

"Then you should try again. You've shown that you keep a careful eye on your funds and I'll put in a good word for you. I don't think they'll turn you down again."

"That's very kind of you," she said, knowing that hardly expressed her gratitude. "I can't begin…"

He stopped her with a shake of his head. "Civil servants who are truly serving their communities need the funds with which to work. I'll do everything I can for you."

Jackie felt as though she'd made a valuable friend for Maple Hill.

When the evening was over, she walked the visiting board members to their cars, then returned to the main doors to find Hank in the middle of a cluster of men who'd attended the reception. Amid their suits and ties, he stood out in his uniform of jeans and chambray shirt. But they were all laughing heartily, with good-natured pushing and shoving, as though they were twelve years old.

Ricky had never been like that, she remembered. But then, all his friends had been privileged, jaded men like him. They hadn't taken pleasure in anything, as she recalled. Except women they weren't married to.

As Jackie approached the steps, Hank broke out of the group and the other men disbanded to head off in different directions across the parking lot.

Hank took her arm to help her up the steps. "Where's

your coat?" he asked. "And why are you wandering around an icy parking lot in your condition?"

"In my office," she replied, unused to being interrogated but not entirely unhappy about it. With her father in Miami, it wasn't often that she had a man concerned for her welfare. "And because this is America, I can walk across an icy parking lot if I want to."

He ignored that smart sally. "When does your leave of absence start?"

"The day the baby's born."

"Don't you have to prepare?"

"I've done this before," she replied as he pulled the doors open. She went inside. "I already have a bag packed. I've made plans to take the girls to Haley and Bart's. Everything's handled."

He smiled. "No wonder you run a tight city. You going home?"

"As soon as I go upstairs to get my coat and purse."

"I'm going downstairs to close up my office. I'll walk you out to your car. Wait for me here."

"I'll be fi—"

"Wait for me," he repeated, then loped off toward the basement stairs.

He was back in time to help her on with her coat. "Where are the girls tonight?" he asked.

"I have a regular baby-sitter," she said as he stood aside while she locked the ballroom door. "She's at the house when they get home from school and helps me when I have nighttime obligations or weekend duties." The door locked, she took his arm and started for the main door. "In fact, she's dating someone who works for you. He repairs furnaces, I think."

"Oh, right. Jimmy Elliott. Good man. She's a smart girl."

"She really is. My girls love her."

"Is she going to be able to take care of the baby, too?"

"She's willing to try, but we'll have to see how it goes. I'm going to take a four-week leave. If I had any other kind of job, I could take longer, but it's not as though I can count on someone else to do my work."

He stopped them in the middle of the parking lot. There were only two cars there—his van and her spiffy red Astro.

She held on to him as they walked toward it over a wide patch of ice.

"Extended model," he noted of her van. "Useful with the children."

"I sometimes pick up guests of the inn at the airport. It's nice to have the room. Hank?"

"Yeah?"

"Thank you for acting so quickly tonight. You saved the evening."

"It's all in a day's work for one of Whitcomb's Wonders." He patted the hand she held on his arm. "You're welcome."

She felt that touch so deeply that even the baby moved. The simple affection in it reminded her of the richness of the friendship they'd shared as teenagers, and how it had subtly developed into feelings that changed her from girl to woman—and eventually ruined their relationship. The lover in Hank had been angry when she'd tried to explain why she had to stay, but if he'd still been her friend, he would have listened.

"Why didn't you ever get married?" she asked.

They'd reached her car, but she made no move to un-
lock it. The cold night air swirled with their breath, but
she felt warm because they could finally talk peacefully.
"No time?"

He nodded. "Also, no inclination. Until I decided to
come back home. I feel as though my professional life
was a success, but my personal life never really started."

"Marriage doesn't define your personal life," she
said with a wry expression. "If I'd judged myself on
mine, I'd have given up long ago."

"Then what do you think defines it?"

She knew the answer to that. "How much you're willing to love. How long you're willing to hold on in hope."

"But you held on to Ricky for fourteen years, and ultimately it didn't matter, did it?"

"No, it didn't," she replied.

But she hadn't been talking about Ricky.

He couldn't know that, of course. Probably didn't
care. They'd planned to meet again to make their families happy, and because they wanted to do the civilized
thing and be friends again.

She wanted that. But right now, leaning against the
car, with his body blocking the wind, his eyes smiling
down on her, his easy presence offering a comfort she
hadn't felt in years, she wanted more.

But she couldn't have it. She straightened up, unlocked the door with her remote and let Hank reach
around her to open it.

"I'll follow you home," he said.

"It's only three blocks. Look," she said, catching the
sleeve of his jacket as he would have turned away. He
had to understand this. She had to put him at a distance

in order that the friendship, at least, might live. "You don't have to look out for me. All the time I was married to Ricky, I pretty much took care of myself and the girls. I'm smart and I'm competent and I don't need a man to look after me."

He considered her a moment with that possessive look that once made her feel so special, then put one hand on the top of the door and the other on the roof of the car, trapping her in between.

"Every woman needs a man to care about her," he said softly. "It's a law of nature. Just as every man thrives on the attention of a woman."

She had to say it. He wasn't getting the message.

"We're not going to have that kind of relationship," she said firmly, folding her arms on the mound of her stomach. She was sure it made her look more ridiculous than determined.

"Says who?" he asked with smiling belligerence.

"Says me. We can be friends, but nothing more."

"There's already more than that in your eyes," he said mercilessly. "And please don't dictate to me. I didn't like it when I was a kid, and I'm even worse about it now."

She lowered her lashes and tried to turn away from him, but it was impossible. He had her backed into a corner. Her only choice was to brazen it out.

"You see memories," she insisted. "Not feelings."

She wished she hadn't said that, because now he looked more deeply into her eyes. She prayed her soul wasn't visible.

"The hell I do," he denied.

"I'm the mother of a ten-year-old!" she said desperately. "And I'm eight months pregnant, for God's sake! My face is puffy, my ankles swell and I waddle!"

He put a hand to her chin, turning her face toward the streetlight illuminating the parking lot. "I don't see much of a difference from the young woman I remember."

She put a hand to his chest. "Hank! I'm not a woman anymore!"

She heard her loud declaration on the cold night air and felt as though the words formed into icicles and hung right over her head.

He blinked, clearly amused. "What?"

She sighed, wishing she'd told him she had to work late and had avoided this whole conversation. "I'm a mother, an innkeeper, an elected official. And I'm tired and disillusioned. There's nothing in me of the girl you remember. Maybe you want there to be, but there isn't. Trust me."

She was beginning to think she'd finally gotten through. He listened to her with a frown between his eyebrows, his eyes roaming her face, the frown continuing as though he saw what she'd told him.

Then he caught her in his arms and pulled her to him, pressing her close as though there wasn't seven-plus months' worth of baby between them. One of his hands caught her hair and tipped her head back.

He looked into her eyes and she tried hard to hide from him everything she felt. She tried to be the woman she'd been before she'd met him the afternoon he'd moved in.

But she could tell it wasn't working. The desire she felt must show in her eyes, and the ticking his touch caused in the heart of her womanhood, pregnant though she was, must be lighting her face because there was a small smile on his lips.

His head came down, his mouth opened over hers and made a bald-faced lie of everything she'd told him.

She tried not to respond, but it had been years since she'd been kissed with genuine passion. Even when the baby she carried was conceived, Ricky had made love to her with the purpose of recommitting himself to their marriage, but it had been done with more desire than affection, more need on his part than sharing.

But this was all about her. Hank kissed her tenderly but without the gentle uncertainty of a first embrace. This said he knew her, and inexplicably, in spite of everything, he treasured what he knew. The kiss praised her, revered her, and when she responded, every neglected emotion of the last ten years of her life clamoring to be noticed, he deepened the kiss and she kept pace. Their tongues warred, explored, his hands wandered over her body and managed to make her feel naked despite a wool overcoat.

His palm settled on her backside. She fidgeted a little, sure it was now broad as a barn, but his fingers closed over her, pressing her even closer. The baby stirred between them until Hank finally drew back laughing. "A kiss shared with three is an odd feeling."

She couldn't agree with him, primarily because she couldn't speak. Astonishment clogged her throat. The woman in her not only lived, it was jumping up and down.

"I'll follow you home," he said again. "And when we meet this weekend, I don't want to hear any more of this you're-not-a-woman idiocy."

He held her arm while she got in behind the wheel,

now a very tight fit, then he closed her door and walked across the parking lot to his van.

Oh, God! Oh, God! Oh, God! she thought. *This can't happen. I can't let it happen. He'll find out and then I'll lose him again!*

But he wasn't that easily dismissed, and she could still feel his hands all over her, remember how it felt to be worshiped with a kiss. For a woman who hadn't known such things since the last time they'd made love all those years ago, it was impossible to walk away a second time.

"YOU KNOW," Bart Megrath said, his breath puffing out ahead of him as he and his companions ran around the high-school track, "you can do this indoors now, on machines!" He pulled his hat farther down over his ears as they rounded a turn in ragged formation. Cameron Trent, in the outside lane, ran a little faster to keep abreast.

"Yeah!" Cam said. "We could be doing this *in*doors!"

Hank frowned at Bart on his left, then at Cam on his right. He'd run the high-school track before breakfast since he'd moved back to Maple Hill.

"You know, it was your idea to join me," he reminded them. "You don't *have* to be here."

"We *wouldn't* have to be here," Bart corrected, "if you hadn't volunteered us for the city basketball league. I was happy being a couch potato."

"You're starting to get a gut."

Bart made a horrified sound. "I am not!"

"You are, too. This is good for you. You spend ten hours a day in your office chair. It's nice that Maple Hill has a good lawyer, but we don't want to have to point at you and laugh and call you 'fatty' behind your back."

Bart gave Hank a shove. "Haley's told me stories about your brutal persecution of her when you were kids, but I thought she was exaggerating. I'll have to reconsider."

"We're going to the bakery after this, right?" Cam asked, keeping up as they rounded the far end of the loop.

"No, we're going to Heart's Haven Health Bar for breakfast. An all-white omelette and fruit."

Bart made a scornful sound. "Yeah, right. Like that's going to happen."

"Food eaten after exercise," Cam contributed, "is burned more quickly."

"Well, that's an argument for sugar if I ever heard one." Bart picked up speed, but instead of turning for another lap around the track, he went straight toward the sidewalk and freedom. "Follow me, Cam!" he shouted over his shoulder.

Cam took off in his tracks.

"Hey!" Hank called, but with the speed they'd picked up, his voice floated back to him, unheard. And with it, a whiff of sweet aroma from the bakery several blocks away. All right. A cruller did have more appeal than an omelette with egg whites. Chucking health considerations aside, he followed them.

"You're already in good shape," Bart said to Hank as the two of them settled into opposite sides of a corner booth at the French Maid Bakery. Cam sat beside Hank. "We helped you cut firewood yesterday, we installed new cabinets in your kitchen the day before that. We could probably enter the Olympics in the shotput competition. What is this compulsion for physical exercise?"

"Unlike you, garbage gut," Hank replied, taking a large bite of cruller, chewing and swallowing, "I have some standards when it comes to appearance."

Unoffended, Bart ripped a maple bar in half. "I have a wife. They feed you. And if you compliment the food, there are rewards beyond imagining."

"That's Hank's problem." Cam tore open a packet of non-dairy creamer and poured it into his coffee. "Not the wife, but the need for 'rewards beyond imagining.'" He underlined the last three words with a lascivious lift of his eyebrow.

Hank gave Cam a dark look. In the brief amount of time that he'd known him, he'd proven to be a loyal, hardworking employee and seemed determined to be a good friend. But he was also insightful and intuitive, and Hank hated being read by anyone—particularly if that person was right. Since he'd walked back into Jackie's life he thought about her all the time, memories of the old days vividly clear. He couldn't help but wonder what making love to her would be like now that they were adults. "A psychologist as well as a plumber?" he grumbled.

"Anyone can see that you have strong feelings for the very pretty and very pregnant Ms. Mayor. And that her cool demeanor and advanced pregnancy and the months ahead of no physical contact even if you *can* warm her up are making you crazy. Am I right?"

"Ah," Bart said with a pleased smile. "So Haley wasn't just indulging in wishful thinking when she said she was sure there was something between you."

Hank made a palms-up, noncommittal gesture. "I'm determined there will be. She's as determined there won't."

"She said there was a look in Jackie's eyes as well as in yours. And the high-school-sweetheart relationship is strong stuff."

"I know. But we caused each other a lot of pain. That can be hard to get past."

Cam spread a cube of butter on a cream cheese Danish. "But you were kids."

"Things hurt more when you're kids," Bart said. "They last longer. But you went on to be a great success, Hank. And she had a rotten husband, but her children are great and the whole community seems to love her. Isn't it time to put the old stuff away?"

Hank leaned into the corner of the booth and sipped at his coffee. "I took her home the day of the ribbon cutting at Perk Avenue and she said she was angry because I came back. Not simply because I'm here, but because she decided not to leave with me when we were kids so that I could live my dreams unencumbered. And then I came back. She let me go, had a rotten marriage, and now after her great sacrifice, I've given up and come home."

Bart frowned. "You didn't 'give up.'"

"I know. I explained that. She's just not rational about it."

"Then maybe that isn't the truth. Maybe she doesn't know why she's angry with you, and she just said that to try to explain it." Cam turned toward him, clearly warming to his theory. "So, that's a good sign. Because in my experience, when a woman is angry at you and not making sense, that's usually because she has feelings for you, and just can't accept them for one reason or another."

"If Jackie has feelings for me she can't accept, why is that a good sign?" Hank asked impatiently.

Bart shook his head as though Hank were simple. "Because feelings always win out. Don't you know *anything* about women?"

Hank rolled his eyes and finished his coffee. "I thought I did, but maybe I don't. Sometimes I'm sure there's something there, then the next minute she seems to hate me. Still, I'm working on it."

"You can get to her," Cam advised, pointing his plastic fork at him, "through her children. Make friends with them, and you've got it made."

"And you know this how?" Hank demanded. "You have no loving wife with children in tow that I've seen?"

"Just passing on what I've observed," Cam replied. "My brother did it. He fell in love at first sight with his dentist, but she had four little boys and wouldn't give him the time of day because she thought he could never be serious about a woman with that much responsibility. So, when the oldest one's baseball coach got sick, Jake saw his opportunity. He volunteered to coach the team, got Sandi to help him set up a pizza party after the games, and watched the boys for her one night when she had an emergency with an abscessed bicuspid."

"You're a step ahead already, Hank," Bart said, folding his empty paper plate in half. "We baby-sat the girls the other night when Jackie had a meeting and her babysitter was busy. All they could talk about was you. Had quite a conversation with you the day of the ribbon-cutting, apparently."

Hank explained what he'd told the girls.

"Well, you must have made a good impression. Erica is very interested in whether or not her mother's getting any kissing action."

Cam leaned an elbow on the back of the booth. "So am I. Is she?"

Hank slapped his elbow off its perch, then gave him a teasing shove out of the booth. "None of your business. Come on. We have work to do."

"Isn't that employee abuse?" Cam asked Bart, who threw their trash away and followed them out the door. "Do I have a case?"

"I'll look it up for you," Bart promised unconvincingly as they all loped back to the cars they'd left at the high school.

THE GOOD COUNCILMEN looked skeptical. The bad councilmen looked hostile. Jackie couldn't help that they lined themselves up in her mind under categories of good and evil.

"It's going to cost us a fortune," John Brockton said with controlled anger. "And we've spent one already with all the man-hours devoted to the homeless shelter and the refurbishing of the basement for commercial enterprise—a project far outside the city's mission, if you ask me." He happily ticked off the changes Jackie had implemented. He'd opposed every one. Fortunately, she and the good councilmen were sometimes able to sway him.

"I thought you told me the night we lost power that you wanted something done about the wiring," Jackie challenged.

"If we repair what's in place," John said. "I don't think it's necessary to rewire."

"All I'm asking for," she said reasonably, "is that we call for estimates."

"Why don't we just ask Whitcomb to do it?" Alan Dartford asked. "We all know his work and respect his ethics. He'll do a good job for us."

"We have to put the work up for bid," John said.

"Technically, we don't," Paul Balducci corrected. "We have to put bids out county-wide. Besides Whitcomb, that leaves Dover Electric, and there's a suit against them for the Connecticut River Lumber fire, so we don't have to consider them. And Brogan and Brogan closed out everything but their retail shop when Patrick Brogan died last month."

John Brockton looked thwarted. "Under the circumstances, we should be able to look beyond the county for an electrician."

Alan rolled his eyes. "Why would we want to do that?"

John exchanged a glance with Russ Benedict, who usually supported his opposition to Jackie's every move. He owned a construction firm that would have put up Brockton's brother's fast food franchise on the highway if the deal hadn't fallen through.

"Because," John said finally, "I think it's bad enough that she advances every plan or program that squanders employee man-hours and wastes taxpayers' money. I don't see why we should also have to employ her paramours, further wasting…"

The gasp of indignation was still caught in Jackie's throat when John Brockton was suddenly yanked out of his chair, his shirtfront caught in a fist. Hank's fist. Jackie had invited him to stop by City Hall to give her an estimate she could pass on to the councilmen.

Russ Benedict, a short, rotund man with glasses and a shiny black suit, got to his feet. Neither Alan, nor Paul stirred, simply watched the proceedings with interest.

"Hank!" Jackie said in astonishment.

"That's assault, Whitcomb!" Russ shouted, his voice high and raspy. "Leave him alone!"

Hank ignored him. "You owe the mayor an apology," he said quietly to John. Brockton managed to swallow, though his head was tipped backward and both his hands on Hank's wrist failed to dislodge it from his shirt. John's face took on a purple tinge. "Now would be nice."

Evelyn, taking notes at the end of the table, looked on in wide-eyed disbelief.

Russ Benedict turned to his fellow councilmen. "Are you just going to sit there?"

Paul Balducci smiled. "Yes," he replied.

Jackie stood and came around the table to Hank's side. "Let him go," she ordered firmly.

"When he apologizes," he said, applying a little more pressure.

"No-o!" John whispered brokenly.

"How much air does he have, Baldy?" Hank asked Paul Balducci. "You're an EMT."

"Five to seven minutes," Paul replied, his hands laced comfortably over his stomach. He was in his middle thirties, a widower with three children. "Of course, with Brockton it'd be difficult to assess brain damage since he starts out with an advanced—"

"That's enough!" Jackie decided it was time to get tough. She frowned at Paul. "Nice professional behavior on your part. And you!" She glared at Hank and tugged at his wrist. "Let him go."

"I will. The moment he apologizes."

"You will do it now!"

"I'm going to call the police!" Russ shrieked.

Alan Dartford grabbed his arm and yanked him down into his chair. "Shut up, Russ."

"Hank!" Jackie warned.

A small squeak of sound emitted from John's mouth.

Hank leaned closer. "What was that?" he asked amiably.

The room fell still.

"I'm...sorry!" came out just above a whisper.

"That's more like it." Hank lowered his hand and eased a gasping Brockton back into his chair. "Now, I know you give Mrs. Bourgeois trouble all the time about city affairs, but I also know she's smart enough to deal with you. But when you impugn her honor as a woman, or as a public servant, you'll have to deal with me. Are we clear on that?"

John had a coughing fit, then glared at Hank. "You *were* lovers!" he said in that pained whisper.

"That was seventeen years ago." Hank's voice was dangerously quiet. "When we were kids. You have no reason to suspect her of impropriety, either with me personally, or in the matter of this bid, except in your own small mind." He looked at the other councilmen.

"Of course not," Alan agreed.

Paul shook his head. "We know better."

Russ's jowls quivered. "Well...I thought it looked as though she might have, you know...maybe could have...um..." As Hank's expression pinned him to his chair, he grew paler. "John said...well, obviously he was wrong. I mean, it's clear that she...didn't..."

"I'd like to adjourn this meeting," Jackie said, going back to her chair before she fell down. There was a great pressure in her stomach and her back, and her nerves were shot. "It's clear nothing positive will be accomplished after…"

"If I might interrupt, Ms. Mayor," Hank said, taking an empty chair beside Alan Dartford, "I'd like to give you this formal bid for consideration before you close the meeting." He picked up a folder he'd apparently placed on the table unnoticed when he'd come into the room. He passed it to Alan, who passed it to Paul Balducci, who gave it to Jackie.

She opened it to register the bid in the minutes of the meeting. Scanning it, she saw that it included new wiring throughout done in phases so that the daily operations at City Hall would not be interrupted. The entire system would be converted to circuit breakers, outlets would be added, and all the computers in the building would be connected on special dedicated lines.

Thinking it sounded like everything the building required but could not afford, Jackie checked the total and saw a zero.

She looked up at Hank in surprise. "There is no total," she said.

He nodded, seeming to enjoy her perplexity. "Zero *is* the total."

She stared at him a moment, then said blankly, as though repeating it would help her understand, "Zero is the total."

"That's right. I'd like to donate my work to the city."

"What?" three councilmen asked simultaneously. John Brockton simply stared suspiciously, one hand soothing his throat.

"I'm volunteering to donate my work to the city," Hank said again. "Switching to circuit breakers will improve safety and efficiency, and it'll also reduce your insurance on the building. With my plan, you won't have any more embarrassing situations like the night of the Board for the Homeless Foundation reception."

"But…without charge?" Balducci asked, obviously shocked.

Hank shrugged. "Right now the city can't afford it and I can. I'm not ashamed to admit that I'll benefit with public relations perks."

"Damn right you will," Alan Dartford said. "I'll tell everyone I know. I move that we hire Hank Whitcomb to rewire City Hall."

"I second the motion," Russ Benedict said before Paul Balducci could do it.

Jackie still couldn't quite believe it. "You're sure?" she asked Hank.

"I am," he replied.

She blinked at him, then looked at the small group assembled around the table. "It's been moved and seconded that we contract Hank Whitcomb to rewire City Hall. All those in favor?"

There were three Ayes.

"All opposed?"

"No," John Brockton whispered.

"Motion carried," Jackie said. She turned to Evelyn. "Let the minutes record the bid to show that Hank Whitcomb is hired. Meeting adjourned."

Hank stood to shake hands with Paul and Alan while John Brockton rushed from the room with Russ in pursuit.

"Mr. Whitcomb!" Jackie said from the head of the table.

He looked up. "Yes, Ms. Mayor?"

"Would you stay for a moment please?"

Paul, Alan and Evelyn left and Hank moved to take the chair at a right angle to Jackie.

The moment the door closed behind the good councilmen, she punched Hank angrily on the arm. "What is wrong with you!" she demanded.

CHAPTER SEVEN

DESPITE THE COOL MANNER in which Jackie had taken the vote then ended the meeting, she was flustered. He liked that.

He rubbed his arm. "A broken bone, quite possibly."

"Don't get smart with me," she threatened, on her feet with exasperation, "or I'll punch you in the other one! What's wrong with you?"

"For a mayor," he said gravely, "your PR skills lack a certain one-of-the-people kind of sty—"

"That's exactly my point!" she shouted, trying to lean her hands on the table, but the baby got in her way. Further frustrated, she came around the table to growl right over him. "When I'm being the mayor, I'm not the woman you're trying to charm into dating you! I'm…I'm one-of-the-people, as you put it. You don't come to the defense of my honor with physical violence!"

"I don't care what role you're assuming," he retorted calmly, but with the very conviction he'd felt when he'd walked into the room and heard Brockton accuse her of showing favoritism to her paramours, "you're a woman above all else, and when you're dating me, the safety of your person and your honor are my responsibility!"

"That's antiquated!" she accused.

He shrugged. "That's me."

"I'm not dating you."

"We have a date for tomorrow."

"That's a one-time thing!"

He sighed and shook his head at her. "Jackie," he admonished gently. "Stop kidding yourself. It's all still there. Everything we felt as kids and more. Accept it."

She opened her mouth to speak, but nothing came out. She put a hand to her back and rubbed. He caught her around the waist and pulled her into his lap.

She struggled for a moment, but then it must have felt so good to be off her feet that she stopped. He rubbed gently where she'd rubbed, and uttering a small groan, she closed her eyes.

"Damn it, Hank," she complained.

"Yeah, I know." He kept rubbing.

"I'm pregnant!"

"It's not like I haven't noticed."

"Who in their right mind wants to take up a relationship with a pregnant woman?"

"A man who never got over the woman who just happens to be pregnant."

"You got over me," she said, leaning her forearm on his shoulder. He felt her weight relax against him. It was the best feeling he'd had in months. Maybe years. "You became a great success."

"At first," he said, massaging up her spinal column, "I think I was trying to prove something to myself. Or my father. I'm never entirely sure who's behind my efforts to accomplish things. Then I loved the work. Until it took too much of me and I had to find my life again."

"Yeah," she breathed quietly. "I understand that. My

marriage took so much effort, I sort of lost myself for a while. Do you think," she asked with a worried frown, "that seeing each other again made us need to…what? Recapture the past? Find ourselves again?"

"Possibly. Or what we had just reignited. It was pretty hot stuff, remember?"

There was a pained look in her eye for a moment, then she did something totally unexpected. She leaned her head on his shoulder and seemed to abandon the moment to his care.

"I never meant to hurt you so much," she whispered.

The soft, tearful sound tore at him. "I had no intention of hurting you. Can we just forgive each other and move on from here?"

There was a moment's silence, then she lifted her head, her cheeks pink, her eyes moist, and asked anxiously, "Do you think that can happen?"

"If that's what we want," he asked, "why can't it?"

Her face crumpled and she wrapped her arms around his neck. "Trouble is, I don't know what I want," she said, small sobs moving her and the baby against him in tantalizing tremors. "Can we just be friends again for now?"

He held her to him, a little disappointed but ready to accept whatever she could offer. "Friendship's good," he said. And it was a foundation for building his plan.

She sat with him another moment, then pushed herself to her feet, swiping her hands across her eyes and visibly pulling herself together.

"Thank you," she said, smoothing the skirt of her blue jumper. "I'd better get back to work before someone finds the mayor in tears and reports to Brockton that the sky is falling on Maple Hill."

"Right. I've got things to do, too." He took his cue from her suddenly brisk mood. "About dinner tomorrow."

"Yes?" Her expression was concerned. She didn't want him to cancel. That was hopeful.

"Your place," he said, remembering Cam's advice about winning over her children. "Six o'clock. I'll bring everything."

"Uh…okay." She seemed taken aback by the suggestion. "You cook?"

"No, I get take-out. Shall I rent a kids' movie?"

"Yes. Sure."

"Anything particular they haven't seen or wouldn't mind seeing again?"

She still appeared confused. "I can take a poll and call you."

"Good idea. See you tomorrow."

SHE WAS WEARING the same look the following evening when she answered his knock on the door. She wore overalls over a long-sleeved red shirt, and the dramatic color made her gray eyes even more silver and her short cap of curls like pale copper.

She pulled the door wider to let him in and he was immediately assailed by her daughters. Erica took one of the bags from his arms, and Rachel, who appeared to be wearing a pillowcase, jumped up and down beside him as he followed Erica to the kitchen. Cam had apparently had the right idea.

"What are we gonna eat?" Rachel wanted to know, pulling a stool up beside him as he placed the bags on the counter. She climbed up to peer into them.

"Chicken noodle casserole from the Maple Market

Deli," he said. There was immediate and enthusiastic acceptance. Haley had given him the tip. "Salad, cheese bread and chocolate cake with ice cream."

"Can we have that first?" Rachel dug into the bag and pulled out a half-gallon of vanilla ice cream with both hands.

He laughed. "Someday when you eat at my house, we can have dessert first," he said. "But your mom's probably more traditional. Would you put that in the freezer, please?"

Rachel put the ice cream down, leaped off the stool, then carried the carton to a tall, cream-colored side-by-side.

"Erica, can you set the oven on warm, please?" he asked.

She hurried to comply. He took the still-hot foil container out of a bag, but held it away from her when she tried to take it from him.

"It's too hot," he said.

She opened the oven door for him, then hovered at his elbow as he put in the container. She closed the door and both girls followed him to the counter.

He removed the flat package of foil-wrapped cheese bread and put it in the oven, too. The girls followed him back and forth across the kitchen like faithful retainers.

He took out the makings of a salad. Without being asked, Erica retrieved a large stainless steel bowl from under the counter and handed it to him. Then she brought him a cutting board.

He handed her a plastic bag of chopped and washed greens.

She found kitchen shears, cut open the bag, and emptied it into the bowl while he chopped green onions, radishes, and red and yellow peppers.

"Rachel doesn't like onions," Erica advised him. "You have to put her salad in her bowl before you add the onions."

"Got it," he said. He pulled three bottles of dressing out of the bag. "Want to put those on the table, please?"

"Yeah. Did you bring salad sprinkles?"

And he was sure he'd thought of everything. "What's that?"

"It's okay." She pointed to the shelf above his head. "They're in there on the turny thing."

He opened the cupboard and found a lazy Susan full of spices. Taller than everything else was a plastic bottle half-full of what the label said was salad topping containing soy nuts and other flavorful ingredients.

He handed the bottle to Erica, who hurried to put it on the table already set for four.

While he worked, Hank saw Jackie putting out wineglasses. She poured milk into them. She also placed a single brass candlestick with a purple candle in the middle of the table and lit it.

She looked up from her task and caught his eye, a curiously serene expression in hers. He wondered if she was thinking, as he was, that this was the way their lives were supposed to be, had they been a little more mature, a little less volatile.

"Want us to taste the cake?" Rachel asked, atop her stool once more. She pointed to the plastic dome in the bottom.

He was about to put her off again, then Erica stood on tiptoe to look into the bag. She smiled at him. "To make sure it isn't poison, you know? Somebody should check."

"Now, would I invite myself to dinner," he asked playfully, knowing he was being worked, "and bring poison?"

Jackie came to stand on the other side of the lunch bar that separated the kitchen from the dining room. "It's a game we play," she explained, leaning her forearms on the bar. "Sometimes to get them to eat their dinner, I let them preview dessert to make sure they eat their liver, or vegetables, or whatever nutritious food I'm promoting at the time."

"Ah." He pulled the container out of the bag. "Insidious," he praised. He removed the lid, cut a sliver, divided it into three pieces and offered them on a napkin Jackie provided.

The girls were enthusiastic.

"You can bring take-out to us anytime," Jackie said, savoring the fudgy frosting.

"Mom said you were gonna bring a movie." Rachel wrapped both arms around his large one. "Which one did you bring?"

He remembered with a spark of amusement his mother's puzzled expression when he returned to the office after a run to Hill Hardware for supplies.

"I have a message for you from Jackie," she'd said.

"Yeah?"

"It's weird."

"What isn't? What'd she say?"

"She said to tell you, *'Toy Story II.'*"

"Great. Thanks." He carried a box of supplies to the cabinet in the back.

She came to stand behind him and swatted the back

of his head. "You don't think you're going to get away without explaining that."

He explained.

She raised her eyes heavenward. "Thank you, God. You inserted his brain at last!"

"Toy Story II," he said now to Rachel.

She looked into the empty bag. "Where is it? Can we put it in the VCR? I know how to get by all the commercials so when it's time to watch, the movie will start."

He pointed to the hall closet where Jackie had placed the jacket she'd taken from him. "It's in my pocket."

Rachel leaped off the stool and ran to the closet.

Erica shook her head at her sister's youthful foibles. "I'm glad you're here," she said. "Everybody else's mother has a husband or a boyfriend except ours."

"Really." He heard Jackie's groan as he sliced tomatoes. He looked up to grin at her.

"Nobody ever takes Mom anyplace. Except Grandpa, when he's around. But he's in Miami. Can you put the tomatoes *in* the salad? They don't look as pretty, but the salad tastes better."

"Sure." He stacked the slices and chopped them up. "Where would your mother like to go?"

"She always says…" Erica closed her eyes and cleared her throat, apparently preparing to impersonate Jackie. Jackie, fortunately, had gone to the closet to help Rachel.

"God," Erica said, making a hand gesture Jackie used unconsciously while talking. "I could use a month in Bermuda."

She had Jackie's voice down pat, complete with a note of end-of-the-rope exasperation. She opened her eyes again. "Your mom says she'd watch us if our mom can ever get anybody to take her."

He nodded, scooping the tomatoes onto the blade of the knife and dropping them into the salad. "It's nice that part of her wish is taken care of."

"Yeah. You have to do the other part."

"I see."

"And she doesn't like to fly, so you'd probably have to take a cruise."

"I'll look into that."

"Look into what?" Jackie had reappeared while Rachel, videotape secured, set up the VCR.

Erica opened her mouth to explain, but Hank wisely placed his hand over it. "Let's let it be our secret," he said into her ear.

Erica beamed and lowered his hand. "She loves surprises!"

Jackie looked from one to the other worriedly. "Can we clarify that I only like *good* surprises?"

"This is a *great* one!" Erica said.

Hank handed her the salad bowl and she carried it to the table. He removed the cheese bread from the oven and passed it to Jackie, potholder and all.

"What were you talking about?" Jackie whispered.

"A surprise," he whispered back.

"Vegetable or mineral?"

He thought about cruising with her under the stars. "Celestial," he replied, turning to fold a tea towel to get the chicken dish out of the oven. Jackie was still standing there when he went to take the dish to the table.

"Celestial?"

"Yeah."

"Erica talked you into taking me to an observatory?" She was teasing, but she was closer to the truth than she knew.

He walked past her with the chicken. "In a manner of speaking, yes. Anything missing?" He put the chicken down on the tea towel and checked the table.

"The chocolate cake," Rachel teased.

Hank couldn't remember when he'd enjoyed a dinner so much. The chicken noodle dish was pretty passable, and the girls had seconds. Jackie had lots of salad and three pieces of cheese bread. Hank drank his milk and took in the scene. The plan was working.

The Bourgeois women were a beautiful bunch. They talked playfully about hiring him on in a sort of nanny-maid capacity because of his ability to provide good food without any of them having to cook it.

"Then, what would we do with Glory?" Jackie asked.

"She's gonna marry the man who works for Hank," Rachel said.

"She *hopes* she's going to," Erica amended. "And anyway, even if she gets married, she'll still have to have a job."

Rachel pointed her index finger in the air. "I know. Glory can watch the baby, and Hank can watch us."

"Hmm," Jackie considered with a sidelong glance of amusement in Hank's direction. "Two nannies. That's going to cost us quite a bit."

"But Hank's going to bring all the food, so we won't have to buy any!"

Erica looked at her in complete disgust. "If Mom's paying him to take care of us and bring the food, she's paying for everything anyway."

Undaunted, Rachel kept thinking. Her face brightened suddenly and she said, as though wondering why it hadn't occurred to her before, "Maybe if we asked his mom, she'd just *give* him to us. Then we wouldn't have to pay him, but he'd be here all the time. And he'd bring the food."

As Erica laughed hysterically and Jackie, maintaining a straight face, explained the dark qualities of slavery, Hank studied Rachel as she listened intently to her mother. He wouldn't be surprised, he thought, if she became CEO of her own company one day—a brilliant product making her the talk of Wall Street. That little brain never stopped working. He had to remember to ask Jackie about the pillowcase Rachel wore.

Erica and Rachel cleared the table and served dessert.

"Is Erica okay with a knife?" Hank asked softly.

"We have a serrated cake server," Jackie replied. "And she's careful."

"What about Rachel's pillowcase?"

Jackie put a hand up to hide a smile. "It's her own design. I think she's looking toward a career in fashion. Unfortunately, the pillowcase was Erica's. We came very close to bloodletting. Rachel paid Erica for the pillowcase, and Erica gave her a deal on it since we'd gotten it on sale. So—all's well that ends well."

That was a philosophy he could endorse—if he was sure this plan to win Jackie over would pay off. The more time he spent with her, the deeper his feelings ran. And the more he saw of her children, the more he thought a lifetime with them could be a very good thing.

But Jackie wasn't ready for more than friendship. That was okay, he told himself. Time—and her children—were on his side.

THEY SAT ON THE SOFA to watch television, Hank and Jackie side by side, Erica on the other side of Jackie, and Rachel in Hank's lap. They reached the mutual agreement that they were all too full for popcorn.

Hank was surprised to enjoy the movie almost as much as the children did. The girls' laughter was infectious, and even Jackie's sense of silly was sparked by the combined efforts of the toys.

After the movie, Erica went upstairs to do her homework, and Rachel went to bed without protest. Jackie had walked halfway up the stairs to tuck her in when the telephone rang. She turned to come down.

"I'll answer it," Hank shouted to her. "Take your time on the stairs." He picked up the kitchen phone. "The Bourgeois residence."

"Um...hi?" a young, uncertain male voice said. "This is the Yankee Inn. May I speak to Jackie, please? It's important."

"Hold on," he replied. "She'll be right here."

Jackie waddled toward him from the stairs, a hand to the small of her back. "Who is it?" she whispered.

"The inn," he replied. "Something important, he says."

"Hey!" a demanding voice shouted from upstairs. "Aren't you gonna tuck me in, Mom?"

Jackie closed her eyes in a bid for patience. "In a minute, Rachel," she called as she took the phone.

"I'll go," Hank said. He pulled the stool up for her. "Sit down. I'll make coffee when I come down."

He took the stairs two at a time as Jackie's voice soothed the young man on the other end of the line.

He found Rachel sitting up in bed, waiting expectantly. The moment he appeared, she fell back against her pillows with a giggle.

"Your mom got a call from the inn," he explained, "so I volunteered to do the tucking. How did your dad handle this? Do I do the feet first?"

"He was always at work," she said, head tipped up to watch him. "You can do my feet first."

"Okay." He made a snug bundle of her feet, then tucked the blankets in at her waist and at her shoulders. She giggled again. "Can you breathe?" he asked, sitting on the edge of the bed beside her.

"Yeah." She beamed at him, apparently happy in her inability to move. "You did a good job. Now you have to read me something."

"The *Wall Street Journal*?" he teased. "The works of Shakespeare?"

She giggled again and turned her head toward her bedside table, where a thick book with gold-tipped pages rested. "We're reading *The Mouse Chronicles*. There's a red ribbon on the page."

He reached for the book, found the ribbon and flipped it open.

"The part where Mama Mouse goes to fix dinner and doesn't have any food." She wriggled a little in her tight confinement, clearly anticipating.

He read in a high falsetto, "'What shall I do? My babies are hungry and the cupboard is bare. And the cat's asleep under the table!'" Rachel giggled at his voice, but stared with rapt attention.

Erica wandered in in white flannel pajamas patterned in large red hearts. "How come *you're* reading?" she asked, walking around the bed to sit beside Rachel, who slid over to make room for her.

"Mom's on the phone, so Hank's tucking me in."

"I think that makes you a boyfriend," Erica said. "Officially."

He was scoring points here right and left. "I don't think it's official until your mom says so."

"Keep reading," Erica prompted, "and we'll report on whether or not you did a good job."

"Fair enough." He turned the page and read on, feeling smug.

JACKIE GOT AS FAR as Rachel's bedroom door and stopped, touched by the scene. The girls lay side by side, Rachel under the covers and Erica atop them in the pj's Jackie had given her for Valentine's Day. Hank sat on the edge of the bed, leaning back on an elbow and reading from the book he'd propped against Rachel's feet.

The three of them seemed to be sharing the pleasure of each other's company and enjoyment of the story. The tale was one of Rachel's favorites. It was about a mother mouse and her two babies and their struggle to get through the winter. They worked together to insulate their little floorboard hole by weaving hairs from the household's dog and cat. They made forays into the kitchen at night for crumbs on the table or the counter, and replaced the bows in their hair with threads taken from the frayed edges of the tablecloth.

Every time Jackie read it, she related it to their struggle to get on with their lives.

When Hank finished and closed the book, Rachel sat up in bed. "That's just like Mom and Erica and me," she said.

Erica smiled. "Except for the part about weaving

dog and cat hair." She seemed in a mellow mood and made the correction with humor, not malice. "And you bought the food. We didn't have to fight a cat for it."

Rachel seemed to understand the difference. "And me and Erica have to work together to help Mom with stuff even though Erica hates me most of the time."

"I don't hate you," Erica corrected. "I just think you're weird." To Hank, she added, "She made that weird pillowcase dress out of *my* pillowcase, you know."

"I asked your mom about that," he admitted, still relaxed. "That was a pretty clever notion, Rachel. But you probably should have used your own pillowcase."

"The design on hers was better." She reached back to grab her pillow and hold it so close to his face that he crossed his eyes exaggeratedly. Both girls giggled. "See!" Rachel exclaimed. "It has baby animals. I wanted a grown-up dress."

Erica rolled her eyes. "Grown-ups can't usually fit into a pillowcase."

Rachel swatted her with the pillowcase. Thanks to Erica's mellow mood, laughter ensued rather than mayhem. She snatched the pillow from Rachel and whopped her with it. When Hank tried to intervene, he was whopped as well.

In a moment they were a chaotic tangle of flannel-clad limbs flailing the air amid shouts and high-pitched squeals of battle.

Jackie was just about to intervene when Hank rose to his feet, a child caught under each arm.

"Mom!" Rachel screeched with laughter. "Help us!"

"I saw the whole thing." Jackie walked into the room feeling a happiness she'd thought she'd stopped believing in. Ricky had seldom played with the girls like this. And it had been years since a look into Ricky's eyes made her feel the palpitations she felt now as Hank looked at her, his eyes filled with laughter. "You two started it," she said breathlessly.

Erica, still dangling from his arm, glanced up at her, her dark hair half covering her face. "We want you to make him official."

"Official?"

"Your official boyfriend. We want him to be, but he says it isn't official until you say so."

She hedged. "He's my official friend. How's that for now?"

Both girls frowned at her, then Erica brightened. "And he's a boy, so…so…what's a word for something that's true, even though it isn't official?"

Jackie couldn't think. She loved the sight of him with his arms full of her girls.

"Technically," Hank suggested.

"That's it. So, if he's a friend and a boy, technically, he's your boyfriend."

"Yeah!" Rachel shouted as he dropped her onto the bed.

"Look at what you did to my great tucking-in job," Hank said, easing Erica to her feet also. Both girls reached up to hug him. He bent down to accommodate them. "Everybody's untucked. I guess I'll have to leave it to your mother after all."

Jackie went to cover Rachel, then realized she held the cordless phone in her hands. *That's right,* she thought, a little alarmed by her forgetfulness. *I came up here to give him the phone.*

"Here," she said, thrusting it into his hand and pointing Rachel back to her bed when she would have climbed out again. "I picked up your mom on call waiting. There's some kind of power problem at the church, and they're having a deacons' meeting tonight."

He groaned and was stabbing out the number as he walked into the hallway. "You'd think," he said, "that a place with so many candles would be able to cope."

Erica tried to follow him, but Jackie pulled her back. "That's a business call, Erica," she admonished gently. "He'll need privacy."

"I wish he lived here," Rachel said. "I really like him."

Erica nodded. "I think," she whispered, "that he likes us more than Daddy did."

"Your father loved both of you very much." Jackie was sure that was true, though Ricky had never understood how to show his love. She was always trying to make sure they knew he cared.

Erica nodded wisely. "I know, but he didn't really like it when we hung around him. Hank does."

"You can't base a decision like that on one dinner and a movie," Jackie said.

Erica looked at her as though she was surprised to understand something her mother didn't grasp. "Yes," she insisted. "You can."

Once Rachel was securely tucked in, Jackie hugged her, then turned out her light.

"If we could vote," Rachel whispered loudly as Jackie and Erica walked toward the door, "it would be two against one, Mom!"

"But this is a monarchy," Jackie turned to explain. "Not a democracy."

"What does that mean?"

"It means I'm the queen, and you do as I say."

She pulled the door partially closed on Rachel's protest.

In the hallway, Hank was grinning. He'd clearly heard her remark. "All of us?" he asked.

She fought an answering grin, but lost. "Just my loyal subjects," she clarified.

"What about your neighboring…" he groped for the right word to continue the role-playing.

"Kingdom?" she asked, thinking she really had to get him out of the house before she got too comfortable with his easy presence. "You, of course, are free to do as you please."

He made a low, sweeping bow. "Then I must be away, your highness. I am beseeched to relight the torches at the…vicarage." He frowned. "Vicarage is the wrong period, isn't it?"

She nodded. "I think so. What would it be? Abbey?"

"I think that's it."

"*What* are you guys talking about?" Erica asked, looking from one to the other in puzzlement.

Hank pinched her nose. "That's how adults play—when the guy isn't the official boyfriend—with words. Good night." He started to back away. "I'll call you."

As much as Jackie had wished he would leave for her peace of mind, now that he was going, she wanted to hold on to him.

"I'll walk you out," she said, then added to Erica, "I'll be right back, sweetie."

"Take your time, Mom," she said. "I'm still finishing my math homework. Bye, Hank."

"Bye, Erica."

He waved and started away, then Rachel called through her half-open door, "By-ye!"

"Bye, Rachel!" he returned.

Jackie caught his arm and walked him to the stairs. "Go, before they try to follow you."

"I have a great place at the lake," he said as they made their way down the stairway. "You'll have to bring them by sometime. I'll bet they'd love it."

"On the far side," she said. "Just about opposite your mother's. She pointed your lights out to me one night when she baby-sat for me at her house."

He laughed as they reached the bottom. "Hoping you'd wander over on your own, no doubt, and we'd make peace and provide her with a horde of grandchildren."

Jackie stopped at the hall closet, tugged his jacket off a hanger and held it open for him. "Yes. She's about as subtle as my daughters."

He shrugged lightly. "Don't worry about it. We're still two independent people free to do as we please. We've had the obligatory date, so whatever happens now is completely up to us."

She nodded, turning away from him to open the door. That was a pretty cut-and-dried assessment of their situation, and suddenly she didn't feel quite that independent. It felt so right to have him in this house, sitting at her table, reading to her children.

And the date hadn't been *that* obligatory, had it? Or maybe it had. Maybe that was why he'd chosen to bring dinner here rather than take her out somewhere. He hadn't wanted to be seen dating an elephant.

But he'd argued for the date, hadn't he? She couldn't quite determine how much of this warm and wonderful evening had really happened, or how much was in her imagination.

Then he pinched her chin in a sweet, affectionate gesture, gave her a quick, chaste kiss and ran down the porch steps to his van.

"Bye!" she called—probably a little too eagerly. She sounded like one of her children.

"I'll call you this weekend," he promised, climbing into the van.

It wasn't until he'd driven away with a tap of his horn that she remembered with great disappointment that the girls were going on a Sunday School fun trip this weekend with Adeline chaperoning. And Jackie had promised to cover the desk at the inn.

Doesn't matter, she thought dispiritedly as she tidied up the kitchen. *This can't possibly work out.*

No way at all.

Guilt was already beginning to nibble at her insides, telling her that he should know.

She'd done what she thought was right at the time. But he wouldn't think so.

So what did she do now? Her girls thought he was wonderful, and she was just beginning to remember what a very special boy he'd been. And what a thoughtful, kind and deliciously sexy man he'd become.

God. The church wasn't the only place in this town that needed light!

CHAPTER EIGHT

ON FRIDAY NIGHT, Jackie imagined what she would do with her weekend if she had only herself to think about. March was a quiet month for guests at the inn, and she dusted the old leaded glass lamp on the front desk as she thought.

The girls had left with Adeline and the rest of their class two hours ago, there was no pressing city business left undone, and the house was clean. Hank had said he'd call, but she'd had no word from him so far. That was probably for the best. She needed time to herself.

She would eat ice cream out of the carton when she got home sometime after midnight. She would watch a movie with love scenes in it because she never did that with the girls around and her mind seemed preoccupied lately with how long it had been since she'd had sex. She would take a shower uninterrupted by "Where are my shoes?" "Can I have a banana?" or "Erica won't let me have the remote!"

She would spritz herself with White Diamonds and wear the black lace negligee she'd bought just before Ricky died and never got to wear. She would pretend that she was a cool career woman with the world on a string, rather than a mother and a civil servant who did indeed look like two women rolled into one.

The front door opened to the ring of a melodic little bell and Jackie raised her head with the smile of greeting she demanded of all desk clerks. And then she noticed her father, six feet, two inches of handsome male in brown pants and jacket over a mossy green turtleneck. Adam Fortin had a thick thatch of pure white hair, and a white beard and mustache with touches of gray in it. He was just beginning to get a little thick around the middle.

"Dad!" Jackie exclaimed, delighted to see him. He hadn't been home since the previous fall.

She'd started walking around the desk to welcome him when she realized there was something else wrapped around him that was not clothing.

It was a woman. At least, she thought it was; she'd never seen a form quite that perfect, and for a moment wasn't convinced she was alive. But she had to be. She was walking, although she was holding on to Jackie's father so tightly, she could be getting her propulsion from him.

When Jackie reached him, he wrapped his free arm around her, his other arm still caught in the woman's. He smelled of something masculine and herbal, not the fresh Old Spice he'd always preferred. But his grip was strong and reassuring, and Jackie was delighted that he was back.

"You look as though you're going to deliver that baby tonight!" he said, holding her away from him. "I thought you were due in April."

"I am." She drew one hand away to pat her water-melon-sized middle. "It's just a particularly healthy little guy."

"It would be such a relief to have a boy in this family. Here. Let me introduce you to Sabrina Bingley." He drew the beautiful woman forward. "Bree, my daughter Jackie Bourgeois."

Sabrina offered her hand, her knuckles directed upward almost as though she expected Jackie to kiss them. She gave Jackie's hand the barest of squeezes.

Jackie disliked her. She knew it was impulsive and unreasonable to form an opinion so soon, but she couldn't help it. The feeling had begun the moment she'd laid eyes on the woman, and grew stronger as she offered Jackie a cool smile.

Sabrina was almost as tall as Adam, and wearing an off-white wool outfit with clinging pants, a long top belted at a waist that was certainly no more than twenty-two inches around. A fringe wool wrap in an oatmeal color draped her shoulders, making her look like something off a Paris runway.

Short dark hair framed a very beautiful, unfreckled face. Dark blue eyes were assessingly frank. *You look like Dumbo,* they said.

Quickly dismissing Jackie, she looked around the inn. "Beautiful old place," she said. "Maine oak banisters."

Jackie wondered how she knew that. Bree apparently read her mind.

"I'm a decorator in South Beach," she explained. "I could do a lot with this place."

Jackie had mixed feelings of horror and relief. Horror because she loved this old place just as it was with its old wood, worn floors, fieldstone fireplace discolored from 260 years of keeping family and guests warm, the patina of age sitting on everything like gray in an old woman's hair. In her two years as manager, she'd struggled to restore the old fixtures and furnishings rather than replace them. She didn't want "a lot" done with them.

But she'd feel better if her father had brought the woman here as an employee rather than as the… companion she appeared to be.

"You're on vacation, Bree," Adam said, wrapping his arms around her shoulders. "And Jackie won't let you touch a thing. She connects with her ancestors here, or something. She loves its age."

"Well, I do, too," Bree said, fixing Jackie with a condescending smile. "I was just talking about a little freshening up. If guests think a place is being neglected, they won't come back."

"Our repeat business," Jackie said with a forced smile, "is about seventy percent."

Sabrina patted Jackie's arm. "I suppose this area doesn't have that much to offer, does it? Adam, I'm dead on my feet. Can we retire?"

Jackie struggled to remember that her father had brought this patronizing snob.

"Why don't you two sit in the parlor for half an hour?" she suggested. "I'll bring you a brandy and have Honorine tidy up your suite." Home for Jackie's father was a suite of rooms on the third floor.

Adam took her chin in his hand and kissed her cheek, completely unaware of the tension. "No need. I'm sure it's fine. I'll open a few windows, shake out the blankets. Come on, Bree."

He caught Sabrina's hand and tugged her along toward the elevators. "John's bringing our things in," he said. John was the night bellman. "Would you ask him to park the Caddy in my spot when he's finished? And tell him to be careful. It's a rental."

"Sure."

She wanted to follow him, plead, "Tell me you're not serious about this woman!" But he put an arm around Sabrina as they waited for the elevator and she leaned into him like a kitten.

"Oh, God!" Jackie groaned to herself.

She was distracted from her concerns for a few moments by a call for reservations, followed by a call from Haley. She was at work, she said, and wanted a comment on John Brockton's plan to impeach Jackie.

"What?" Jackie demanded.

Haley was silent for a moment. "You didn't know," she asked finally, "that Brockton and Benedict are mounting a campaign to have you impeached?"

"No, I didn't."

"Something to do with assigning business favors to your lover." Haley sounded more intrigued by the reason than upset. "Are you and my brother finally…?"

"No!" Jackie shouted at her. When John, pushing a luggage rack stacked with seven or eight beige and green tapestry bags, stopped to look at her inquiringly, she shook her head to assure him that she was fine and that he could continue to the elevators. Then she lowered her voice and wrapped her hand around the rim of the mouthpiece. "I am so pregnant I have neither the desire, nor probably even the ability, to accommodate a man!" That wasn't entirely true. She did certainly have the desire, but she was determined no one would know that but her. "And your brother and I have decided that we can be friends. Friends! That's all! Brockton's just being hateful. Can he even do this?"

"Yes," Haley replied. "I checked the city's charter. All it takes is two councilmen to form a recall committee. But the decision on whether or not to proceed is made by a judge. Brockton's out to get you, and Benedict's going along because he doesn't want to lose his business."

"I know."

"So, what's your statement?"

"I'll save it until the hearing. Then I'll have a lot to say." Actually, she had a lot to say now, but none of it was printable. Jackie put a hand to her suddenly aching head. Another line began to ring. "I'm sorry, Haley, I've got to get that."

"Okay. Talk to you later. And you know I'll give you all the support you need."

"I know. Thanks. Bye." She drew a breath and answered cheerfully, "Front desk."

"Jackie, this is Sabrina." The tone was clipped and superior—guest to peon. And it suggested a major problem.

"Hello, Sabrina," Jackie said pleasantly.

"The heat light in the bathroom doesn't work." That news was delivered in the same way a doctor might tell a patient, "You have three months to live." "I have been on a plane for twelve hours and I was about to take a quick shower. Fortunately, I flipped on the heat lamp first, otherwise I'd now be wrapped in a towel and freezing to death."

And that would be bad? Jackie asked herself.

"I'll send someone up to change the bulb," she promised.

When John returned with the luggage cart, she handed him a replacement bulb she'd retrieved from the supply closet. He was twenty and taking drama classes at Amherst. He got on his knees in front of her. "Please don't make me go up there again! She made me hang her suit bags in the closet, put her train case in the bathroom, place all her other cases in the middle of the bed, and then open them. She sent me for ice, then asked me to call the restaurant and place her room service order. And she stared at me the whole time, ordering me around like a field general. Please, Mrs. Bourgeois. And there was something weirdly sexual about it—like ordering me around was arousing her." He clutched her hands theatrically. "I think she's a succubus."

Jackie giggled, then frowned at him, urging him to get to his feet. "We're it tonight, John. Do you really want to see me on top of a ladder?"

He wrapped his arms around her. "I'll put you on a pedestal if you'll hire someone else for an hour to go up there."

"I've changed thousands of these in my career as innkeeper," a deeper male voice said. Jackie and John turned in surprise. Adam stood there, apparently having heard everything. Or at least John's last plea.

"Mr. Fortin!" John said, standing straighter, his complexion going pale. "I…I…"

"Not a problem." Adam took the corrugated box containing the bulb from Jackie and started back toward the elevators. "I would have given you a big tip, though, John," he added with a grin over his shoulder. "Can you have breakfast with me in the morning, Jackie?" he asked as he punched the up button.

There went her sleeping-in plans, but she'd happily abandon them to find out what on earth her father was doing with such a dragon. "Sure, Dad. I'd love to."

"Good. I'll pick you up and we'll go somewhere that won't remind you of work." The elevator doors parted and he stepped aboard.

As the doors closed again, John turned to Jackie with a look of dread. "Am I fired? Do you think I'm fired?"

Jackie shook her head. "I own the inn now, John, and you're not fired. I think she's a pill, too, but we have to be courteous, okay? She's a guest."

He closed his eyes, drew a breath of relief and nodded. "Thank you. I'll give you a kidney, my liver, anything. Just say the word."

"I'd settle for a mocha."

"Right away." John hurried off in the direction of the restaurant.

He hadn't even delivered the mocha when Sabrina called again. "It isn't the bulb," she said, the b's in the last word enunciated with royal displeasure. "Your father has put it in and taken it out several times and there is still no warmth in the bathroom."

Jackie wondered if it had occurred to Sabrina that her presence in the room was providing too much chill for a simple bulb to counter. Aloud, she said, "Can you live without it tonight, and I'll have it looked at in the morning?"

"I'd prefer not to," Sabrina replied simply.

Jackie drew a breath for patience. "Then I'll see what I can do. I'll be in touch."

She dialed Hank's number, happy to have an excuse. Time alone be damned.

"Whitcomb," he replied.

She explained the problem. "I'm sorry," she added. "I know you probably thought you were finished for the week and could finally relax, then along comes…"

"An opportunity to see you," he filled in for her. "That's a good break whatever time it is. I'll be right there."

She hung up the phone, a ray of light invading the grimness of Sabrina's arrival and Haley's phone call. Hank sounded as though he wanted to see her.

And she was a little horrified by how much she wanted to see him.

HANK RECOGNIZED A DRAGON when he saw one, even if it was wearing an ivory peignoir. Jackie had told him simply that the warming light in the bathroom of her father's suite wasn't working, changing the bulb hadn't helped and that housekeeping had brought up a ladder for him. But John Granger, her night bellman, had shared the elevator with him. He'd warned Hank about Jackie's father's guest.

Sabrina opened the door to him, yards of flimsy fabric hanging from the arm that held it open. She looked him up and down with an expression that reflected disdain for his chambray shirt and jeans, mingled with interest for what might be underneath.

Then Adam Fortin appeared behind her with a surprised greeting and her interest was quickly banked.

"Hank!" Adam said, pumping Hank's hand. "It's great to see you. What are you doing here? Last I heard you were responsible for bringing Traveler Two down safely."

Hank began to explain but Sabrina interrupted by giving Adam a long-suffering smile. "Could you two talk while he works? I need my shower."

"Sorry. Of course." Adam led Hank into the old-style but sumptuous bathroom. As Jackie had promised, a ladder stood in place right under the light.

Hank flipped off the light and examined it closely. It took only a moment to determine that the problem was simply a loose connection. While he set about fixing it, Adam sat on the rim of the tub, continuing their conversation.

Hank told Adam about his sudden realization that he had nothing in his life but his work and his very occasional trips home.

He described his business and the men who worked for him part-time.

Holding a hand down to Adam, he asked, "Would you pass me the light, please?"

Adam handed up the new one. Hank installed it, then Adam went to flip the switch. Brightness and warmth instantly filled the room.

"Thank goodness," Adam said, helping Hank fold the ladder. "If Sabrina had had to wait any longer for her shower, I'd have never heard the end of it."

Hank couldn't imagine loving a woman who made a man accountable for things he couldn't control. But every man to his own taste.

"Well, now you're safe." Hank carried the ladder out into the living room.

"You're finished?" Sabrina sat in the middle of a blue and orange chintz sofa, reading a magazine. She looked up in surprise, eyelashes fluttering.

"It was easily fixed," Hank replied politely.

"Thank you," she said, grabbing a robe that lay on the sofa beside her and hurrying off for her delayed shower.

"You're welcome," Hank said to Adam. "I'll take the ladder down to housekeeping."

"You don't have to do that."

"I'm going down anyway."

Adam opened the door for him. "Have you and Jackie…you know…"

"We've agreed to be friends," he said, then he grinned. "Well, *she's* agreed to be friends. I have other plans."

Adam looked vaguely troubled. "Have you… talked?"

"Yes." He nodded wryly. "We just don't agree about the direction of our relationship, so I'm letting her believe friendship's good enough for now."

"I'm pulling for you. I always thought you'd be good for each other." Adam shook hands with him.

With a wave goodbye, Hank headed toward the elevator with the ladder. After meeting the dragon, he wasn't sure he should trust Adam's opinion on who would be good for whom.

He found John behind the front desk.

"Mrs. Bourgeois is taking a break," he said. "Just prop the ladder up against the wall there, and I'll take it back to the supply closet."

"Mrs. Bourgeois go to the restaurant?"

"No. She put her coat on and went outside. Said she needed some air."

Hank took his tool box out to his van, which was

parked around the side, and scanned the grounds for a sign of Jackie. The night was crisp and cold, the ground covered with snow that crunched underfoot.

His tools stowed, he walked under a pergola at the side of the inn. It was covered with the naked vines of a clematis that would have beautiful pink flowers in the summer. Moonlight gleamed on the snow-covered lawn, which eventually sloped to a spring that ran along the back of the property. He could hear its musical movement as it rushed along, a beautiful sound in the nighttime quiet.

That was where he found Jackie, standing at the top of the slope. A decorative little bridge crossed the stream, but he guessed she didn't dare risk slipping on it.

"Jackie," he said quietly, afraid of alarming her in the dark. But she was apparently deep in thought and he had to say her name again before she heard him.

She turned to him, only the contours of her cheeks visible. She wore a big, dark coat, her hands buried deeply in its pockets. She looked almost pitiful for a moment, then he saw the brilliance of her smile as he approached.

"Hank," she said. There was a sort of sudden, desperate relief in her voice, as though she truly was glad to see him. It was all he could do to play it cool. Eagerness, he was sure, would send her running.

"Hi." He went to stand beside her, arms folded against the cold—and to prevent him from reaching for her. "Thought you might like to know the light's fixed."

"Bless you," she said. "What was the problem?"

"Just a loose connection. I only get to bill you for the minimum."

She sighed. Her breath puffed out around them, a

white mist in the darkness. "You could name your price for this one. If I'd had to listen to her complain one more moment, I'd have been forced to slap her. She should pay you, too, for saving her from bodily harm."

"I'll bill her," he teased, "and see what happens. What's your father doing with her anyway?"

"Haven't a clue. They just came back tonight and I haven't had a chance to talk to him yet. But he's picking me up for breakfast tomorrow. I can't imagine what he sees in her."

He pointed out the obvious. "She's a young, beautiful woman with a great body."

"But my mother was a sweet, gentle woman. This one's a…a…"

"Dragon?" he helped.

"Yes! So what's the appeal?"

"He's getting older," Hank speculated. "Maybe she's visible proof that he's still got it—if he thinks he's in danger of losing it."

"That's such a cliché."

"Life's full of them. And try as we do to be unique, we all succumb to the same fears and foibles."

"You didn't. You went off to make your mark, and you did it."

"Yeah. Then I got lonesome and came home. That's an old story, too."

"Still, all I did was become notorious. The woman whose husband died in another woman's arms. The mayor they tried to impeach."

"What?" he demanded.

"Brockton wants me recalled for giving city business to someone with whom I'm having intimate relations."

"No one will believe that."

She turned and took several steps away from him. "I know. I just worry about the girls. They've been subjected to so much junk this past year…."

Her voice sounded high and strained.

He reached her in one stride and turned her to face him. There were no tears on her cheeks, but he could see them in the misery in her eyes, just a breath away.

He wrapped her in his arms, tucking her sideways so that he could draw her closer. "It's all right," he told her, stroking her hair. It was cold and silky under his hand. "You're entitled to be tired and discouraged and sick of all you've had to put up with. You want to shoot at tin cans or something? Break crockery? I remember you used to like to stomp around when you were angry."

She sniffed, apparently refusing to let the tears fall. "I was seventeen then. If I stomped now, the ground would shake in Connecticut. And you might find yourself delivering a baby."

"Oh, please." He laughed lightly and kissed her forehead. "I guess it's just another kind of engineering skill, but I don't have it. Why don't I hang around until you're off, then I'll take you to my place where you can get a different perspective on things? I know your girls are with my mother this weekend."

Her eyes, still glossed with unshed tears, looked at him with uncertainty. "I can't just…"

"Why not?"

"Because we'd be proving just what Brockton suspects."

"I doubt that he's out and about at this hour. I'll take

you home whenever you're ready to go. At 1:00 a.m., or after breakfast tomorrow."

A charmingly embarrassed look crossed her face. "Hank, I can't..."

"I didn't think we'd make mad passionate love in your condition," he interrupted to assure her. "But I have four bedrooms, each with a view of the lake. Two of them have a fireplace, and one of them has a fireplace between the bedroom and the bath so that you can sit in the tub and watch the firelight."

She sighed longingly. "That's the one I'd want."

He laughed. "Good choice. That one's mine."

She shoved him in exasperation. He laughed and caught her hands. "I was teasing. I thought I'd cook for you, let you rest awhile, then take you home."

He could see that she found the idea tempting, so he stopped pressing.

"I'd have to bring my beeper," she warned.

"That's not a problem."

"Something to eat," she bargained, "a look at the lake, then you'd have to take me home."

"Okay."

"You won't try to coax me to stay?"

"I won't say a word."

"I'm off at eleven."

He glanced at his watch. It was 9:42. "I'll pick up some groceries," he said. "And be back for you at eleven o'clock. Come on. I'll walk you back. The path is slippery."

CHAPTER NINE

THE FIRST THING Jackie noticed about Hank's property was the quiet. There were fewer homes on the far side of the lake where his sprawling two-story split-level was located. The darkness seemed to amplify the silence.

The second thing she noticed was the fragrance. There was little vegetation in early March, but the sharp freshness of winter filled her nostrils and the smell of woodsmoke lingered in the air.

"A couple from Washington, D.C., built this two years ago," she told him, "as a refuge from their hectic life. He was a senator from the southwest, I think. They weren't here very long."

"New Mexico," he said, "according to my Realtor. He lost big when tech stocks dropped, so they had to sell."

He took her arm to help her up six steps that led to a broad deck. He pointed to a bare corner of the deck. "First thing I did when I moved in was buy a huge gas grill that goes right there, and a long table with chairs and a big umbrella. Unfortunately, business got really good almost right away, so I didn't have many opportunities to use them before the snow set in. I'm looking forward to spring and summer."

"I'd love to cook outside," Jackie said, huddling into

her coat as he unlocked a large front door with a leaded glass window in it. "But our back yard is so small, I have to barbecue on the porch. Since there's no room to sit there, the girls and I have to run up and down with the plates and the food. Ricky had no patience for it."

"This deck runs all around the house," he said, pushing open the door. "And I own five acres on each side of it. Lots of room to eat on the deck while the girls are running around the property, playing with the dog."

"My girls?" she asked in confusion.

"Of course," he replied.

"But we don't have a dog."

"I know. You should, though."

She was used to reciting her arguments to the girls. "No one's home during the day. It wouldn't be fair. And I couldn't expect Glory to look after them and a dog."

"Does she like dogs?"

She hesitated. "I'm not sure. It's never come up."

"Just wondering," he said, pushing her gently into the house. "Jimmy raises Black Labs."

Whatever Jackie might have replied to that was blocked by a gasp of astonishment when Hank flipped on a light. He walked her into a huge room with hardwood floors and a vaulted ceiling. The walls were painted a warm off-white, and a deep fieldstone fireplace dominated one side of the room. The stone hearth was strewn with colorful cushions and potted plants.

Large sectionals in an oversize green-and-beige check formed a conversation area around the fireplace. Farther into the room, several overstuffed chairs in coordinating fabrics were clustered around a rough-hewn coffee table, and there was a padded oak bench and two chairs that matched it filling up another space by one of a series of long windows.

"The Senate could meet *here!*" she whispered.

"Yeah." He took her coat, then pointed her to the sofa in front of the fireplace. "The corner of the sofa reclines," he said, putting her coat on a hook near the door, then crossing the room to the brass wood box on the hearth. "Make yourself comfortable. I'll get a fire going and find you something to eat."

"I had a mocha at the inn," she said. Then she made a face. "Decaf, of course. The first thing I'm going to do when this baby is born is drink an entire pot of caffeinated coffee."

He laughed. "I've got to have the real thing myself. Didn't you have anything to eat?"

She sat in the corner of the deep sofa and reached to the outside of it for the handle to make it recline. There was none.

"How does this…?" she began, but Hank was already there, reaching between her and the sofa arm for the control hidden beside the cushion. His hand brushed her hip as he found the handle and tugged. She was tipped slightly backward and her feet came up, propped comfortably against the elevated bottom of the seat.

For an instant she was in a complete dither. The spot on her hip where his knuckles had brushed felt hot, as though someone held a match to it.

I'm going insane, she thought, in a state of mild panic. *It must be hormones. Or maybe the stress of my life is turning me into a sexual deviant. It is deviant, isn't it, to think about sex all the time when you're almost eight months pregnant?*

"What?" he asked worriedly, frowning over the dismay that must be showing in her face. "Is that uncomfortable?"

"No, no," she denied quickly, forcing a smile and wriggling into the enveloping upholstery. "It just surprised me. It's very comfortable."

He appeared unconvinced. Still frowning, he put the back of his hand to her cheek. "You're flushed," he observed. "You probably shouldn't be doing so much this late in your pregnancy."

She swatted his hand away. "I'm fine. This is my first weekend as a bachelor girl in...well, ever! At work, I was thinking about going home to eat ice cream out of the carton and watch Jay Leno while I had a bubble bath."

He laughed lightly. "Sorry, but that's not going to happen here. No ice cream, and no bubbles."

She sighed deeply, pretending disappointment. "I thought you went shopping."

He laughed again. "I guess my ideal staples are different from yours."

"All right, what do you have?"

"Ah..." He reached to the back of the sofa for a fleece blanket with which he covered her. "I can fix you a cold sandwich, a grilled sandwich, soup, chili, stew, fruit, Oreos, bacon." He looked inspired suddenly. "How about a BLT? You always used to order those when we were dating."

A bacon, lettuce and tomato sandwich. She hadn't had one in ages. "I'd love that. Can I have another choice, too?"

He straightened and smiled teasingly down on her. "You want chili with it?"

"No. An Oreo."

"Sure. What to drink? I don't have decaf coffee, but I have some herbal tea Parker gave me."

She blinked in surprise. "Our Parker? The massage therapist?"

"Yeah. It's chamomile and something. I haven't had the nerve to try it. Shall I brew a pot?"

"Yes, please."

"Okay. You relax, I'll get the fire going, then make your sandwich."

She watched him kneel before the grate, jeans encasing his neat backside. He'd been leaner when they were kids, she remembered, but even then he'd had an athletic, beautifully formed body. She'd loved watching him, clothed or naked.

Their physical relationship had been a development of the last half of their senior year. Hank's father had died in April, and Hank had mourned their wasted relationship. He'd wept, and Jackie had tried to offer comfort. In his grief and her helplessness, comfort had come in the only sure way either could communicate true feelings.

Lovemaking had become as much a revelation as a pleasure. It had been a shock to both of them to see how deeply they loved and understood one another.

Or so they'd thought.

She remembered suddenly how he'd refused to listen to her reasons why she couldn't leave Maple Hill with him as they'd planned, and the shock she'd felt that he could hurt her that way.

Then she remembered, too, the truth she'd never told him. They were probably even. In the light of adulthood and all that had happened since, refusing to listen to reason seemed like such a paltry offense.

She closed her eyes against the sight of him, reminded of how impossible her desire for him was. She felt tears form under her eyelids, but held them back. She'd once cried enough tears to flood the lake, and that hadn't changed anything. She had two beautiful daughters, work she enjoyed, a comfortable living and good friends. She had no right to whine simply because she'd really only loved one man in her lifetime and the fates decreed that she couldn't have him.

She heard flames crackle as Hank's fire apparently took, then felt warmth emanate from it. Resigned to what must be, she felt consciousness drift away.

THE FIRE BRIGHT, Hank went to the sofa to ask Jackie if she wanted fruit or chips with her sandwich and saw that she'd fallen asleep. Filled with tenderness, he leaned over her to readjust the blanket and stopped when he saw the tears on her cheeks.

He could have sworn that a moment ago they hadn't been there. Had she been holding them back and sleep released them? She did have a lot to worry about—her father's demanding girlfriend and the threat of impeachment the two latest worries in the life of a single mother who was also a public official.

He wished he could keep her here and protect her from everything that could hurt her. But she'd never stand for that. He'd just have to do the best he could for her tonight. He went into the kitchen to make her sandwich.

He'd put mayonnaise, lettuce and tomato on toasted wheat bread and was draining the bacon for two sandwiches on paper towels when Jackie walked into the kitchen ten minutes later. She had the blanket wrapped around her, her cheeks pink, her eyes still heavy.

"I fell asleep," she said apologetically. "Is there anything I can do?"

The tears had dried on her cheeks, he noted, leaving faint tracks of mascara. There was something charming about it that touched him, but he knew she wouldn't appreciate having it brought to her attention.

"Everything's ready." He put the bacon on the sandwiches and handed her the plates. "You want to take those back to the fire, and I'll bring the tea."

She smiled at him over her shoulder. "Don't forget the Oreos."

He took the bag off the tray and held them up. She smiled her approval and disappeared into the living room.

He poured boiling water over the teabags in the simple brown pot and caught a whiff of something medicinal and unappealing. He put the lid on the pot and consoled himself with the thought that Jackie might like it.

And apparently she did. She was on her second cup, her sandwich almost finished, when she reached into the open bag of cookies and took one.

She watched him note the action. "I know," she said, taking a bite. She chewed, put a hand to her chest as she moaned in approval, then swallowed. "I'm not finished with my sandwich, but I'm taking advantage of the girls being gone to live recklessly."

He arched an eyebrow. "This is reckless? A cookie before your dinner's finished?"

She smiled and nodded. "I guess to someone who sends men hundreds of thousands of miles into space, that doesn't seem reckless, but when you're a mom, any flouting of the rules is reckless. And you never risk it when there's a possibility the kids will see you. But mine are miles away tonight."

"You seem to enjoy being a mom." He topped up her teacup. He'd be able to do that a few more times, because his remained untouched after the first sip. Whatever curative properties it might have, chamomile was vile-tasting stuff in his opinion. "Will it still be fun with three?"

"Oh, sure," she said with the casual confidence of experience. "When I had Rachel, I was shocked by how much more work two children were than one, then you fall into the rhythm of who needs what and when and what makes them happy, and somehow it's all programmed into your brain and you no longer notice the effort. It doesn't diminish the way you worry about them and their safety, but you're just no longer aware of what it costs you to keep them happy. I'm sure three will be no different."

"Of course, you'll still be mayor."

"Right. But my baby-sitter will stay on, hopefully, and your mother and the ladies at church will be helping me in the beginning. It'll all come together."

His sandwich finished, he leaned on his elbow and watched her snag another cookie. She talked bravely, he thought, but she looked desperately as though she needed rescue. Or at least help. "What are you going to do to sustain *you?*"

She cast him an amused smile and bit into the cookie. "I just don't think about it. Most mothers don't think about it. Somehow, keeping your children happy and functioning sustains you."

"Maybe the mother part, but what about the person? The woman?"

She opened her mouth to reply, but he interrupted quickly with, "And don't tell me she doesn't exist. I've kissed her."

"There's just no time for her," she said with a shrug. "I never liked her much anyway. Nothing she ever did turned out quite right."

"She was going to go away with me," he reminded her quietly. "That would have turned out. We might have struggled, but it would have turned out. We'd have had the kind of marriage where you support and sustain each other, rather than what you had with Ricky."

She looked suddenly weary. "Let's not go there tonight, Hank."

"I'm trying," he insisted intrepidly, "to make you see yourself. There's a whole part of you you're ignoring. That's not good for you."

She dropped the half-eaten cookie on her plate and picked up the rest of her sandwich. "You've been gone too long to know what's good for me," she said with more conviction than anger. "And how would you know, anyway? You came home because you didn't have a life? That suggests a whole part of your own life was ignored."

"True. But at least I recognized the problem."

"Yeah, well, for me it's not a problem. I didn't like being married, so it doesn't really matter if the woman in me ever finds another man. I don't intend to get married again."

The words seemed ludicrous coming from such a beautiful woman ripe with pregnancy. And they weren't helping his cause at all.

"Oh, don't look so surprised," she snapped, suddenly impatient. She dropped the sandwich to her plate, put the plate aside and pushed herself laboriously to her feet. "I know you kissed me and I reacted. Sex is great, living with a man just to get it wouldn't be."

Hank sprang to his feet, following her to the hook where he'd hung her coat. "Do you think that's all marriage has to offer?"

"No," she said, yanking her coat down. "In my experience, it has nothing to offer. I just thought you might think I'd want to be married for the sex. But I don't. I *don't.*"

SHE WAS PROTESTING TOO MUCH. She could hear it in her own voice. Instead of being convincing, she came off sounding like a frustrated old maid who said she didn't want any because she couldn't get it.

Which was just about true at the moment. She'd felt all softened and vulnerable in this warm and wonderful house, enjoying his sandwich and his cookies and the attentive way he covered her with a blanket. But it didn't change what was. Nothing would ever change that. And she was impatient with herself that she kept forgetting.

Then she caught sight of her reflection in the mirror near the door and gasped at the sight of her mussed mascara. The tears she'd thought she'd suppressed had fallen when she was asleep.

Hank turned her to him, framing her face in his hands and running his thumbs over her cheeks. "What hurts so much," he asked, "that you cry in your sleep?"

She wanted to pull his hands away, but his touch did something to her, made her want to believe that nature and fate could be thwarted, that there was some way they could be happy together.

"I'm pregnant," she said in a suddenly frail voice. "I feel like crying about everything." Tears crowded her eyes now and she drew a ragged breath, trying to hold them back.

He put a gentle hand to her shoulder and rubbed down to her elbow. "Maybe you'd feel better if you indulge that feeling once in a while. While you're awake and can enjoy the release."

She took a step backward, out of his reach. "No. I'm a mother. I'm a mayor. I have to keep it together."

He took a step toward her. "Everyone has to let go once in a while."

She shook her head firmly, the threat of tears making her voice raspy and frail. "I have to go."

"Why?" he asked gently. "The kids are gone. Why don't you spend the night here?"

"You promised you wouldn't try to make me stay."

"I'm not trying to make you stay. I think you *want* to stay. I'm just trying to make you admit it."

She put a hand back to the doorknob. "I have to meet my father for breakfast."

"I'll drive you in in time," he promised.

"No, no!" she shouted, her voice gaining sudden power in her need to escape before she fell apart. Then she remembered that she couldn't escape. Her car was in the inn's parking lot. Hank had driven her here. "Just…just drive me back to the inn and don't say anything."

"Nothing at all? Not 'fasten your seat belt,' or 'are you warm enough?' or…"

She pointed a threatening finger at him. "Hank. If

you say one more word, I won't be responsible for what happens to you."

He seemed willing to accept that with equanimity. "I've always faced up to the consequences of my actions." He waggled his fingers at her in a come-and-get-me gesture. "Come on. Do your best. Because I'm going to keep talking. I'm going to tell you that you want to stay with me because all the feelings we had for each other as kids are still alive. They've lain dormant all these years, but now that I'm back, you're going to have to stop pretending that you're fine, that your life is just the way you want it."

"Hank," she said, tears streaming down her face at the utter injustice of having to deal with this all over again. "Believe me when I tell you it can't be."

He shook his head at her. "Sorry. I believed you seventeen years ago when you told me it'd be better if you didn't come with me. This time I'm going with what I think is best. We are meant to be together. I'm going to make you love me again."

She closed her eyes so that he couldn't see that she already did. Had never stopped.

He was reaching for his jacket, about to comply with her plea that he take her home, when the baby gave her a firm and punitive kick to her spine.

"Ow!" she complained before she could stop herself, putting a hand to her back and the other to Hank's arm.

He wrapped his arm around her and drew her back to the sofa. "What?" he demanded. "Pain? Contraction? You want me to call your doctor?"

The baby kicked again, this time to the front. She winced and leaned back against the pillows. "No," she groaned. "It's just kicking, I think, but geez! The baby must be in a temper."

Hank sat beside her, putting a gentle hand to her belly. "Well, no wonder. He's fighting for space amid all your suppressed stress and emotion." He grinned. "And he knows what's going on inside you. He knows you're fibbing when you say you don't want it to work out between us."

"I didn't say I don't want it to work, I said I'm sure that it can't. I've been another man's wife, I have two children, and as angelic as they were when you brought dinner over, they can be that devilish when things aren't going their way." She sighed and finished wearily, "Seventeen years is a long time. We've grown in different directions."

"If that was true," he said, putting a pillow against the arm of the sofa and lifting her feet so that she lay the length of the cushions, "we wouldn't find ourselves in the same place, comfortable together despite the past."

"You're comfortable?" she asked doubtfully as he pulled off her shoes and spread the blanket over her.

"I am," he confirmed. "And you are, too. You just don't want to admit it to yourself and let it be. Baby settled down?"

She put a hand to her stomach, where all was quiet for the moment. Her back hurt and her ribs felt as though someone was wedging them apart, but she was getting used to that.

"Yes."

"Good. You stay here where I can keep an eye on you, then I'll take you to meet your dad in the morning."

He flipped the lights out so that all she saw was firelight. It danced cheerfully and silhouetted Hank's figure as he knelt before it to add another log.

All the stress and tension of the evening left her. She thought that strange in light of the fact that nothing had changed; all her problems remained in place.

She closed her eyes and listened to the sound of Hank stirring the fire, his footsteps across the room as he locked the door, then into the kitchen, where he probably checked the back door and made sure the stove was turned off.

A little wave of comfort stroked across her body, seemed to pat her shoulder and tell her to relax.

She heard a sound nearby and opened her heavy eyelids to see Hank sitting on the end of the sofa beyond her feet.

"Go to sleep," he ordered gently, draping an arm over her ankles and catching a blanketed foot in his hand. "Everything's all right."

"For the moment, anyway," she qualified, closing her eyes with a sigh.

"That's all we have." His voice came to her through a long tunnel as her awareness began to drift. "Moment to moment."

HANK AWOKE TO DARKNESS and a definite chill in the air. The fire had gone out and the furnace had turned automatically to a lower nighttime setting. He pressed the winding stem on his watch for illumination and saw that it was 3:17.

Jackie was curled up under the blanket into as tight a ball as she could achieve. She needed another blanket, and he could use one himself.

He reset the furnace, then got the fire going again to take the chill away until the furnace warmed up the air. Then he sprinted upstairs to the linen closet for blankets. He was opening one out over Jackie when she said his name.

The plaintive sound of it in the darkness made his pulse accelerate.

"I'm right here," he said, adding the second blanket.

She caught his hand as he tucked the blanket around her.

"I'm cold," she complained. "Really cold."

"I just got the fire going again," he said, trying to free his hand to give her the third blanket, but she seemed unwilling to part with it.

"Cold," she said again.

"Okay. Can you sit up?"

She didn't sound entirely awake, but he could feel her shuddering under the blanket.

"Sleepy," she said, "and cold."

Smiling in the darkness, he reached under her to lift her upper body, heavy with her pregnancy. He sat under her, wrapped the third blanket around his shoulders, then tugged her toward him. Her bulk made it awkward, but the moment she realized that his arms promised warmth, she propped herself up and literally fell into his arms and turned her face into his chest.

"Mmm," she said with a heavy sigh.

"Mmm," he thought, enfolding her in the wings of his blanket and smiling again at her little moan of approval.

He wasn't giving up, he thought, until they were curled up in the darkness together every night.

CHAPTER TEN

HANK AWOKE to pale daylight and found Jackie still in his arms, watching him. She looked warm and rumpled, and there was something in her expression from the old days—love, admiration, affection. But there was a curious sadness there, too, that confused and worried him.

He gazed into her eyes, trying to assess the strength of this enemy to their happiness. There were dark layers in the depths of the soft gray—pain, he guessed. The pain he'd caused her? he wondered.

No. He didn't think so. He wouldn't see love and affection there, too, would he, if he'd caused the sadness?

She put an index finger to his lips and smiled. "You still smile in your sleep."

He caught her fingertip and kissed it. "Because I had you in my arms."

To his complete surprise, she leaned forward to plant a light kiss on his lips. "That was the best night's sleep I've had," she said, "since Erica was born. Thank you."

If he was calculating the amount of time spent sleeping, it was the worst night's sleep he'd had since he helped bring the astronauts home last August. But discounting that, it was the most delicious six hours he'd spent since he'd left her and Maple Hill all those years ago.

"My pleasure," he said softly. "I intend to do this for you every night."

She smiled, but that sadness filled her eyes again and she pushed her hands against his chest and tried to lever herself to her feet. It was a job for two. Hank slipped out from under her, and catching her hands, pulled her to a standing position.

She groaned with the effort, then the sound turned to one of exasperation. "Next time I decide to have a baby at this age," she teased, looking carefully away from him as she searched for her purse, "remind me that it makes me move like a Buick without wheels."

He went to the hearth where she'd left the large leather pouch and handed it to her. "Next time you decide to have a baby," he returned, "I'll be involved enough to do that."

She scolded him with a look.

He spread his arms helplessly. "What do you want from me? It's not going to go away. We have to deal with it. *You* have to deal with it."

"Hank, don't start," she admonished quietly. "Do you know where my shoes are?"

He pointed to the floor in front of her.

She looked down at them in dismay, then put her arms out for balance as she tried to push her feet into them. But her feet had swollen overnight and the task was impossible. She couldn't even bend over to retrieve them, and she looked up at him pleadingly.

He folded his arms and stood his ground. "You tell me what the sadness is about," he said, "and I'll get you your shoes."

She pretended surprise. "What sadness?"

He didn't fall for it. He put a hand to the side of her face and traced the delicate skin under her eye with his thumb.

"The sadness right here, under the smile and the strength. That's what's keeping us apart, isn't it? Not the fact that I left and you stayed."

For an instant, he saw horror in her expression that he'd read that much. Then the old resolve to do what she had to do took over and that glimpse of vulnerability was lost.

"You agreed that we'd be friends," she said judiciously, "and friends don't torture each other." She walked to the other end of the sofa where his Romeos lay, stepped into them, and with a so-there! look in his direction, shuffled determinedly toward the bathroom.

Accepting defeat, he snatched her shoes off the floor with one hand and stopped her halfway to the bathroom. He caught her hand, held it palm up and slapped the shoes into it.

"I'm remembering," he said irascibly, "that things usually had to end up your way."

She closed her eyes a moment, her expression darkly amused. "Yeah, well, that stopped right after you left. Thank you for getting my shoes." She stepped out of his and headed for the bathroom.

Jackie, Hank thought, made space travel seem simple.

"WHY DON'T YOU join us for breakfast?" Adam Fortin asked Hank. He and Jackie and Hank stood under the inn's red- and gray-striped awning.

Jackie smiled in Hank's direction, hoping her father would interpret the look as seconding his invitation, but that Hank would understand she didn't want him to come. She hadn't liked the hopeful look in her father's eyes when Hank pulled into the inn's parking lot with Jackie in the passenger seat.

"Thanks, but I have to get to the office." Hank shook her father's hand.

"It's Saturday," Adam protested.

Hank grinned. "Electrical and plumbing emergencies on Saturday mean overtime. You two have fun."

Grateful that she was about to escape an embarrassing explanation, Jackie offered Hank a cheerful goodbye. Her wish that he have a good day never left her lips.

He cupped the back of her head in one hand and covered her mouth with his in a firm, lengthy kiss. Then he freed her, gave her a look that told her she couldn't expect everything to go her way, and climbed into his van.

Jackie was both indignant and delighted and wasn't sure which emotion deserved free rein. Adam chuckled, put an arm around her shoulders and led her to the sporty little Cadillac Catera he'd rented. "I'd better get you some food," he teased, "to put into that open mouth."

The Breakfast Barn was a favorite hangout of locals, huge amounts of simple but delicious food served at a reasonable price. A nineteenth-century dairy barn housed dozens of tables, a long counter with bright red stools and a banquet room at the back where Kiwanis, Rotary and The Revolutionary Dames held their weekly meetings.

Brick-red walls were decorated with old farming tools, photos of patrons and the city league teams the restaurant sponsored. Each booth and table had a bud vase of flowers appropriate to the season. This morning, sprigs of hawthorn and pine filled the vases.

"God, I love this place!" Adam slipped into a booth opposite Jackie and closed his eyes as he inhaled the aroma of bacon and spicy Portuguese sausage frying, the smells of coffee, of citrus and melon and the perfumes and aftershaves of the men and women beginning their day at the Barn. "The only thing that comes close to the down-home sincerity is the small-town pubs in England."

"I'd wager you didn't meet Sabrina in a pub," Jackie said, pulling off her jacket and letting it fall to the seat. When she looked up again, her father studied her with a frown.

"What kind of a welcome-home remark is that?" he asked, then was distracted by the waitress, who brought menus and poured coffee.

"Well, Adam Fortin, as I live and breathe!" The short plump woman had a curly up-do colored an unconventional shade of burgundy. She was a good friend of Adeline Whitcomb. "Heard you were home. Hi, Jackie."

"Rita, how've you been?" he asked genially. "I got in last night. And you keep forgetting this is no longer home for me. I live in Miami now."

"'Cause of the decorator?" Rita interrogated him with the ease of long friendship.

"What decorator?" he asked, clearly convinced she couldn't possibly mean the one he'd brought to town with him just the night before. He'd apparently lived in Miami long enough to have forgotten the Maple Hill information pipeline.

"The princess you brought with you."

Jackie couldn't help enjoying his stammering while he tried to decide whether to be offended by the remark or astonished that someone across town already knew— a mere ten hours after the fact—that he'd brought a woman home with him.

Curiosity won over sensitivity. "How could you possibly know about her?"

Rita Robidoux smiled and leaned an elbow on the back of Jackie's side of the booth. "Adeline was already in this morning. The board of Revolutionary Dames meets at 7:00 a.m."

That failed to clarify things for him. "And how did she know?"

"John Granger's mother is our secretary. I waited on them." She shook her head pityingly. "I heard all about the heat lamp in the bathroom. Sounds like a bit of a prima donna to me."

Jackie saw her father's eyebrows beetle and decided it was time she intervened. "I'll have a Denver omelette with egg substitute," she said quickly, "and fruit instead of potatoes and toast. Daddy?"

"The usual," he said with a frown, handing back his menu.

Rita took it from him. "How can you say you live in Miami," she asked with a provincial tilt of her chin, "when you can walk into a restaurant in Maple Hill and order 'the usual'?"

She walked away before he could attempt to answer, knowing Adam's "usual" was bacon and eggs over hard, hashbrowns and whole wheat toast.

Adam looked at Jackie in affronted disbelief. "Is there no civility left in this world?"

Jackie shrugged. "Not judging by Sabrina." Since the subject had already been opened for review—with a sledgehammer—she felt safe continuing the discussion. "What are you doing with her, Dad?"

He took a sip of coffee, probably counting, she guessed.

"I like her," he replied with strained patience. "I met her on the cruise, we had a good time together, and she enjoys being with me." When she looked skeptical, he asked stiffly, "You don't think that's possible?"

"Of course I do." It occurred to her that at this point in time she was the last one to question who took up with whom, but she put that reasonable thought aside, more comfortable with her filial disapproval. "I love your company. Your granddaughters love your company. All the inn's employees love it when you come home. And it is home, Daddy. You just don't like to think of it that way anymore because Mom's no longer here. Well, guess what? The rest of your family still is, and after two years of your quest for whatever it is you're searching for to prove your desirability or your virility or to come to terms with the fact that you're still alive when Mom isn't, you're…you're making everyone wonder when you'll come to your senses."

"Oh, really." He leaned toward her on his forearms. "Well, let me tell you something, missy. I have never lived my life to conform to Maple Hill's expectations. I love everyone here, but you know they'll gossip about anything and everything."

He fixed her with a steady look and she met it unflinchingly. "Yes, I know that. But what about your granddaughters' expectations? They haven't had you for any length of time in two years, and then you come home with a woman a third your age and a snob to boot."

"My granddaughters and I understand each other very well. You don't have to…" He paused abruptly when Rita brought a twelve-ounce glass of orange juice to the table—part of his "usual."

"You don't have to remind me of my duties as a grandfather," he said more quietly. "And you should be the last one to rake me over the coals. At least I'm trying to keep my heart alive. You haven't cared about your emotional life since you realized what a tragic mistake you made with Ricky. Judging by the surprised look on your face when Hank kissed you, you haven't a clue what's going on between the two of you."

She sighed patiently. "Daddy, how would you know what's going on between us. You haven't even been here."

"John likes to talk as much as his mother does," he replied. "And I'm not the only one in the family this town is worried about. You should have gone with Hank when you graduated."

She stared at him openmouthed. "You knew what I was up against. And he wouldn't even let me explain!"

"If you hadn't chickened out at the last minute," he said mercilessly, "you'd have made him listen."

"Dad…!" she gasped.

He put a hand to his forehead, took a sip of juice, then sat back in the booth and shook his head regretfully. "I'm not saying you didn't live bravely with your decision and do the absolute best you could in an impossible situation, but damn it, Jackie. Now's your chance to fix it."

She'd have loved to believe that, but she knew better. "Some things can't be fixed, Daddy."

He sighed deeply. "Everything can be fixed—just

not easily. And if he's moved back here and apparently still in love with you, you're going to have to either move to Miami with me so you don't have to see him every day…" He studied her face and seemed to see that that very thing was already taking its toll on her. "Or…fix it," he added softly, reaching across the table to take her hand.

She knew he was right, but she felt fairly sure that an attempt to "fix it" would end it. And the love that had evaded her all those years ago and now offered itself so generously a second time would be lost to her forever.

She couldn't think about that, so she turned the discussion back on him. "Are you expecting Sabrina to fix things for you?"

He shrugged. "Right now, I'm not sure. We like a lot of the same things, she's smart and funny and she thinks I am, too. She had two weeks between jobs, so I invited her to meet my family. I know she can be a little demanding, but she owns a business with twenty-three branches. She has to be forceful and in charge, or everything would fall apart. Don't take it personally."

He was right. At least he was willing to take a step out in faith and see what happened. As his daughter, she had to honor that.

"When can the two of you come for dinner?" she asked, leaning back as Rita arrived with their food. "Unfortunately, the girls are gone until Sunday night. A church group outing with Addy Whitcomb."

He rolled his eyes. "How is Addy? Still supervising the world?"

"Now that we have a space station," she laughed, "she's going interplanetary."

He nodded. "That's our Addy. So you're alone for the weekend?"

She was afraid to reply on the chance he intended to invite her to join them and become better acquainted with Sabrina. "Alone with mountains of laundry, payroll for the inn and city paperwork. I should get a lot done in the peace and quiet." That barrier erected, she asked amiably, "What are you two doing?"

"Sabrina has a friend at Amherst she wants to see this afternoon," he replied, "and tomorrow she wants to just drive and see the Berkshires."

The Berkshires were magnificent. Sabrina did show good taste there. "Shall I serve as concierge and make reservations for you to have lunch at De Marco's?"

He looked pleasantly surprised by the offer. "Thank you. I'd appreciate that."

"Sure." She grinned as she passed him the pepper. "In exchange you have to promise me that you won't make her my stepmother."

Teasingly, he yanked the pepper away. "How about if I just flaunt our May-December romance to the Revolutionary Dames and get the whole town talking?"

Rita had reappeared unnoticed and sloshed coffee into his almost empty cup. "The ship's sailed on that one, Fortin. We already are."

THE WEEKEND was painfully short. Jackie did get the laundry done and prepared the inn's payroll. She had lied about having to do paperwork for the city, but was tempted to go into the office on Sunday anyway to catch up on correspondence.

But that might mean running into John Brockton,

and she didn't want that to spoil her solitude. Monday would be plenty of time to learn the details of his impeachment plans.

So she sat alone in her living room Sunday afternoon and tried to absorb the quiet. The moment the girls got home, it would be gone. She'd adjust immediately; she loved the sound of their voices. But when she was stressed, she longed for the precious gift of having the house to herself.

She didn't seem to be able to enjoy the last few hours of her day, however. She found herself wondering why Hank hadn't called—and hating that it worried her.

She told herself she hadn't expected him to call. She'd told him that nothing could come of their fragile relationship and she sincerely believed that. But somehow the possibility that he finally did, too, was upsetting.

Would he just give up on her now and find another woman to pursue? There were certainly enough single women in town wanting to pursue him, according to Haley. Maybe now he'd want to meet that niece of Addy's friend.

She went into the kitchen to bake cookies and put the subject out of her mind. Instead, she got a clear mental picture of enjoying her plate of sweet treats with him at the tea shop. And she remembered the perfect BLT he'd made her, and the bag of Oreos they'd shared.

She was about to paint the inside of her eyelids black in the hope that images couldn't form there when the front door burst open and Addy appeared with Erica and Rachel. Everyone spoke at once, souvenirs were shoved in Jackie's face, and she found the madness of the moment a delicious relief from the constant image of Hank's face.

As the girls carried their bags upstairs, Addy gave Jackie a hug. "We had a wonderful time," she reported, "and you'll be pleased to know that they were cooperative and well-mannered every single moment."

Jackie narrowed her eyes in teasing suspicion. "You wouldn't be trying to kid me."

Addy laughed. "Not at all. They're great fun to be with. You have every right to be proud. So, when are we going to decide on colors?"

Jackie blinked. "Colors?"

"Wedding colors," Addy replied.

Jackie laughed. "You took my daughters off for a weekend and now one of them is getting married?"

Addy swatted Jackie's arm. "*Your* wedding. Rachel insists there's going to be one. Erica thinks you'll fold and won't be able to commit to Hank. Which do you think it's going to be? If I'm going to be mother of the groom, I'll need a little time to shop, to..."

Jackie wasn't sure which opinion was more upsetting. She swatted Addy back. "Ha, ha. I've seen him several times, we do enjoy each other's company, but I promise you there's no need to run out shopping."

Addy made a face. "You're sure? The girls and I were planning a shower and everything."

"I'm sure, Addy." Jackie hugged her then opened the door. "But if anything changes, you'll be the first to know."

"I look good in blue," Addy said as Jackie walked her out onto the porch. "And green. Yellow makes me look jaundiced, and pink just isn't me. Lavender, though, is..."

"Addy!"

"I could buy an Easter outfit that'd do double duty."

Jackie decided the only way to turn her off was to

pretend she wasn't talking. "Thank you. The girls seem to have really enjoyed the weekend." She walked Addy down the steps and to her car. "Poor things never see anything but school and me."

Addy opened the driver's door. "A man in their lives would be a nice addition. You should see Hank in a tux."

"I have," Jackie reminded her. "Our senior dance was formal."

Addy made a dismissive sound. "That was before he had shoulders."

"Good night, Addy," Jackie said firmly.

Addy sighed. "Good night, Jackie."

It took the girls an hour of talking on top of each other over milk and cookies to settle down. They'd bathed and changed into pajamas, but still looked wide-awake.

"What did you do while we were gone?" Erica asked. She leaned both elbows on the table and propped her chin in her hands. Not precisely the good manners Addy had just praised her for, Jackie thought, but while they were eager to share their experiences was not the time to quibble. "Did you have a date?"

Rachel seemed excited at the possibility, but Erica looked as though she already knew the answer. She wondered why her oldest child felt sure her mother couldn't commit.

"I did, as a matter of fact," Jackie replied, putting her coffee cup casually to her lips. "Hank took me out for a sandwich after my shift at the inn on Friday."

Both girls sat up and stared at her in astonishment. "He did?" they asked simultaneously.

She nodded, deciding to withhold the part about going to his place and staying the night.

"We had a very good time."

Erica continued to stare, then asked, eyes widening, "Did he kiss you?"

Jackie wasn't sure what she was doing here. She shouldn't be encouraging them to think he could become a part of their lives, but she couldn't pretend he'd simply disappear, either. Something had to be done. And soon.

Erica pointed to Jackie's face. "He did kiss you!" she exclaimed. "Your cheeks are pink!"

"Yes, he did." There was little point in denying it when she'd been seen through like a window. "But just once."

"Was it nice?"

"Nice. Yes."

"Did he take your clothes off?" Rachel wanted to know.

Erica turned to her impatiently. "Don't be stupid! Mom's pregnant."

Rachel looked surprised by her sister's angry reaction. "On TV whenever they kiss, they start taking each other's clothes off."

Jackie focused on Erica. "What have you two been watching? I thought I told you to stick to Disney and Nickelodeon."

"Ashley Browning told me," Rachel explained. "She gets to watch whatever her parents are watching." She frowned at Jackie in sudden worry. "It hurts to have a baby, you know. There's a lot of yelling and screaming, 'cause the baby has to come through your belly button."

Erica collapsed on her folded arms, laughing hysterically.

Jackie wasn't sure she could deal with this tonight, though she had a little difficulty suppressing her own smile. She knew right where she'd put the children's book on childbirth she'd bought, certain that such questions would come up as delivery approached.

She urged the girls to put their dishes on the counter, then ushered them upstairs. "That part isn't quite right," she said gently, snatching the book out of the case in the hall. "It does hurt, but the doctor has medicines that take away the pain and help the baby come safely. Climb into bed and I'll read to you about how it happens."

Rachel scrambled eagerly under the covers. Jackie noticed that Erica, who'd laughed knowingly at her sister's misinterpretation of the facts, hung by the door.

Jackie patted the edge of the mattress beside Rachel. "Would you like to join us?"

Erica wandered unhurriedly toward them. "I know what happens, but some stuff is…you know…blurry."

Jackie nodded, covering her as she climbed in beside her sister. "Right. Well, maybe this will clarify it." She opened the book and began to read.

JACKIE AWOKE Monday morning feeling huge and heavy and very depressed. According to Haley, John Brockton and Russ Benedict would file charges against Jackie today. And while she didn't think Brockton had a leg to stand on, simply raising the issue would plant doubts in some people's minds and was bound to make everything she did as mayor just a little more difficult. She had to watch her every step.

She'd been through worse, she told herself as she woke the girls cheerfully and made pancake batter. Of course, the whole world hadn't known then that her husband never loved her enough to be faithful, and she hadn't been carrying an anvil in her stomach, either.

And she'd managed to forget what she'd done to Hank seventeen years ago. Well, she'd never forgotten, but she'd been able to bury it by reminding herself of her pure intentions.

While the girls ate, she checked the kitchen calendar, her mind too cluttered with her own problems to allow her to remember if Erica or Rachel had anything going on after school. A quick look told her the girls' schedules were open, but she had an ultrasound right after lunch. She'd had one scheduled at four months, then gotten a cold and canceled the appointment. She'd been unable to find a spare moment since then to reschedule, and a normal pregnancy had removed any urgency to do so. But her doctor insisted she have one as she approached her ninth month.

She grabbed an energy bar and a commuter mug filled with milk and drank and ate on her way from the school to City Hall.

John, Russ and a tall, slender man they introduced as the impeachment committee's attorney handed Jackie a thick sheaf of papers before she'd crossed the lobby to the stairs. They'd invited Haley and a representative from the radio station, apparently making a media event out of filing charges.

City employees stood in the doorways of all the open offices with varying degrees of anger or approval on their faces. Some watched from the second-floor railing, and she noticed Addy and Parker in the basement doorway.

A light flashed from the direction of the stairway, and

Jackie looked up to see Haley lower her camera with a rueful wave.

"You can't do this!" Evelyn, Jackie's secretary, appeared from behind her, her lunch and her briefcase still in hand. "It's wrong, and you know it!"

Jackie pulled herself out of her depression and smiled at Evelyn, then at John Brockton. "No, it isn't, Evelyn. It's what the whole process is about, and many of our Maple Hill ancestors fought for that very thing—the right to expect honesty in our government." She held up the sheaf of papers toward Haley, giving her a moment to get another shot, then smiled confidently at her audience. "The recall hearing will give me the opportunity to prove that I'm the honest one, and that John Brockton and Russ Benedict are—" she paused to consider all the things she'd like to say about what she thought they were, then remembered that she was trying to prove herself fit to govern "—not," she finished pleasantly. "Back to work, everyone. Maple Hill doesn't run itself."

"May I have a word with you, Ms. Mayor?" Haley asked at the bottom of the stairs. Her polite, professional expression hid an uncertainty Jackie identified and understood immediately. Haley was just doing her job.

"Please," Jackie said. "We'll talk in my office."

Evelyn held up a paper bag from the bakery. "I thought we might need sugar today. I'll make the coffee."

Jackie led the way upstairs. "Bless you, Ev." To Haley, she said, "You can't teach that kind of clever crunch-time thinking."

"So, what's your strategy?" Haley asked as she and Jackie sat at the small sofa in her office. "I know you think you can beat this because everyone loves you and your family, but I want to make sure you're covering all the bases here."

Jackie nodded. "Of course. I want to read this through first, then when I know what I'm up against, I'll get a lawyer and be prepared."

Haley took notes. "Bart says he'll volunteer his services. You deny any suggestion of impropriety in your administration?"

"Unequivocally," Jackie replied firmly.

"Without reading the charges?"

"I have never at any point in my service done anything even remotely illegal or self-serving. I don't have to read the charges to know that."

Haley nodded. "Good. Perfect pull quote." She put down her pen. "Can I have another maple bar? Or should I be thinking about fitting into a bridesmaid's dress?"

Jackie picked delicately at a giant apple fritter. She'd hate herself later, she knew, but this was now. She took a long pull of decaf coffee, thinking that even a long pull didn't equate to a short sip of the real stuff. "Have you been talking to your mother? Or my girls?"

Haley shook her head. "Rita at the Breakfast Barn. She said Hank, Bart and a couple of the guys in Hank's office had pie and coffee there after basketball practice last night. He picked up the tab, then forgot to pay it. Apparently everyone was teasing him about being in love. Said he'd performed very poorly during practice. Couldn't focus. He's usually their high scorer. And Friday night, I couldn't reach him and I couldn't reach you. Simple coincidence, or two loonies finally coming to their senses?"

Jackie leaned back against the sofa cushions, balancing her coffee on the padded arm. Life was too complicated today to try to lie about anything. She told Haley about Hank picking her up Friday night, and her staying until morning.

"I was stressed, he can be very comforting," she said, as though there was no other way to explain it. "I had the first good night's sleep I've had in years. But…that's all."

"Jackie." Haley touched her arm. "When it's right, it's right. I had a tough time coming to terms with that, too, because I didn't want to put my faith in anyone after what Paul Abbott did to me. I'm sure you feel that way because of all that Ricky put you through. But Hank isn't like that. You know he isn't."

"I know." Then she expressed the concern that had been bothering her since Saturday morning. "But he hasn't called me since."

"There's some kind of power crisis at the senior housing complex. He was supposed to come for dinner last night and canceled."

"Oh."

"Why don't you call him?"

"It's just not that simple."

"Ha! Because you're in politics, you think everything has to be complicated and intricate, but it doesn't. You love him, he loves you…"

Jackie looked at her watch. "Don't you have ads to sell or pages to paste up or something?"

"Ads are sold," Haley said, "and the computer does the paste-up now. But I can take a hint." She put her cup down on the coffee table and picked up her large briefcase-purse.

"Can you have lunch today?"

Jackie shook her head regretfully. "Thanks, but I have a doctor's appointment this afternoon."

"Everything okay?" Haley asked, her brow furrowing.

"Everything's fine. Just an ultrasound. Maybe tomorrow?"

"Sure. You and the girls are coming to Mom's birthday celebration Sunday, right? I ran into your dad and invited him, too." She grinned wickedly. "I met Frosty Fanny."

Jackie laughed aloud at Haley's assessment of Sabrina. "Is she invited, too?"

Haley hunched her shoulders apologetically. "It was only polite."

"Of course it was." They stood, Haley helping Jackie up. "We'd love to come."

"Two o'clock?"

"We'll be there."

Jackie had Evelyn hold her calls and spent the rest of the morning reading the charges filed against her and the copy of the charter the committee had provided, the section on Impeachment highlighted.

Most of the accusations were transparently vindictive, and served more to indict Brockton's motive than to prove guilt on Jackie's part.

He cited her absence at several meetings, all of which had occurred because her children were ill or she was— and the council had been notified the day before so that Paul Balducci chaired the meeting in her place and with her notes on matters on the agenda.

He termed her efforts for Perk Avenue "influence peddling," and asked that the situation be investigated.

He asked for an audit of the funds for the project for

the homeless, suggesting there was ten thousand dollars less in the account than had been given them. But that money had been paid to the builder and she felt certain John knew that.

Only the suggestion that she was improperly funneling work Hank's way had any possibility of sticking.

They had been high-school sweethearts, and she was now offering him work in her capacity as mayor. But she was sure she could prove one had nothing to do with the other.

If only she didn't look into anyone's eyes, she thought as she fell back dispiritedly in her chair. Because she did feel like Hank's lover—probably because she wanted to be. They hadn't been lovers in seventeen years, but she'd change that tomorrow if she could.

She decided she'd better phone Bart.

CHAPTER ELEVEN

PETE MARCOTT, Maple Hill's radiologist, spread gel on the mound of Jackie's stomach and gave a long, low whistle as he wiped his hands. "That baby must be lying stretched out, like on a lawn chair. Either that, or there are three other babies in there hiding behind him and evading our womb-spying technology."

Jackie raised her head to glower playfully at the tall young man who looked more like a Chicago Bears quarterback than a kind and gentle doctor. "Don't even tease about that, Pete. I have enough turmoil in my life right now."

He frowned as he put the convex probe to her stomach. "I heard about this impeachment foolishness over breakfast this morning. What's going on, anyway?"

She felt Pete guide the probe over her stomach. She explained about John Brockton's resentment of her when she was just a councilwoman, his shock and disapproval when she was named mayor, then his eagerness to thwart or subvert her every move ever since.

"Then I encouraged Bridget and Cecilia to get that spot on the square for the tearoom when he'd promised his brother he'd be able to put a Cha-Cha Chicken franchise there. Unfortunately, his brother didn't have the financing together in time, and lost out to Perk Avenue. He blames me." She sighed. "Now he's really out for blood. You would think that since everyone knows he…"

Pete shushed her abruptly.

"What?" she asked, all senses suddenly focused on the procedure. "Something wrong?"

He held up a hand for silence, his eyes on the viewing screen.

Her heartbeat accelerating, Jackie followed his gaze and saw the swirling stuff she always had difficulty identifying as anything on other proud mothers' ultrasound prints. She looked up at Pete, really beginning to worry about that frown of concentration.

"Pete, what it is?" she demanded, worry turning almost instantly to fear. This was her third child, and though the last thing she needed to worry about after what had happened with Ricky was another life, this baby was part of the family. She'd lived with it for eight months, her girls nuzzled it and felt it kick. She wouldn't let anything be wrong. "Tell me!" she said firmly. "What is it?"

He gave her a quick, apologetic glance before turning back to the screen. "Nothing's wrong, Jackie. It's just that…" His long index finger pointed to the screen and a small, pulsing spot of light. "See that?"

"Yes."

"That's his heartbeat."

"Oh!" She felt excitement blunted by concern. "Is there something wrong with it?"

His finger moved across the screen to another pulsing light. "Here's another one. My joke about three other babies hiding behind the first one wasn't so far wrong. Except that it's only one. You're carrying twins, kiddo."

In view of the morning she'd had, the chaos that was her life and the potential for disaster that was her growing relationship with Hank, all she could do was put a hand over her face and swear. And hope that he was wrong and it was possible to give birth to one healthy baby with two hearts!

"I know," Pete said apologetically, pushing a button to print the image. "I'm sorry. It's a shock. But both babies appear to be perfect. You want to know the sex?"

Oh, God. She couldn't unscramble her thoughts, couldn't find words, couldn't…couldn't… "Ah… okay."

"Boys. Both boys. And you're probably looking at an earlier delivery date, here," he said. "At the size of these guys, there's no way you're going to go full term. I'll call your OB-Gyn and see if he can see you right now."

Her appointment with Sam Duncan was a blur. He was sympathetic, trying to buoy her with the assurance that the twins were in perfect health so far. "You'll have to ease up a little, delegate more at the office, make the girls help you at home."

She was still too stunned to give him the look that suggestion deserved. Her co-workers were overworked as it was, and her girls meant well, but they were children. Their good intentions were forgotten in a minute when the invitation to play or a favorite television show intervened.

"I want to see you next Tuesday," he said as she walked out of his office. "Before, if you have any problems at all. Call me anytime."

She walked halfway around the lake. She was going to have two babies instead of one, four children instead of three. One whole extra life would depend upon her, Jackie Fortin Bourgeois, who'd so irretrievably screwed up her life that there was probably no saving it. What was God thinking?

By the time she was on her way back to City Hall, the shock and confusion had turned to fear and panic.

She couldn't breathe. She tried stopping in the middle of the parking lot at the back of the building, hoping to drag in a deep breath. But it didn't seem to be there.

She tried to fight off the panic. This was silly. There was breath in her lungs. She knew there was. She just had to calm down and breathe. Faith Hill had a song about it. Breathe. Just breathe. It was early afternoon, lunch breaks over, and the parking lot was almost empty. She judged the distance to the back door against her absence of air and emitted a little squeak of dismay.

Then she noticed Hank's van behind the big, bare oak, the sliding side door open as he seemed to be inventorying supplies and making notes on a clipboard. He leaned away from the van in her direction, apparently searching for the source of that sound.

He caught sight of her and asked in puzzlement, "Jackie?"

She had no air to speak, so she stretched out a hand toward him.

He tossed the clipboard into the truck and ran toward her, his eyes concerned as they looked into hers.

Even had she been able to speak, she could not have told him how glad she was to see him. It was curious, she thought, that he was a source of part of her problems, yet that didn't seem to matter now. She'd be fine if he would just wrap his arms around her.

As though he read her mind, he did just that. "What is it?" he asked, one arm tightening on her while the other tipped her chin up so that he could explore her face. "Are you having contractions?"

She shook her head, gasping for air. There was a scary, rasping sound when she tried to breathe.

"Can't breathe?" he asked, putting a hand to the baby as though that would somehow help.

She nodded, trying again and feeling a whisper of air come through. Encouraged, she breathed in again and felt her lungs expand. She held on to Hank as he led her toward the van.

"I'll take you to the hospital," he said, opening the passenger door and lifting her into his arms. He put her into the front seat.

She shook her head desperately.

"No time to argue," he said, trying to back out of the van and close her door.

She grabbed his hand and held on. "I'm…I'm fine now," she said, her voice soft and raspy between more gulps of air. Her chest rose and fell and she continued to breathe deeply so that he could see she could do it. "I'm…breathing."

He looked somewhat relieved, though still concerned. "Well, that's good, but I think we should know why you almost stopped."

"I can tell you," she said. "Can you just…get in?"

He closed her door and the sliding door, then ran around to the driver's side and climbed in behind the wheel. "Jackie, I'm taking you…"

She grabbed a fistful of the front of his jacket and pulled him toward her until he was kneeling between the seats. "Hold on to me," she pleaded.

"But you're…" he protested, clearly confused by her behavior.

"Please," she whispered breathlessly. Tears filled her eyes and she had the most awful feeling sobs were going to be the next step in this weird mood progression.

He noted her brimming eyes, and with a frown of consternation wrapped her in his embrace. "All right, take it easy," he said, rubbing gently up and down her spine. "Whatever it is, we can fix it. Just relax. I'm right here."

She held on and wept for what felt like an hour but was probably only moments. She allowed herself the luxury of sinking into the comfort and security of his arms and forgot about all the really difficult elements in her life. For the space of time he held her, she let herself believe they could be fixed, that the impeachment hearing would prove Brockton didn't have a case, that she could explain to Hank what had happened seventeen years ago and he'd understand. He might even forgive her.

She raised her head from his shoulder and looked into his face, trying to gauge if that was possible. But beneath the kindness and concern of the moment, she saw the strength, the toughness that made him who he was, and couldn't decide if those qualities would work in her favor or not.

In the interest of getting through the next few weeks, she allowed herself to believe that they would. Then, after the babies were born, she'd try to explain.

One superhuman effort at a time.

HANK WASN'T SURE what was going on, except that the longer he held her, the more even her breathing became, and for the moment that was all he needed to know.

She drew slightly out of his arms and looked at him, her eyes a little frantic. They seemed to be trying to read his, and for a moment it looked as though they didn't like what they saw. He wondered if his love for her was visible. It troubled her that he continued to care, though she considered their relationship hopeless.

Yet she'd come to him. She'd asked him to hold her—even demanded it. So what did that mean? That he couldn't trust what she told him, obviously.

Then she seemed to relax and come to some sort of decision. She hugged him fiercely for a moment, then smoothed his hair in a gesture that just about unraveled him. "You must think I'm crazy," she said.

He levered himself into the driver's seat. "I've thought so ever since the day you told me you were staying in Maple Hill. But what's going on today?"

She drew another deep breath that seemed to go through her without obstruction. "Just a panic attack, I think," she said calmly, a weird serenity taking over.

"Over the impeachment?"

"Partly." She smiled grimly. "And partly because I just learned I'm carrying twins."

Twins. Two for one. That sounded like a deal to him rather than a worry, but then he didn't have to give birth to them. Keep them healthy and happy and raise them to be good and honest citizens along with two other children.

He used to think raising children would be scary, but

he didn't anymore. Growing children with her had real appeal. But she probably wouldn't want to know that now. He scanned his mind for something positive to say that wouldn't sound patronizing. Concrete help, he realized, was probably the best thing.

"We'll get you some help," he said, putting a hand out to touch her shoulder across the gap between the seats. "My mother's already mobilizing her ladies for you. I'll…I'll do whatever you need me to do—drive the girls to school and pick them up, do your shopping, run errands."

She put a hand to his forearm and rubbed gently—another gesture that turned his spine to noodle. "Thank you. Unfortunately, that'll only substantiate Brockton's accusations."

"Do we care about that?"

"Technically, no. But if I'm going to have to defend myself against them, we'll have to be more… circumspect."

"I'm your friend." He hated having to settle for that. "That allows me to help, despite whatever spin Brockton might put on it. For starters, I'm taking you home."

"I have…" she tried to protest.

"Evelyn can cancel whatever was on your calendar," he insisted, pulling the seat belt gently around her, having to expand it to its farthest reaches to make it fit. "You can call her from home."

"I have to pick up the girls…"

"I'll do that."

"Hank…"

"You need to rest and get your bearings. I'll make you a cup of tea, you can put your feet up and try to restore yourself before we make plans for the next few months."

She frowned at him. "You haven't heard a thing I've said about being careful."

"Yes, I have," he corrected, then indicated the empty lot. "Do you see anyone around?"

"No."

"Then what are you worried about? Just sit back and relax."

SHE HAD TO ADMIT that it was nice to have him puttering around her house. He'd put her in her favorite chair, pulled off her shoes, covered her with a knitted throw then disappeared into the kitchen to make tea. She liked the sound of drawers opening and doors closing—the knowledge that he was occupying her space, touching her things.

Twins, she thought with fatalistic amusement. Two babies. She put a hand to her stomach, where she'd often thought a tiny contortionist was growing—there'd been kicks in so many directions at once. But she had two babies in there.

She wasn't sure why laughter bubbled up, but it did. And it was somehow liberating and soothing to let it free.

"Now, that's more like it," Hank said, carrying in a tray with a pot and two cups. "Are you thinking about how delighted the girls are going to be? They seemed so excited about one baby. Imagine when they learn they'll each have a baby to fuss over."

Jackie was feeling less desperate, but she couldn't help a groan over the reality of what she faced. "Oh, Hank." She took the tea he offered and smiled grimly. "One baby keeps you up for months in the beginning. Two babies will be awful. I'm sure they won't be cooperative enough to sleep at the same time, to not wake each other up, to respect the fact that I often have 8:00 a.m. meetings. Addy's lining up her friends to help me, but you can't expect volunteers to stay the night and get up with screaming babies."

He placed the tray on the coffee table and took the loveseat opposite her. He seemed to be giving the matter thought. "You need a husband," he said. "Someone with the right and the responsibility to stay the night and get up with screaming babies."

She shook her head. "I've had one. They don't do that."

"I'd be happy to prove you wrong about that."

Jackie put her cup down to her lap and let several seconds tick away. The house was quiet; she knew she hadn't misheard him. And he didn't look as though he was teasing.

"Hank," she said finally. "That would never work."

He seemed unimpressed by her rebuttal. "You always say that, yet when you needed help, you came to me."

"You were in the City Hall parking lot."

He shook his head. "You were glad I was there. You needed me, and you came to me."

She looked down at her cup, afraid he'd see how true that was. "You can't propose to me out of some misguided wish to set the past right," she said, her voice faint and stiff.

"That's not it and you know it," he objected, placing his cup on the tray with a small bang. "And if either of us has to set the past right, it's you."

She looked up at him then in mild panic, wondering if his remark suggested that he knew.

He met her eyes, and though they studied hers, she

saw no evidence there that he referred to anything other than their last argument.

"I'm asking," he said, "because I love you. I've always loved you. I loved you the whole time we were apart. And you love me. You might deny it, but it's always in your eyes, in your touch."

She fought for calm. "I do love you," she admitted, expecting to see triumph in his eyes. But all she saw was a sort of awed wonder. "But I don't think we should do this to save me from sleeplessness." When he would have protested that that wasn't the reason, she shook her head to stop him. She couldn't believe he was offering what she'd wanted all her life, and she had to refuse. "After the babies are born and I get my life organized, maybe we can…talk about it?" *And maybe by then I'll have the courage to explain—and you'll have the generosity to understand.*

But it wasn't something she could simply confess on the spur of the moment. She needed the right place, the right time.

He leaned toward her, his elbows on his knees. "You think time will make it easier to accept how stupid we were as kids?"

"No," she said with a pleading smile. "You can't imagine how many times I've wished we'd handled that differently. But it'll help me get to an even place where I can think clearly, and deal with only one life-altering decision at a time."

"All right," he agreed finally. "Later. But I'm not going to just disappear until then. Brockton will have to—"

The sound of the doorbell pealed through the house. Jackie lowered her feet off the hassock, but Hank stopped her with a raised hand and went to answer the door. She leaned against the back of her chair with great relief that he'd been distracted from the subject of marriage.

Her father walked into the living room, his brow knit with worry, Sabrina following in his footsteps.

"What happened?" he asked, coming to sit on the hassock near her feet. "I called at your office to talk to you about dinner, and your secretary said you decided to come home after your doctor's appointment. Is everything all right?"

Dinner! She'd completely forgotten about having invited her father and Sabrina. She smiled apologetically at Sabrina, who seemed to be trying to pretend concern for Jackie while looking around the old house with the same greedy expression she'd worn when surveying the inn. She was probably thinking about painting everything white, laying down carpet, reupholstering.

Jackie turned her attention back to her father. "I'm fine," she said, squeezing his hands. "Just a little stunned. I'm having twins, Dad."

"Twins!" He grinned broadly, the reaction the word seemed to engender in everyone. Then he appeared to reconsider from her point of view and asked anxiously, "How do you feel about that?"

"Worried," she replied. "Overwhelmed. Fortunately Hank was around to make me a cup of tea and keep me sane. I'm calmer now and maybe, almost, cautiously…excited."

He kissed her hand. "The girls will be ecstatic."

"I know." That thought did give her pleasure. "About dinner, what say we all go—" She'd intended to suggest they all have dinner at the Old Post Road Inn, but her father interrupted her.

"Actually, I was calling to tell you that Sabrina had accepted an invitation from the McGoverns at the same time that I accepted your invitation."

"Before, actually," Sabrina put in apologetically as she settled on the loveseat. "I thought you'd understand if we rescheduled for tomorrow. Our treat, of course. And not that the Old Post Road Inn isn't…charming, but I thought we'd go to Springfield to the Firelight."

If there were any pretentious people in down-to-earth Maple Hill, it was the McGoverns. He was a retired stockbroker who'd made millions for some of his clients, and she behaved as though all his success were hers. And if there was any restaurant Jackie didn't like because it carried elegance to an uncomfortable level, it was the Firelight. Her father looked embarrassed. She forgave him for not standing up for his family. She had a new understanding of what it was like to have your life proceed almost without your control.

She patted her father's hand. "Tomorrow will be fine, but I'm not sure the girls have the right frame of mind for the Firelight."

He nodded. "I'd prefer the Breakfast Barn myself."

Over her father's head, Jackie saw Sabrina force a frail smile that she strengthened when Adam turned her way. "Sure," she said. "Whatever everyone else wants."

"Now, since I can't visit with my granddaughters tonight," Adam said, "what about if Sabrina and I pick them up at school and take them for ice cream?"

"Uh…okay." Jackie was eager to share her news

about the twins, but knew they'd be thrilled to see their grandfather. The news could wait until dinner.

Hank returned from the kitchen with the coffee carafe, cups, and cream and sugar. It was the old plastic set Jackie kept on the kitchen table, and she saw Sabrina look it over with distaste.

They visited for half an hour, Sabrina rhapsodizing about the Berkshires and how it was ripe for some stylish touches.

Jackie caught Hank's eye across the room and noted the amusement there. She also caught Sabrina glancing at him often, making remarks about the provincial qualities of Maple Hill. She confessed relief at finding intellectual life in Amherst, presuming, Jackie supposed, that since Hank had just moved home from Florida, he'd share her sophisticated views.

He was polite, but generally silent.

Just before three, Jackie called the school to tell them the girls' grandfather would be picking them up. Then Adam and Sabrina left on their mission.

"Is she horrid?" Jackie asked as Hank gathered up cups. "Or is it me?"

"She's horrid," he confirmed.

"What do you suppose my father sees in her?"

"What's missing in his life since your mother died," he replied without pause.

"But my mother was nothing like that."

He carried the tray to the kitchen, then came back to sit opposite her again. "It's not that, it's just she makes him feel something—excitement, sexual eagerness, whatever—and that's getting him over the awful feeling of being dead himself. When I moved to Florida, I dated a scuba-diving, beach-bunny surfer in her early thirties who was as different from me as it was possible to be. But she was attractive and she liked me and that brought me out of the sinkhole I fell into when I had to leave Maple Hill alone. It lasted about a month and we finally parted by mutual consent."

She smiled. "I can't imagine you on a surfboard."

He laughed. "Well, that's because I didn't spend much time on it. Usually I was under it, or chasing it, or trying to outswim it after I fell off so it didn't decapitate me." He sobered slightly. "You spent a couple of years in Boston right after that. Did you finish school, or were you looking for something, too?"

The smile froze on her face.

HANK WONDERED about that look. It crossed her face often now—a sort of horrified guilt whenever he talked about their relationship growing more serious.

"Did you love someone there?" he asked gently, quietly. He hated the thought that there'd been more than just Ricky in her life since the two of them had been lovers, but he had to be realistic. She was beautiful and smart, and scores of men must have found her appealing.

He wasn't sure what to do when her eyes brimmed suddenly with tears. They seemed to surprise her as much as him. She closed her eyes and drew a breath.

He went to sit on the side of her chair and wrapped his arms around her. "It's all right," he said. "You don't have to tell me about it. But I can see there's something unresolved from that time."

She leaned into him with a vulnerability she seldom displayed. He could feel a tremor in her.

· "Is it anything I can take care of for you?" he asked, concerned by her abject misery.

She held tightly to him and shook her head. "No," she said finally, drawing another breath. "It's something I have to do."

He framed her face in his hands and looked into her eyes. "But it involves me, I can see it when you look at me. So why don't you let me help?"

That expression reappeared, stared him in the face, then slipped away when she lowered her lashes and looked up again. "I'll explain it all," she said in a half whisper, "as soon as I can think clearly again. I promise."

"Okay," he said, seeing that she needed out of the discussion. As much as he wanted to understand the problem, he didn't want to torture her with it. Whatever it was, he wasn't going to let it get in his way. "Why don't I take you and the girls to dinner if your father and Sabrina have other plans? As a celebration of the news about twins." Then it occurred to him that she might like to tell the girls in private. "Or would you prefer that to be just a family moment?"

She gave him a look that melted something inside him—one that surprised him after the misery he'd seen in her only moments ago. It was filled with warmth and affection and something deeper she seemed able to acknowledge even if she didn't know what to do with it. It said he belonged.

"What about the Breakfast Barn?" she asked. "The girls love strawberry waffles, and an omelette sounds really good to me."

He tried to act as casually as she did. "Sounds good to me, too. I'll haul some wood in for you while we're waiting for the girls." He indicated the almost empty brass wood box.

"Actually," she said, scooting toward the front of the chair, preparing to push herself to her feet. It seemed such an ordeal for her. "I wanted to talk to you about adding outlets in the girls' rooms."

He stood in front of her and offered his hands. She pulled herself up with a sigh and a groan. "There's only one in each room in these old homes, and while we've modernized the rest of the house, their rooms need a little work. Their clocks and bedside lamps take up the outlet, but I was thinking if we put one across the room, I could get them each a disc player to help numb the fact that they'll have a lot less of my attention while I'm adjusting to the twins. Want to have a look?"

She led the way upstairs. She explained what she had in mind, and Hank offered options. Darkness had fallen and they were still discussing it when there was a great commotion downstairs.

"They're home," Jackie said.

Hank laughed. "You're sure? It sounds more like bumper cars going through."

She caught his hand to pull him along with her as she headed toward the hallway to greet them.

The girls rounded the landing and were heading up to the second floor, their eyes alight, their cheeks flushed.

"Twins!" Erica squealed. "We're having twins!" She wrapped her arms around her mother, who'd stopped in the middle of the hallway, clearly disappointed she hadn't been able to tell the girls herself.

"Sabrina says she could tell even before the doctor

told you," Rachel reported, getting in on the hug, "because one baby doesn't usually make you so big."

Hank put a hand to Jackie's shoulder, trying to massage away the strain he could see stiffening her back.

Adam appeared on the landing, out of breath. "I'm sorry, Jackie," he said. "Sabrina was excited and spilled the beans without thinking. Hello, Hank."

Hank returned her father's greeting and rubbed a little harder on her shoulder, knowing she was struggling with a careful response. "I doubt she does anything without thinking," she said finally. "But it's all right. Enjoy your dinner tonight."

Adam shook his head. "I'm sure she didn't mean…"

Jackie cut him off with a wave of her hand. "It's okay, Dad. Have fun."

He studied her another moment, then waved and went back downstairs to let himself out.

Erica seemed to understand the mild tension. "Grandpa was mad at her for telling us," she said, then smiled brightly. "But I don't see what difference it makes. We're going to have two babies! Two!"

"One for Erica," Rachel said, "and one for me."

Jackie kissed each head. "Don't I get one of them?"

"Just for diapering," Erica teased. "We get to play with them."

"And get up with them for midnight feedings?"

"Casey Carlisle's mom has a nanny for Casey's little sister," Erica said, "and the nanny lives there."

"Can guys be nannies?" Rachel asked. "'Cause we could have Hank be the twins' nanny, then he could live here. He's not getting to be your boyfriend fast enough."

"He can't be a nanny," Erica pointed out reasonably,

"because he has his own business already. If he's going to move in here it has to be because he marries Mom."

"Is that gonna happen?" Rachel asked hopefully.

"They have to fall in love."

"How long does that take?"

Jackie gave Hank an apologetic glance. "Don't you love having your life dissected in the upstairs hallway? It takes longer than we have right now. Hank's taking us to dinner." She shooed the girls toward the bathroom. "Go wash your hands, and Rachel, change your shirt for one that doesn't have ice cream on it."

Giggling and pushing, the girls went to do as they'd been asked.

Jackie led the way downstairs. "Sabrina is trying to separate Dad from his family," she said, giving rein to her anger now that the girls were out of hearing. "She's done everything she can to annoy me and thwart my efforts to get us all together. She's hoping I'll stay out of their way and she can have him to herself."

He stopped her at the bottom and caught her shoulders. "She can't do that and you know it. Your father's very devoted to you and the girls."

"Then why is he going to the McGoverns' with her, when he was invited to dinner here? She said she'd accepted that invitation first, but I'll bet she didn't. She probably sought it out rather than come here. And there was a day when nothing would have kept him from putting us first."

"He'll catch on to her," he insisted. "You just have to let him discover her tricks for himself."

She subsided slightly and folded her arms. "I hope he does that before I'm forced to kill her."

He wrapped her in a hug. "I hope so, too. I'd hate for you to do life in maximum security just when you're falling in love with me again."

She wrapped her arms around his neck, her large belly pressing into his groin. "I don't recall saying that exactly," she taunted.

He kissed her quickly, gently. "I don't either. Why don't you just say it clearly so we can both remember."

To his complete shock, she looked into his eyes and said with grave conviction, "I love you, Hank."

"I love you, Jackie," he replied, kissing her again. Less gently this time—less quickly.

A corner of his mind not occupied with the miracle of her admission heard giggles on the stairs.

CHAPTER TWELVE

"ALEX AND AUSTIN!" Erica suggested. They'd finished dinner and dessert and Erica made a list of twins' names on her napkin while Jackie and Hank lingered over second cups of decaf.

"Do the names have to match?" Rachel asked.

Interpreting that to mean did they have to start with the same letter, Jackie shook her head. "They don't have to. But twins names often sound alike or start with the same letter."

Rachel sat up brightly, all her inherent verve glistening in her eyes. "What about Barney and Baby Bop?"

Erica looked at her as though she were a bunch of broccoli. "Baby Bop is a girl!" she said in complete exasperation. "And that's a stupid idea."

Jackie fixed Erica with a firm look. "It's not stupid. They're names that are familiar to her."

Erica looked horrified by her mother's tolerance. "I'm not going to the same school with a kid called Baby Bop."

Jackie laughed. "You won't have to." She patted Rachel's hand. "Keep trying," she encouraged. "Something a little more…special."

"Justin and Joey," Erica said. "Or Justin and JC."

Hank raised an eyebrow in question.

"Singers with 'N Sync," Jackie explained.

"Ah, well, how about Scottie and Bonzi?" Hank contributed.

It was Erica's turn to look confused.

"Portland Trailblazers," he explained. "I'm just trying to get into the spirit of the thing."

Rachel frowned and rested her chin in her hands. "It's too bad they're not girls. Girls' names are better."

"What about Adam and Alex?" Hank suggested.

"After Grandpa!" Erica said, writing it down. "That's a good idea, Mom. And Alex is a good name."

"Do you like them?" Jackie asked Rachel.

She yawned widely. "Yeah. But I want mine to be Adam."

Erica rolled her eyes. "You don't get to just pick one."

"I can if I want!"

"That's stupid."

"You're stupid!"

Jackie smiled wryly at Hank. "Civility's breaking down. Time to go home."

Hank paid the bill and they walked out of the restaurant, he and Jackie between the girls to prevent bloodshed. Hank wrapped an arm around Jackie's shoulders as they started across the parking lot toward his van.

They were intercepted almost immediately by John Brockton and Russ Benedict. Before anyone could react, John Brockton raised a camera to his eye and light flashed in their faces.

"You still maintain there's nothing going on between you two?" he asked with a smug smile.

Hank grabbed John's shirtfront in a fist and yanked the camera from him.

"No!" Jackie shouted, putting her hand on Hank's where his knuckles dug into John's throat.

Hank ignored her. He gave John a shake. "You look pretty prepared here, Brockton," he said, holding up the camera in his free hand. "Are you stalking us?"

John was perspiring, but he seemed to know he had an advantage. "You still maintain…" he said again, "that there's nothing going on?"

A crowd had begun to gather around them.

Jackie tugged on Hank's arms. "Hank, the girls," she whispered urgently.

Hank hesitated a moment, then flung John from him so that the man staggered backward into the hood of a truck.

Jackie drew Hank back, holding his arm with both of hers. She then wrestled the camera from him and handed it to Russ Benedict, unashamed of whatever it immortalized. "Let's just go," she said quietly, seeing her career dissolve in disgrace.

"Hank's going to be our dad!" Erica said vehemently, stepping up to John Brockton, her manner aggressive and fearless. Jackie watched in astonishment. It was Hank who caught her arm and pulled her back. "He can be with us if he wants to be," she continued, resisting Hank. "And you leave my mother alone!"

"Yeah!" Rachel stepped forward to put her two cents in. "We're going to get married 'cause they were kissing."

Jackie withheld a groan.

Hank scooped Rachel up in one arm, holding firmly to Erica with the other.

Jackie decided it was time *she* did something. She couldn't leave her defense to her children. The only thing she could think of was probably foolish and maybe even dangerous, but it was a solution.

"Hank and I are engaged, John," she said with icy courtesy, not even considering the repercussions of her statement.

Complete silence greeted the words. Erica and Hank turned to look at her.

And then it hit her. Her heart began to thud. She'd just told a parking lot filled with her friends and neighbors that she was engaged to Hank Whitcomb. She couldn't decide if she felt horrified or exhilarated.

"And if you still consider that that makes his work for us a kind of business nepotism," she went on, angling her chin, "you might remember that he's rewiring City Hall for no charge. I don't think you have a leg to stand on."

"Really." Haley appeared beside them, taking notes. Bart took Rachel from Hank and glowered suspiciously at John.

"What's going on?" he asked Hank. "We just got here. You need a lawyer?"

The two councilmen stalked off to the restaurant.

"Have you set a date for the wedding?" Haley asked with a detached interest that belied the twinkle in her eye.

Jackie turned to her with a quelling look. "Don't you ever cook?"

She held up her cell phone. "Mom called. Her car was broken down at the market. We picked her up and took her home and thought we deserved a cup of coffee. So. A wedding?"

John Brockton was gone, but the need to carry on

with her story remained, Jackie realized, as the audience they'd collected lingered. She was sure they didn't know whether to believe her or not. Suspicion once cast on a public figure or a celebrity would attach itself to that person until they were cleared without a doubt, or the whole thing simply blew over.

But impeachment proceedings would not blow over.

"After the babies are born," Hank said for her when she hesitated too long. "Too much to do before they come."

Haley blinked. "Did you say ba-*bies?* Plural?"

"Yeah!" Erica smiled broadly and wrapped her arms around Jackie.

Rachel clapped. "We're going to be flower girls!" she told Bart and Haley. "And Mommy's having twins!"

Haley squealed and hugged Jackie and the girls. Then she giggled and she embraced her brother. "You're in for it, Hank."

Hank laughed. "Thanks to you, I'm accustomed to dealing with challenges."

Bart grinned at him. "I presume I'm in line for best man? And baby-sitting?"

Hank shook his hand happily. "Yes, on both counts."

Jackie felt another panic attack coming on.

With a glance at her face, Hank reclaimed Rachel and started moving toward the van.

"You do realize you're front page news," Haley warned them, "and there's nothing I can do about that."

Jackie frowned and nodded.

"Good. Then two o'clock Sunday." Haley reminded them of Addy's birthday dinner. "Can you bring fruit salad?"

Jackie nodded. Conversation bubbled around her as

they drove home, but her mind was too cluttered to allow her to participate. While Hank fielded the girls' questions about John Brockton and reassured them that the man could do nothing to hurt them, Jackie prayed that was true. The girls had been through so much with their father's death, and Erica had suffered especially with the rumors about Ricky's involvement with other women.

When they got home, Jackie put the kettle on while the girls milled around Hank, clearly delighted at the prospect of him becoming a part of their lives.

Jackie carefully avoided his eyes while she bustled around the kitchen with cups, cocoa, tea and coffee.

"Can I get a new dress for the wedding?" Rachel wanted to know as she climbed onto Hank's knee.

"We'll all get new dresses for the wedding." Erica stood beside him, leaning an arm on his shoulder. "What color, Mom?"

Jackie was losing her ability to breathe. The harmless deceit had seemed like such a good idea. Actually, when she watched her children with Hank, the whole thing seemed like such a good idea.

Of course, it was all likely to blow up in her face, but she didn't know how to apply the brakes. And in the deepest places in her heart, she could admit to herself that she didn't want to.

"What color do you like?" Hank asked Erica.

"I like yellow," she replied. "Like daisies."

"I want a purple dress," Rachel said excitedly. "Like Barney!"

Erica groaned. "See? We'll never be able to agree."

Hank smoothed the hair out of Erica's face. "Well,

do you have to wear the same color? Can't you wear yellow and let Rachel wear purple?"

Even Rachel winced. "That'd be ugly."

Hank turned to Jackie with a laugh. "Help me out here. Our wedding's about to be thwarted by a fashion crisis."

"What color are you going to wear?" Rachel asked him.

"I have to wear a suit," he replied gravely, "and I have only one. It's gray."

"What'll you wear, Mom?" Erica came to take the plate of cookies while Jackie carried the tray of mugs to the table. "Will any of your stuff fit you after the twins are born?"

Jackie let her mind linger longingly on the time when she would not be bearing this weight. Comfort and a wardrobe would be hers again. She couldn't resist a little shudder of delight.

She caught Hank's eye and saw a watchfulness there that concerned her—and served to bring her back to reality.

"Can we decide on a color tomorrow?" she asked, handing them their cups. "I'm pooped right now. And *Castaway Kids* is on."

The girls scrambled off, cups held carefully, to watch their favorite program.

Jackie sat at a right angle to Hank and drew a breath, wondering how she could explain what she'd done.

"The engagement was a ploy to save us from the suggestion of an affair," he said, leaning across the table toward her, reading her mind with alarming clarity. "But it's developing into a plan you can support, isn't it?"

"Yes." It would have been pointless to deny it. "But we have a million details…issues…to work out."

One really big one, she thought with burgeoning panic.

THERE IT WAS AGAIN, Hank thought. That pleading look that told him nothing about what troubled her, only that she needed him to understand.

"All right," he said, taking a sip of his coffee. "We'll talk about it when you're ready. But I'm moving in tomorrow. You're starting to look pale and more stressed than usual."

"Hank," she said worriedly. "Brockton's out to get us! If you move in…"

"It'll prove we're serious," he interrupted. "I'm not leaving you alone at this point. So I'll take over the home duties so you can concentrate on whatever you need to do to fight the impeachment and set up things with the city so it doesn't fall apart while you're on leave. Now that we know you'll deliver early, we'd better make sure nothing happens to endanger your pregnancy. If he sees us acting like a family, making wedding plans, it'll destroy his ability to make you look like a reckless, loose-living city official."

"But we'll be *living* together!"

"Yes, but the scandal in that is having sex." He lowered his voice in deference to the miss-nothing little girls. "And that isn't safe in your condition."

Her first reaction was a smile, as though she liked that idea. Then she bit her bottom lip, apparently deciding that his solution came with its own problems.

"What about your business?" she asked.

"You handle both," he replied. "I'm sure I can do the same."

"There'll be two lively children," she reminded him, "and two little babies in this house."

He nodded. "I can count. The girls and I do fine together, and I don't have much experience with babies, but I'm sure I'll learn."

She gave him a sweet smile and reached along the table to cover his hand with hers. "You *did* admit to coming home to get a life, but a thriving business, a wife and four children makes you a bit of an overachiever."

He caught her hand in his and assumed a teasingly superior air. "Story of my life." Then he felt regretful of the strained circumstances. "I'm sorry the situation is so lacking in romance."

She clutched his hand more tightly and uttered a little sound like a laugh with a sob in it. "When you're this huge and tired," she said, "and this much under siege, it's terribly romantic to have someone insist on taking care of you."

He brought her hand to his lips and kissed her knuckles. "When life settles down—" he waggled his eyebrows wickedly "—I'll want a few things in return."

She came to wrap her arms around his neck and kiss the top of his head. "I hope so," she said.

He thought that a curious answer. But then he felt the twins move strongly against his shoulder as she leaned over him, as though they'd tumbled over each other.

She gasped and put a hand to her belly.

Hank stood quickly and pushed her gently into his chair. "Are you all right? That felt like more than a simple kick."

She expelled a sigh and smiled tiredly, rubbing where

the action had been. "They're very busy lately. Tidying up, maybe, and getting ready to move."

He reached over and pulled her teacup toward her. "Maybe I should move in tonight," he suggested.

She shook her head. "I'll be fine. The activity probably just seems more extreme to me because I know there're two of them in there. They've settled down now."

He hated the thought of leaving her, but he, too, was going to have to put a few things in order at home if he was going to spend the next few months here. And if his mother was having car trouble, he'd probably have to pick her up in the morning and take her to his office before he moved his things.

"I'll pick up the girls for school in the morning," he said, "so you can have a little extra time to sleep."

She made a face at him. "Thank you, but that's not necessary. I'm fine, and as soon as I get a good night's sleep, forget about Brockton and just concentrate on my children and my job, I'll be even better. Go home, Hank.

"There's a key under the pot of geraniums on the porch. Erica's always losing hers, so I keep an extra. Bring your things in whenever it's convenient."

He leaned over her and looked into her eyes. She framed his face in her hands and brought it down to kiss him chastely. "I can't believe I let you go," she said, a catch in her voice.

He cupped her head in his hand and kissed her soundly, lengthily. "I can't believe I went," he said. "I'll see you tomorrow."

He went to say goodbye to the girls, who offered their cheeks for kisses without moving their eyes from the television. Fatherhood, he decided as he let himself out, was going to be a revelation.

JACKIE WAS A LITTLE SURPRISED that business at City Hall could go on as usual despite the fact that her entire life was about to undergo enormous change—twins, marriage and the threat of professional destruction.

Haley stopped by to take her for a mocha at Perk Avenue.

"Do you know how many calories there are in a mocha?" Jackie asked her as they sat at a small table with mismatched chairs. "I think the twins are going to come out carrying free weights."

Haley settled in across the table and smiled apologetically. "I thought the chocolate would steady your nerves when I tell you that you're front page news this issue."

Jackie rolled her eyes. "The impeachment?"

"That, and your confrontation with Brockton in the Breakfast Barn's parking lot. I'm sorry. It embarrasses you, but it shows Brockton for what he is, which is important as you fight the impeachment. I talked to Rosie Benedict—they're splitting the sheets, you know—and she told me Brockton has been following you, waiting to see you and Hank looking cozy."

Jackie's mind was too turbulent to decide if this was good or bad for her cause.

"Brockton dared me to use his photo of you and Hank," Haley went on, "so I'm going to."

"Haley…"

Haley raised a hand to interrupt her protest. "But I'm using it with a sidebar about your engagement with a little background about your high-school romance and our families' long friendship so that people understand your relationship isn't just a flaming affair."

Jackie put a hand to her forehead, feeling as though stress had tightened everything from her head to her toes. "And this is considered hard news?"

Haley leaned toward her, her eyes grave. "The only real issue Brockton has with you is your relationship with my brother. So we have to prove that it's not a tawdry thing. And the fact that Hank's doing the work gratis takes any threat out of the suggestion of nepotism. We have to make that clear." Haley sighed, snapped her biscotti in two and offered half to Jackie. "I'm sorry it puts you in the spotlight, but ultimately, it's the best thing for you."

"How did I change from the woman people seldom noticed—including my husband—to the center of a public scandal?" Jackie bit into the thick cookie.

"Brockton's trying to make it into a scandal, but it isn't one. That's why we have to be aboveboard about everything."

"Then maybe you'll want to include that Hank's moving into my house today." She chewed and swallowed, everything so beyond her control she wondered why she was worried. There seemed to be little she could do to affect the course of events.

Haley grinned broadly. "No kidding. So, you really are engaged?"

Jackie nodded. "We really are. The girls are thrilled."

"And you?"

Jackie avoided Haley's probing gaze. "I've loved him most of my life."

"Then everything should be fine. Cheer up. Don't

worry about the impeachment. None of the charges will stand." She reached across the table to pat Jackie's hand. "Things are looking up for you at last, woman! Jackie Fortin's going to win one!"

Jackie returned her friend's smile, wanting to believe that. If she were to balance the blessings against the hard knocks in her life, the blessings would far outweigh the problems she'd faced. She had the girls, the house, her work, good friends.

And now, it seemed, she had Hank, and while she knew she should tell him the truth about their shared past before they got married, she didn't have to do it yet. She could just enjoy this time together, pretend there was nothing between them until the twins were born. Build up to the truth. Then, maybe, he'd be so much a part of her little family that he'd consider that his blessings outweighed her truth.

She could only hope.

HE'D PICKED UP THE GIRLS and was fixing dinner when Jackie got home. He smiled and waved a spatula at her over the counter. "Hi!" he called. "Lasagna and green beans with bacon. You'd better have an appetite."

Erica poured milk into two glasses while Rachel set the table.

The girls stopped to greet her with hugs and a giggly ebullience.

"Your sister bought me a mocha in the middle of the afternoon." Still holding the girls to her, she walked around the counter to watch him toss the beans in a bacon-and-onions mixture. "It's a plot to make me look as though I'm carrying triplets, isn't it?"

He leaned down to give her a quick kiss on the cheek. "Not at all. I just want those boys to be born big and strong so they can pull their weight around here as soon as possible."

Jackie looked into Hank's smile and was suddenly overwhelmed by the sweetness of having him here when she came home after a grueling day, and seeing the girls cheerful and apparently happy. That situation had never existed with Ricky. He usually wasn't home for dinner, or if he was, she was fixing dinner, he was watching television and the girls were in their rooms or playing outside. Dinner had never been an eagerly awaited family time.

With her arms still around the girls, she leaned into Hank with a grateful sigh. And he did just what she hoped he'd do. He dropped the spatula and turned to her, wrapping the three of them in his embrace.

"Thank you," she breathed into his ear as his cheek rested against hers.

"My pleasure," he whispered back.

"Can we have a tickle fight?" Rachel asked, crooking her index finger and threatening Jackie with it. "Glory says her family always had tickle fights when she was little. They're really fun. Everybody ends up on the carpet."

Jackie drew away from Hank with a lingering glance that punctuated her thank-you. Then she turned her attention to Rachel. "Honey, if I got on the carpet, it would take heavy equipment to get me up again."

Rachel made a face. "What's that?"

"You know, those big yellow trucks that haul heavy things around. Like tractors and cranes."

She looked disappointed. "You mean we have to wait until after the babies are born?"

Jackie nodded. "I'm afraid so."

Rachel turned to Hank, who'd gone back to the green beans. "Now that you're the dad, you can say we can have a tickle fight."

"I'm not ticklish," he said with unconvincing nonchalance.

With a child's acute perception of adult weakness, she attacked him. "You are, too!" she cried victoriously. "You are, too!"

He dropped the spatula and backed into a corner, his arms pressed to his side as he tried to fend her off, already laughing. Erica joined the attack.

Jackie left them, Hank's phony shouts for help mingling with the girls' high-pitched squeals of delight, and went upstairs to change out of her binding clothes and into her robe.

She found Hank's shirts and jeans in her closet, and an unfamiliar shaving kit on the counter in the bathroom. She felt a little thrill at the knowledge that he was sharing her room.

Dinner was delicious. The girls talked nonstop and Hank didn't seem at all bored by their childish tales and observations. He asked questions, learned about their teachers and their friends, then Jackie joined in when the conversation worked its way around to the wedding.

Guilt pinched her viciously, but she ignored it. As though there was nothing in the world to steal away her happiness, she agreed that pink would be a nice color for her and the girls to wear—a decision the girls had come to after Hank said he liked to see women in pink.

"Not a chauvinist opinion," he said when Jackie arched an eyebrow. "Just an aesthetic one. Seems no matter what a woman's coloring, when you put pink on her, her cheeks become a darker shade and her eyes brighten."

"And how many women have you put in the pink?" she teased when the girls went to dish up ice cream.

He grinned. "You're the only one I'm counting. How do you feel?"

She stopped to analyze the afterglow of their delicious meal, her new and exhilarating sense of well-being, the inexplicable mother-high of knowing her children were happy, and admitted without reserve, "In the pink. Definitely."

She helped him clean up while Erica did her homework and Rachel bathed, then curled up with him on the sofa to watch the news.

They tucked the girls in.

"Where are you gonna go on your honeymoon?" Erica asked, leaning up on an elbow.

"We'll have the twins," Jackie said, pushing her down again and tucking the blankets in around her. "There won't be time for a honeymoon. They're going to keep all of us very busy until they're about three."

Erica frowned. "I think you're *supposed* to have one. So you kind of get to know each other when you're all by yourselves."

"Hank and I have known each other for a long time, remember?"

"Yeah." Erica was up on her elbow again. "But that was as friends. Won't it be different to be married? I mean, don't you have to get to know each other like a husband and a wife?"

For an instant, Jackie wondered if she was talking about lovemaking. Then Erica clarified her question. "I mean, you'll have to balance the checkbook and share the van. Daddy never liked that stuff, remember?" To Hank she added, "Mom forgets to write things down in the checkbook, and sometimes she forgets to put gas in the van. Daddy used to get mad about that." She fell grimly quiet.

Hank came up behind Jackie and wrapped his arms around her. "I love everything about your mom. That doesn't mean we won't sometimes annoy each other and even quarrel, but you can disagree without getting angry, and she's the only woman I ever want to be with. We'll see about the honeymoon. Maybe after the twins are a couple of months old."

Then Hank released Jackie and eased Erica back to her pillows, pulling the blankets up under her chin. "I don't want you to worry about things anymore," he said, leaning down to kiss her cheek. "I'm here to take care of you. Everything's going to be fine. This is going to be a good family."

Erica wrapped her arms around his neck and squeezed. "I know. Good night."

"Good night, Erica."

"I'm still awake!" Rachel called from her room.

"A good family except for her," Erica grumbled as Jackie and Hank crossed the hall.

Jackie stopped on the threshold of Rachel's room and looked in. "You've already been tucked in," she said gently but firmly. "And you've had your water and you've got your bear."

Rachel sat up, clutching the bear, the soft glow of a

nearby night-light putting her in shadow. "But I haven't been tucked in by a daddy in a long time," she said. "Can I do it again?"

Before Jackie could reply, Hank pushed her gently aside and went to Rachel's bedside. She hunkered down with her bear and Hank pulled the covers up over her shoulders and tucked them in. He leaned over her to kiss her hair.

"Good night, Rachel," he said.

"When can I call you Daddy?" she asked.

Jackie felt a stab of emotion in her chest. Hank smoothed Rachel's hair. "I won't officially be your dad until your mom and I get married."

Rachel sighed. "Is it okay…if it's not officially?"

There was a moment's pause, then Hank cleared his throat. "It's okay with me. Is it okay with you?"

"Yeah," she replied. "Good night, Daddy."

Another pause. Another throat clearing. "Good night, baby." Hank kissed her again, then pulled the door partially closed behind him.

Jackie opened her arms to him and he wrapped his around her, having to tuck her into his side, around the obstruction of the twins. "Okay, whatever paternal sternness I might have had is dissolved into a puddle of adoration. I hope you're not going to count on me for discipline."

In a moment, she'd be able to laugh about that with him, but for now, she, too, was a puddle of adoration— for him. Her heart had ached for years over the casual and often minimal effort Ricky made with the girls, and how they'd clung to every little show of affection.

Things would be different with Hank.

"Usually, all they need is a little direction," she said, leading him toward the stairs. "But you'll have to toughen up or they'll learn quickly to use your easy-going ways against you."

He held her arm as they walked down the stairs. "I never thought of myself as easygoing."

"Their father was often tense and preoccupied. You do lighten the atmosphere. Another cup of decaf while we watch TV?"

"Sounds good to me. You sit down, I'll get the coffee."

THE HOUSE WAS QUIET when they went to bed shortly after ten.

Giving Jackie a few moments to adjust to the fact that her room was no longer her own, Hank looked in on the girls, pulled the blankets over Rachel's protruding feet, then pushed Jackie's door open to find her standing at the foot of the bed, contemplating a length of black lace.

She looked up a little guiltily. "I could wear this," she said, color in her cheeks, "but frankly, it's itchy. My skin is so dry." She rubbed her belly unconsciously as she spoke.

"Or you could wear nothing," he bargained, taking the negligee from her and tossing it at a chair, "and make me and your itchy skin happy."

She made a face. "This body's pretty ugly," she said, crossing her arms over the big chenille robe she'd put on. "I put the lights out even when I'm alone in here."

He scolded her with a look and went into the bathroom for a bottle of moisturizing cream he'd noticed earlier, when he'd been putting his things away.

He emerged and held up the bottle. "Wouldn't this help?"

She shrugged. "I forget to use it. Or I'm too tired."

He took her hand and drew her gently toward the bed. "Let me do it for you," he suggested softly.

SHE DIDN'T WANT him to see her veiny and bulbous belly and breasts. But he'd already tossed the blankets aside, was plumping pillows up against the headboard, then helping her off with the robe. His touch was gentle, almost clinically detached as he left her socks on and pulled the blankets up to her hipbones.

He sat on the edge of the bed beside her, straightened her nearest arm and put her hand on his shoulder. He took cream in his hands and worked them up and down her arm from shoulder to elbow, then elbow to wrist. He used his fingertips and the heel of his hand, up and down, then up again. She began to feel as though that side of her body had been sedated.

She tried not to think about his hands as he worked on her other arm. But her mind refused to budge from the delicious sensation of him massaging her.

Even as a boy, he'd had a delicate but powerful touch. He used it now, pulling her toward him, leaning her into his shoulder as he applied a dollop of cream to the middle of her shoulder blades. He rubbed up and down her spine, across her shoulders, up one side and down the other, skimming the cleft of her buttocks.

Sensation ricocheted inside her.

He eased her back to her robe, which protected the

sheets, and worked on the point of her shoulders. Gently, almost studiously, he applied cream to the dry skin of her breasts, then over her enormous belly.

He shifted focus for an instant to smile at her. "You okay? I can't feel you breathing."

She nodded briefly in response, certain her lungs weren't working. Nothing was working but her nerve endings. She felt a curious edginess that seemed out of place in a massage.

Then his fingertips traced the curve of her belly, and some emotional knot inside was suddenly and dramatically undone.

Oh...my! She thought. *This can't be hap—oh, God!*

IT TOOK HANK A MOMENT to understand what was happening. While trying to pretend a detachment he didn't feel at all, he noticed a mild quiver wherever he touched, a little gasp in her breath as his fingertips smoothed cream into the chapped skin between her belly and her thigh.

She moved suddenly and he thought he'd hurt her.

He stopped to look up at her, saw a flush in her cheeks, a furrow on her forehead, and a sudden, desperate movement of her hand reaching for him.

He caught it in his cream-slick fingers just as she uttered a soft little cry he remembered from long ago.

He experienced relief and a touch of arrogance. Jackie was having an orgasm. He ran his free hand over her belly, doing what he could to prolong it.

JACKIE FELT THE MOVEMENT throughout her body, the languid warmth, the little waves of sensation, the exquisite freedom from the fear that she'd never know that feeling again.

She emerged from the sudden and unexpected fulfillment in astonishment. She hadn't experienced it in the last three or four years of her marriage—even when the twins had been conceived. Yet Hank hadn't even touched her intimately.

She was elated, embarrassed, shaken.

"How…did that happen?" she breathed.

Their hands still joined, he leaned over her to plant a light kiss on her lips.

"Nuclear power," he replied. "We've always had it."

When she could think again, she felt a glow of happiness, a blossoming sense that this was all too good to go bad on her. She wanted to give it a couple of days, to let Hank settle in, to let herself adjust to the wonder of having him within reach, then she would tell him everything.

He would understand. She was growing more confident of that. And then nothing would stand in the way of her and her daughters' happiness. Or Hank's. She would love him as no other woman had ever loved a man.

CHAPTER THIRTEEN

JACKIE HAD four delicious days before Addy's birthday party at Haley and Bart's. The family routine was quiet and sweet and the girls seemed to thrive under it.

Hank got the girls up, made breakfast, managed to find all the critical items that managed to get lost in the morning rush—shoes, homework, field trip permission slip. He drove the girls to school while Jackie got up, took a shower and dressed with the promising smell of fresh coffee in her nostrils.

She made breakfast for herself and Hank, and they ate it together when he returned. Then he drove her to work. He walked her up the stairs to her office, kissed her with the tantalizing promise of what awaited them when there was no longer thirty pounds of babies between them, then went down to the basement to his office.

Glory picked up the girls in the afternoon and stayed with them until Hank and Jackie got home. Glory had started dinner several times. "I've got to learn something about cooking," she explained with an embarrassed smile. "I really like Jimmy and he can't even make coffee."

Her spaghetti sauce was delicious, but her meat loaf the following night had the consistency of a brick. Fortunately, Addy arrived with a pork and noodle casserole.

"Do not buy me anything for my birthday," she said firmly, placing it in the middle of the set table. "All I want is to be surrounded by my family." She smiled beatifically at Hank. "Now that they've finally come to their senses."

"We already have your present!" Rachel said, "It's…!"

Erica covered her mouth. "You're not supposed to tell."

Addy looked dismayed.

"Come on, Mom," Hank teased, trying to take her coat. "You know you always say that the day before your party, knowing your gift will already be bought. Pretty transparent ploy."

She held on to her coat and frowned at him. "All right, but it would have showed more delicacy if you hadn't pointed it out. Especially since I just brought you your favorite casserole and prevented you from having to eat hardened clay."

Glory, shrugging into her jacket, stared mournfully at the black lump. "I don't know what I did wrong."

Erica patted her arm. "You tried. That's what counts."

Addy hooked her arm in Glory's and led her toward the door. "Oven was too hot, that's my guess. Sometimes the wrong pan can do that to you, too. I hear you're dating Jimmy Elliott."

"Yes."

"Now, that's a nice boy. Likes my brownies."

"Really? I didn't know he liked brownies."

"He does. Without nuts. I have a great recipe…"

Addy opened the door. "See you Sunday, Addy," Jackie called. "Have a good weekend, Glory."

The women, their attention focused on brownie recipes, ignored her.

"If she's your mom," Erica asked Hank when they gathered around the table, "then we can call her Grandma."

Hank nodded. "She won't care that it's still unofficial."

After the girls were tucked in for bed, Hank and Jackie followed their routine of a last cup of decaf while watching an hour or two of television, then went upstairs to bed.

Under the covers and flannel sheet, Hank wrapped his arms around Jackie, her back to his chest. She felt as though she sank into him, physically, emotionally, even spiritually. She let herself be overtaken by the security he represented in her turbulent life, the steadiness that was such a part of him and the generosity he offered every time she turned to him.

The only heartache was the knowledge that she might have had this for the past seventeen years as well. But she didn't dwell on that because everything had been different then. She had him now, though. She had him now.

She reached a hand back to touch his face. "I love you, Henry Jedediah Whitcomb," she whispered.

He kissed her neck. "I love you, Jacqueline Denise Fortin Bourgeois Whitcomb."

"Not officially Whitcomb," she reminded him.

He nuzzled into her hair. "Officially doesn't seem to count around here."

HANK COULDN'T QUITE BELIEVE how much he enjoyed family life. True, it had been less than a week and the girls were being particularly sweet and helpful, and Jackie's usual tendency to resist his every suggestion was blunted by the growing weight she carried and an exhaustion clearly visible in her face. He was also very much aware of his value to the group.

The girls seemed fascinated by his presence and were always nearby, either to ask permission for something or to tell him where the seldom-used melon-baller was in the kitchen and advise him against using the hot cycle on the dryer because it didn't work.

If he settled in the big chair to watch the news or a ball game, Rachel sat in his lap and Erica curled up on the arm of his chair.

Jackie seemed to love those moments, even though it meant she couldn't get near him. She gave him a smile that said she absorbed his love through her children. It surprised him that he understood that.

Yes. He was going to love married life, he thought. Even though two new babies would complicate their schedules and no doubt shred everyone's nerves for a while, they would adjust and the love would expand to encompass all of them. He'd never understood before how flexible love was—or how inexhaustible. He found himself wishing his father were around to see the successful man he'd become, personally and professionally. But he dismissed the thought, realizing that personal demons prevented the man from enjoying his own life. He'd probably be unimpressed by Hank's successes—or unaware of them.

He and Jackie had made a fruit salad for the party that he packed into a cooler with a frozen ice pack. "Where would you go on a honeymoon?" Erica asked, handing him the can of whipped cream to top the fruit with when they arrived.

Rachel knelt on a chair and watched the proceedings.

He put the back of his wrist to his forehead in a theatrical gesture and replied in the voice he remembered Erica mimicking, "A month in Bermuda, I think!"

Erica laughed.

"When I get a honeymoon," Rachel announced. "I'm going to Disney World!"

Erica shook her head pityingly. "That's where little kids go. You're supposed to go someplace romantic."

"What's romantic?"

"Where you can kiss and hug."

Rachel looked confused. "Can't you kiss and hug on the teacups?"

"You can hug and kiss anywhere," Jackie said, walking hurriedly into the kitchen, the girls' coats over her arm. "But we don't have time right now. We're going to be late." She handed Erica her coat and helped Rachel with hers.

Hank caught her as she shooed the girls toward the door and showed her that you could also hug and kiss anytime—even when late for a birthday party.

Haley and Bart's house was filled with family and friends—Addy, the guest of honor, Haley and Bart's fifteen-year-old foster son, Mike, Adam and Sabrina, Jackie and Hank and the girls and several of Addy's friends. After a potluck lunch, everyone gathered around the dining room table where an enormous birthday cake decorated with pink flowers and a telephone receiver to signify Addy's work with Hank held a place of honor in the middle of a lace tablecloth.

Mike, who seemed very fond of Addy, teased her about the large number of candles and the possibility of the fire department responding to the smoke.

Addy took it all good-naturedly and blew out the candles, her friends helping so that she would get her wish.

"What did you wish for?" Haley asked.

"She can't tell," Rachel intervened, "or her wish won't come true."

Haley leaned down to kiss the top of Rachel's head. "Well, what if we try to guess. Is that okay?"

Rachel turned to Erica for a ruling.

Erica turned to Jackie. "Is it?"

"Um...I think the you-can't-tell rule only applies until you're fifty," she said, then grinned slyly at Addy. "And Addy's way, *waaay* over that."

The decision was met with laughter from the group and the threat of a throttling from Addy.

"Because if you wished for grandchildren," Haley said, "it comes with a guarantee."

Addy patted Jackie's stomach. "I know. Four of them! Do you believe it?"

"Five," Haley corrected.

For a moment, Addy didn't understand. Then Haley and Bart exchanged a look of utter ecstasy, Jackie shrieked and the room exploded with sound.

Hank found Bart in the melee as the women surrounded Haley. He wrapped his arms around him, because now that he had a glimpse of what having children was like, a handshake simply wasn't enough. "Congratulations," he said, clapping him on the back. "When's this going to happen?"

"Middle of October," Bart replied.

Bart had lost his pregnant wife several years ago, and Hank studied his face for any sign of remembered grief. But he seemed completely happy.

"I'm good with it." Bart nodded, apparently reading Hank's mind. "What you lose stays with you always, but you find you're able to go on and things can still be wonderful. Better than you deserve, even."

"Yeah." Hank could agree with that. Of course, he hadn't experienced the same degree of loss Bart had. Jackie hadn't died, just gone out of reach. But he'd reclaimed her after all so he hadn't lost anything—simply gained four children in the process. A pretty good deal all in all.

The women surrounded Bart and drew him into the circle, and Hank noticed that the only one not part of the weeping, laughing knot of guests was Sabrina. She had pasted on a smile, but she looked completely bored with the goings-on. She drifted toward the high-backed settee where Hank stood.

"Loud group," she observed, swiping the back of the settee with a hand before she leaned against it in her white woollen dress.

"Babies are cause for excitement around here," he answered.

"Seems there're a lot already."

"Some believe there are never too many."

She turned slightly toward him and said more quietly, "I'll bet there weren't many at NASA."

He nodded. "That's why I came home."

Obviously finding him as dull as the children, she wandered away toward a window that looked out onto the garden.

Haley suddenly flew into his arms. "Did you ever think you'd be this happy?" she demanded. "You getting Jackie and four beautiful children, and me getting pregnant?"

He loved seeing her so happy. "No, I didn't. But we've both always been pretty good at getting what we wanted."

She hugged him again. "But for a long time, I didn't even know I wanted this."

He held her close. "I know. Fortunately, Bart did. Jackie didn't know she wanted me, either, but I straightened her out. You women don't know how lucky you are."

She squeezed him tightly, then stood back to smile into his face. "Any other day I might dispute that, but today I think you're right. Can you imagine how wonderful next Christmas is going to be around here with Mom acquiring five grandchildren in one year?"

He nodded seriously. "I hope she appreciates what we've done for her."

The cake was cut and chairs were carried in from the kitchen so that everyone sat in a large, irregular circle eating cake and ice cream. Hank was helping Rachel with a scoop of ice cream that had fallen off her plate and onto her jumper when he heard a small commotion at the other end of the room. Jackie, who'd been helping Haley serve, looked pale and in pain. She fell into a chair her father quickly vacated, and Hank went immediately to her side.

She breathed through her mouth, her eyes closed.

"Nobody panic," she said, puffing. "I'm okay. Just…just the babies turning around, I think." She put a hand out. "Hank?"

He laced his fingers in hers. "Right here. You're sure that's all it is?"

Her puffing breaths slowed and she opened her eyes, obviously analyzing how she felt.

"I think you should call your doctor to be sure," Adam said. He leaned over her from behind, his face tight with concern.

"No, I think I'm okay," she insisted with a small smile for Hank. "This has happened a couple of times. I think they just forget they're in a cramped space and stretch out."

"You're sure?" Hank asked. "It'd just take a couple of minutes to run you to the hospital and check for sure."

"No." She was adamant. "It didn't feel like a contraction, just a…"

"Hank's right," Adam insisted. "Remember when you carried Henry, you had to spend the last three weeks in bed."

The room fell silent. Hank, focused on his concern for Jackie, failed to realize for a moment what was wrong with that simple sentence.

Then he saw panic take over Jackie's expression, saw the same panic in Adam's face when she turned to him. Then both of them looked at Hank, and somewhere behind him, his mother's voice asked in confusion, "Who's Henry?"

And that was when Hank felt the sky fall on his head. Henry. Jackie had carried a child named Henry. After him. That was the secret she couldn't share, the truth that brought guilt to her face so often when she looked at him. Probably the reason she'd decided not to leave with him that fateful day seventeen years ago. She'd been pregnant! With *his* baby.

Adam's lips worked as though he intended to say something, but couldn't quite form the words. He turned to Jackie again. She was ashen now.

Hank's mind churned with all the details that didn't make sense. If Jackie had had his baby, his mother would have told him. Haley would have told him.

But Jackie had gone to Boston, he remembered. Was it possible that she'd gone before it had been obvious to anyone?

But she'd come back just two years later.

Without a baby.

Confusion was morphing into anger, and anger was quickly becoming rage. Jackie had given away his baby!

"Jackie," Adam whispered, his face contorting with apparent horror, "I'm sorry!"

Jackie wrapped her arms around his neck and hugged him. "It's all right," she said quietly. "It's all right, Daddy."

Everyone looked at everyone else, frozen in a startled tableau. Then Haley began ushering everyone into the kitchen. "Come on," she said briskly. "Let's finish our cake in there."

"But…what's wrong?" Erica wanted to know, coming toward her mother. The tension was so palpable, her child's radar had picked it up.

Bart caught her arm and led her toward the retreating group. "She's fine," he said, "because Hank's going to take good care of her." With that he gave Hank a speaking look that Hank noticed but ignored.

"Mommy?" Rachel asked worriedly.

"It's all right," Jackie said in a strangled voice. "Go ahead with Uncle Bart. I'll come and get you in a minute."

Adam tried to begin to explain, but Jackie stood and urged him toward the kitchen. "I have to tell him, Dad."

"But, I want to ex—"

"No," she said. "I have to."

Clearly torn between honoring her wishes and doing what he thought best, Adam finally settled for standing in front of Hank and telling him firmly, "I'm sure your years with NASA have taught you to get all the facts, then think them through before you make a decision on something. I'll consider you less of a man if you don't do that now."

"Daddy," Jackie pleaded.

With a last worried look in her direction, Adam pushed his way through the swinging door into the kitchen.

The moment they were alone, Hank turned to Jackie, feeling as though an inferno raged inside him. "You had my child!" he accused.

JACKIE WANTED TO DIE. She knew people used that expression all the time to exaggerate their desperation, but at the moment, if it hadn't been that her children needed her, she'd have happily fled the earth.

She'd planned to tell Hank carefully, to remind him of how much they now had together and how much they could have if he would only understand. But the news that he'd had a child no one had told him about had been announced in front of his astonished family and friends—and not even by Jackie herself.

She'd known it didn't pay to be selfish, but she'd so hoped she'd be able to preserve her little bit of heaven by waiting until the moment was right.

She wanted to bawl, to sob, but he'd only think she was playing on his sympathies, so she swallowed against the burning sensation in her throat and held his gaze with cussed determination.

"Yes," she replied. "I did. I tried to tell you...."

"When?" he demanded, taking several paces away from her as though he found her distasteful. "When did you try to tell me? I don't remember once in seventeen years—"

"That day," she said, struggling to maintain control. Everything inside her shook with emotion and old pain.

And new pain.

"I tried to explain why I couldn't go with you," she went on, "but you—"

"You said you thought it'd be better if you stayed behind," he said, taking several angry steps back to her. "You never once mentioned a baby."

"You talked over me," she returned quietly. "You didn't give me a chance. Then you stormed away."

"Well, what about the seventeen years since?" he roared at her. "Why didn't you call or write?"

Oh, God, she thought, steeling herself. Anguish squeezed her lungs and made air escape in a painful sound. She had to pull herself together. The hard part was coming.

"And where the hell is he?" he asked, both arms spread out to indicate the child's absence. "Where is Henry?"

"I..."

"Did you hate me so much for not listening to your explanation that you couldn't even raise him yourself?"

"Hank, I..."

"What? What! Did you give him away to someone

you thought could give him the things your struggling engineer couldn't? Did you find him some high-society family on Beacon Hill?"

"No!" she shouted back at him, her meager composure evaporating as the horror of that time came back in vivid detail. "I had him for five months and I would never have given him to anybody! He's dead! He isn't here because he's dead!"

When Henry died, she used to make herself say the word—*dead.* Not passed away, or gone, but dead. She knew it was the only way she'd accept it. She'd thought herself so strong to be able to do that, so she was surprised to discover that saying the word now could hurt even more than it had then. She didn't know if it was because his father was hearing it for the first time, or because she now had growing children and was forced to confront the real depths of Henry's potential and therefore the real magnitude of her loss.

Hank fell silent, pain a dull force in his eyes. "Dead," he said finally, as though he, too, needed to hear the word again to believe it.

"He had glycogen enzyme deficiency," she said, holding on to the back of a straight chair before lowering herself into it. Her back ached abominably. "He was weak from the very beginning, but he was diagnosed at about a month. They told me there was no cure, and that he wouldn't survive very long." Her mouth began to quiver as she remembered looking into Henry's eyes and seeing Hank there, knowing that the part of him that was his father made him fight to survive. But in the end, nature was stronger than the baby's will. "He fought to stay with me for…for five months. Then…he couldn't…fight anymore."

HANK COULD NOT REMEMBER anything in his life hurting this much. Shock, anguish, loss, all beat through him from head to toe and limb to limb, making him feel as though he had burrs in his bloodstream, hooks in his lungs. His heart throbbed against his ribs, feeling like the claw end of a hammer.

He found that he, too, had to sit. "What…what was it again?"

"Glycogen enzyme deficiency," she repeated. "Glycogen is produced in the tissues, particularly the liver and the muscles, and it's changed into a simple sugar as the body needs it. I guess in simplest terms, his body couldn't feed itself."

His brain had a mental image of an infant struggling to survive—*his* infant—and anguish and anger tumbled over themselves to take control of him. The anguish was too painful, so he gave the anger free rein.

"Why didn't you tell me you were pregnant?" he demanded.

"Because you had big plans," she replied, sniffing and dabbing at her eyes with a tissue. "I wanted you to have your dreams."

He bolted out of his chair, energized by his fury. "The dream that came first with me," he raged at her, "was you and the life we'd make together."

She didn't want to hurt him any more, but her own anguish was beyond control. "That must be why you shouted me down and took off without looking back when I tried to explain why I couldn't go with you."

"That's not fair," he said with quiet vehemence.

She shook her head at him and replied in the same tone. "None of it was fair."

He paced away from her, hands in his pockets, then stopped at the sofa and turned back to her. "I can't believe you didn't even call me to tell me he'd been born."

A sob swelled inside her. "I knew there was something wrong from the beginning."

"Did you think I couldn't deal with that?" he shouted. "That I'd somehow require he be perfect before I claimed him?"

"No!" she screamed at him. "It was because it hurt so much! It seemed futile to subject you to that when nothing could be done." As Jackie heard herself speak the words, they sounded hollow and absurd, though they'd made sense in her abject misery at the time.

But judging by Hank's expression, he accepted them at their current value. "How can you look at me and say that?" he asked in angry disbelief. "I was his father. I should have known him. He should have known me. You deprived me of five whole months of having a son and him of having a father!"

He was absolutely right. Her parents had pleaded with her at the time to call Hank. But she'd been so destroyed herself, she hated the thought of doing that to him when his mother reported that his letters said he was doing well. Jackie had lived with the guilt ever since.

"I told him his father loved him," she whispered.

"I should have told him myself! How could you have prevented me from doing that?"

"Is loving you an excuse?" she asked, knowing his answer even before he roared it.

"No!" He came back to her to look down into her face, his own tortured with pain. "Because I don't believe you did. How can a mother keep her son from his father and claim she did it for love?"

She wondered how she could make him understand that her own grief and pain had warped her thinking. But he didn't wait for an answer. He stormed out of the house, and an instant later, she heard the van drive away with a screech of tires.

The door to the kitchen burst open and her father rushed out, sitting beside her and wrapping her in his arms. "Jackie, I'm so, so sorry," he groaned. "I can't believe that after all these years of keeping it from everyone, I blurt it out in front of Hank. You'd just gone so pale and I was worried that something would go wrong with…"

"Daddy, it's okay," she reassured him, though tears began to fall in earnest. "It's okay. I should have told him long ago. It's my fault."

"I wanted to come out here and make him understand, but Addy thought…"

"Addy thought that he'd be hurt and angry," Addy said, coming to stand over them, placing a hand on each shoulder, "but that he'd understand. Seems I was wrong."

"No, you weren't." Haley appeared with a cup of coffee, which she handed to Jackie. "He just needs a little time. You can understand that it was a shock. He's a planner, an organizer. He feels vulnerable when he's surprised by things. And most men get angry when they feel vulnerable. Drink this, Jackie. It's decaf, but it's hot."

Jackie obliged her with a sip, then decided it did feel good going down, warming her chest where a cold rock seemed to have formed. She rubbed at it, needing to make contact with her babies. "Where are my girls?" she asked, suddenly horrified by what they must have thought when they heard her and Hank screaming at each other.

"Bart took them out in the back yard when the shouting started," Haley replied.

Remembering how angry Hank had been, Jackie was sure they must have heard something—even outdoors.

She clung to her father's hand and, putting her coffee down, caught Haley's in her free one. "I'm so sorry your party was spoiled."

"Oh, please." Haley held Jackie's hand in both of hers. "Don't be silly. I'm just sorry...it all happened."

"And it was a wonderful birthday," Addy said. "Thank you for the beautiful sweater."

Jackie was suddenly exhausted beyond bearing. "You'll understand if I excuse myself," she pleaded to Haley.

"Of course. Why don't I take you home?"

"I'll take her home," Adam said. "I'll go get the girls and put them in the car, then I'll come back for you."

"I'm okay, Dad."

"Just wait here for me," he ordered.

"Adam," Sabrina said, "we're supposed to meet the McGoverns for a drink at their place before the theater."

Jackie looked up at her in surprise, having completely forgotten she was there.

Adam, too, seemed taken aback by her presence. "Get Jackie's coat, will you please?" he asked her, ignoring her agenda alert. He then went through the kitchen for the girls.

Head in the air, Sabrina headed for the study, where Haley had put their coats.

The ride home seemed eternal. Jackie sat in the back of her father's Cadillac, the girls pressed in on each side of her, exceptionally quiet. She wondered if her father had asked them not to talk about what had happened.

She waited until they reached the house, then went upstairs with the girls while her father and Sabrina stayed in the kitchen. She had no idea how to explain all that had happened to Erica and Rachel, but knew she had to try.

The three of them sat on the bed in the room she'd shared for the past few days with Hank. The jeans and flannel shirt he'd changed out of for the party were thrown over a chair, and the smell of his aftershave clung to the bedclothes still disturbed from the nap she'd taken just before they left.

Erica seemed to understand that she needed help. "You had a baby named Henry," she said.

Jackie nodded.

"But not with Daddy." When Jackie drew a breath, Erica added gently, "Uncle Bart took us outside, but we could still hear you."

"No. Hank was my boyfriend then. Way before you were born. Way before I married your dad."

Rachel leaned into her. "But if Hank was just your boyfriend, you couldn't have a baby. You have to be married to have a baby."

"No, you don't have to be married," Jackie corrected. "But it certainly makes things simpler for everybody if you are. Hank and I were planning to move away together, but when I found out I was going to have the baby, I didn't tell Hank because I was afraid he'd want to stay here and wouldn't go to school, and I didn't think that would be good for him."

Erica looked confused. "But then Henry didn't have a dad."

Jackie nodded, pain swelling in her all over again. "I did the wrong thing. I thought it was the right thing to do at the time, but it wasn't."

"And Henry got sick and died."

"Yes."

Rachel wrapped her arms around Jackie's stomach as far as they would go. "Were you sad?"

"I was very sad."

"Did you cry?"

"For a long time."

"Now Hank's mad at you," Erica observed, "because he never got to see Henry."

Jackie nodded, the affirmative catching in her throat.

There was a long silence while they all sat together in the quiet room.

"Is he coming back?" Erica finally asked.

Jackie tried never to give the girls a noncommittal answer to any question, but this time it was the only one she had. "I don't know," she said.

HANK DROVE TO GLOUCESTER at the opposite end of the state. He hadn't intended to, he just kept driving and looked up at some point in the darkness and saw the monument to the New England fisherman.

He stopped at a small diner for a cup of coffee, filled up the gas tank at a neighboring station, then headed for Boston.

He tried to think as he drove, but his mind was so completely occupied with pain that all he could do was control the car. His brain wouldn't allow for anything else.

Once he reached Logan International Airport, he turned around and headed west. He stopped for coffee again, and when the waitress pointed out that his hands were shaking and he should probably eat something, he ordered bacon and eggs. His stomach refused the bacon and the hash browns, but he ate the eggs and the toast.

As he drove west on Interstate 90, his brain began to look for something to occupy it. He saw a picture in his mind of Jackie with a baby in her arms and quickly pushed it away. Work. He could think about work. And all he could think was that he'd have to move Whitcomb's Wonders to another town. He couldn't stay in Maple Hill now. He couldn't look at Jackie every day and remember that she'd deprived him of his child.

Then he remembered that he'd promised the Maple Hill Manor Private School outside of Maple Hill that he'd see what was wrong with the illuminated marquee, and he was supposed to meet with Holden Construction to talk about doing the wiring on a development up the hill from the Old Post Road Inn. And all his "wonders" lived in and around Maple Hill. How could he leave?

Well. He'd have to move out of his office at City Hall at the very least. He couldn't stand the thought of running into Jackie every day.

Then he remembered that he'd promised to rewire the building, and that his promise was part of the city council minutes. Doing the job from an office outside of the building to make the next month or so easier on himself when he had everything he needed right in the basement would be foolish.

All right, then. He'd stay in the building. But there was no question now that he had to move out of Jackie's house. He wouldn't be able to be that close to her every day and not want to berate her for what she'd done, and he couldn't do that in front of her children.

Yes. He was moving out first thing in the morning.

He was in Auburn, about fifty miles from Maple Hill, when he remembered that he'd promised Rachel he'd put lights in her dollhouse, and Erica that he'd help her with her science project. And he'd promised Jackie that he'd add that outlet to their rooms. Not that he cared about his promise to her, but she thought the disc players the outlets would accommodate would help the girls feel less neglected when the babies arrived, so he wanted to do it. He'd stay until the twins were born because he'd promised the girls he'd take care of them, then he was out of Jackie's house, and the moment he'd finished rewiring City Hall, he was out of there, too.

But he was moving into Jackie's spare bedroom the moment he got back to Maple Hill.

He heard the plan collapse around him.

CHAPTER FOURTEEN

JACKIE AWOKE to the aroma of coffee brewing and something sweet in the oven. She sat up, her heart thumping in excitement. Hank was back! Then she remembered that her father and Sabrina had stayed the night in the spare bedroom, insisting she shouldn't be alone after the emotional upheaval and the unexplained contraction. Sabrina had smiled bravely when he canceled their theater date with the McGoverns.

The vicious headache and generally foggy feeling reminded Jackie just how horrid yesterday had been. She'd lain awake for hours during the night, too grief-stricken to cry, knowing that she'd probably never see Hank again.

At the thought, she sank back against her pillows. She would have given anything to be able to spend the day in bed, but this was a teachers' in-service day at school and she had to figure out what to do with the girls. She had City Hall business to conduct, an impeachment proceeding to fight and babies to prepare to deliver. There was no downtime in her immediate future.

She allowed herself to sob in the shower, to indulge herself with the memory of the last week and how stupid she'd been to let things play out as they had, then dried herself off, blew her hair dry into a somewhat messy, flyaway style that was mercifully fashionable these days and pulled on a khaki jumper over a white blouse. It made her look like a Humvee, but it was comfortable. She put a hand to her aching back and headed to Erica's room. It was empty. As was Rachel's.

She went downstairs and spotted the girls at the table, chatting happily as they ate waffles with strawberries and whipped cream.

"Dad," she exclaimed as she walked into the kitchen, "thanks for cooking, but you don't have to…"

She stopped short at the sight of Hank working at the stove.

Her heart rocketed in her chest. He'd come back! They could talk. Perhaps she could make him…

No. He pulled a plate out of the oven and carried it to her place along with a bowl of berries. When he gave her a cursory glance and a polite "Good morning," she knew he was there simply for the benefit of her children.

Her heart fell like a dropped bowling ball.

Actually, the bowling ball was an interesting metaphor, she thought with gallows humor as she returned his terse greeting and took her place at the table. She did look as though she'd swallowed several.

Well, she'd have a talk with him when the girls went upstairs to get their school things. If he was here because he thought he owed her something because of the impeachment hearing, she would set him straight. If he was here for the girls, that was noble of him, but if she and Hank had no future together, it would be easier on the girls in the long run to make that clear now.

"When did you get back?" she asked Hank civilly,

ignoring the fact that he probably didn't care to speak to her.

"About four-thirty this morning," he said, pouring a cup of coffee, which he brought to her. "Your dad and Sabrina were in the spare room, so I sacked out on the sofa."

"Grandpa's going to take us for a ride today." Erica pushed the napkin holder her way. "He went to get gas for the car."

Hank avoided her eyes and went back to the counter to replace the coffee carafe.

Jackie glanced at the clock. "Did Grandpa just leave?"

"A few minutes ago," Erica replied. "Sabrina wants to go shopping, but Grandpa wants to go hiking. He says we need to burn off some steam."

"We can call Hank Daddy now." Her waffle gone, Rachel ate the rest of her strawberries with a spoon, lost in a world of her own where they were a perfect family, unaware that her mother had fixed things so that the dream was dashed forever.

Erica gave Jackie a knowing glance. She understood what had happened, but with the optimism Jackie had taught her to indulge, probably believed that things would work out. Hank was back, wasn't he?

She wished she had the innocence to believe that, too.

Ten minutes later her father returned.

"Are we ready?" he said, handing the girls their jackets from the hallway. "Thanks for spelling me, Hank."

Hank nodded. "No problem, Adam. Where you guys off to?"

"Some unknown destination." Adam leaned over Jackie to give her a hug. "I'll call you if we're going to be later than 2:00. I've got an appointment with the dentist at 2:30. Sabrina!"

Sabrina stumbled into the kitchen, elegantly turned out in bright pink fleece, but an air of martyrdom hovered about her. With a cursory good morning to Jackie and Hank, she went out to the car, clearly unhappy at the prospect of spending the day with children.

Unaware, the girls shrugged into their jackets. "Want me to fix dinner tonight?" Adam asked Jackie, then turned to Hank with a neutral expression. "Or are you going to be here? In which case I don't want to intrude."

"I'll be here," Hank replied, "so I'll fix dinner. Why don't you join us?"

"Great. We'll bring dessert."

"Six o'clock."

"Perfect."

As her father hurried off with her children, Jackie braced herself to confront Hank about his presence here.

But the kitchen door opened again and Rachel raced back in, bear-shaped backpack slapping against her blue coat. Jackie turned away from the table, prepared to answer a question or find some misplaced treasure.

Her services weren't required, however, as Rachel ran to Hank. He dried his hands on a tea towel, then braced them on his knees to look into her face. "Hey, Snooks," he said with a smile. "You forget something?"

"I forgot to kiss you goodbye," she said, reaching up to loop her arms around his neck.

He circled her small body with his two hands and kissed her cheek as she smacked him noisily. Then she looked into his eyes with a big grin. "Bye, Daddy," she said.

That was why she'd really come back, Jackie knew. She wanted to be able to say the word.

For an instant, the man who handled most emergencies with skill and calm looked defeated. Then he swallowed, cleared his throat and pinched her chin. "Bye, baby," he said. "Have a good day."

"You, too!" she sang as she raced toward the door. "You, too, Mommy!"

The door closed behind her with a bang that vibrated for several seconds.

Hank came to the table and sat at a right angle to Jackie, his eyes just as turbulent as they'd been yesterday afternoon, though now a glaze of exhaustion lay over them. He pointed to the closed door. "Rachel and Erica are the only reasons I'm back," he said coolly, "and only until the twins are born. Between now and then you have to find a way to explain to them that I'm not staying."

He was well within his rights to be angry with her, but she didn't think she could stand it if he'd returned simply to make that point over and over again until she delivered.

"I did explain to them yesterday that you might not come back," she said quietly, but without the penitence she'd previously shown. "Maybe you should be the one to make them understand why you did. Because if it's just for the opportunity of beating me over the head with what happened, I don't think it'll help them in the long run because I'm the one who's going to have to deal with them when you're gone. I'll do a better job if I'm emotionally intact."

"Why should you be?" he asked, looking her in the eye. "I'm not."

"Hank, I can't change it." She pushed her half-eaten breakfast away and leaned toward him, desperate to make him understand, or at least try. "I was wrong. I take full responsibility, even though you walked away from me when I tried to tell you I had to stay because I was pregnant. I never called you, but you never called me either. I can't tell you how I regret doing that to you, and no matter how I try, it won't change how you feel. So why don't you go now? I'll make the girls understand."

He shook his head mercilessly. "You took away my prerogative to assume my responsibilities when Henry was born. You're not going to do it again. These aren't my children, but I made them a promise to take care of them and I'm going to do it."

"For a while," she reminded him with the same brutality. "Your promise to them wasn't conditional as I recall."

"Don't try to blame this on me," he said coldly.

"Why not?" she shrieked at him, finally unable to take another moment. "I know this is awful for you, but can you think for a minute what that time was like for me? An eighteen-year-old girl in a strange city with a dying baby, the man she loved gone to follow his dreams? You can't forgive me, but I think God has. I died a thousand times myself during those five months. I think I've expiated my sins."

HANK DIDN'T WANT to think about her with a dying baby in her arms. She'd been a warm and wonderful friend and lover in those days, and he could only imagine the intensity of her pain at losing her child. But he'd lost Henry, too, and thanks to her, he hadn't even known it. He'd been at school, studying, partying, completely oblivious to the fact that a thousand miles away his son was born and died.

He could see the agony in her eyes, but somehow that served only to deepen his own.

Yet his fury didn't negate his need to stay. His work was here—several major projects underway—and he'd promised the girls. But something else kept him—grief for what Jackie must have endured, an empathy he didn't want to admit to but felt strongly all the same. He felt her pain. He loved her.

He just didn't think he could forgive her.

"I'll take you to work when you're ready," he said, and left the kitchen to take a quick shower and change his clothes.

When he came back downstairs, the kitchen was empty, and he hadn't heard her upstairs. He looked out the kitchen window and found her using his stool and trying to climb in behind the wheel of his van. He knew she could no longer climb into hers. Seems she didn't fit behind his wheel, either.

He helped her off the running board, where she'd stranded herself, unable to sit behind the wheel and unable to step back down to the pavement because the stool had overturned. Then he reclaimed the keys he'd given her last week. He walked her around to the passenger side and helped her in, expanding the seat belt and handing it to her.

Her face was blotchy and tear-stained, her eyes puffy, her nose red. He felt like a heel. He had to remind himself that his position was justified. They drove to City Hall in silence.

In the parking lot, Jackie tried to climb down without his help, but her belt was looped through the strap of her purse and she appeared close to a meltdown when he came around to help her. The purse freed, he offered her his hand, but he could see as she tried to turn toward him that trusting her to step onto the narrow running board, then down to the pavement without mishap was tempting fate. So he scooped her out, then set her on her feet. She hit him with her purse and walked awkwardly toward the door, a tragicomic figure whose being was now so allied to his that he finally understood in that moment that half his rage and pain over Henry was because she hadn't allowed him to share her pain.

He left the van in the lot and strode toward the street and the French Maid Bakery. He ordered an Americano and a maple bar to go, then turned to leave with it and spotted Bart and Cameron in a booth in the back. Bart waved him over. The last thing he wanted at the moment was company—particularly company privy to what had happened yesterday—but if he went to work he'd have to face his mother, and that would be worse. Bart moved farther into the booth to make room for him. He looked natty in a pin-striped suit.

"You're back!" Bart observed.

Hank nodded. "Obviously. You got court today?"

Bart frowned at him, hesitated, then said, "Yeah. I take it you two haven't made up yet?" Bart handed him a napkin from a dispenser on the table.

Hank shook his head and took a deep sip of coffee. Then he ripped his maple bar in half. "I don't think we're going to."

"Why not?"

With an apologetic glance at Cameron, Hank turned

to Bart and said impatiently, "Because I won't be able to forget that because of her I never saw my son. Come on. Cameron doesn't want to hear this."

Cameron rolled his eyes. "My father's a drunk and my mother's in jail. Other people's problems don't embarrass me. And that puts me in no position to criticize, so feel free to talk. Is her honor the mayor being difficult?"

Hank absorbed Cameron's information with surprise, then drank more coffee. "It's what she does best," he said finally.

"And you're going to let this be it," Bart asked, "because she tried to save you from the pain she endured?"

Hank turned to his friend in disbelief. "It was a baby, Bart, not a common cold. I lost my son without ever seeing his face."

Bart was silent for a moment, then he said grimly, "So did I. I understand what you feel."

Engrossed in his own misery, Hank had momentarily forgotten that Bart had lost two unborn babies when his pregnant wife died in a plane crash. Hank had sat with him for hours on end, day after day to prevent him from slipping into the darkness yawning at his feet— similar to the one that beckoned Hank at the moment.

"I'm sorry," Hank said, offering him half his maple bar. He suddenly wasn't very hungry. "I'm not usually this self-indulgent, but damn it! I had a son!"

Bart was silent. Hank wondered if it was because he really had nothing more to say, or because Hank had reminded him of his own loss.

"Hard to find fault with a woman who wants to protect you from anything," Cameron weighed in with quiet detachment. "So many of them either want what you've got or want to blame you for what they haven't got. I mean, she was wrong, but she was thinking of you."

Hank finished off his coffee. "You don't have kids."

"No," Cameron admitted.

"Then I'm not sure you could understand."

Cameron shrugged. "I know what it's like to be alone. I thought that gave me the right to tell you to think twice if that's how you're going to end up."

Hank really liked Cameron Trent. He hadn't known him very long, but that didn't seem to matter. He was genuine, willing to put himself out for the job and never complained about the pay or the conditions. It was hard to fault a man like that.

"Thank you," he said simply, though gratitude wasn't precisely what he felt.

Cameron chuckled. "And get the hell out of your face, right?"

"Right."

"Okay." Cameron glanced at his watch. "I'm due at Perk Avenue in ten minutes anyway. Hot water pipes are whining. I'll call in when I'm finished." He slid out of the booth and strode away.

Hank moved to the free side of the table.

"Where'd you go last night?" Bart asked. "Addy and Haley were frantic."

"Gloucester," Hank replied, taking a bite of maple bar.

Bart raised an eyebrow in surprise, then went to the coffeepot on the counter, brought it to their table and re-filled their cups.

Hank swallowed the hot brew gratefully.

"You love her," Bart offered, resuming his place.

"Yes," Hank replied, feeling his own grimness settle

inside him as though it had plans to stay, "but I can't forgive her."

Bart leaned back in the booth and pinned him with a look. "You're sure it isn't yourself you're having trouble forgiving?"

Hank grew immediately defensive. "What do you mean?"

"If you'd listened to her when she tried to tell you she was pregnant," Bart said, "you'd have known your son." He explained that he knew that detail of their relationship by adding, "Haley went to Jackie's last night and stayed with her for a couple of hours. They talked."

Hank raised both hands in disbelief, then brought them down to the table with a crash that shook the napkin holder and sloshed the coffee. "I don't understand how I get to be the villain in this! I've got to leave before I ram a silk carnation down your throat."

Bart nodded. "Just remember what you were always telling me when Marianne died. 'It's not going to stop hurting if you don't stop focusing on the pain.'"

"Put a sock in it." Hank slipped out of the booth.

"Did you forget that the impeachment hearing's today?" Bart called after him as he headed for the door.

Hank stopped in his tracks, sure there was a stunned look on his face. He had forgotten. And she hadn't mentioned it. Well, he thought, pushing his way outside, they weren't each other's problem anymore. Only the children mattered.

"BUT, YOUR HONOR," Brockton said as the judge for the impeachment's preliminary hearing refuted the claim that Jackie had advanced her own interests when she'd encouraged the addition of Perk Avenue on Maple Hill Square. "Those women are friends of hers. They…"

The judge, a middle-aged man from Springfield, had made short shrift of most of Brockton's claims. "This is a small town, Mr. Brockton. Everyone knows everyone. And I understand the only other claim on the spot was one…" He consulted his notes. "A Cha-Cha Chicken franchise that wasn't prepared to purchase the building." The judge looked up pleasantly. "The interested party was related to you, I understand."

John squared his shoulders. "That's right, Your Honor, but he was going to put in a restaurant that would have offered more jobs and brought in more revenue. I had nothing to gain from my brother's business."

The judge frowned at him. "I've examined the records, Mr. Brockton, and found nothing to prove that Mrs. Bourgeois profited from Perk Avenue in any way. Mr. Megrath, however, has provided me with a statement from Mr. Benedict's wife that says in part that you're a silent partner in Mr. Benedict's construction company, and had your brother purchased the building, you'd have profited in the renovation for which your brother intended to hire Mr. Benedict."

Jackie turned to Bart in astonishment. He winked at her and returned his attention to the judge.

"Let's move on to your last claim, Mr. Brockton," the judge said.

Jackie shifted nervously—or tried to. She felt so enormous this morning, so weighted down that the best she could manage was a small fidget.

John cast a dark glance in Jackie's direction and faced the judge. "Everyone in town is aware that Mrs.

Bourgeois and Hank Whitcomb had a relationship when they were teenagers."

"And how is that relevant now, Mr. Brockton?"

He pointed to the judge's bench. "You'll notice the photographs included with the Committee for Impeachment's report. The mayor is seen in several instances in intimate circumstances with Mr. Whitcomb. We believe that the relationship is once again active, and that the presence of Mr. Whitcomb's office in City Hall, and the fact that Mr. Whitcomb was hired by the city to..."

"He's rewiring City Hall at no cost, I understand," the judge put in.

"But Mr. Dancer hired him to replace the light fixtures, and I know he's being considered for the homeless project."

Bart stood. "Your Honor, Mr. Whitcomb and Mrs. Bourgeois do have a relationship..."

Did have a relationship... Jackie amended to herself, noting Hank's absence in the room.

"But his employment by the city," Bart went on, "has nothing to do with Mrs. Bourgeois. The city manager is empowered to hire on his own for jobs under a certain amount, as this one was. Those over that amount require the approval of the council. Further, Mr. Whitcomb was hired because of his excellent reputation. Mr. Brockton has done everything within his power to make City Hall a hostile environment for Mrs. Bourgeois. He was a confidant of our former mayor, who is now serving time for fraud. Mr. Brockton had hoped to be appointed mayor in his place, but Mrs. Bourgeois—a relative newcomer to city politics, but a longtime resident of Maple Hill with its best interests at heart—received the appointment instead. We believe that simple jealousy and ill will are at the bottom of this impeachment effort."

"This is pretty flimsy evidence, Mr. Brockton." The judge looked through his notes. "My copy of the invoice for the lights shows that Mr. Whitcomb charged the city three dollars an hour less than standard. And another part of Mrs. Benedict's statement says that you and her husband stalked Mrs. Bourgeois and Mr. Whitcomb."

John Brockton gaped. "We…conducted a surveillance."

"Without legal backup, Mr. Brockton, that's stalking."

"We're an impeachment committee!"

The judge banged his gavel. "You're not anymore. I find no cause for impeachment, but due cause for an investigation of your behavior, Mr. Brockton, and that of Mr. Benedict. Go back to work, Mrs. Bourgeois."

Bart helped Jackie stand as the judge left the courtroom.

And right there, in front of a courtroom packed with citizens who'd come to support their mayor and now applauded her victory, Jackie's water broke.

CHAPTER FIFTEEN

HANK SAT AT HIS DESK, working on Whitcomb's Wonders' accounts receivable. He'd chosen to do paperwork today so that he didn't botch anything electrical. He was too distracted to think clearly. Not very professional on his part, but true all the same.

His mother hadn't spoken to him since he'd arrived that morning. She'd asked him how Jackie's court appointment had gone and he'd told her he'd been repairing a bad connection in the radiology lab at the hospital.

His mother had glowered at him. "I know this has been shocking and painful for you, Hank, but you weren't the only one involved. She was wrong but she acted out of love for you, not because she was being selfish. You should have been at court with her. I'm sure the hospital could have waited." Then she'd gone to work on her quilt. "If you're going to be around the office, you can answer your own phone."

He wasn't sure the hospital could have waited, but he had to admit he'd been grateful for the excuse. All he could think about this morning was babies and children and the horrible injustice of having to lose them before they reached adulthood.

He'd been staring at the Maple Hill Manor Private

School's account on the computer screen without seeing it for five minutes now. He tried to refocus and get something done. He'd sent Cameron to the campus, which was two miles out of town, the previous week to give them an estimate on replumbing the kitchen in a minor renovation.

He hit a function key to access Cameron's estimate. He was just making notes for himself when the telephone rang. His mother pulled up a stitch and pretended not to hear. He hated office work, he thought as he picked up the receiver. It was impossible to concentrate on one task for any length of time.

"Whitcomb's Wonders," he said, still making notes. "This is Hank."

"Hank, it's Bart."

Something in his voice made Hank push the notes away and concentrate on the call. "Yeah? They aren't going ahead with the impeachment, are they?"

"No, the judge denied the petition." Bart didn't sound as pleased about that as he should. "If you cared about the result, you could have shown up."

"Look, the hospital had a power problem," he said defensively. "Don't make judgments when you haven't got the facts. Anyway, Jackie didn't even mention it to me this morning."

"Big surprise. You're not easy to talk to suddenly."

Hank swallowed an angry retort. "Did you want something?"

"Yes," Bart replied. "Jackie's in the hospital."

Hank was on his feet. "What happened?" he demanded.

"Nothing," Bart replied. "She's delivering. She asked me to call your mom and ask her to come down, and to tell you that Haley and I'll keep the girls until she comes home. You can go."

Go? Hurt feelings kept Hank silent for a moment.

"Hank?" Bart prompted.

But there was something else wrong here. "Uh…" Hank was thinking. The girls. Where were the girls? "Adam's got the girls. They went hiking. He was supposed to be back at two."

"Jackie asked me to let him know, but neither he nor Sabrina is at the inn. Where would he be?"

"Jackie's?"

"I just called there."

"He had a dentist's appointment at 2:30." Hank looked at the clock. It was 4:15. "Maybe he took the girls with him."

"Who's his dentist?"

"Heck if I know. Bart, I don't know what's going on, but I'm going to the hospital. You find out, all right? Find out if he made the appointment. We've only got three or four dentists in town."

"Jackie'd know."

"Yeah, but I don't want her to think we don't know where her father and her children are while she's having the babies. It may be nothing, but she doesn't need that added worry now. I'll be there in five minutes." He hung up the phone. "Mom, Jackie's having the twins," he said as he handed her his key to Jackie's house. "Will you go to her place and wait there? Adam and the girls are overdue from their trip. If they call or show up, call me on my cell, okay?"

She stuck her needle in the fabric and was hurrying to get her things together as he walked out the door.

To Hank's complete surprise, he arrived at Jackie's room to find Parker with her, massaging her back. Jackie lay on her side, her back rounded, her hair already matted to her head.

When he blinked at Parker's presence, she explained, "Well, I was in the courtroom along with many of her other friends," she said, and Hank couldn't tell if there was mild censure in her tone or not. "Massage can help a lot in childbirth. If you're taking over," she said, pulling him beside the bed and putting Jackie's hand in his, "she's having a lot of back pain, so press with your knuckles and the heel of your hand, adding pressure with your other hand. They're going to be taking her to the delivery room soon. According to the nurse, twins progress more quickly than single babies. Are you okay?"

He was probably pale. He felt pale. He didn't know what to do, or even why he felt he had to be here, but he did. So he was going to have to be useful. And in the back of his mind was a nagging worry about Adam and the girls.

"I'm fine. I'm staying if you have things you need to do."

She glanced at her watch. "I do have a 5:30 appointment."

"Go, Parker," Jackie said. "Thanks so much."

"Sure. You've got a free massage coming your first day back to work. Bye. Good luck."

When the door closed behind her, Jackie asked wearily, "Where's Addy?"

"Out shopping," he replied, pressing the heel of his hand to her back and rubbing. "I left her a message. How's that?"

"Good. Thank you." She gasped suddenly and rolled onto her back, catching his hand and grinding his knuckles. He turned his hand in hers and held it tightly.

The pain seemed to subside after a moment, but she was panting heavily. When she could speak again, she said with a weak shake of her head, "You don't have to be here, you know. You didn't promise the girls you'd see me through labor."

He kept a grip on her hand when she would have drawn it away. "I wasn't there for Henry," he said. "But I'm here now."

PAIN HELD A TIGHT RED WRAPPER over everything in her mind, and Jackie couldn't decide if his words were intended as a promise of support or a condemnation. Did he mean she hadn't let him be there for Henry, so this would somehow make up for that? Or did he mean that he regretted not being there to help her deliver Henry, so he wanted to help her deliver the twins?

She couldn't analyze, couldn't decide. Another contraction rolled over her, and whether he wanted to go or not, she dedicated all her strength to holding on to him.

She had no idea what was really on his mind. He was obviously determined to honor his promise to the girls to take care of them, but he'd already warned her that it didn't extend beyond her getting the twins safely home.

So this time with him would be over in a day or two at the most. She felt a horrible sadness at that realization, then tried to focus on something else. She didn't want her babies to leave her body in an aura of impending doom. She wanted them to move from womb to world in a state of serenity.

"I wouldn't trade this time for anything," she said, instinctively curling up against the back pain. She felt his knuckles rub into her back. "I like knowing what we'd have been like as adults had we stayed together. I think we'd have been happy, even though we couldn't have saved Henry."

"We'll talk about Henry later," he said, working his knuckles up her spine then down again, concentrating on the spot where a head probably pushed, preparing to make an exit. "Right now you should be concentrating on the twins."

"I want you…to understand about Henry." Another contraction racked her and she rolled back again. He held her hand. It felt like a lifeline as pain seemed to submerge her in a well of blackness. She surfaced again in a few seconds, the pain only slightly relieved. "I want you to…understand," she whispered.

"I do," he said, taking the cup of ice chips from the bedside table and putting it to her mouth. He didn't look her in the eye, she noticed, but concentrated instead on the cup of ice. He was fibbing to appease her. "Want some of this?"

"Don't lie to me, Hank," she scolded gently.

He smoothed her hair. His cool hand felt heavenly against her hot forehead. "Can we deal with that later," he asked, "and focus now on the twins?"

She sighed anxiously. "I don't want them to come into a world where you hate me."

"I don't hate you," he denied.

"You can't forgive me," she reminded. "Same thing."

He took issue with that, putting the cup aside and shaking his head. "It isn't at all."

"People say that all the time," she complained. "I love you, but I can't forgive you. But I don't think that can be. If you love, you're openhearted. And if you're openhearted, you can forgive." Pain rolled over her again and she gripped his hand. She felt herself sink once more into the black well of pain, but only part of it was the fault of the contraction. When it was over, she panted, "You should go."

He grinned and indicated the hand she held. "I'd have to leave without my hand. You don't seem to be willing to let it go."

Jackie smiled sadly and freed him. "I know. Isn't it ironic. All that time I couldn't believe in us, you were so patient and let me lean on you. Now that I've established the habit—it's over."

Energy surged up in him. He didn't know where it came from and couldn't quite define it, but it was strong. "It isn't over," he insisted.

"You can't stay because of..." She was interrupted by pain. Even his grip seemed to provide little relief this time. "Because..." she continued breathlessly, struggling to remain rational, "you feel obligated."

He was analyzing why he *was* there when a nurse came in, pushed him gently aside, and made adjustments to the bed. Then she began to roll the bed out into the hall and toward the delivery room.

"You coming?" the nurse asked Hank.

"Can I?"

"Sure. We'll gown you up and you can keep coaching."

He took Jackie's hand and walked beside the gurney until they reached the delivery room's double doors.

It all happened with amazing rapidity. The nurse had

warned him to expect a twenty-minute pause between babies, but Adam was born at 6:07 and Alex at 6:16. Born a month early, they seemed alarmingly tiny to Hank, but the doctor assured him after he'd removed them for tests that they were fine.

The births were more amazing and more deeply moving than Hank had anticipated. He'd gone to work for NASA because he longed for the excitement, the thrills, the sense of accomplishment offered by the exploration of the unknown. Yet when he saw Adam and Alex screaming their arrival to the world, he realized that the most profound emotion came with the most familiar gift—life.

He'd known that on some level, because he'd come home in search of personal connection. He just hadn't expected that the connection he'd made years ago would still be open—almost waiting for him—and that he'd find his life wrapped up in Jackie's.

Jackie held the boys, one in each arm, her face devoid of makeup but absolutely radiant. They bellowed and she made comforting sounds.

"Your sisters are going to love you," she crooned. "You're going to be so spoiled, and so adored."

Hank didn't know how to repair what they'd done to each other, but knew only that he wouldn't be left out of this. Henry would understand.

He scooped up one of the babies and held him close, studying the pruney little face, the tiny eyes screwed shut as the infant screamed in agitated waves.

"Who've I got?" he asked.

"First one out," the nurse replied. "Adam, wasn't it?"

"Hank, would you call Dad again?" Jackie asked.

"Mr. Whitcomb!" Another nurse pushed open the room's double doors. "Phone call for you."

He tucked the baby back into Jackie's arm. "That's probably him," he said, kissing her forehead. "I'll be right back."

Hank was pointed to the nurses' station, where an aide handed him a receiver.

"Hank, I don't know what the hell happened," Bart said. "Adam never made the dentist appointment, and I got his cell phone number from the inn, but it doesn't pick up."

Hank could see down the corridor to the revolving doors leading outside. Night had fallen and rain came down in a torrent. Adam and the girls were now five hours overdue.

"Oh, God," Hank said, trying not to even consider the possibility they'd been involved in an accident.

"Maybe they got lost and there's no service where they are," Bart suggested. "Haley's on her way down. She's bringing Jackie a change of clothes and blankets your mom made to take the twins home in." There was a moment's hesitation. "I think I'd better call the police."

He was right. "Thanks, Bart," he said. "I appreciate it. The boys are here."

"All right!" Bart's voice lightened. "Congratulations!" There was another hesitation, as though he wasn't sure he'd made the right response, then apparently decided to leave it at that.

Hank hung up the phone and headed back to Jackie's room. He was surprised to hear shouting coming from it as he reached the door. He went in to find Haley trying to calm a clearly agitated Jackie. She brushed at Jackie's hair, which was sticking up in curly spikes.

Jackie caught her wrist to stop her. "If my girls and my father are missing," she shouted, "I don't give a rip how I look!"

Hank went toward the bed, eyes locking with Haley's.

"I'm sorry," Haley said sympathetically. "I wanted to reassure her that Bart was looking everywhere, that she wasn't to worry...I didn't realize you hadn't told her."

He absolved her with a shake of his head. "It's not your fault." It would have been comforting to be able to blame someone else, but not fair.

The focus of Jackie's anger turned from Haley to Hank. She did not look like a woman who'd just exhausted her last efforts giving birth. Haley glanced from one to the other, then excused herself and left the room.

"How dare you not tell me my family is missing!" Jackie accused.

"You were a little busy," he began, reaching for her hand, "I didn't want to endanger..."

"If my children haven't been heard from in five hours," she shouted, "I don't mind being interrupted! It's not as though having the twins means I get to give up the girls!"

"Jackie, be reasonable," he coaxed gently, alarmed that she'd so misunderstood his intentions. "You were in labor. We might have compromised the safety of your—"

"That doesn't matter!"

"How could it *not* matter?" he demanded. "We don't know the whole story and you were bringing new life into the world. I was trying to protect you from—"

"They're my girls!" she shrieked at him, her eyes

brimming. "My babies! My father! How I dealt with the news while in labor should have been my—"

She stopped abruptly midtirade and stared at him as though he'd turned to stone. Or she had.

OH, GOD, Jackie thought, the sudden silence in the room a very loud thing. So this was how it felt to be deprived of knowledge you had every right to know. The reason didn't seem to matter, only the feeling of alienation the withholding of knowledge created. The situations were different, but she finally understood with blinding clarity why Hank couldn't forgive her.

"I WAS TRYING to protect you!" Hank heard himself say, then stopped abruptly. What was it Jackie had said about Henry's birth and death. *It hurt so much, and I couldn't imagine inflicting that on you when there was nothing you could do.*

He grasped suddenly why she'd thought that such a valid excuse. She'd loved him. However misguided her decision—and his—they'd been made with the most sincere and loving intentions.

JACKIE FELT HERSELF dissolve into a puddle of anguish. "I'm sorry!" she said, reaching blindly for Hank. She felt him sit beside her and wrap her in his arms, and she clung to the warmth and strength he provided.

"Bart's called the police," he said. "There's probably some good reason your father hasn't checked in, but just in case…"

"I know you had my best interests at heart. The news

may very well have affected the babies' birth. And I'm so sorry about Henry."

"It's all right." He kissed her cheek and pressed her head to his shoulder. "I understand how you feel. I'm sorry, too."

"I don't know what I'll do," she said in a strangled voice, "if…something's happened."

"Let's not even consider that until there are no other options left."

Hank's cell phone rang.

Jackie's heart pounded. She thanked God for the safe arrival of the twins and begged for the safety of the girls and her father.

Hank's broad grin made her take in a hopeful breath.

"They just called your house from the airport," he said as he closed and pocketed the phone.

She blinked. "The airport?"

"I don't know. They'll explain when they get here. They're on their way. And so's my mother."

Jackie fell back against her pillows, relief flooding through her. "Thank God!" She put both hands to her face, sure she was too spent to cry, but residual hormones made it possible anyway.

She felt Hank's hand in her hair. "It's all right," he said. "Considering you've faced impeachment, given birth to twins, and lost and found your family in the space of one afternoon, I think you're entitled to cry."

She wanted to ask, "And what about us?" But a nurse arrived to wheel her back to her room, and Hank left her to telephone Bart and find a cup of coffee.

As the nurse turned the gurney one way, Jackie watched Hank walk off in the other direction and wondered if this was a metaphor for her future. They'd had an epiphany about each other's feelings a few minutes ago, but was that sufficient for him to want to go back to the way things were when they were planning a pink wedding?

Or would he remember only that he'd put himself out to help her through the birth of her twins while selflessly withholding the news of her missing family, only to have her scream at him like an ungrateful banshee. How many times could he let her hurt him before he said, "Enough!"

CHAPTER SIXTEEN

JACKIE'S ROOM overflowed with family. Thanks to her rather public onset of labor, everyone in town knew the twins had arrived. Flowers crowded every surface and helium-filled balloons bumped the ceiling and danced around the room.

Erica and Rachel stared at their new brothers in the hospital bassinet that had been moved into Jackie's room. The boys shared a single one, apparently feeling no distress at the tight quarters, accustomed as they were to sharing the even tighter space under Jackie's heart.

"We'd driven into the hills," Adam said, "and Bree wanted me to turn around and head back to civilization so she could go shopping, but I thought the girls could use some fresh air and conversation. So I promised we'd hit the mall in Springfield before we came home." He rolled his eyes. "Well, I went down a side road to explore, got turned around, blew a tire and took out my cell phone to let you know I'd be late, and she just lost it."

"She grabbed the phone out of Grandpa's hand!" Rachel contributed excitedly. Erica shushed her, reminding her of the babies. Rachel moved closer to the bed and lowered her voice. "Then she threw it! She told

Grandpa all he ever thought about was you and me and Erica, and what she wanted didn't matter at all!"

Erica wandered over, too. "Then Grandpa told her she was being selfish, and she told him he was being an old coot." She smiled apologetically at Adam. "Sorry, Grandpa. That's what she said."

Adam nodded with a laugh. "I heard her. They probably heard her in Boston. Anyway, it took me a while to change the tire—not as young as I used to be—then to find my way back. By the time we were on our way home, Bree was livid, told me she was not staying in Maple Hill a moment longer, and wanted to be taken directly to the airport."

"She didn't want to stop for her clothes or anything," Rachel said. "We have to mail them to her."

"That's why we called from the airport," Adam concluded. He checked his watch. "Her flight left an hour ago. Whew! I thought I wanted the excitement of a younger woman." He chuckled. "Turns out our hearts make their own connections, and no matter what we do, they'll nag us till they get what they want. I want Maple Hill, grandchildren and maybe the occasional date at the movies with a woman I have some hope of understanding." He winked at Addy.

Addy, on a chair in the corner, smiled wryly. "Oh, really. And what makes you think I'd want that, too?"

He shrugged humbly. "I can only hope."

"Well," she said, her hauteur deflated, "so happens I like the movies, too. But what about your place in Miami?"

"I like it there," he said. "It's a great place to spend January and February. You might like it, too."

Hank stared in stupefaction as his mother blushed.

Bart and Haley reappeared after carrying a load of flowers out to their car. Haley studied Addy's pink cheeks. "Mom?" she asked. "You okay?"

Addy grinned a little sheepishly. "I'm fine."

"Want to come home with us?" Haley asked.

Before she could reply, Adam said, "She's coming home with us to help out with the twins. I'll drive her."

Haley met Hank's eyes and he saw that she'd detected the subtle change in chemistry between their mother and Adam.

"Okay, then." Haley went to hug Jackie, then the girls. "We're off. If you need us for anything, call." Then she hugged Hank, her grip a little more fierce than usual. He could see that she wanted to ask questions and didn't dare.

She and Bart left with a bouquet of balloons.

Adam went to one last, very large flower arrangement. "I'll take this out to the car," he said, "then I'll take Addy and the girls home and you can have a peaceful night's sleep before Hank brings you home."

"Thanks, Daddy," she said as he walked off with the flowers.

"Our little brothers are so cute," Erica whispered. She and Rachel had wandered back to the bassinet.

"I wish I could have both of them," Rachel said, looking from one to the other as though trying to select the more beautiful baby and unable to.

In a rare moment of sisterly understanding, Erica wrapped an arm around her shoulder. "We have both of them. They're our brothers."

Addy stood and put an arm around both girls, then

beamed at their mother. "You can thank their Sunday School teacher for that insightful observation. We're studying families."

Rachel looked up at Hank, who stood on the other side of the bassinet feeling overwhelmingly possessive. "The whole world is our family," she observed seriously. "Did you know that?"

"Uh...sort of," he replied. "Yes."

"And everybody, even the people who are dead, are all one big circle. They're part of us, and we're part of them."

He liked that notion, was amazed that she seemed to understand it. His mother must be powerful stuff in the church basement on Sunday mornings.

"So...Henry's here, too," Erica said, reaching across the twins for his hand. "You'll always have five children. Well, maybe more, you know, if you and Mom..." Unable to decide on the right words to express herself, she concluded, "Anyway, our family starts with five kids. Right?"

Though his throat was tightening and his eyes blurred, Hank swore he could feel his heart mending. "Right," he said with certainty.

Adam returned a moment later, stopping in the doorway at the sight of Addy and Jackie in tears. He turned to Hank in question. The fact that Hank had to clear his throat and draw a breath deepened Adam's concern as he walked into the room.

"It's all right," Hank assured him. "Despite a lot of smart talk, my mother's very emotional. That's something you should know about her. And it's been an emotional day all around."

"Then we'll say good night. Job well done, Jackie." Adam leaned over her bed to hug her.

The girls kissed her, Addy wrapped her arms around her, then embraced Hank. "You did a pretty good job, too, I hear from the nurses. You were a good coach."

He shrugged. "Launching rockets, birthing babies. Big projects are all pretty much the same. You go into it with purpose and determination, and it usually works out."

"Are we forgetting that I was the launchpad?" Jackie teased.

Adam and Addy left arm in arm, the girls dancing off ahead of them.

Hank went to Jackie's bedside. She looked pale, tired and uncertain. He had to fix that.

HANK SAT BESIDE JACKIE, leaning back against her pillows and wrapping an arm around her. She nestled into him gratefully, not sure if this was simply the victorious moment shared by two people who'd endured a long and difficult day, or the coming together of partners determined to share the future.

She felt as though she stood on the tip of a spear, a fall one way promising heaven, the other…

"I understand you have a longing to vacation in Bermuda," he said lazily.

Her heart fluttered. "How did you know?"

"Erica told me. She does a great imitation of you under stress. I thought we'd go in June."

Afraid to presume too much, she asked simply, "Who?"

"You," he replied, "me, the kids, and Glory to help out with them. You think she'd want to come?"

She pushed a hand against his chest to sit up in the circle of his arm and gaze down on him. It occurred to her that she'd looked upon that face in some of her most desperate moments today, and it now felt like her heart's focal point. Did he mean the wedding was still on?

"Are you talking about...a honeymoon?" she asked breathlessly.

"No." Her fragile hope crashed with the simple, forceful reply. Then he added with a smile, "A honeymoon is something we should do alone. Maybe a week in the fall when the boys are able to be without you. We can find a quiet little inn somewhere and never come out of our room. I'm talking about a family vacation in Bermuda. I'm sure the next couple of months will be harrowing. We'll probably all need sun and sand by then."

She stared at him, her heart erupting inside her. Love flowed everywhere, finding every corner in every part of her being. She wrapped her arms around his neck and squeezed with new strength. Life had been such a long, dark haul the last few years that sharing love made her feel as though the Bermuda sun was already beating down on her.

"I love you," she whispered, a sudden and surprisingly virulent sense of heartbreak washing over her because Henry wasn't here. She opened her mouth to express that thought, but he shushed her, putting a hand to his heart and tapping it.

"I've got him right here," he said in a broken whisper. "We'll always have him. Erica said so. All connected. One big circle. And look at the richness of our family now. We're going to be so happy." He cupped her head in his hand and brought her closer to him. "I love you, too. We can get married next weekend."

She hugged him fiercely again, heartbreak dissolving in her overwhelming happiness. "Good. I'm getting tired of you being unofficial."

MAN WITH A MESSAGE

CHAPTER ONE

CAMERON TRENT WALKED around the Maple Hill Common in the waning light of a late-May evening. Fred, his seven-month-old black Labrador, investigated bushes and wildflowers at the other end of a retractable leash.

The dog looked back at him, eyes bright, tongue lolling; he was out and about after sleeping in the truck for three hours while Cam installed an old ball-and-claw bathtub in a Georgian mansion near the lake.

Life is good, Fred's expression said.

Cam had to agree.

Moving from San Francisco to Maple Hill, Massachusetts, situated on the edge of the Berkshires, had been an inspired idea. He and his brother and sister had spent a couple of weeks here as children every summer with their grandparents. It was the only time he could pick out of his childhood when he'd felt happy and safe.

As Cam wandered after Fred, he took in the colonial charm of the scene. A bronze Minuteman, his woman at his side, dominated the square. A colonial flag and a fifty-star flag were just being lowered for the night as Cam walked by. During working hours, the shops and businesses built around the green-lawned square bustled with activity, very much as they had two hundred years ago.

Many of the houses in Maple Hill were classic Georgian, with its heroic columns, or the simpler salt-box style, with its long, sloping roof in the rear. In Yankee tradition, small boats hung from the ceilings of some porches, and many houses bore historic plaques explaining their history. And Amherst, where he was earning his master's in business administration, was a mere hour away.

He had everything he needed right here. Well almost. He missed his brother, Josh, but he was a chef in a Los Angeles restaurant and raising his wife's four boys, and it was good to know he was happy.

Whitcomb's Wonders, the agency of tradesmen Cam worked for as a plumber, had become his family. They were a cheerful, striving group of men who enjoyed working part-time for the company because it allowed them to pursue other endeavors—raise their children, go to school.

Fred came running back to Cam, his head held high so that he could hold on to a giant branch that protruded at least two feet out of each side of his mouth. His tail wagged furiously.

They were in the middle of a serious tug-of-war over the branch when Cam's cell phone rang. Cam tossed the branch, then answered.

"Mariah Mercer from the Manor says they're sinking!" Addy Whitcomb told him urgently. "A pipe in the bathroom burst."

Cam reeled in the dog, who'd just headed off to chase the branch. Repairing the Maple Hill Manor

School was a lucrative job for Whitcomb's Wonders. One of the oldest buildings around, it was a plumbing and wiring disaster. They'd just been contracted to re-plumb the kitchen in the main building as part of a re-modeling project.

"The bathroom in the main building?" he asked.

"No, the dorm. You know, the old carriage house."

"Okay. I'm in town. I'll be there in about ten min-utes."

"I'll call and tell her. And just to reward you, Cam, I'll find you a really wonderful girl."

"No favors necessary, Addy." Addy was Hank Whit-comb's mother. Whitcomb's Wonders was Hank's brainchild, and the men who staffed it provided the source for much of Addy's Cupid work.

"But I want to!"

"No. Got to go, Addy."

Fred was disappointed at no more play but enjoyed the sprint across the common toward the truck. Cam let him into the passenger side, then ran around to climb in behind the wheel. The truck's tires peeled away with a squeal as he headed for the Manor. He'd outfitted his somewhat decrepit old truck to hold his tools and sup-plies so he was always ready to report to a job.

He tried to imagine what could have caused a pipe to burst. Pipes often froze and broke in the winter, but this was spring. And the Lightfoot sisters, who ran the school, had told him that they'd renewed the carriage house plumbing about ten years ago.

He knew that only a small number of children still boarded at the school, and did so only because of long relationships with the Lightfoot sisters, who'd taken over running the school from their mother in the fifties, after she'd taken it over from her mother, and so on all the way back to pre-Civil War days.

Letitia and Lavinia Lightfoot, who both charmed and intimidated the crew working on the renovation, were in their late seventies and still took pride in the bastion of civility they managed in a world they considered both fascinating and mad.

Cam refocused his attention on a series of curves, then exited onto Manor Road, which led through a thick oak, maple and pine woods to a clearing where the school stood, one of the finest examples of Georgian architecture in western Massachusetts. He turned left toward the carriage house, instead of right toward the main building.

It was dark now and all he could see of the carriage house, a replica of the main building but smaller, were its white columns, caught in the floodlights that illuminated the small parking area in the front. He pulled up beside a van, gave Fred a dog biscuit and spread his blanket on the seat. "Relax, buddy," he said, patting the dog's head. "I don't know how long I'll be."

Fred, just happy for the attention, cooperated.

Cam grabbed his basic tool kit and went to knock on the front door. He could hear a great commotion on the other side—children shouting, feet hurrying.

The door opened with a jerk and a little blond girl wearing neon-orange pajamas stood there, pale and breathing heavily. Behind her children ran up and down the stairs with towels and buckets. He heard a boy yelling from upstairs, "Turn the cutoff…it looks like a faucet!"

A younger male voice yelled back, "I don't see it! I don't see it!" he said again.

The little blond girl turned to shout up the stairs, "He's here!"

"Tell him to hurry!" the boy replied.

Cam experienced a weird sense of unreality, as if he'd blundered into a world occupied only by children. Not one adult was in evidence.

"Come on!" The little blonde grabbed his wrist and pulled him inside.

He allowed her to tow him up the stairway, its carpeting soggy. There was water everywhere, inches of it in the narrow upstairs hall.

Water rushed from the bathroom through a large hole in a pipe visible because of the broken tiles in the shower stall.

"Hey!"

The boy's voice made him look down. He saw a woman lying on her back, apparently unconscious, the boy's arm keeping her head out of the water. Her face was familiar. Cam had seen her around the school while scoping out the kitchen in the main building.

He dropped his tool kit on a sink and fell to his knees.

"You're not the ambulance guy?" the boy asked. He was about ten, his dark eyes panicky, his face ashen.

"No, I'm the plumber," Cam replied, putting two fingers to the pulse at the woman's throat. He couldn't detect one, but then, he could never find one in himself, either. "What happened?"

The boy appeared close to tears. "I busted the pipe looking for gold. She came in, slipped on a towel in the water and fell and hit her head. I'm not supposed to move her, right? I mean, she could have broken something."

Gold? Cam didn't even take the time to try to figure out what that meant. He did a cursory exploration of arms and legs and detected nothing out of place. She didn't seem to be bleeding. He decided that getting her out of the water took precedence over maybe causing her further injury.

"Is there a dry bed anywhere?" He slipped his arms under her and lifted her. She was small and fragile. Water streamed from her all over him as he stepped back to let the boy lead the way.

"In here!" The boy beckoned him into a room two doors off the bathroom. Cam noticed absently that the doors had hand-painted signs with kids' names on them.

A pack of children followed them and gathered around the bed as Cam laid the woman down.

She looked younger up close than he'd thought. Her dark hair, now drenched, was pulled back into a tight knot, and she wore a silky, long-sleeved blouse, through which he could see her lacy bra. A long blue cotton skirt lay clumped around her, also heavy with water. She'd struck him as stiff and matronly when he'd seen her at the school. How different his impression of her now.

He wrapped the coverlet around her.

He leaned close to tell if she was breathing. He felt no air against his cheek, heard no sound. Where was the ambulance? He'd taken a CPR course a few years ago, but he couldn't remember it now. So many pumps, so many breaths.

"She's gonna die!" one of the little girls said tearfully.

"No, she won't!" the boy said.

"She won't!" another boy repeated.

"She won't!"

Cam glanced up, wondering why he kept hearing double, then realized he was seeing double, too. Twins.

The woman made a scary, choking sound and the children cried out in unison.

Knowing he had to do something, he shooed the children aside, leaned over the woman, pinched her nose and placed his mouth over hers.

She was cold and still in his arms, like a marble statue.

He blew air into her mouth, raised his head to see if it was having an effect. When he couldn't detect one, he covered her mouth again and breathed into it. After several more breaths, a curious thing happened. He felt the first infinitesimal sign of life as a small, almost sinuous exhalation swelled the breasts under his chest.

Disbelieving, he breathed into her again, and that same subtle ripple occurred in the lips under his.

He put a hand to her ribs, feeling for an intake of breath, even as he gave her another one of his.

When he felt the probing tip of a tongue in his mouth, he thought he was hallucinating—giving her too much of his air, not keeping enough for himself.

Then her lips moved under his, and before he could raise his head in surprise, one of her hands went into his hair in a caress that paralyzed him momentarily into helplessness.

As he hovered above her in shock, her body arched up to his and she expelled a little moan. "Ben," she murmured against his lips.

For an instant, everything in him rose to the challenge. Yes! This was what life was supposed to be about! Man and woman entangled, seeking solace and pleasure in each other, their bodies a mutual haven. He'd have given a lot at that instant to be the Ben she sighed for.

Then reality reclaimed him and he sat up abruptly, the children all staring, not sure what they'd seen.

His heart was beating hard, then his brain snapped to attention. *This kind of thing won't work for you,* it told him. *You have a past. Allison had thought it wouldn't matter, but eventually it did. You're starting over, but you'll only get half the dream....*

The woman opened deep brown eyes, and after a moment of searching the room, a puzzled line between her brows, she focused on him. A small smile of what appeared to be—he wasn't sure...surprise? delight?—curved her pale lips.

No one had ever looked at him that way—as if he represented home at the end of a long journey. He still leaned over her, a hand on the mattress on either side of her, unable to move or speak.

MARIAH SURFACED FROM her chilled dream to find that the last year had all been some kind of terrible misunderstanding. Ben was back the way she remembered him at their wedding—the loving, solid partner around whom she'd centered her hopes, rather than the angry and confused man he'd become after she'd lost four babies and refused to try again to get pregnant.

Then his mouth had been hard and condemning. Now it was pliant and...life giving.

But why were they surrounded by children? They'd never be able to have their own. And he hadn't wanted to consider adoption—

"Mariah?"

She turned at the sound of her name and focused on…on Ashley? Of course. Ashley. She looked at the children circling the bed and remembered that they were not her children, but the Manor's. The kid fix she'd sought when she couldn't have her own.

The euphoria of a moment ago collapsed, and with it came the bitter disappointment that always returned to take hold of her when she allowed herself to think about her marriage, her divorce, all the things she wanted that she'd never have.

She gazed into dark-lashed hazel eyes set in a handsome face crowned with very short dark brown hair.

She put her fingertips to her mouth, recalling those nicely shaped lips on hers and the renewal she'd thought he'd brought to her life.

But he wasn't Ben. He was a stranger. And she didn't care what he was doing here or why she was in bed with the children gathered around her.

The only thing that mattered was that he'd led her to believe the pain was over and life was going to begin again.

It wasn't, though. And it was all his fault.

She raised a hand and slapped him as hard as she could.

CHAPTER TWO

"NO, MARIAH!" BRIAN, standing beside the stranger, caught her wrist. "He saved your life! I broke the water pipe—remember?—and you slipped on the towel and fell and hit your head. He carried you in here. He didn't kiss you. He gave you artificial...you know."

"Resuscitation," Ashley said knowledgeably. "But I think you kissed him."

"Yeah," Jessica said. "I saw it."

"Me, too," Peter confirmed.

"Me, too," Philip chimed in.

Mariah groaned and put her hands to her face. If she didn't get herself together soon, she had no hope for her future. Once the school found out she was French-kissing strange men in front of the children, she'd have to take the job her sister, Parker, had offered her—working in her massage studio in the basement of city hall. Then she'd never get to Europe.

Mariah felt movement on the bed, and when she lowered her hands, she saw that the stranger was gone.

Brian took off after him, calling over his shoulder, "We're going to cut off the water!"

The screeching of a siren could be heard outside.

"I'll let the ambulance men in," Ashley shouted as she left the room.

The children stood back and Mariah sat up. She was horrified that an ambulance had been called.

"I don't think you're supposed to get up," Jessica said worriedly, sitting beside her.

Mariah's intention was to tell her that she was fine, but she realized suddenly that she wasn't. Her head ached abominably, and suddenly everything around her was wobbling.

Two men in white shirts with some kind of insignia on them burst into the room. One cupped her head gently with his hand and leaned her back into the pillows. "What's your name, ma'am?" he asked.

"Mariah," she replied weakly.

"I understand you've had a fall."

That's an understatement, she thought as she battled nausea. The Fall of Mariah Mercer could be a play in three acts.

WITH THE LITTLE BOY NAMED Brian shining a flashlight into the dark corners of the basement, Cam found the cutoff and turned it off. When he raced back upstairs, Brian at his heels, the paramedics were putting a protesting Mariah on a gurney.

"I cannot leave the children!" she insisted. "There are eight children under ten years of age…"

"We're here, dear. We're here." The Lightfoot sisters appeared in the hallway, looking as though they'd just stepped out of a family portrait, circa 1930-something. They wore their usual long black dresses with lace collars. Letitia, the elder sister, had a small gold watch attached to Her generous bosom. Lavinia, younger and smaller, had a sprig of silk violets pinned at the waist of her dress. Cam had had several meetings with them to discuss the kitchen renovation, and he'd found them surprisingly sharp in business, considering their vintage clothing and their charmingly old-fashioned approach to education.

"Ashley called us." Letitia put an arm around the girl's shoulders. "You gentlemen take good care of Mariah!" she admonished the paramedics, who were heading for the stairs. "I know your mother, Matthew Collingwood. I'll have a word with her if Mariah isn't returned to us in perfect health."

The paramedic pushing the gurney cast a smile over his shoulder. "Don't worry, Miss Letty. She'll be fine. Watch the stairs, Charlie."

"Well, now!" The sisters shooed the children toward the back of the house. "While Miss Lavinia calls the janitorial service to clean up the water, we're going to camp here. Where are the sleeping bags from our hiking trip during spring break?"

Jessica and her sisters pulled down the attic stairs and fought over who would climb up to get them.

Letty tried to enlist Brian's help, but he turned to Cam. "I could help you," he whispered pleadingly.

"Ah…I'm sort of using him as my assistant," Cam said. "Is it all right if I keep him for another hour or so?"

Letitia appeared concerned. "If you keep a close eye on him. He's eager to help and sometimes…" She was obviously searching for a diplomatic explanation.

Cam understood. "He'll be right beside me at all times."

Brian gave him a grateful look.

"All right, then," Letitia replied. "Brian, I'm counting on you to do exactly as you're told."

"Yes, ma'am," he promised.

"Good." Cam put a hand on the boy's shoulder. "For safety's sake, I'm going to turn off the power. With water everywhere, I don't want anyone touching light switches, even where it's dry."

"Right."

He was about to ask Miss Letty if she had a flashlight to lead the children in the dark house, when she shouted up the attic stairs, "Jessie, bring the camp lanterns down with you, too!"

Cam grabbed the flashlight from his tool kit and, with Brian glued to his side, hurried back downstairs to shut down the power. He handed Brian the flashlight.

"This is so cool!" Brian said. "Nothing exciting ever happens around here." Then apparently he realized what he'd said and looked sheepish. "I mean, I know it's all my fault and it's caused everybody a lot of trouble. And you probably charge a whole lot."

"Yeah, I do." With all the circuit breakers flipped, Cam and Brian stood in darkness except for the glow from the flashlight. "And the guys who have to clean up the water cost a bundle, too."

Brian sighed. "I was going to take everybody to Disneyland for summer vacation if I found the gold."

Cam turned him toward the stairs and let him lead the way with the light. "You mentioned that before. What gold are you talking about?"

The boy told him a story about a Confederate spy trying to escape to the South with a satchel full of gold. "He was in this building when he was shot, and the Yankees and the Lightfoots who owned the Manor then found the satchel, but not the gold. Everybody knows the story."

"I've never heard it."

"Mr. Groman told me. He teaches here, you know. Some rebel soldier stole it off a train and hid out with it in the carriage house. When they tiled the bathroom floor, they covered up the blood!"

The kid had a flair for theatrics, Cam thought, and was probably destined for a career in front of a camera.

They climbed the stairs, Brian holding the light to his side for Cam's benefit. "But if it hasn't been found in a hundred and fifty years…"

"A hundred and thirty-seven," Brian corrected him.

"A hundred and thirty-seven," Cam said obligingly, "why did you suddenly think you'd find it in the bathroom wall?"

They'd reached the main level. Brian waited while Cam closed and locked the basement door. "Because I thought about it. They didn't find it when they tore up the floor to put down new stuff, so where else could it be?"

"Somewhere in the attic?"

"Looked there."

"And you probably checked the basement."

"A couple of times."

"Maybe this spy had an accomplice and passed it on or something."

Brian frowned. "I guess that could be. But that's not in the story."

They made their way carefully toward the stairway to the second floor. "There's probably an old newspaper account of the incident," Cam suggested. "In the library. Old newspapers are scanned into the computer. Or maybe they could help you at the *Mirror.*"

Brian grinned in the near darkness as they went up

the stairs side by side. "Maybe Mariah will take me," he said hopefully. Then suddenly his expression turned doubtful. "If she can forget that I almost killed her."

Cam ran a knuckle down his own cheek, remembering her slap, and patted Brian's shoulder. "I don't think she was as near death as it seemed. Apologize first, then ask her."

In the bathroom once again, Cam tore out more tiles to get at the pipe connection while Brian held the flashlight for him.

"About your plans for the gold," he said. "Aren't you all going home for the summer?"

"Yeah, but Ashley doesn't have parents, you know. She just has a guardian and he's pretty old. She never gets to stay home with him. He sends her on trips with people she doesn't know and she hates it. They think she doesn't know, but he's going to die pretty soon."

When Cam looked down at him, not sure what to say to that, Brian added with a shrug, "We hear the teachers talking. She's going to have to go live with somebody else. My mom's a movie star."

Cam had difficulty focusing on the plumbing and the conversation. "No kidding?"

"No. She's very pretty, but she's always on a movie set somewhere far away and I stay with the housekeeper. Pete and Repeat's mom and dad are stunt people and they're working with my mom in a movie right now. In Mongolia."

"Pete and *Repeat*?"

"The twins."

"Ah."

"They're really Pete and Philip, but their dad calls

'em 'Pete and Repeat.' Now everyone does. Their dad jumps off cliffs and out of airplanes and over waterfalls. Their mom once jumped out of a building on fire! I mean *she* was on fire. 'Course, the building probably was, too, or she wouldn't have been. She had a special suit on so she wouldn't get burned. Cool, huh?"

"I'm not sure I'd want to be on fire, even in a special suit."

"Jessie and her sisters' mom wants to take them to New York with her to visit a friend of hers. So they don't want to go home for the summer, either."

"Jessie and her sisters are those four dark-haired little girls who all look alike?"

"Yeah, only they get smaller and smaller. Like those toy things that fit into each other. You know?"

Cam had to grin at him. The kid had such an interesting little mind. "Yeah, I know. But what's wrong with meeting their mom's friend? New York's a very exciting place."

"He's a guy."

"Well, so are we. Is that bad?"

Brian seemed to like being considered a guy. Cam had to remind him to hold up the light.

"It's because their mom likes him and they don't want another dad."

"What happened to the first one?"

"He and their mom got divorced."

"Ah. That's too bad."

There was a moment's silence, then Brian announced, "I don't have one."

"What? A father?"

"Yeah. I never had one. And he didn't die and my

mom's not divorced. I mean, he's probably somewhere, but he's not my dad."

Cam nodded empathetically, catching the significance of that detail from the boy's tone of voice. Brian wanted to adjust to that fact but still hadn't.

"I had a father," Cam said, carefully applying pressure to the wrench. "But he was drunk a lot and most of the time it was like I didn't have one."

"Did he beat you up?"

"No. Most of the time he didn't remember I was there."

"Did you have a cool mom?"

Cam wasn't sure how far to carry this empathy. He wanted Brian to know he wasn't alone in an unfair world, but he wasn't sure what it would serve to tell Brian it could get worse than he knew.

"No," he replied simply. "She was gone most of the time."

His mother had been out of jail only three weeks when she and a male friend had been picked up for armed robbery. Cam and his siblings had had the misfortune of being with her at home at the time, their father passed out on the sofa, beer cans and a bottle of whiskey beside him.

With their mother going to jail and their father deemed unfit to raise them, he and his siblings had been placed in foster care. He'd argued zealously that he'd taken care of himself and his brother and sister most of his life—that all the other times his mother had gone to jail his father had also turned up drunk and Cam was the one who had cooked and done laundry and gotten himself, Josh and Barbara off to school.

No one had cared about that. Their grandfather had died, their grandmother was in a nursing home and the three Trent children were placed together in foster care with a middle-aged couple who lived in the heart of the city.

Deprived of the choice of how to live his life, Cam became bent on destroying it. Fortunately, he'd been caught with a few of his friends holding up a restaurant while the owner was closing. A few months in juvenile hall had turned him around. Foster care seemed like heaven after that.

"My mom's always in another country 'cause of the acting thing," Brian said. "What'd yours do?"

"Ah…" He had to think to recollect what had identified her place in his life besides the drugs and the jail time. "She worked in a furniture factory."

"She drink, too?"

Cam was so surprised by the question that he stopped what he was doing to focus on the boy.

Brian shrugged. "It's a statistic that a lot of people who drink do it with a husband or wife or boyfriend."

Cam was sure that was true but he wondered how the boy knew. "Who told you that?"

"My mom's in rehab a lot." It seemed to be something he had accepted. "It happened one time in the summer, and the housekeeper took me to visit her. We had to sit in at this meeting about families of substance abusers."

Cam had never known the politically correct term because there'd been no one to take him to meetings.

"Come on," he said. "We're going out to the truck. Remember to keep your hands off the switches."

"We going to the shop or something?" Brian asked excitedly, taking the lead with the flashlight.

"No. I've got pipe in the truck."

They reached the third stair from the bottom and Brian leaped down, the carpet squishing as he landed. "So, is it cool to be a plumber?"

Cam could feel his soaked shoes and socks and jeans and smiled into the darkness. "Oh, it's way cool."

CHAPTER THREE

MARIAH'S SISTER WAS BESIDE herself with worry when she arrived at the emergency room. "Oh, my God!" she exclaimed, swiping a white curtain aside to come to Mariah's side. "Are you all right?"

Mariah sat up, fine except for pain in the bump at the back of her head. She explained briefly about Brian's search for gold and the resulting deluge.

Parker shook her head sympathetically. "That kid's going to blow up the world one day."

Mariah sighed. "He's the sweetest boy, but I'm going to have to build a cage around him for the safety of the other children."

"And you. Do you have a concussion?"

"Just a mild one. The doctor's worried, though, because I passed out."

"You passed *out?* Did you stop breathing?"

"I'm not sure. I dreamed…" She put a hand to her throat as she recalled a drowning sensation, as if she was falling into a well, unable to draw in air. "Someone gave me…mouth-to-mouth," she explained, remembering with abrupt clarity her grave disappointment when the face bent over her wasn't Ben's but that of some stranger's.

Some stranger she'd just kissed with the desperate need she'd never revealed to anyone.

Someone whose eyes said that he'd felt that need in her.

Bitter disappointment over the loss of her babies, the loss of her marriage, the loss of her mask of stoic courage, had all required that she punch his lights out.

"Oh, God!" She put a hand to her face and groaned.

"Nurse!" Parker shouted.

"Sh!" Mariah lowered her hand and placed it over Parker's mouth. "I'm fine! I just…just remembered something."

"What? You looked as though you were going to slide right off onto the floor."

"I…I was just thinking about the cleanup at the dorm." Mariah frowned apologetically. "I'm sorry, Parker, but the doctor won't let me go home tonight if there isn't someone to watch me. Can you take me home with you, just for tonight?"

"Of course! It'll be fun. I just made carrot cookies."

Mariah tried to look pleased at that. As much as she loved her sister, she had very different opinions about what defined a comfortable environment. Parker was a naturalist, earth-mother sort of woman; Mariah's approach to life was much more traditional.

Parker had a heart of gold, but her sofa was a red vinyl banquette from a Japanese restaurant, and two hammocks suspended from the ceiling constituted her bedroom.

All of a sudden Parker smiled. "Who gave you mouth-to-mouth?"

Mariah closed her eyes again, shuddering as she recalled her poor display of gratitude. His face had been familiar, but she couldn't quite put a name to him. "I think I've seen him at school, or around somewhere...." And then she sat up as it hit her. In the kitchen at the Manor, talking to the man in charge of the renovation.

"He's part of the construction staff at school," she said.

Parker's smile waned. "I was hoping he was young and handsome."

Mariah was confused. "He was young. And if you like that rough look, he's handsome."

Now Parker appeared confused. "But I have regular appointments for all the Ripley Construction guys, and the youngest one's in his late forties. Three brothers and two brothers-in-law."

"Guys who work construction," Mariah asked in disbelief, "get massages?"

Parker shifted her weight impatiently. "Well, of course they do. Massage is very sensible. They sling around heavy stuff all day long, reach and bend. It's very forward-thinking of their boss to see that they have weekly appointments."

"This man was probably in his early to middle thirties," Mariah insisted. "And..." Her attention drifted for a moment as she recalled waking up and looking into his eyes—a soft hazel. "His eyes were hazel."

"Cam Trent?" Parker said, suddenly animated again. "The plumber? I know he's the plumber on the job because my office is near Whitcomb's Wonders. I've gotten to know all the guys a bit."

"Whitcomb's what?"

"Wonders. Guys who can do anything." Parker hugged her as if to congratulate her. "He's gorgeous!

And smart. He's getting an MBA from Amherst. Wants to be a developer. Addy told me all about him."

Parker was so enthusiastic that Mariah had to put a stop to her sister's considerations of romance immediately. "Well, he's not going to want anything to do with me. I hit him."

"You what?" Parker was as horrified as Mariah had hoped.

"I hit him. When I woke up, he was half lying on me, kissing me—or so I thought. By the time I realized he was just…well…I'd already hit him." She wasn't being entirely honest, but it was all her sister had to know for now.

The doctor reappeared with a bottle of painkillers on the chance that her headache worsened.

Parker took them from him and introduced herself.

The doctor held up two fingers and asked Mariah how many she saw. When she answered correctly, he asked her name. He listed three items, then asked her to repeat them. She did.

He told Parker to wake her every four hours to test her awareness. "If she seems confused or uncertain, bring her back in."

Parker drove home to her duplex across the street from the grade school. She held Mariah's arm solicitously as they walked from the car to the front door.

"How's the head?" she inquired as she unlocked the door.

"A little woozy," Mariah admitted, "but not awful."

The lock gave, and Parker pushed the door open and reached in to flip on a light. Sheer fabric festooned the living room, leading from a ring in the middle of the ceiling and catching in drapery loops in each corner of the room. Large, colorful pillows lay strewn around the Japanese-restaurant banquette—her sister's creative approach to a "conversation area." A filigreed cage held a fat aromatic candle, which Parker went to light as Mariah eased herself onto the banquette.

"Lavender and chamomile for serenity," Parker said as the wick caught flame. "In fact, if we mixed chamomile with oil of basil, it'd probably be better for you than whatever's in here." She rattled the bottle of painkillers. "But I'll get you water for your pill, and I'm sure you'll feel better before you know it."

Mariah wanted to believe that. Much as she loved her sister's company, she always felt as if she was in purdah with the rest of the harem when she came here, waiting for the sultan to make his nightly choice of woman.

"I know you hate the hammocks." Parker's voice drifted back to the living room as she disappeared into the kitchen. She returned with a glass of water and the bottle of pills. "So we'll sleep down here. You can have the couch and I'll use the beanbag. Want a cookie?"

"No, thanks." Mariah sat up to take her pill, then handed back the water. "There's no reason for you to stay downstairs, Parker. I'll be fine."

"No, you might need me." She put the glass and pills on the low table and sat beside Mariah. "This happens so seldom that I hate to miss it. You're usually the one who rescues me."

Mariah stretched her legs out in front of her and leaned sideways onto Parker's shoulder. "A little financial help now and then hardly constitutes rescue." Mariah had sent her sister money when her first husband had run out on her and left her owing back rent and many overdue bills. Parker's second husband had supported a mistress on the side with money Parker made waiting tables while she went to school to learn massage. He, too, had abandoned her when the mistress's former boyfriend came looking for him.

"You have to make better choices in men, though," Mariah said sleepily. "Stop supporting them and find someone who'll work with you for a change."

Parker put an arm around her and sighed. "I know. It's just that all that sunshine and harmony we got from Mom and Dad really sank in with me. You were more resistant. You're probably a throwback to Grandma Prudie, who loved them both but was convinced they were crazy."

Grandma Prudie had been their father's mother, an Iowa farmwife who related to the earth, all right, but only because it bestowed the fruits of an individual's labor. She thought her son and his wife's belief in the earth's unqualified bounty, in man's intrinsic goodness and life's promised good fortune were poppycock. And she'd said so many times before she died.

Mariah had loved her parents' generous natures and their obvious delight in everything, but she'd never been able to understand such innocence in functioning adults. Until she'd finally grasped that—whether deliberate or simply naive—it brought them aid from everyone. Neighbors admired their sunny dispositions and gave them things—firewood, a side of beef, help with bills—so that they could maintain a lifestyle everyone else knew better than to expect. This had confused Mariah for a long time, until she concluded that it was still proof of man's basic goodness—his willingness to support in a friend what he knew he couldn't have for himself.

"I feel that my life's been very blessed," Parker continued, "and that I have a lot of blessings to return. So I try to help those in need."

Mariah yawned. "Yeah, well, some people are just in want, Parker, not need. It's noble to help, but not to let yourself be used."

"I know. I'm off men for a while. How 'bout you?"

"I'm off them forever."

"That isn't healthy. You want children."

Mariah sat up to frown at her. "Park, have you missed the last year of my life? I'm not going to *have* children."

Parker took advantage of the moment to place a pillow on the banquette and reach into a bamboo shelf for a folded afghan. She pointed Mariah to the pillow and covered her with the crocheted blanket.

"I know you're not going to give birth to them, but there are other ways to get them. Just because Ben wouldn't do it doesn't mean you can't do it on your own."

Mariah was about to shake her head, then decided that would not be a good idea. She simply placed it on the pillow, instead. "I don't want them anymore. It's just all too much trouble. Children should have two parents, and men are just too determined to form a dynasty, you know?"

"Well, Ben was. But that doesn't mean they all are." Parker's voice suddenly changed tone from grave to excited. "And a gorgeous plumber has just breathed life back into you! It could be fate has plans for him to give you more than simply oxygen."

Mariah groaned and leaned deeper into the pillow. "Park," she said, her sleepy voice muffled. "Don't even start."

She drifted off to her sister's reply: "Sometimes, Mariah, fate moves whether we're ready or not."

HANK WHITCOMB HAD ARRIVED to work with the cleanup crew. Cam met him in front of the carriage house while carrying his tools back to his truck. He'd long ago walked Brian to the Lightfoot ladies' residence on the other side of the campus, where they'd taken all the other children when the water cleanup had proved too noisy and disruptive for them to stay. It was 2:00 a.m.

Talking with him was a small, very pregnant dark-haired woman with a camera around her neck and pad and pen in the hand she held up to stifle a yawn. She was Haley Megrath, Hank's sister, and publisher of the *Maple Hill Mirror.*

She and Hank came to his truck as he set his tools down on the drive.

"Hi, Cam," Haley said with another yawn as she walked past him toward the steps. "You'd think people could have their crises during the day, when plumbers and reporters are awake, wouldn't you?"

"Yes, you would. Maybe the *Mirror* could launch a campaign toward that end."

She waved and kept walking. "I'll see what I can do. 'Night, guys."

"I'll wait for you and follow you home," Hank called after her.

She turned at the top. "I'm fine. Go home to Jackie."

"I'll buy you a mocha at the Breakfast Barn on the way."

She grinned. "Okay. Who cares about Jackie." She blew him a kiss and disappeared inside.

Hank opened the lid of the truck's toolbox for Cam. "One of our more dramatic messes," he said with a laugh. "Hey, Freddy!" He patted the back window as Fred's head appeared. The dog was barking excitedly. Hank leaned an elbow on the side of the truck as Cam put away his tools. "I hear you rescued Mariah Mercer from drowning."

Cam shook his head. "That's a little overstated. Brian—one of the kids—held her head out of the water. I just carried her to a bed."

"Where you gave her mouth-to-mouth and she French-kissed you."

Cam frowned. "No, she didn't."

"Yes, she did. Ashley told me." Hank grinned. "She's thrilled about it. She adores Mariah and thinks it'd be wonderful if she could find a husband."

Cam gave Hank a shove out of his way as he dropped pipes into the back. "Yeah, well, I don't think Mariah Mercer has designs on me. After she kissed me, she slugged me."

"Really?"

"Yeah. Probably a reaction to the bump on the head, or something. No big deal."

"So I can tell my mother you're still on the market?"

Cam opened the passenger side of the cab to let Fred out, the gesture half practical, half vengeful. The dog leaped on him elatedly, then went right to Hank, who always had treats in his pockets. Fred backed Hank up to the side of the truck, his paws on his chest, alternately kissing him and barking a demand for treats.

Pinned to the truck, Hank reached into a pants pocket. "How big is this guy going to get?" he asked, quickly putting a biscuit in the dog's mouth. "He doesn't beg—he just mugs you for what he wants!"

"I'm not sure. I guess some Labs get to a hundred pounds or more. Jimmy didn't tell me that when he sold him to me." Jimmy Elliott was a fireman and another of Whitcomb's Wonders.

Treat in his mouth, Fred ran off around the side of the carriage house.

"You must be beat," Hank said. "You have a class in the morning?"

"In the afternoon. I'll be fine. I'm a little wired, actually. Letty brought us coffee and I don't think she bothered to grind the beans."

Hank took a key out of his jacket pocket and offered it to Hank. "Why don't you go take a look at the lake house," he suggested. "You and Fred can even sleep there if you don't want to go back home tonight."

Cam tried to push the key away. "Hank, I appreciate the offer to buy your house. There's not a place in town I'd like better. But I keep telling you—I don't have the cash."

Hank nodded. They'd argued this before. "We'll find a way to keep the payments way down."

Hank had married Jackie Fortin, the mayor of Maple Hill, a brief two months ago. In doing so, he'd acquired two little girls, ages seven and eleven, and infant twin boys. He'd bought the big house on the lake as a bachelor, but now found that the old family home Jackie occupied was closer to school for the girls, and closer to city hall for Jackie and for Hank, since the office of Whitcomb's Wonders was located in its basement.

Cam had mentioned once at a party Hank had held how ideal he thought the house was, how warm and welcoming after his cramped apartment behind the fire station.

"We'll put a balloon payment at the end," Hank said, "and by then you'll be a well-known developer. Since you have plans to save our colonial charm rather than replace it with malls and movie-plexes, you'll be popular and make big bucks."

"That's a little optimistic."

"It never hurts to think positive." Hank took his hand and slapped the key into it. "Even though that hasn't been your experience in the past. You have control now. You're not dependent upon neglectful parents, and you don't have to worry about a selfish wife. Do what *you* want to do."

Cam was touched by his concern and grateful for his support. "You're pretty philosophical for a NASA engineer-turned-electrician. You didn't get zapped tonight while standing in all that water, did you?"

"No." Hank grinned and braced his stance as Fred came running back to them. "I'm charged on life, pal...charged on life. Oof! Go look at the house. Fred needs room to run. And someday you'll want to think about getting married again and having children."

Well, he was right about Fred needing room to run, anyway. Cam closed the dog in the car, said good-night to Hank and the cleaning crew still working, waved at Haley, who photographed them, then headed for home.

But somewhere along the way he took a turn toward Maple Hill Lake and Hank's house on the less-populated far side of it.

He pulled off the road onto a private drive that led through a high hedge, and into the driveway of the two-story split-level. He would look through it as Hank suggested, get the notion of buying it out of his system. Then he could just settle down, keep working and going to school so that he could finally achieve the goal for which he'd come here. He wanted an MBA behind him before he bought the old Chandler Mill outside of town and turned it into office space and apartments.

He'd talked to Evan Braga about it, and he thought the idea was sound. Braga was another of Hank's men who did painting and wallpapering, and sold real estate on the side. He'd been a cop in Boston and had come to Maple Hill for the same reason Cam had—to start over. He hadn't said why and Cam hadn't asked.

Anyway…if he was going to buy a house in Maple Hill, it should be one of the classic salt boxes or Georgians that were such a part of the area's history.

But he loved this house. From the moment he'd arrived at Hank's party all those months ago, he'd felt as if the house had a heartbeat.

He let himself in and flipped on the light in the front room. Fred stayed right beside him, intimidated by the new surroundings. As Cam walked from room to room, he became aware of details he hadn't noticed before. The master bedroom had a fireplace that was also open to the bathroom, which had two sinks and vanities, a sunken tub and greenery growing all around it. It was probably what a Roman bath would have looked like.

He could imagine lying in the tub after a particularly grueling and dirty day in the pipes, and being warmed by a real fire. Here was a tendency toward hedonism he didn't even realize he had. Each of the three bedrooms upstairs had a private bath.

He walked back downstairs to look around outside and Fred went wild, running through the tall grass that rimmed the lake, chasing imaginary quarry in the dark. He stopped to sniff the air and bark his delight to the woods across the road.

The property spread for five acres in both directions, and except for Fred's footsteps, there was nothing but the sound of insects. The natural perfume of the dark quiet night took his breath away.

A broad deck ran all around the house, and Cam remembered Hank saying that when he'd bought the place, he'd anticipated having barbecues and inviting his friends. But Whitcomb's Wonders had been more successful than even he'd imagined, and family life had kept him too busy.

Cam looked at the covered gas grill in a corner of the porch, and the wide picnic table beside it. "I could have the guys over for a barbecue," he thought aloud. He could get a small boat and go fishing.

As a child, he'd never been able to bring anyone home because of the unpredictable condition of his parents. He'd dreamed of inviting friends over, hosting parties, having a Christmas open house the way his friends' parents did.

A curious hopefulness stirred in the middle of his chest. He could do that here. He could…maybe… someday…give some thought to getting married again, having a family.

"Oh, whoa!" he said to himself.

Fred, hearing the command and thinking it applied to him, came racing back. Cam caught him as he jumped against his chest.

"I'm getting carried away here, Fred," he said, going back to the front door to make sure he'd locked it. "That's the trouble with having a cold, grim childhood and a selfish wife. You get a glimpse of warmth and happiness and you become this greedy monster, wanting more and more."

Fred raced around his legs, apparently seeing nothing wrong with that.

Cam tested the doorknob and, finding it secure, led the way back to the truck and the little apartment behind the fire station. So he had cardiac arrest every time the alarm went off. He was learning to live with it.

He didn't need the house. And so far his life had taught him that you didn't always get what you needed, much less what you wanted.

CHAPTER FOUR

THE ALARM SHRIEKED in Cam's ear. Without moving his head from the pillow, he reached out to slam it off.

Blessed quiet.

He'd finally gone to bed at 4:00 a.m. and set the alarm for seven. There was too much to do at the school today to allow for eight hours' sleep. But certainly he could steal another fifteen minutes.

Fred, however, had other plans. The Lab, awake at the foot of the bed and waiting for the smallest sign that Cam was awake, leaped onto his chest and bathed his face with dog kisses.

Cam tried to push him away, but he was weak after the all-night session and the measly three hours' sleep. The dog plopped down on top of him and chewed on his chin.

Cam knew if he didn't get up he'd be eaten. It would be done with affection, but he'd be eaten.

"Okay, Fred, that's enough," he said calmly but firmly, pushing the dog off.

He sat up to swing his legs over the side of the bed just as Fred decided he'd cooperated long enough and it was time for some serious extreme wrestling. Growling, large mouth open in what Cam thought of as his alligator mode, Fred attacked.

Cam's body, unfortunately aimed toward the edge of the bed, went over the side, dog atop him and gleefully pretending to kill him.

MARIAH HEADED FROM THE CAR where Parker waited, along the little walkway to the stairs that led up to Cameron Trent's apartment. She'd awakened this morning determined to apologize to the man who'd given her mouth-to-mouth resuscitation and been slapped for his efforts.

Provided the man was Cameron Trent. And provided he would even want to listen to her. She intended to reassure him quickly that she would take only a moment of his time, then she would never darken his doorway again.

She climbed the stairs, rehearsing her little speech. "Mr. Trent, I apologize for slapping you. I thought you were my…" No. That was too much information.

"Mr. Trent, I apologize for slapping you. I was in a sort of dream state and your lips were…" No, no! Too revealing of feelings she didn't understand and he was bound to misinterpret.

"Mr. Trent, I'm sorry I hit you. I awoke to see a stranger leaning over me and I…I…"

Okay, get it straight! She told herself firmly. *Don't stammer like an idiot.* Maybe a simple "I'm sorry." He'd know what she was sorry about, so there was little point in belaboring why it had happened.

She checked the note in her hand. Apartment E. Parker had called Addy at the Breakfast Barn, where she always had breakfast with her cronies, and learned Trent's address.

She stopped in front of the end apartment upstairs,

pulled aside the screen door and, bracing herself, knocked lightly twice. The door squeaked open.

She heard a commotion beyond the door and concluded he must have the television on. She knocked a little louder. The door opened farther, making the commotion inside more audible.

But it wasn't the television. Someone was being attacked! By…dogs? In Maple Hill? The man's cries sounded desperate. She looked around for help, but Parker couldn't see her from the car.

She couldn't just walk away. This man had possibly saved her life; the least she could do was make an effort for him.

She looked around for a weapon and, finding none, simply took a firm hold of the handle of her purse, burst through the door and ran toward the sound.

In a bedroom at the back of the apartment, she found a sight that chilled her. The man whose face she'd awakened to yesterday now lay half on and half off the bed, his legs trapped in the blankets while a huge black beast, fangs bared, attacked him unmercifully, sounding like one of the dogs of hell unleashed.

She fought a trembling in her limbs and advanced, swinging at the glossy hindquarters with her purse. "Stop it!" she shrieked at the animal. "Get out! Get out!" The dog yelped and withdrew onto the bed, eyes wide. Encouraged that she'd made it retreat, she followed it, purse in full swing.

"Whoa!" the man shouted.

His directive didn't register, however, as she climbed onto the bed in pursuit of her quarry. "Get out of here you—"

Her threat was abruptly silenced as something strong manacled her ankle, effectively dropping her facedown into the bedclothes.

Momentarily blinded and unable to move, she felt a cold chill as she heard a menacing growl just above her.

"Fred!" Trent shouted. "Down! Now!"

She heard the dog's claws connect with the hardwood floor.

Fred? Cameron Trent had been viciously attacked by a dog named...Fred?

CAM WAS SURE HE WAS hallucinating. First of all, there was a woman in his bedroom, and that hadn't happened in a long time. Second, she appeared to be an avenging angel determined to rescue him from Fred's morning wake-up ritual. An angel he'd rescued himself just last night. Only, she hadn't reacted like much of an angel.

It took a moment before he realized her determination to save him included hitting his dog with a leather purse that resembled something Evander Holyfield would hang from the ceiling and beat with boxing gloves. And then he reached up and caught her foot.

She plopped down in the middle of his mattress, skirt halfway up her legs, one shoe off, the other dangling from her toe. He experienced a sudden visceral need to put his hand to the back of her thigh and explore upward.

Fortunately—or unfortunately—his foster parents' civilizing influence had taken root in him and he simply freed her ankle and got to his feet. Then, remembering he was wearing only white cotton briefs, he wrapped an old brown blanket around his waist as she rolled over.

She wasn't happy.

He wasn't surprised.

For an instant he simply absorbed the steamy look of her in his bed. She wore another long-sleeved silky blouse, pale blue this time, and another long skirt—black. Her hair was in a tight knot at the back of her head; her cheeks were flushed from exertion.

Nothing about her should have been seductive, but there she was amid his rumpled bedclothes, knees bared, one tendril of dark hair falling from her right temple. Her eyes smoldered.

He concluded that expression was probably fueled by anger or embarrassment, but what it contributed to the picture she made was powerful. He wanted her. Badly.

But what was she doing here?

Fred, standing near the edge of the bed, leaned a long neck and tongue forward and slurped her bare knee.

She shrank back with a little cry.

"Fred!" Cam caught the dog's collar and made him sit. Fred complied, apparently totally affronted.

"I'm sorry," Cam said quickly as Mariah looked around herself, her cheeks growing rosy. So it was embarrassment. "I know that appeared brutal, but it's a game we play. Fred's just seven months old and very frisky. The snarling and teeth flashing are phony. He's just trying to get me up for breakfast."

She drew a deep breath and something inside her seemed to collapse. He wasn't sure what that meant, but he didn't like the look of it. Her eyes lost their smolder and filled with the sadness he'd seen in them last night.

Instinctively, he reached for her waist to pluck her off the bed and stand her on the floor. In her stocking feet, she barely skimmed his shoulder. "I appreciate the rescue, though," he said, his hands still on her. "I'll bet that purse packs a wallop."

She put her hands on his and removed them from her waist. "Where *is* my purse?" she asked stiffly.

It had gone over the side of the bed when she'd fallen. He went to retrieve it for her. It weighed a ton.

When he came back with it, she was hunting for her second shoe. Then she looked beyond him and gasped. Fred, whom he'd lost track of when he'd scooped her off the bed, had it in his teeth.

"Fred, give me that shoe!" she demanded, going toward the dog with a hand outstretched.

"Mariah…" Cam began to caution, but he was too late. The dog had darted off toward the living room, tail wagging, and Mariah went in pursuit.

Cam followed, catching up with them in the kitchen. Mariah had one end of the shoe and Fred the other. This could not end well.

"Mariah, don't pull!" he ordered. Then to the dog, he said in the authoritative tone he'd learned in obedience class, "Fred, give!"

It never worked in class, either. Fred was an independent thinker.

Cam finally grabbed the dog around the jaw and pried the shoe from his teeth. There was a small tooth hole in the side of the black leather flat, and slobber on the toe. He wiped it off with the tail of the blanket wrapped around him and handed the shoe to her.

She snatched it from him and slipped it on, the smolder back in her eyes. "Thank you!" she snapped. "I came here in an attempt to be a thoughtful human being, and thanks to you and Mr. Astaire here—" she pointed in the direction of the dog "—or is it Flintstone? Regardless, I've been harassed and embarrassed!"

"I'm sorry you were embarrassed," he said reasonably, "but I didn't expect visitors this morning."

"Then you should have locked your door." She marched back to the bedroom, where she'd left her purse. "I thought you were being killed!"

He tried to placate her with "You were very heroic."

"No, I was mistaken." She made that correction grimly as she shouldered her purse.

"Is that such a terrible thing?" he asked quietly. "Or is it just that making mistakes is new to you?"

She blew air scornfully. "I've made a lot of mistakes. But I'm trying to change the pattern."

Fred had followed them back to the bedroom and she leaned down to stroke the dog's head. He reacted with his customary enthusiasm and was about to lick her face.

Cam caught him before he could connect, but Mariah surprised him by leaning down to take one of Fred's kisses, then laughing as she nuzzled his face with her own.

"It's okay, Fred," she said. "I know you didn't mean any harm. I'm sorry I yelled at you."

Cam, now completely confused about her—and just as captivated—asked innocently, "Aren't you sorry you yelled at me?"

HE WAS GORGEOUS NOW THAT she observed him with all her faculties at work. She hadn't appreciated the width of his shoulders last night, the odd gold color of his eyes. His good looks weren't a feature-by-feature thing but rather a whole impression made by confidence and humor playing in the rough angles.

She frowned and folded her arms. "Did I yell at you?"

He pretended hurt feelings in a theatrically dramatic sniff. "Yes, you yelled at me. You blamed me for what you called your 'embarrassment,' and here I was the one wearing nothing but my skivvies when you burst in. And in danger of being puppy chow, if you'll recall."

She wanted to laugh. Nothing made her laugh these days—except children and dogs. "You assured me you were in no danger."

He folded his arms over that formidable chest and looked away in a gesture of emotional delicacy. "Because I didn't want you to risk yourself further on my behalf."

She still managed to keep a straight face. "Well, I appreciate that. I have to go."

She headed for the door again, but he caught her halfway across the living room and turned her around. His hand was warm and strong and stopped her cold though he applied no pressure.

"What was the thoughtful reason you came?" he asked. There was something urgent in his eyes.

"Oh." She sighed, realizing she'd never offered her apology. "I forgot." She angled her chin, hoping to put him off by appearing haughty. Men usually hated that. And she did not want to be attracted to this one. "I came to apologize for slapping you last night. I was…" What was it she had rehearsed? He was gazing into her eyes and she couldn't remember. "I was sort of dreaming and you…and I…" She stopped, hating that she was stammering like a twit. She squared her shoulders and tried to go on. "When I woke up, I thought you were…" She did everything humanly possible to avoid completing that sentence, avoid uttering the word that dangled unspoken.

"You thought I was kissing you?" he prompted, apparently having no such compunction.

He didn't really appear self-satisfied, but there was an artlessness to him she didn't trust at all.

"Yes," she admitted, making herself look into his eyes. "I'm sorry."

She tried to leave again, but he still had her arm. She felt a sudden and desperate need to get out of there.

"What?" she demanded impatiently.

"I haven't accepted your apology," he reminded her.

She cocked an eyebrow at him. "What?"

"Well, how I react to this," he explained in an amiable tone, "will be determined by why you hit me."

"I just told you! I was dreaming and I…"

"I know, but if you were angry at me because you were disappointed that I *wasn't* kissing you, that requires a different response altogether."

She knew where this was going and she didn't want any part of it. Well, she did, but only for purely selfish reasons. She missed the intimacy of marriage. Not the sex, necessarily, but the touches, the pats, the…the kisses. And though she'd sworn there would never be another man in her life, she was still allowed to miss what a man brought to a relationship. Wasn't she?

"I thought you were…" She even hated to say his

name aloud. It brought back memories of those last awful few months of her marriage when she'd shouted it pleadingly, begging Ben to understand how she felt.

Cam waited.

"My…husband," she said finally.

His eyes closed a moment. "You have a husband?"

That was her out. She had simply to say yes, and he'd lose interest in this unsettling morning exercise. Freedom was one small word away.

She opened her mouth to speak it but heard herself say, instead, "My ex-husband."

He looked cautious. "You want him back?" he asked gently.

For the first time in a year she faced that question directly. Did she want him back?

"No," she whispered. "But I miss…" It was hard to say.

"You can tell me," he encouraged her softly.

The words clogged her throat. What had begun in amusement and sexual challenge was all of a sudden filled with real emotion.

"I miss trust," she finally admitted, her voice barely audible, even to herself. He tipped her face up as if to help himself hear. "I miss holding hands, telling stories, and I miss…" She had to say it. "Kisses."

And that seemed to be all he had to know. This was no longer about what she'd felt last night when she slapped him, but what was suddenly between them now as she admitted need and he responded.

His mouth came down on hers with tender authority. The sureness in the hands that framed her face told her to leave it to him; he knew what he was doing. And he did.

The touch of his lips was familiar from last night, and she experienced none of the awkward newness of first kisses. He was confident, she was willing, and the chemistry was its own catalyst.

His mouth was dry and warm and clever, his hands sure as they moved over her back, down her spine, stopping at the hollow just below her waist, then moving up again.

She met his lips avidly, basking in the almost-forgotten comfort of the shelter of a man's arms.

HER RESPONSE WAS FAR MORE enthusiastic than Cam had expected. He wasn't entirely sure what was happening here, except that it wasn't what he'd originally intended. He'd been teasing her, playing with their previous connection, trying to taunt the stiffness out of her because...he wasn't sure why. Stiff, tight women weren't his type. And neither were small ones. They made him feel huge and inept and afraid to move.

But she wrapped her arms around him gamely, dipped the tip of her tongue into his mouth with tantalizing eagerness, combed her fingers into the hair at the back of his neck and somehow touched something inside him that seemed to rip in two everything he thought he'd decided about women since his first wife, Allison.

Then without warning she sagged against him, dropping her forehead to his chest and remaining absolutely still for several seconds. When she raised her head, her eyes were stormy with something he couldn't quite define.

She punched his shoulder as if to release some pent-up emotion. But it didn't seem to be anger.

"Now you're going to have to come back tomorrow," he said, trying to lighten the abrupt sadness in the room, "and apologize for hitting me again."

"So this is what's taking so long," a female voice said from the doorway.

Cam looked up and Mariah started guiltily out of his arms.

"Parker!" she said, her voice sounding strangled. "I'm sorry I kept you waiting. I thought the dog was devouring him and came in to…"

Parker glanced at Cam, still partially wrapped in a blanket, then listened interestedly as Mariah tried to explain, then gave up. It did sound ridiculous.

"Oh, never mind." Mariah looked up at Cam, opened her mouth to speak, then apparently decided against it. "Goodbye," she said, instead. She walked past Parker and out the door. Fred whined.

"Good morning, Parker," Cam said politely, feigning a normalcy the situation denied.

Parker, who'd always been warm and kind to him the few times they'd met in city hall, now studied him with a measure of doubt. "Mariah's my sister," she said.

He nodded. "Hank told me." He explained briefly about Fred and his growling game. "It was 4:00 a.m. when I got home. I pulled my shoes and socks off on the porch because I was drenched, came in with an armload of stuff and kicked the door closed—or thought I had. When Mariah heard Fred playing, she assumed I was in trouble and came in to rescue me."

"That kiss was a thank-you?" she queried.

"No," he replied. "You should probably ask her what it was."

She nodded and prepared to leave. He walked her to the door, where she stopped and smiled. "She's a very nice girl who's had a very bad time recently."

He leaned a shoulder in the doorway. "The ex-husband?"

Parker looked surprised. "She told you?"

"Only that she had one."

"He was a good guy," Parker explained, "who turned out to be a bastard. I'd hate to have that happen to her again."

"Don't worry, she's learned to defend herself," he said with a wry smile. "She keeps hitting me."

Parker frowned. "She came to apologize for that."

He laughed lightly. "She did. Then she hit me again." He straightened and assured her seriously, "I'm not a bastard. My background isn't pretty and I wouldn't claim to be a good guy, but I'm not a threat to anybody's safety, either."

She studied him, as if deciding whether or not to believe him. Then she finally nodded. "Okay. I'll take your word on that. Otherwise, I know how to massage your shoulder into your eye socket."

"Rough women in your family," he noted with a grin.

She smiled pleasantly and hurried down the stairs.

Cam closed and locked the door, fed Fred, then decided against cereal in favor of stopping at Perk Avenue coffee shop on his way to work. He deserved a little sugar after what he'd been through this morning.

In the bedroom, he yanked off the blanket, delved into the closet for fresh jeans and a sweatshirt and started toward the bathroom, but something sparkling in the middle of the bed caught his attention. He reached for it and found that it was a little gold hoop with three tiny beads—an earring. Mariah's earring.

He tossed it in his hand, remembering her leaping to his rescue, sprawled in the middle of his bed, leaning into him as he kissed her.

He had to draw a breath to clear the images. He didn't need this. If he did intend to get involved with a woman, he wanted some buxom, uncomplicated ray of sunshine who'd want to make a home, raise children and help him forget all he'd lost or never had.

He didn't need a tiny brunette with troubled eyes who'd had "a hard time."

He tossed the earring again as he headed for the bathroom, caught it, then stopped with a growl of complaint when it bit into his hand. He opened his palm to find that his overzealous grab had caused the sharp post to jab his ring finger.

A metaphor for his involvement with her? he wondered.

CHAPTER FIVE

THE SECOND MORNING AFTER the deluge, Mariah encouraged her little troupe to finish breakfast so that they could get to school on time. They were rushed this morning. Mariah had overslept—something she never did—and it had taken Ashley's violent shaking to wake her up.

"I'm sorry I have to hurry you," she explained, shooing the girls upstairs to brush their teeth. "I know it's all my fault, but we can still be on time if we put some effort into it."

"We were late yesterday," Philip said, "and nobody cared."

"That was because of the excitement the night before. But today it's our responsibility to be punctual."

"There's still no carpet," Amy complained as she and the other girls started up the stairs.

Mariah nodded. "We have to wait for the wood to dry. It'll be replaced at the end of the week."

"So, where do you think the gold is?" Peter asked Brian as the three boys, teeth already brushed, shouldered their backpacks.

Brian considered. "Cam says I have to do more research."

"Well, where else could it be?" Philip asked.

"I'm thinking maybe in…"

Mariah missed whatever it was he thought as he lowered his voice to a whisper.

Brian had dropped Cam's name at every opportunity since the flood. The boy had acquired status among the other children because the man who'd rescued Mariah had asked him to help. He was clearly enjoying his popularity.

Mariah tried not to think about that night—or yesterday morning. Her behavior in Cam's apartment had to have been a result of her embarrassment at discovering that he hadn't been in danger at all, simply playing with Fred. Added to that was the fact that she hadn't seen a partially naked man in a long time, and the fact that the hormones she'd been sure had died with her marriage were still very lively. She had to have lost her mind just a bit.

Otherwise, why would she have practically asked him to kiss her?

Why would she have enjoyed it?

Why could she still feel his lips on hers twenty-five hours later?

It didn't matter, she told herself briskly, pushing chairs up to the kitchen table. Unless there was another plumbing emergency, she wouldn't have to see him again. And if there was, she could ask one of the Lightfoot sisters to attend to it. They were full of praise for his work—and his charm.

Even Parker had nice things to say about him, though she'd found them in each other's arms.

"He seems to be a gentleman," she'd insisted, when

Mariah had grumbled in response to her question about what had been going on when she'd walked in on them.

Mariah hadn't denied it, but wondered why, if he was such a gentleman, he made her feel such unladylike things.

The girls bustled down the stairs, dragging backpacks.

Mariah rounded up her little group and led them outside, locking the carriage house door behind her. They went down through a lane of swamp maple to the school playground, where all the day children were gathered, waiting for classes to begin. A lively basketball game was under way, several girls were jumping rope and a coed group competed for daredevil notoriety on the monkey bars.

Janie Florio, a third-grade teacher, waved at Mariah from the basketball hoop, fulfilling her role as playground monitor.

Mariah returned the wave and was about to wish the children a good day, when she realized they'd already dispersed into their playgroups without giving her a second thought.

Little ingrates, she thought good-naturedly as she climbed the stairs to attend a meeting with Letitia Lightfoot.

Letty hadn't specified the reason for the meeting, but Mariah could only assume it had to do with the flood. A lot of damage had been done in the carriage house, though mercifully it was mostly superficial and covered by insurance. She would probably suggest Mariah be more vigilant, more of an authority figure with the children than the friend she strove to be.

Letitia's office was clearly not dedicated to the needs of the children. Everywhere else in the building the rooms were cheerfully academic—blackboards, maps all over, alphabets and musical notes running above the picture rails. Here, there were big cozy chairs, frilly lamps, a mantel covered with family photos, lace curtains at the window.

The other Lightfoot sister sat behind a smallish rosewood desk and pointed Mariah to a chair patterned in cabbage roses.

Mariah sat, sinking into the old springs. Letty, she thought, looked severe. She couldn't have heard about the kiss, could she? Of course not. The only other person who knew, aside from herself and Cam, was Parker, and she wouldn't have told.

Such behavior had been irresponsible, very inappropriate in a woman hired to guard the safety of young...

"Mariah," Letitia said without preamble, "we've finally decided to close the dormitory at the end of this school year." She sighed after she spoke, as if making herself say the words had taken a lot of energy. "I'll be contacting the parents and Ashley's guardian today to let them know. I'd like you to tell the children."

Mariah wasn't shocked; the rumor had circulated for some time. But she was upset at the realization that she'd lose her charges, not just for the summer but forever.

And what about Ashley, whose guardian was ill, and Brian, whose mother was in and out of rehab? What would they do without the stabilizing influence of the Maple Hill Manor School? Public schools were wonderful, of course, but the Manor's program was set up to take special care of children in their unique situations.

"I don't want you to worry about your position here," Letty continued. "We've all grown very fond of you. It's clear you're destined to work with children and we'll find another spot for you by September. Lavinia thinks we need an office secretary, but I think your special talents would be wasted behind a desk. We'll come up with something suitable, if you'd like to stay on as much as we'd like you to."

Mariah smiled gratefully. "I so appreciate that, Letty. But, you know that I've been planning an extended European trip. Maybe this is the time for me to go."

Letty frowned with maternal displeasure. "Well, I'd hoped you'd gotten over that notion. When you hired on, you told me it would be just for a year, that you had this trip planned to tour Europe and learn about art, but I'd put it down to the dreams of a woman who'd lost so much and wanted to escape. I thought you might feel loved and wanted here and decide that escape wasn't the answer."

"I don't want to escape, Letty," Mariah denied gently. "I just know now that marriage and family aren't for me, so I may as well get out there and find out what it is I do want—and try to learn something in the process."

Letitia leaned her elbows on the desk and smiled benevolently at Mariah. "Marriage with *that* man wasn't for you, and neither is having babies in the traditional way. But there's so much more to marriage and family than what you've known."

Mariah shook her head firmly. "I don't want that anymore, Letty. I have other plans. And while I appreciate your concern and affection for me, I have to do what I have to do."

"So you *are* bent on escape."

"It's not escape. It's exploration."

Letitia stared at her a moment, then smiled. "Well. When you return from your exploration, we'll find a place for you if you'd like to work with us again. But until then, we have a lot to do here until the school year's over. Is your heart still in it?"

"Absolutely," Mariah replied firmly.

"Good. Then please explain to the children, and we'll try to spoil them to help cheer them up."

Mariah nodded. "I'm worried about Ashley. Do you have any idea what Walter Kerwin's intentions are for her if he should…"

Letitia shook her head. "That isn't really our business, Mariah. But I'll be speaking with him today, and if he shares any information about that, I'll let you know."

"Thank you, Letty."

"Are you going shopping today?"

Mariah nodded. Every Tuesday morning she replenished the dorm's groceries and picked up special requests for the children.

Letitia delved into a bottom drawer of her desk and surfaced waving a ten-dollar bill. Mariah stood to take it from her. "Would you buy me a quarter pound of raisin clusters? Dark chocolate."

Chocolate was Letitia's one indulgence. Mariah had trouble finding fault with that.

"Of course." Mariah started for the door.

"And about the flood…"

Mariah stopped in her tracks, prepared to take the heat for Brian's gold-digging fiasco. She turned, shoulders square, "Yes?"

Letitia shook her head. "We had Brian's grandfather here in the old days and he set the lawn on fire with a magnifying glass. Unfortunately, we'd just mowed, and it caught a bank of raked grass and burned several acres. We had his mother, too, and she had the same problems when she was in high school that she has now. We had to expel her."

"Mercy."

"Yes. I know there's nothing you could have done to prevent what happened, but it was costly, and we must try to make Brian understand that even if he finds the gold, he'll owe it all to us should he destroy the house."

Relieved, Mariah nodded. "I've already explained that."

"Good. Then enjoy your day."

Mariah left Letitia's office and headed for the cafeteria, hoping to get a quick cup of coffee before she went into town. Because she'd been rushed this morning, she hadn't put up her hair or taken care with her clothes and she felt sort of unguarded, and therefore unprepared. She felt sure caffeine would help.

The cafeteria was filled with workmen, a circumstance the Manor staff had grown used to and mostly ignored. As she stepped over lumber in the dining area, she could hear saws whine, the staccato beat of hammering and the sound of male laughter. She went behind a long counter where lunch was usually served and into the kitchen.

Though the Manor had made arrangements for the public school to cater lunch at tables now set up in the gym until the renovation was complete, a coffeepot was always going in the kitchen for the staff and the workmen.

She took a thick pottery cup from a tray on the stain-less-steel counter and filled it with the steaming brew. She turned to find a quiet corner in which to drink it—and ran right into Cam Trent, who was coming up be-hind her.

She uttered a little cry of dismay as the coffee sloshed; he danced back a step, and she put a hand to her cup as if to hold the coffee in. The hot brew sloshed all over it and she cried out again.

"Mariah!" Cam took the cup from her, caught her wrist and led her to the sink, where he slapped on the cold water tap and dunked her hand under it. "I'm sorry. I thought you saw me."

"I had my back to you," she pointed out, though her brain seemed focused on the touch of his fingertips at her wrist. "How could I have seen you?"

He turned her hand over under the water, his glance at her friendly but unsettlingly sharp. "I sensed you be-fore I saw you," he said. "I thought it might have been the same for you."

She ignored that, determined just to get out of there. Her pulse was fluttering.

He shut off the water, dried her hand with the tail of his shirt, then inspected it. The pad of her thumb was red where the hot coffee had burned her.

"Come on. I can take care of that." Still holding her hand, he drew her with him out the kitchen's back door.

She pulled against him. "But my coffee…"

He wasn't listening. In another moment they were in a parking area filled with tradesmen's trucks. He led her to a green pickup that had seen better days.

He opened the passenger-side door and was immediately assailed by Fred, who kissed Cam's face and whopped him with a dexterous paw.

"Hey, Fred." Cam patted the dog's flank, then reached around him and into the glove compartment. He extracted a first aid kit.

Fred licked Cam's ear while Cam delved inside. He finally held up a small tube of something. "Hydrocortisone cream," he said as he placed the kit on the roof of the cab. Holding her injured hand palm up, he squirted a small amount of white cream into it.

He rubbed it in gently.

She tried to think of something else. She'd felt flustered and befuddled this morning, and had put it down to oversleeping and then hurrying to prepare for school. His gentle, circling touch didn't help. That is, it soothed the burn but did nothing for her flustered feelings.

"Better?" he asked.

"Yes, thank you," she replied. She looked at her thumb and not at him. Then she focused on the dog, who was overwhelmed by her attention. He kissed her cheek, her forehead, her hair.

"Fred, show some manners!" Cam commanded, pushing him back onto the seat he was about to fall off of.

"That's all right." Mariah patted the dog and nuzzled him. "My husband got our retriever in the divorce and I miss her a lot."

CAM, STANDING SLIGHTLY behind Mariah, put the tube back into the first aid kit, studying her, thinking there was something different about her this morning. She seemed a little less controlled. Then he realized that her hair wasn't scraped back and tied in a knot. It fell to the middle of her back, thick and glossy and the color of walnut. It softened the line of her face, darkened her eyes to midnight. Light rippled in it as she nuzzled Fred. Her hair made Cam feel lustful. He hated being such a cliché, but he couldn't deny his reaction.

"Have you had breakfast?" he asked.

She stepped aside, giving him more room than he needed.

"No, I overslept. But I don't really have time. I have to go shopping and then there's—" A wild rumbling in her stomach interrupted her.

"Sounds like you'd better make time," he said, pushing Fred to the middle of the bench seat. "Besides, I have something of yours."

She looked puzzled. "What?"

"I'll tell you over breakfast," he said, bargaining, "then I'll take you wherever you want to go shopping. I have to pick up a few things, too."

She eyed him doubtfully. "Aren't you supposed to be working?"

"I came in to see if they were ready for me, but they're ironing out some kind of problem with the plan, and I can't start until tomorrow. Climb in." He held the door, waiting for her to comply.

She finally did, giving him a brief but stimulating glimpse of a jeans-clad derriere as she swung into the seat. He pretended detachment, locked her in and closed the door.

He was not only a cliché, he decided as he walked around to his side, but a pubescent cliché.

The Breakfast Barn was everyone's favorite place to

begin the day. When things were starting slowly everywhere else, it was alive with activity—businessmen and -women, morning walkers, gossip groups who'd been getting together for years and solved their own and the world's problems over scrambled eggs and coffee.

The Barn was a huge room lined with booths and filled with tables in the middle. The walls were covered with photos of the city teams the restaurant had sponsored, of parties held there, of patrons celebrating one success or another. It was home away from home for much of the population of Maple Hill.

Cam spotted an empty booth near a window and pointed Mariah to it. He followed her across the room, weaving in and out of tables, noting the speculating glances of friends and neighbors.

Rita Robidoux, a fixture at the Barn, was upon them immediately with menus and glasses of water. "Coffee?" she asked.

"Please," Mariah said.

"Regular?"

"Yes, please."

"Coming right up." As she turned away from Mariah, she waggled her eyebrows at Cam, a silent comment on the worthiness of his breakfast companion.

He gave her a teasing frown of disapproval. "Do you know Mariah Mercer?" he asked politely for Mariah's benefit.

Mariah smiled. "No, we've never—" she began, but Rita was already filling her in on herself.

"You're the dorm mother at the Manor," she said, offering her hand. "Came here from Chicago after a divorce, to be near your sister, Parker Peterson. You never get out to breakfast because you're always overseeing the children's breakfast, but you show up occasionally at dinner with Parker when the Lightfoot ladies give you a day off."

Mariah blinked in astonishment as she shook Rita's hand.

"The rumor," Cam said gravely, "is that Rita has radar and a surveillance truck that she uses to stake out single men to see if they're husband material for the single women on Addy Whitcomb's list. They're a team."

Rita smiled sweetly. "The details are a little off, but essentially, that's correct. I'll be right back with your drinks."

Mariah laughed as Rita wandered off. "So how many women have she and Addy tried to marry you off to?"

"So far I've resisted," he replied. "It helps, too, that Addy's son is my boss. If she tries to crowd me into a date, Hank finds a plumbing problem for me."

"You don't want to get married again?"

"I used to think I didn't."

She'd been perusing the menu but raised her eyes questioningly. "What changed your mind?"

He knew the menu by heart and pushed his aside. "Maple Hill, I think. The folks all seem happy, love their spouses, their children, their community. I used to want that in the beginning."

Now she put her menu aside and focused her attention on him. "The beginning? Of your life or of your first marriage?"

He leaned back as Rita returned with two cups and a little bowl of creamers, and poured their coffees. She put the pot down on the table, took their orders, then was gone again with another discreet waggle of her eyebrows at Cam.

He put sugar and cream in his coffee, wondering just how much to explain. It was all so grim, and he preferred to think ahead.

"Both, I guess," he replied, choosing to skim the surface of the issue. "I come from a family dedicated to substance abuse and making one another miserable, so as a kid I just didn't believe the cozy families I saw on television. A few of my friends seemed to have them, but I was sure when all their guests were gone, they were just like my family—loud and angry."

He offered her the cream. She shook her head. "Allison, my wife," he said, "chose politics over me."

She looked up from placing her napkin over her knee. "You mean, you didn't want her to go into politics? Or she found someone else in politics?"

"First one, then the other," he replied. "My parents have both done time," he said, needing to get past that fact. "My mother's still in prison. Allison was a judge's daughter I'd met at a party. I told her about my family. She said it made no difference to our relationship. I think she even meant it, until someone noticed what a brilliant lawyer she was and asked her to run for local office. I supported that, but someone found out about my family history and decided we should lie about it."

Mariah looked skeptical. "That wouldn't be good, would it? I mean, considering how determined politicians are to unearth what they can use against one another."

He nodded. "That's what I thought. And though I don't like to remember my childhood, I'm proud we survived it. And it's not as if I can erase it."

"So she thought she'd have a better chance without you," she guessed.

"Precisely. She's now married to her campaign manager."

"Who's 'we'?"

For a moment, he wasn't following her.

"You said you were proud 'we' survived it."

"Oh. I have a younger brother and sister. Josh is a chef in a restaurant in California and has a family. Our little sister, Barbara, took off for New York to be a model. She used to write at first, then she stopped. The last thing we heard was that she had an interview with the Ford agency. She was excited. I can only guess it didn't work out."

"Have you tried to find her?"

This part was still difficult after all this time. "When her phone didn't answer and she didn't return our calls, I contacted the Ford agency. I was right. They'd decided not to represent her. They had no forwarding address for her. We even hired a private detective and he couldn't find her."

She said nothing, just waited for more.

"A year later, a call came from a police officer in New York, telling us that Barbara had died from massive injuries sustained in a motorcycle accident. She was twenty-two."

"Cam, I'm sorry," Mariah said fervently.

He nodded. "The worst part for Josh and me was that for whatever reason, she didn't feel she could call us. I imagine she felt rejected and just didn't think she could come home, even though we sent her to New York with a return ticket."

She reached across the table to put a hand over his. "Now, there's no way you can blame yourself for that. You can understand her pride being stronger than her need for family, but you can't feel guilty about it. Maybe…maybe she figured after dealing with your parents, you'd seen enough of people who couldn't achieve. She was wrong, of course, but people in pain don't think very clearly."

He sat in quiet surprise. He'd always looked for the blame in himself. Although their parents had been horrid, he and Josh and Barbara had always stuck together. He'd thought he must have failed in some way to make her understand that whatever happened, she would always be a part of their triumvirate and could seek shelter there anytime. He'd never considered that she might have stayed away to spare him and Josh yet another family failure.

He digested that possibility and felt it soothe him. He finally smiled at Mariah. "That's an openhearted thought," he said.

She inclined her head—the closest she could come to taking a bow in the confining booth. "My family was good at understanding the souls of people and things, if not at dealing with them very realistically.

"My parents were sort of retread hippies. We lived in communes, in trailers, with friends. The best period of our lives was when we farmed for a cousin of my mother's who'd bought a place as a tax shelter but didn't want to live there. My parents were in heaven and Parker loved it, too."

He was happy to listen to her talk. She smiled absently and the usually rigid line of her shoulders seemed to relax.

"But I'm a city girl at heart," she continued, sitting back in the booth, her hands in her lap. "My dream is to visit all the great European capitals, learn about Western European art and work on my own."

"You planning a trip?"

She nodded. "In my situation at the school, it's been easy to save. And while my ex-husband wasn't willing to share the dog, I did get half our savings account and the proceeds from the sale of our home. I'll be going this summer, I think."

He felt the smallest pang. Somehow, Mariah leaving felt like…like a missed opportunity. As if he were standing on the brink of something important as it was backing out of reach.

"Money goes pretty quickly when you're spending it and not making more," he felt obliged to caution.

She leaned toward him, lowering her voice. "No!" she said, pretending surprise. "I thought it just multiplied in your purse, like an amoeba or whatever it is that splits in two."

Okay, he had that coming. He stared her down when laughter replaced the seriousness in her eyes, and leaned toward her. "Well, never having carried a purse, I didn't think that. I thought the bills fooled around in your bank account and generated…interest."

She laughed. "Actually," she said, "I paint signs and wall plaques. Gift shops in San Francisco and Chicago carry them for me and I have a dealer in Boston and a separate account to keep track of sales to make sure I am making a profit, and I'm doing well. In fact, I reserved space at St. Anthony's Spring Fair the week after next."

"Right." He knew about the fair. "Evan Braga belongs to the parish, and I promised to help the men's club with their booth. It's food, I think."

"Who's Evan Braga?"

"He works for Hank, too. He's a house painter, and in his spare time, he sells real estate. We're going to collaborate someday when I buy that old Chandler Mill site and give it a face-lift."

"When is that going to happen?" she asked, reaching for her coffee cup.

"I'm working on a master's in business administration. I'd like to know more before I start speculating with large amounts of money. Although Evan thinks we should do it now." He grinned. "When the time comes, you'll be welcome to invest your sign fund in my project."

She shook her head. "I should be long gone by then, drifting on a gondola and sketching the doge's palace."

The little pang he'd felt the last time she said that doubled in size.

"I hope you find what you're looking for," he said.

To his surprise, she straightened, appearing just a little defensive. "I'm not *looking* for anything," she said. "I just want to see Europe. Why is that so bad? Parker makes that same criticism. I'm not running away. I'm just…just…"

While she sputtered in an attempt to explain herself, he reached across the table to put a hand over hers. "Hey," he said quietly. "I meant that I hope you'll be happy. That's all. I wasn't implying anything, or suggesting…"

She was still for a moment, her eyes locking with his, their dark depths curiously troubled, her lighthearted mood gone. Then she withdrew her hand.

"I don't see why a woman can't go to Europe," she said, lowering her voice as Rita approached with steaming plates, "without everyone presuming it's an act of cowardice."

There was a commotion as Rita placed a veggie omelet with whole-wheat toast in front of Mariah, and sausage and eggs with biscuits at Cam's place. She pulled ketchup and Tabasco sauce out of her apron pocket, surveyed the table, left and returned instantly to top up their coffees.

"All set?" she asked cheerfully.

Mariah liberally poured Tabasco on her omelet. "Yes, thank you."

Rita observed that and raised an eyebrow at Cam.

"Thanks, Rita," he said quickly, hoping to forestall a comment.

She grinned and walked off.

Mariah ate in silence.

Cam wondered at her spurt of temper and tried to approach conversation from another angle.

"Brian's a cute little kid," he observed. "Resourceful, too. He helped me a lot the night of the flood. Trying to make up for it, I think."

She glanced up at him, her expression softening. She spread jam on a toast point and nodded. "He's a sweetheart. Really a boy—rambunctious and inquisitive and just smart enough to check things out for himself if he wants answers. That's how he got into trouble. He's convinced there's gold stashed somewhere in the carriage house."

"He told me. Said he was going to take the other kids to Disneyland over the summer if he found it." He frowned at her. "I'd have thought kids who are away from their families for most of the year would be eager to go home for the summer. But he filled me in on his mom and Ashley's guardian."

She closed her eyes a moment, thoughts of the children's summer vacations obviously making her even more grim.

So his new conversational gambit hadn't been such a good idea after all.

"It's so sad," she said. "Brian's mother's kind of a flake, and Ashley's guardian intends the best for her but just doesn't know what to do with a little girl. And now he's ill, and she's eventually going to have to adjust to another household."

"Whose?"

"I don't know. Whoever he puts in charge of her care."

"At least the Manor's familiar ground."

That statement seemed to deepen her distress. He was beginning to wonder if he'd lost his social skills altogether.

She put down her piece of toast and said, "The dorm's closing with the school year. They need more room for classes. I think as the Lightfoot sisters get older, maintaining a living space, insurance on the kids, all that day-to-day stuff, is just getting too expensive and worrisome. Letitia just told me this morning."

"I'm sorry." She looked on the verge of tears. He passed her his handkerchief. "Does that mean you're out of a job?"

She stared at the handkerchief in surprise, then up at him. "I didn't think guys carried these anymore."

"Addy gave me a monogrammed twelve-pack for

Christmas," he said with a smile. "It's part of her plan to pair up single men and women."

"How so?" she asked, dabbing at her eyes. "Does she intend you to tie a woman to you with them?"

He considered that. "I don't think so, though that does have possibilities. You get weepy, I lend you my handkerchief, you offer to launder it, then we have to get together again so that you can give it back to me. Second date guaranteed."

"I could put it in the mail," she said.

He made a face at her. "Now, that would be just plain obstructive. I'll expect you to find me and return it to me."

She picked up her toast again, took a bite and chewed, clearly working off her dismay over the dorm's closure.

"They'd find another job for me," she said finally, "but I doubt there'll ever be a better time to take my trip."

"How long do you intend to be away?" he asked.

She shrugged, scooping up a bite of omelet. "Until I see no more reason to be there, I guess. Maybe a couple of years."

"Well, then, you may be back just in time to invest in my Chandler Mill project."

"Maybe." She brightened again. "Or maybe I'll have such a good time on my own, answerable to no one, that I'll decide to stay forever."

"So, you never intend to remarry?" Now that she looked relaxed again, he felt safe asking.

"Heavens, no," she denied with quiet vehemence.

He guessed that her obvious determination suggested

that she'd been very much in love and therefore very hurt by the divorce.

"The next man you meet might make you happier than your ex did," he said.

"Has nothing to do with that," she replied, studying the toast as though reading something in it. "Time was I could have been happy anywhere."

"What changed?" he asked carefully.

She sighed, put the toast down and sipped at her coffee. "Him," she said finally. "I did, too. And we'd had everything going for us in the beginning. When we failed, I guess I just lost faith in the old dreams."

"What were they?"

Suddenly Rita appeared to top up their coffees, but when she took in the concerned expressions on their faces, she gave Cam a worried look and moved on.

She shrugged. "Oh, babies, swing sets in the backyard, Sunday-afternoon drives, August vacations, a big yellow dog." She swung her fork in the air as if to erase what she'd just said. "Doesn't matter. They're gone."

He found that puzzling. "But one failed marriage doesn't mean you can't have all those things."

She looked him in the eye and said with the grimness of someone who'd learned to live with hard facts, "No, but three miscarriages and a stillbirth do."

CHAPTER SIX

CAM STARED AT HER in bleak surprise. She wished she'd kept that information to herself. She hated pity. But under the friendly antagonism, he was charming and interested, and all the suppressed details of her life seemed to be forcing their way to the surface.

"It's fine," she said quickly, busying herself with her omelet. "I'm fine. I've adjusted."

"Abandoning your dreams isn't a healthy adjustment," he argued.

"I had little choice. It used to be that I could conceive but never successfully carry a pregnancy. Now even my chances of conceiving are down to one in a hundred."

"What about adoption?"

She could hear all her old arguments with Ben in her head. "My husband wanted his own baby, and I just didn't want to try anymore. And I didn't want another woman to carry it for me."

He didn't ask why she didn't, but she felt obliged to explain.

She stopped eating and laid down her fork. "I think because I kept trying to get pregnant, even though every miscarriage was devastating. I can't tell you how awful the stillbirth was. I'd finally thought I was going to have a baby, then I stopped feeling movement." She experienced the same tormenting emptiness she'd known when the doctor told her her suspicions were correct and she'd lost the baby. "She was dead. I felt dead. Ben held me and we cried, then he started talking about trying again and I finally realized that while he might have loved me in the beginning, now all our life together meant to him was having a baby. And someone else's baby wouldn't make him happy. It had to be his. And it didn't seem to matter what the effort put me through." Her voice sounded strangled even to her own ears. She took a sip of coffee, then pushed her plate away. "I told him I'd be happy to adopt a baby, but I wasn't going to try again to get pregnant. He said I was being selfish."

Cam remained silent for a moment, then made a sound of exasperation. "Your dreams don't deserve to die because he was a jerk."

"Most men want their own children," she countered. "That's what everyone everywhere has. And that's fine. Maybe you're all entitled. I just don't want to have to deal with it again. I can't have babies, so I've just chosen to go my own way."

He was quiet, simply watched her with an expression that was both sympathetic and disapproving.

To forestall further discussion, she added, "And that's something to which *I'm* entitled."

He finally nodded, pushing his plate away and reaching for his coffee. "You're absolutely right. It's your life, and if your decision is to shortchange it, you have every right to do that. Where do you have to go shopping?"

She opened her mouth to take issue with him, but he'd waved Rita over for the check.

That was fine, she decided. He didn't have to understand. They were just two people having breakfast, going shopping.

"Oh. Almost forgot." Before they slipped out of the booth, he reached two long fingers into the chest pocket of his denim jacket, extracted something and put it in her palm.

Her missing earring! She'd assumed she'd lost it during the flood.

"Thank you," she said. "Where was it?"

"In the middle of my bed," he replied, just as Rita appeared.

Mariah felt the color rise in her cheeks, found herself wanting to explain, then decided against it. Even Parker had been hard-pressed to believe Mariah had thought Cam's dog was killing him and rushed into his bedroom to rescue him.

Cam handed Rita a bill considerably larger than the check required. "Keep the change," he said with a grin, "and your silence, please."

"No, hold on." Rita pocketed the check and bill and began to stack the plates. "I'll bring your change. I'd much rather be able to talk about what I overheard."

Mariah looked at Cam, uncertain if she was teasing or not.

Cam put his cup and saucer on top of the stack she'd collected and held it there, effectively stopping her tidying.

"Remember when you were making candles and held the dripping form over your sink and managed to seal the drain shut? Who fixed it free of charge because I was there, anyway, to connect your new washer and I had a free afternoon?" He gazed into her eyes. "And you were a little short of ca—"

"Yes!" she said impatiently, anxious to stop him. She glanced around surreptitiously. "I remember."

"Good," he said pleasantly. "Because I'd hate to have to charge you for it."

"I gave you fudge," she whispered.

"I know, and it was delicious. But when you consider that was four or five billable hours…"

"Okay, okay!" she said quietly. "The fact that her earring was in the middle of your bed will never leave my lips." She looked disgruntled. "But that's prime information, you realize. Addy would pay me off in a quilt to know that!"

He smiled. "If I hear a whisper of it anywhere, I'll come after you." He raised his hand from the top of his coffee cup and they grinned at each other. Mariah couldn't tell if this had been a teasing exchange or his threat was serious.

Rita smiled pleasantly at Mariah. "It was nice to meet you. I understand you have a booth at St. Anthony's Spring Fair." When Mariah appeared surprised, she added, "I'm chairman of the setup committee. I saw your name on the list next to your sister's massage booth. I've wanted one of your signs for a long time." She picked up the stack of plates. "Have a good day, you two." And she walked away.

Mariah was stunned. "Were you teasing her?"

He slipped out of the booth and offered Mariah a hand. "Of course. It was just a reminder that she owes me. She'll be quiet."

Mariah accepted his hand and, grabbing her purse, got to her feet. He retained her hand and led her through the maze of tables to the door. When she caught her trailing purse on the back of an empty chair, she turned to free it and saw Rita standing near the kitchen in the middle of a knot of four waitresses. They were all watching her and Cam and smiling.

CAM WAS FASCINATED as Mariah shopped for the children. The twins needed batteries for their CD players, Ashley wanted styling gel, Jessica had lost the last of her hair clips, Amy and Jalisa begged Mariah to rent the latest Olsen twins movie and Julia wanted Sweet Tarts.

"What are Sweet Tarts?" Cam asked as he carried the bag from the drugstore to the truck. Fred stuck his head inside, searching for treats.

"It's a very sour candy the kids love." She rescued the bag and folded it, intending to keep it on her lap. "Don't let them give you one. It takes a full day to recover."

Cam took it from her and placed it in his storage box in the bed of the truck. He'd had a canopy over the back through the winter and spring, but removed it with the advent of warmer weather.

When he returned to the cab, Mariah was feeding Fred a dog treat. Fred sat up in the middle of the seat, taking the small bites offered him with gentlemanly restraint. When Cam fed him treats, he stood in danger of losing his arm as far as his elbow.

"Where'd you get that?" he asked in surprise.

She smiled at him. Now that they were no longer talking about the past, she seemed comfortable with him. "I bought it from that bin at the counter while you were checking out the *Playboy* magazine."

"I was looking at *Popular Mechanics,*" he corrected her. "You had your back to me."

"I take care of children," she said. "I have eyes in the back of my head."

"Well, you should have them checked. They didn't work when you sloshed coffee all over yourself."

"Who's the centerfold this month?"

"Some pretty little redhead from a Balkan country."

"But you weren't reading it."

"It said so on the cover."

"And you noticed this because *Popular Mechanics* was right next to it?"

"Um, yeah. That's it. Probably placed alphabetically."

His biscuit finished, Fred gave Mariah a large slurp up the side of her face. She giggled and wrapped an arm around the dog as Cam drove off.

At the grocery store, Cam and Mariah split up. He bought anchovies, black olives, salsa-flavored corn chips, a bag of bagels and one of pecan-chocolate-chunk cookies. He picked up a six-pack of Sam Adams beer. When they met near the checkout as planned, Mariah frowned into his cart. "No meat?" she asked.

He shook his head. "I eat out. I just snack at home."

She made a face. "On anchovies?"

"Sometimes I bring a Caesar salad home from the deli. It's not a real Caesar without anchovies, so I put them on myself."

He peered into her cart and saw a colorful, sugary cereal. "Is that good for children?" he challenged.

She held up the box of Cheerios under it. "This is for weekdays with a banana and yogurt. The other is for Saturday mornings so they can have something fun."

"What about the caramel corn?"

She shifted her weight. "That's for the stash I keep in my room." Her direct look into his eyes dared him to criticize.

"In your bedside table?"

"The kids are too smart for that. It's in a hat box in the top of my closet."

He grinned. "Now I know where it is."

She grinned back. "But you're not likely to find yourself in my bedroom, are you?"

He knew she was determined that this attraction could go nowhere, but he hated to turn his back on the possibility.

"Life is filled with the unexpected," he said, falling into line behind her as she wheeled into one of two checkout lines. "Where to after this?"

"The chocolate shop," she replied over her shoulder. "Letty needs raisin clusters. Then the library. I promised Brian I'd try to find a book on the incident at the Manor that led to the story about the gold."

Cam smiled proudly. "He took my advice about needing more research."

Mariah pushed her cart forward as the woman in front of her, groceries paid for, moved on. She began stacking her purchases on the conveyor belt.

"You've become his hero. He drops your name all the time in conversation with the other children. And they're in awe that he got to help you fix the plumbing. You've given him real prestige."

He squeezed by his cart to reach under hers for the flat of two-dozen yogurts she'd stored on the bottom rung. He placed the flat on the conveyor, not sure what to say about her revelation. He'd never been anybody's hero. Well, maybe his little sister's, but that had been a long time ago.

She smiled at his surprise as the clerk continued to scan the contents of her cart. "Does that embarrass you, Cameron?" she asked softly.

He saw a curious sweetness in her eyes over that question and felt an almost uncontrollable urge to kiss her. But he'd already done that once and it had only served to confuse both of them. And after threatening Rita into secrecy, he couldn't very well romance Mariah in the middle of the Maple Hill Market.

So he bluffed it out. "I think it's the forty dollars an hour. I repaired my boss's kitchen sink on Sunday, with the help of his two daughters, and now the youngest one wants to be a plumber. Maybe we should introduce her to Brian. If there's chemistry there, they might grow up to be plumbing moguls."

Her smile deepened, as though she read his mind and his ruse to cover up. Then he got the oddest impression that she wanted to kiss him.

The moment stretched. Their eyes held, her lips parted and she leaned slightly toward him. He felt as if she touched him, drew him toward her.

Then the clerk called out a total—twice—and the moment was over. Mariah gave the clerk an apologetic smile and wrote a check.

They carried their purchases out to the truck, and Cam put them in the covered box. Mariah leaned her elbows on the bed of the truck and peered in to make sure her two-dozen eggs were carefully placed. Fred stuck his head out the back window, kissing in their direction.

"Do you ever run contraband in there?" she teased. "Illegal aliens? People in witness protection?"

He closed and locked the lid. "No, but I have been known to put smart-mouthed annoyances in it."

She gave him a superior glance and let herself into the passenger side. Fred leaped on her and Cam caught her just as she would have fallen out again. He braced his knee on the running board and propped her up on it.

"I'd better put him in the back," he said, trying to reach around her to open the window all the way so that Fred could get through.

"No, no!" she insisted, wrapping an arm around his neck to steady herself. "He was just being affectionate. He shouldn't be banished for that."

As she spoke the words, their gazes locked and that look from a moment ago was back in her eyes. He couldn't ignore it a second time.

He kissed her with all the conviction he felt that there could be something between them. She seemed to respond with the same belief, a tenderness in her touch, a welcome in her he'd never experienced with a woman before.

Allison had been confident and passionate—qualities he'd appreciated because tenderness had been unknown to him at that point in his life. Other women in his life since then had been eager and daring, almost bold in their attempts to prove that their hearts weren't involved, simply their bodies. He'd be a liar if he said he hadn't appreciated that to a point.

But something about this connection with Mariah was different. He didn't understand it entirely, but he'd never quite connected on this level before—something between all-out passion and uncomplicated intellect.

He wasn't entirely sure what to make of it.

When he finally raised his head, she said breathlessly, "I meant…the dog shouldn't be…banished for it. Not you."

He kissed her again, quickly, just to show her that she couldn't banish what was clearly present and waiting to be explored. Then he put her in her seat, pushing Fred out of the way to make room.

"You can't banish me—I'm driving," he said, then closed the door on her and walked around the truck.

When they came out of the chocolate shop, she handed him a small white bag of chocolate-dipped pretzels. "It's just a thank-you for breakfast," she said offhandedly, "and for making all these stops."

At the library, in the section on local history, they found several diaries of Letitia and Lavinia's great-aunt, Aletha Lightfoot. Mariah tucked them under her arm. "There might be a reference to what happened," she said hopefully.

Cam handed her *A History of Maple Hill, 1858 to 1900*. "This might have a mention, too."

"If Brian rips up the rest of the house," she threatened teasingly, "I'm coming back to get you."

Cam sighed. "I can only hope that happens."

He checked his watch and found that it was almost noon. "Want to go to Perk Avenue for lunch?" he asked.

She opened her mouth to reply, but nothing came out. She was debating the issue with herself, he guessed. He was abjectly disappointed when she said no.

"Back to the Breakfast Barn?" he persisted.

She shook her head again, glancing around in the quiet little library. There were two older people at a worktable toward the middle of the room. Otherwise, they were alone. "I can't, Cam. I have things to do. And…"

He knew what was coming. He didn't want to hear it, intended to ignore it, but she did have the right to say it. He listened patiently.

"We should keep things simple," she said, looking into his eyes with clear reluctance. "I'm going to Europe and you're building your life here. Nothing can come of our attraction. Okay?"

"No," he replied with a smile. She'd admitted attraction. That was important. "First of all, life is never simple, so you can't expect to contain something as far-reaching as love—"

"Love?" she disputed, her voice a little loud. Then she glanced around again, and seeing that they'd disturbed no one, she repeated more quietly, "Love? We—"

"I know." He cut her off before she could build up a head of steam. "It isn't love. We don't know each other well enough. But it's something, and I don't intend to hide from it or try to escape it."

She drew a breath—probably for patience—and firmed her stance, the library books caught in front of her like armor. "Did you hear nothing I said over breakfast?"

He nodded. "I did. It all related to your life with another man. That has nothing to do with us."

"It related to *me*," she corrected him. "Me! The woman who's lost four babies!"

He nodded again. "I'm sure that was awful, and your husband's reaction to you was brutal. What you're missing here is that I'm not him. I have no problem with adoption. And if we understand this isn't even love yet, why are we even talking about children?"

"Because if it turns out to be," she said, her voice rising to a desperate whisper, "it'll become an issue!"

"No, it won't. But why don't we wait to have this argument until it turns out to be?"

She faced him stubbornly, and he knew what she was thinking. It *would* turn out to be. So the best thing she could do for herself was keep her distance.

"I think it would be smarter to just save ourselves from that." She dug into her purse, extracted her library card and marched to the desk. He followed and waited patiently while a slender young woman behind the desk scanned the books and handed them across the counter.

Mariah thanked her, then pivoted and walked past Cam as though he wasn't there.

He followed, planning strategy. He wasn't usually good at plots. He was a very straightforward person. But if she was determined to make it difficult, he could do what it took to get the result he wanted.

She waited in front of the locked passenger-side door without looking at him, her chin at a challenging angle.

He ignored her and walked around to his side, unlocking the door. Fred ran at him and he pushed him back into the truck. "Good boy," he said, ruffling the dog's ears. Then he glanced at her over the top of the truck. "Are we holding this relationship together long enough for me to drive you home?" he asked.

She rolled her eyes at him. "Don't be ridiculous, Cam."

"You race into my bedroom," he challenged, "you kiss me as if you've been waiting for me a lifetime—twice—then you claim to read my mind and decide what I do and don't want out of life without even bothering to ask me." He let all that sink in, then asked calmly, "And *I'm* ridiculous?"

She rolled her eyes again, walked around the truck to the driver's door, pushed him aside and climbed in behind the wheel. Fred whined ecstatically as she slid along the bench seat as far as she could.

"Would you please take me home?" she said.

He slipped in behind the wheel and started the motor. With the dog crowding her, Cam didn't have much room to move without touching her—a situation she was trying hard to avoid, considering the way she had her left arm placed across her body to avoid contact.

They were both silent as he pulled out of the parking spot, turned onto Maple Street, then headed out of town toward the Manor.

Mariah's other arm was wrapped around Fred, and the traitorous dog kissed her ear all the way to the school. Cam turned onto the long, maple-lined drive, the trees now bright with small, spring-green leaves. Soon the leaves would be as large as dinner plates. He wondered if Mariah would be gone by then.

He stopped at the junction that led straight to the main building, then made a left toward the carriage house. It was at the top of a slope and had to be approached on foot. He pulled to a stop at the bottom.

Mariah hitched her purse over her shoulder and reached around Fred to push open her door.

"Wait a minute!" he commanded.

She faced him in surprise. Even Fred didn't bolt from the truck as he always did the moment a door opened.

Cam got out, walked around and snapped his fingers for Fred. The dog jumped to the ground and stood right beside him. Cam offered Mariah a hand down. "Just because you insist on being difficult," he said, "doesn't mean that I want to be sloppy. Watch your step."

He unlocked the storage box in the back, retrieved her bags and set them aside in the bed until he had them all out, ignoring her open arms, ready to take them from him. He relocked the box, then gathered up her groceries and other purchases.

"You don't have to..." she began, then stopped when he started up the hill.

She ran around him, Fred following her, and hurried ahead to open the front door. He walked in, through the foyer and past the stairway, still bare of carpet, and into the kitchen. He placed the bags on the large oak table.

She offered her hand, looking uncertain of him.

On one level, he hated that. He'd enjoyed the laughing camaraderie they'd shared at various times throughout the morning. She'd enjoyed his company, and she'd felt safe with him.

But on another level, he guessed, it might be good that she wasn't sure what to make of his reactions. She seemed so sure of her perception of things, wrong as she was, and if she found him unpredictable, it could only help his cause.

He took her hand, keeping his manner casual. Actually, it wasn't what he felt at all. The more time he spent in her company, the more he longed to hold her, kiss her, make love to her so that she would never be able to question what they could mean to each other.

But he had a strategy here. He had to be cool.

"Thank you for a lovely morning," she said. He saw vague disappointment in her eyes. She'd wanted him to kiss her.

"I enjoyed it, too," he replied amiably.

"Thank you for understanding," she added, following him as he walked to the door. Fred hung back, licking at her fingertips.

"I don't understand," he corrected her. "I just refuse to spend valuable time arguing. Goodbye. Come on, Fred."

She said nothing until he was halfway down the slope, then she called, "Thanks again."

He waved and kept going. Fred took several paces back to her but came when Cam called him.

If he stayed away, Cam wondered, would absence make her heart grow fonder? He doubted it, but his choices were slim at the moment.

He opened the passenger-side door to let Fred in, then walked around and got in behind the wheel. Fred looked longingly back at the house and whined.

Cam patted his head. "I know," he said. "Me, too."

CHAPTER SEVEN

SATURDAY NIGHT MARIAH and the children sat around the kitchen table that she'd covered with newspaper and painted some of the signs she would sell at the fair. She'd outlined several with simple designs that would be enhanced, rather than harmed, by less-than-perfect painting.

She'd told the children several days ago about the closure of the Manor's boarding program and their reactions had been surprisingly calm. But she knew sometimes the announcement of major changes in their lives took several days to process. They were just beginning to talk about it among themselves today. She'd thought the painting project would relax them and make them comfortable enough to share their thoughts with her.

"Our mom's coming with her boyfriend to get us when school's over," said Amy, dipping her brush into yellow paint for the center of a stylized daisy on a Bloom Where You Are Planted sign.

"We don't like him." Jalisa painted a blue kitten in the corner of a Quiet—Baby Sleeping sign.

"You haven't even met him, so you don't really know if you like him or not," Mariah said reasonably. She put clear sealer on several signs she'd painted last night after the children had gone to bed.

"We want her to get undivorced and marry our old dad again." Jessica, her sign finished, dipped her brush desultorily in the water jar and watched it turn colors.

"He got married again to another lady, Jess," Mariah reminded her. "You went to the wedding."

She nodded. "Yeah, but maybe *they'll* get divorced and he and Mom can start all over."

"Uh-uh," Amy said. "'Cause Margie's gonna have a baby." Margie was their father's new wife. "So he has to stay."

"Well, what about us?" Jessica demanded, dropping her brush in the water and sitting back, folding her arms pugnaciously. "How come he didn't have to stay with us?"

"Sometimes married people aren't happy together anymore." Mariah tried to explain the unexplainable. "So they can't live together the way they did before. But that doesn't mean he doesn't still love you. Even if he has another little girl with Margie."

Jessica blew air, clearly disgruntled. "Well, I don't like it."

Ashley, carefully painting the white petals on a daisy, looked up from her work to smile at Jessica. "At least you get to be with your mom. I never get to be with people I know when I'm not at school. And now I can't come back here."

Brian, screwing eye hooks into the tops of the finished signs in order to attach chain, put a finished sign aside and shook his head. "Well, I can't, either, but you don't see me whining about it. I'm going to find the gold and go wherever I want to go."

Ashley leaned her chin on her hand, the paintbrush

in her fingers forgotten. "Wouldn't it be cool if that could happen? But where would we go after Disneyland?"

The question seemed to perplex Brian. "We won't go anywhere. We'll just stay there."

"You can't live at Disneyland."

"Why not? They have hotels and stuff."

"I know, but it's a place to play. After you have a vacation, you have to go back to your real life."

He met her gaze with a surprisingly jaded glance for a ten-year-old. "Yeah, but you and me don't have a real life. We live with people hired to take care of us. That's not like having a real life. So I don't see why we'd have to go back to it."

Ashley considered that, and her optimism appeared to dim.

"You're both forgetting how lucky you are that your guardian, Ashley, and your mother's housekeeper, Brian, take good care of you. There are a lot of children in the world whom nobody cares about. That's really sad."

"We have neat parents," Peter said. He clipped chain onto the eye hooks with special, user-friendly hooks Mariah had attached. "We go parasailing in the summer, and waterskiing."

"We jumped out of an airplane last summer!" Philip said.

Mariah shuddered. The Franklins loved their boys, but their idea of fun was daunting to her. The boys, however, were thriving, and Peter, at least, exhibited the same daredevil proclivities their parents had. Philip was less adventurous.

"But it's gonna be weird not to come back here." Peter frowned at his brother. "If we end up in a military school, I'm running away."

"Me, too," Philip seconded.

"Running away never solves anything." Mariah handed a finished sign to Julia, who carried them to the counter where several dozen signs lay to dry. "And I think you're all putting the cart before the horse."

Every pair of eyes looked up at her at the strange metaphor. "Imagine," she proposed, "that Santa's reindeer were behind the sleigh instead of in front of it. What would happen?"

"They'd go backward," Amy said.

Ashley shook her head. "They wouldn't go anywhere. They're supposed to pull."

Mariah nodded, happy to be understood. "So, if you plan for what's going to happen before it happens, you could be all wrong. What you expected to turn out badly might turn out well, but you've already run away, so you'd never know that. You haven't gotten anywhere. You've put the cart before the horse."

Brian frowned. "I thought we were talking reindeer and a sleigh."

She opened her mouth to explain, then caught the laughter in his eyes. He was teasing her.

Ashley sighed. "Okay, Peter and Philip might end up in a good school, and Jess's mom's boyfriend might be a really neat man, but I don't think Brian and I are going to be surprised. Things are always the same for us. His mom's always gone, and I have all these people I don't know in my life. We have to make some plans."

She was absolutely right, but Mariah held fast to her

plea for caution. "I'm sure the adults in your life are making plans for you. You don't have to worry."

Ashley and Brian exchanged a doubtful look and went back to their tasks.

Later that night, after the children were in bed, Parker called.

"I have a new portable chair for the studio," she said eagerly. "Free massage if you want to try it out. I'll bring it over."

"Only if you want to be showered with chocolate and wine," Mariah replied, tugging at the back of her neck where the long nights working on her signs, the stress of worrying about the children and memories of Cameron Trent had all balled into an aching knot. Her sister's healing hands were just what the moment called for.

"Be right there," Parker promised.

They had a glass of wine, shared the quarter pound of Turtles Mariah had bought for herself when she'd shopped for Letitia, and Mariah duly admired the new chair, then sprawled on it to help Parker adjust it.

"Head's just a little high," she said, lifting hers off it so her sister could make the adjustment.

"Try that," Parker advised.

Mariah lay on it again and sank into rapturous comfort. "It's perfect."

"All right!"

Mariah caught the scent of spearmint, violet and roses that Parker had dried herself and sprinkled into her bath. Her sister's hands settled on her shoulders and began to do their work.

"Has he called?" Parker asked, her thumbs kneading Mariah's spine.

Mariah felt herself sink into a level of consciousness once removed from her daily struggle. "Who?" she asked.

"Cam," Parker replied. "Who else?"

"No." Mariah kept her reply simple, unwilling to turn her concentration from the delicious massage.

Though Parker's hands remained firm and apparently focused, her voice took on a suspicious note. "What did you say to him?"

Mariah hesitated before she replied, allowing herself to bask in the comfort of relaxing muscles, knowing that once she answered, the sweetness of this raglike state would be lost.

"You may as well tell me," Parker prompted. "I'm not going away."

"I don't want you to go away." Mariah sighed, her voice vibrating with the strength of the massage. "I just want you to be quiet."

"Fat chance."

Mariah felt the vigorous assault of the sides of Parker's hands across her back from shoulder to shoulder and couldn't help but believe that was some kind of retribution. Even if it did help relax her further.

"I know you saw him on Tuesday," Parker said, working farther down Mariah's back.

Reluctantly, Mariah forced herself to surface from the stress-free depths of comfort. "Did Rita squeal?" she asked, remembering the promise Cam had forced from the woman.

"No." Parker sounded perplexed. "I haven't seen Rita. But Kelly Patrick has a standard Wednesday-afternoon appointment when she gets off work at the Barn."

Mariah had an instant memory of a group of waitresses smiling as they watched her and Cam leave the restaurant.

"She saw the two of you," Parker added.

"I don't even know Kelly Patrick."

"It's Maple Hill," Parker reminded her. "Everyone knows everyone. And we have certain favorites we'd like to see happy."

"I'm happy."

"You're lonely."

"I'm independent."

"You're trying to escape your loneliness."

Mariah sat up, annoyed. "The whole world thinks people are only happy in pairs. I don't happen to agree. And while I appreciate everyone's concern, I'd like it better if they didn't feel obliged to offer advice on my—"

Parker pushed her back onto the chair. "I'm not the whole world. I'm your sister. And I feel that if you're ever going to be happy, you have to stop living in a box."

"A box?"

"A box. You've closed your life up so that all you have in it is me and the children."

"And I'm about to rethink *you!*" Mariah protested as Parker worked at the back of her waist.

Parker ignored her and continued. "You're running away to Europe because you believe every man is going to be like Ben, but you're wrong."

Mariah sat up again, her efforts to relax completely shattered. She fought off Parker's attempt to continue the massage and climbed off the chair. "I asked Cam what he wanted out of marriage, and he said a loving wife and children."

Parker spread her arms in exasperation. "Well, what is so awful about that? Of course he'd want a loving wife and children. But that doesn't mean he'd harass and berate you because you couldn't give him his own. I'm sure if you explained—"

"I did explain."

"And?"

Mariah turned away from her sister's persistent inquisition and went into the kitchen. She tested the signs and plaques with her index fingertip and, finding them dry, took tissue out of a package she'd opened on a kitchen chair and began to wrap them.

Parker stood beside her, taking the wrapped signs from her and placing them in a box on the floor.

"And," Mariah finally replied, "he said he'd be open to adoption if he found himself in such a situation."

"Then, what's the problem?"

Mariah sighed and stopped as she prepared to wrap a Quiet—Baby Sleeping sign. It was the one Jalisa had painted with the blue kitten. "The problem is that Ben and I were in love." She held the sign to her and looked into Parker's eyes, remembering how she'd felt when he'd asked her to marry him. She'd been so happy, certain she'd found a lifetime of joy and fulfillment. "And then I got pregnant, and we were happier than I thought it was possible to be. He was so attentive to me, so loving—as though I was something very precious."

Parker nodded with understanding, putting a hand on her arm and rubbing gently. "Then you lost the baby."

"Yes. Then I lost two more, and by the fourth pregnancy, it was like having our own baby became a matter of honor for him. I felt pain and grief, and he never gave me time for that. He just wanted to try again—to force nature to do what it didn't seem to want to do." Pain filled her chest. It occurred to her that it was like an attack of the heart. "Stephanie had a lovely face, tiny fingers and toes. I held her and got to look at her almost-perfect body, and I just couldn't do it again. Ben held us and cried with me, but started to give me that pep talk I knew by heart. 'I know this is tough, Mariah, but we can't let it defeat us. We were almost successful with this one. We have to try one more time.' And I knew I just couldn't do it."

Parker took the sign from her, put it aside and wrapped her arms around her. "Life makes some people smarter and stronger and others weaker and downright stupid."

"He just wanted his own baby."

"But he wanted it more than he wanted you to be happy. That's not fair."

Mariah pushed her sister away to look into her eyes. "I think maybe it's an instinctive thing, you know? Some impulse or longing placed in men to keep the human race going. A need to see the imprint of your features on future generations, so that the world knows you've been here."

"Yes. That's probably true to a point. But even those impulses have to allow for some exceptions to the rule. Nothing in this world survives without a backup plan. On some level, Ben wasn't man enough to subordinate his ego to your inability to carry a baby to term."

Mariah nodded grimly. "The thing is, he'd known me for a long time, lived with me and loved me for four years. We were everything to each other. And he couldn't come to terms with my inability to carry a baby to term. How can I expect another man to be any different?"

"Because you were only everything to each other as long as he thought you could give him what he wanted. When you couldn't, his love evaporated. Makes you wonder if those years you thought were filled with love and happiness really were."

Mariah sighed, demoralized. "Makes me wonder if I even have the ability to assess my own life."

"Of course you do. The fact that he changed on you isn't your fault."

"Just goes to show you how uncertain love is, anyway. I mean, it's so nebulous to begin with, an emotion dependent upon someone embodying all the things we need in life but can't supply ourselves. We develop this grand feeling for the person because he or she's our other half. But life, time and nature change us, and pretty soon we're not who we were in the beginning. So love dissolves."

Parker studied her with a frown. "Well, you paint a pretty bleak picture! I don't think real love does dissolve. I think it makes adjustments."

"Parker, you've been divorced twice. And you were in love each time you got married."

Parker shifted her weight. "I know. But I fall for needy souls. So whenever I need something, they don't come through for me because they're too busy fending for themselves." She hugged Mariah again. "Are you okay?"

Mariah smiled. "Of course I'm okay."

"Good. Then I'm leaving before you completely disillusion me about love. I still believe in it."

She gathered up her purse and motioned at her massage chair. "And I have a date tomorrow."

"You do?" Mariah picked up the back end of the chair to help Parker out to her station wagon. "Anyone I know?"

"I don't think so. His name is Gary Warren, and he works for Hank Whitcomb, too. He's landscaping my duplex. He's also been coming for massages. He's so easy to talk to."

Hank's men, it seemed, were everywhere. And insinuating themselves into the lives of every woman she knew. She took most of the weight of the chair while Parker unlocked the back of the wagon. Together they pushed in the chair.

Mariah hugged her. "Have a wonderful time and keep believing in everyone and everything as you've always done. Just be on the lookout for selfish qualities and don't let yourself get serious if he has any."

"Right. And you try to be a little more hopeful. You're helping raise children, remember. You have to make them feel there's hope for the world. Particularly if they're not coming back to you next year."

Mariah waved her sister off in the darkness, then went back into the house. She wrapped up the remaining signs and packed them into the box, deliberately trying to keep her mind blank.

Cam's face appeared in her mind's eye.

Okay, it was hard to keep her mind blank. But she was not going to indulge it with thoughts of men and love. She would think about her booth.

After several years of doing flea markets, she now had a double-size vinyl pavilion to shelter her wares in case of strong sun or rain. She'd made Peg-Board screens on which to hang the signs, had a card table for doing business and her own cash box. She had to remember to wipe everything off and buy more hooks. Those always seemed to get lost in storage.

She should get a pretty vinyl tablecloth, make a note to pack cold drinks for herself and Parker, and remind Letty and Lavinia that they were watching the children for her.

She also had to remember to go to her storage locker and retrieve a box of signs with Christmas motifs she'd printed two years ago but never sold. She'd ended up in the hospital, losing Stephanie, instead of at the crafts fair the signs had been intended for. And she had to think about something easy for dinner for the children that night.

There. She shook off the pain the thought of one of her babies always brought and congratulated herself on being organized.

The box all packed, she locked the front door, checked the back door, then put the wineglasses and snack plates in the dishwasher. She shut off the downstairs lights and started up to her room.

The house was quiet, the old grandfather clock downstairs ticking its comforting time, the refrigerator humming, the bedsprings creaking as the children turned over in bed.

She hated the prospect of them leaving in two weeks. Since she'd taken over dorm-mother duties last year, her life had revolved around them. The job had been challenging at first, and she'd wondered if God hadn't known what he was doing when he kept her childless.

Then she found her feet with the children, discovered

they weren't so much troublemakers as trouble finders, and soon all their qualities, even the ones that kept her on her toes, became very dear to her.

How well they functioned in spite of the turmoil in their lives away from school amazed her.

She found herself wishing she could keep them all with her this summer. Then she realized there would be little point to that if they weren't coming back in the fall.

And anyway, she was going to Europe.

Her mind went instantly to what would happen to Ashley and Brian. The Morris girls would be fine because their mother loved them and they had each other. The Franklin boys had sunny dispositions and positive attitudes, and parents who always seemed to get away from filming when the boys had a birthday or something special happened.

But Ashley's guardian was dying, and Brian's mother was a flake. Still, as Letty had reminded her, where the children attended school next fall was none of the Manor staff's business.

Mariah wondered if she should call Ashley's guardian and offer to find a good boarding school for the little girl. Letitia would probably discourage it, but she'd have to give it some thought.

She showered, pulled on a cotton nightgown and went to climb into bed, then noticed the light on in her closet. She walked into it, pulled the worn cord to turn the light off and was about to close the closet door, when she heard movement above her head.

She looked up into the closet, a shudder running along her spine. A mouse? she wondered. A raccoon?

Letty had told her that they occasionally had a problem with varmints in the carriage house's attic.

She blinked and looked again. It if was a mouse, it must be a particularly clever one, because it had created a large square of blackness where a ceiling tile should have—

She hadn't even completed the thought, when something fairly large glanced off her head and bounced off the clothes rack and into her hands. She screamed, certain it was alive.

Then she felt cold metal and realized it was a flashlight.

That was followed instantly by a cry of alarm and the pitching downward through the hole of hands, arms and a head with cobwebby dark hair.

Mariah reached up instinctively, then she fell to the floor of the closet—along with half her clothes and Brian.

Landing on his back beside her, one foot trapped in the belt of her raincoat, the other caught in one of her shoe pockets tacked to the closet wall, he smiled at her hesitantly, his face smeared with dust.

"You'll be glad to know," he said seriously, "that the gold isn't in the attic."

CHAPTER EIGHT

CAM HELPED EVAN BRAGA assemble the Men's Club booth on the large lawn that usually served as the playground behind St. Anthony's School. Also pressed into service were Hank Whitcomb and his brother-in-law, Bart Megrath. It was very early Saturday morning the first day of the fair, and none of the other vendors had arrived. Jimmy Elliott was baby-sitting Fred for the weekend.

"Wouldn't it be better to buy one of those aluminum things that's easy to carry," Hank asked as he and Bart hauled lumber from Cam's truck to the designated spot in the roped-off area. "And sets up in five minutes?"

"Undoubtedly," Evan replied. He and Cam followed with more pieces. "But an older member of the club provided this booth when his kids were in school, and they've always used it. They see no point in buying some newfangled contraption now." He grinned at his companions. "And that's a quote from the last meeting."

That Evan belonged to this group of older, staid and spiritual men, when church seemed like the last place you'd find him, always amazed Cam. Yet Evan attended regularly.

They had the basic box assembled in half an hour. It was about three times the size of the usual booth.

Cam was about to return to his truck for the slab of wood that would serve as the counter, but Evan loped toward him, waving him back.

"No, we're not going to need that part," he said.

"Won't you want something to rest the food on when you take the money?"

Evan shook his head. "We're not doing food."

"You told me you were making German dogs with peppers."

"Yeah, that's what we usually do, but the wife of one of the men suggested we try something else this year."

Evan went to the open back of Hank's van, pulled out a rolled-up carpet and put it on Cam's shoulder.

Cam balanced it while waiting for Evan to heave a large, plastic-wrapped package out of the rear. "What kind of booth requires a Persian rug?"

"I'm not telling you until it's up."

"But you volunteered me to help in it. I have a right to know what we're doing."

"That's why I'm not telling you. You'll rabbit on me. Come on."

Cam followed him warily across the lawn. "Is it a kissing booth? I'm more open-minded than you think."

"It's not a kissing booth."

"You're not going to dress me in a bra and pass me off as a bearded lady."

Evan laughed. "No. But that's a thought for next year." They walked into the booth through the side left open by the missing counter and Evan dropped his burden in a corner.

"Just put the rug in the middle. Guys?" he said to Hank and Bart. "Can you get the chairs and the table?

Hold on, Cam. The school's janitor is supposed to have left a ladder just inside the front door for us."

Cam unrolled the carpet, and by the time he'd walked over it to settle it into place, Hank and Bart were back with the table and chairs and Evan had an eight-foot ladder.

"The table goes on the rug," Evan directed, "and the chairs on either side. "Cam, want to grab the cabana?"

Cam looked around in confusion. "Cabana?"

Evan pointed to the plastic-wrapped package in the corner.

Cam complied. He removed the contents as Evan climbed the ladder, and discovered it was an old-style beach tent, or cabana, complete with wide blue-and-white stripes and tasseled ornamentation.

Evan threw the heavy fabric over and his companions leaped up to pull it down to fit over the booth. A peaked top rested neatly over the one-by-ones they'd nailed along the top of the booth so that they met in a point in the middle.

"How's it look?" Evan asked from the ladder.

Hank and Bart stepped back to look.

"The point's just a little off center!" Hank shouted. "Pull it to the left. There! Perfect!"

"Looks great!" Bart praised. "You're not jousting or anything, are you?"

Evan climbed down the ladder. "No. We're telling fortunes."

"What?" Cam demanded.

"We're telling fortunes," Evan repeated. "Cam, you're on from eleven to one o'clock, incidentally."

"You told me we were making hot dogs," Cam reminded him. "I have no fortune-telling skills."

"You have no hot-dog-making skills, either," Hank observed. "You burned mine when we watched the game at my house."

Cam drilled him with a look. "That's because your daughter was showing me she could stand on her head and I had to extract her from the recycle box when she fell in."

"We're not claiming to be psychics," Evan said, handing him a large snow globe of a cabin in a cluster of trees near a lake. "It's a carnival game. Here's your crystal ball."

Cam tried to return it. "I can't make up that kind of stuff. People will want their money back."

Evan put it in the middle of the table. "No, they won't. It's a fund-raiser for the school. Will you quit whining? Nobody will expect you to contact their dead relatives or really see into their futures. Just make up something about fame and fortune, and you'll be fine."

Accepting defeat, Cam told him grimly, "I can see into your future, buddy, and it isn't pretty. I see traction, around-the-clock nursing care, insurance claims…"

Ignoring him, Evan tacked a sign to the front of the cabana that coaxed, Come Inside For a Message From the Future."

"I thought churches didn't believe in this sort of stuff."

"No one's taking it seriously." Evan handed him another plastic bag. "Here're your robes and turban," he said. "You might want to try them on before your shift. Let's go to the bakery. I'm buying."

Cam clutched the plastic bag to him. "Turban?" he asked in horror.

Hank took the bag from him, tossed it onto the table and laughed hysterically as he wrapped an arm around his shoulders and led him back to his truck.

MARIAH HELPED PARKER SET UP her booth—a simple vinyl tent affair bedecked with garlands of silk nasturtiums. Her new massage chair stood in the middle of the small space, and an end table nearby brought from home held her business cards and literature about massage.

When they were finished, Parker helped Mariah assemble her pavilion, put up the screens, then hang the signs.

"I'll give you a lunch break and watch your booth, if you'll do the same for me," Parker bargained.

"Sure." Mariah delved into the cooler she'd brought and handed her sister a commuter mug containing sweetened iced tea with a slice of lemon. She also handed her a bag of misshapen peanut butter cookies.

Parker bit into one and made a sound of approval. "You and the kids have been baking."

"We have."

"At lunchtime," Parker said, peering out onto the lawn now covered with booths in various stages of construction, people bustling around in their preparations, "St. Anthony's Men's Club usually does German dogs with onions and peppers. They're to die for."

"Sounds wonderful. You can go first, though."

"No, you. All I had to do was lug in the chair. You had all kinds of stuff to get ready. Oops. Got a live one." A young woman stood inside Parker's booth, studying the handout. "Thanks for the tea and cookies."

"Sure."

Mariah had sold a fourth of her stock by eleven o'clock.

She was rearranging signs to close up bare spots, when Letitia and Lavinia walked by, the children clustered around them.

Ashley noticed immediately that some of the stock had been sold. She pointed to a large sign Mariah had painted herself and placed at the top. It read Live Well, Laugh Often, Love Much. "That's my favorite. I wonder why nobody's bought it yet?"

"I'm sure it's waiting for just the right person," Mariah replied. "We'll divvy up the money you all made today," she told the group, "so you'll have extra money to spend when you come back tomorrow."

"After lunch," Ashley said excitedly, "I'm going to have my fortune told."

"I'm going to buy a candy apple!" Julia said.

"I'm going to play the Wheel of Fortune." Brian held up two one-dollar bills. "It only costs fifty cents, and the girls win dolls and the boys get trucks."

"All right! What do the adults get?"

He shrugged. "I don't know. Probably books, or something." She guessed that was the dullest thing he could think of.

"Well, let's move on and see if we can find the cakewalk," Lavinia proposed. "I'd love to win a chocolate cake."

"A wish I applaud," Letitia said, shooing the children before them. "Good luck, Mariah. We'll see you at closing time."

Mariah waved as they started away and several young girls wandered into her booth, giggling.

She'd picked the top-twenty girls' names out of a baby book and made several for each, some with butterflies, some with flowers and some with kittens. She sold two Sarahs, a Brittany and a Bailey.

In addition to the children earning money, she realized, checking the contents of her cash box, her European trip account was doing well.

She was famished when Parker appeared to relieve her at just after noon.

"You're sure you want me to go first?" she asked. "I know you've been really busy, too. Your hands must be aching."

Parker flexed them happily. "They're used to this. And I've signed up three new regular weekly customers. Go ahead. I'll be fine."

"Okay. I'm starved." Mariah grabbed her purse from under a folding chair and took off down the fair's lively midway.

Her first stop was a booth with handcrafted jewelry. She found a necklace made of silver beads she knew Parker would love, admired a star-shaped brooch for herself, then decided against it, opting to put the money in her Europe fund, instead.

She pitched pennies and played the ring toss to no avail, but joined in the cakewalk and won a butter brickle cake. The children, she knew, would be thrilled to have it for dessert tonight.

She carried the cake to her car, delivered the necklace to Parker, who gave her a squeal of delight and a big hug, then continued on her way. She signed up for a quilt raffle and was getting serious about finding something to eat, when she noticed the striped tent and the invitation to Come Inside for a Message From the Future.

She wasn't sure why that intrigued her, but it did. Gypsies with bangle bracelets and wild eyes had always fascinated her. She parted the striped folds and peered in. It would be fun to pretend that there was some mystery about her future.

CAM WAS MAKING a bundle for the Men's Club. He'd told a dozen fortunes and was beginning to feel comfortable with his turban and Hungarian accent. The face-enveloping beard and mustache, however, must have been made of something smelly and flea-bitten. He was continually having to scratch under it.

He was wondering if fortune-telling could be a lateral career move from plumbing, when a familiar dark head peeked inside the tent. His first thought was that Mariah knew he was working the booth and had stopped by to say hello, or to remind him that she didn't want to see him again.

But he realized as she looked around and stepped hesitantly inside that she had no idea who was under the robe and behind the thick, dark beard.

She peered at him, hesitated, appearing to consider a hasty exit.

"Come in, Princess," he said with a thick roll of *R*s and the slur of consonants that seemed to give him some authenticity, if not exactly credibility.

She peered around again.

"I was expecting a Gypsy," she said. She wore jeans that clung to her flat stomach and slender limbs, and a white blouse with pink roses. Her hair was caught up in a loose knot, bangs fringing her forehead. She looked very young; nothing about her indicated all she'd been through in life.

"I am son of Othar, prince of the Gypsies," he said, beckoning her toward the table with an index finger bejeweled with a ring probably taken from a bubble gum machine. It, and the other three he wore, had come with the costume. "Come, Princess."

She took several more steps to the table, smiling. "I meant a Gypsy *woman*."

"Ah," he said, sweeping a hand toward the chair. "In my family, the gift of prophecy is passed from father to son. The women are not quiet long enough to hear the stirrings of dreams."

She sat down, leaning forward and smiling. "And how do you hear them?"

He made a broad gesture upward with his hands. "They're in the snow."

"Well…" She pointed to the sun streaming through the open slit of the tent. "It's May, Gypsy prince. Almost June."

He framed the globe in front of him with his hands, passed them over it as though casting a spell, then picked it up in one hand, spun it theatrically, then placed it right side up on the table. Snow swirled like a blizzard inside it.

"In my tent," he said softly, "it is only…the future!" He added the last two words in a dramatic whisper.

"Yes, well. Here's my five dollars." She put a bill on the table. "Your sign says that gets me a message from…the future!" She repeated those two words with the same whispered note he'd used.

"I see…" He leaned closer, narrowing his gaze on the globe as if having difficulty reading it. "I see…children."

"Yes," she said. "There are children in my present life. Are you one of the Manor's parents?"

He cupped his hands around the globe without touching it. "No, this is the *future*. There are children in your *future*. A yellow cottage with climbing roses on the picket fence."

He chanced a glance up at her and saw her staring at him. Had she forgotten he was in a role?

Had he? He found himself wanting to give her back her dreams.

"Ah!" he said.

"What?"

"A ship."

She hesitated a moment, then asked with bald cynicism, "I'm going into the merchant marines?"

He frowned over the globe. "No. You are a passenger."

"Oh. A Caribbean vacation?"

"No. I see you at the Louvre, the Prado, the National Gallery."

He heard her intake of breath, and wondered if he'd gone too far. Thinking that if he had, he may as well go for broke, he continued. "Later, you will meet a handsome stranger. Together you will find the yellow cottage and the children. You will have an easel in a room with a dormer window facing north. It looks out on swings in a backyard, a yellow dog."

She stared at him in silence, a dreamy wonder in her eyes. As he watched, her expression hardened to suspicion.

MARIAH FELT HERSELF inhale his message from the future like oxygen. She took it into her lungs, into her bloodstream, willing to believe in this blue-and-white tent with a snow globe for a crystal ball and a playful Gypsy charlatan across the table and that he was telling her the truth.

How could he have known? she asked herself as she tried to get a grip, tried to reason this through. A few people were aware she planned a trip to Europe, but not many knew she was going on a self-conducted art tour—just Parker and the Lightfoot sisters. And the swings and the yellow…

Reality fell on her like an anvil. She stood and reached across the table, yanked on the bristly beard and slapped off the turban. She looked into a roughly handsome face with hazel eyes. "Cameron Trent! You…you liar!"

"I wasn't lying, Mariah," he denied. "I was indulging your dreams. You should be doing that for yourself."

He reached a hand out toward her and she batted it away angrily. "Don't try to talk around it! You pretended to be someone else and used what you knew about me to…to…"

"Give you your five dollars' worth?" he finished for her. He folded his arms and wisely kept his distance.

She was furious. She had a vague misgiving about why she should be so upset about a fortune-telling booth clearly intended as harmless entertainment, but she was too angry to be rational.

"Five bucks for a dream?" he added. "Cheap at twice the price."

She snatched up her five dollars and jammed it into the side pocket of her jeans. "I'm taking my money back. I thought you were supposed to be cooking hot dogs for the Men's Club."

"They changed their minds about what they wanted to do."

"Well, I think you should have stuck to food!" She knew she was being ridiculous, could see that in his eyes. Unable to explain or defend herself, she pivoted to leave.

Strong fingers manacled her wrist and turned her to face him.

"Do you even know why you're so upset about this?" he asked.

She tried to yank free, unwilling to discuss it.

He held firm. "Because my phony glimpse into the future, tailored to what I know you want, reminded you that you do still believe in your dreams. And Europe isn't the only thing you want. You want the handsome stranger, the cottage and the children. You bought into it because you believe."

She opened her mouth to remind him that she couldn't have children. He seemed to read her mind and interrupted with, "Adopted children, foster children. Any kind of children."

"Let me go," she demanded coldly.

He did.

She slapped the five dollars back into his hand, reminding herself that it was for the school, then she hurried out. She ran into Letitia and Lavinia and the children, who all had corn dogs and pizza and invited her to join them. What she really wanted to do was run to her car, but she drew a deep breath, instead, noticed a family of six leaving one of the many picnic tables set up near the playground equipment and ushered everyone in that direction.

"Are you all right, dear?" Lavinia asked solicitously.

She smiled, nodded and swallowed the barbed anger she felt at the discovery that she did still want all those things she'd turned her back on. Which was insane, because all the effort to acquire them did was cause her pain.

She really could have slugged the phony Gypsy prince for reminding her of it.

CERTAIN HE'D JUST RUINED whatever fragment of chance remained that he could make a friend of Mariah Mercer, Cam put his beard back on, dusted off his turban and placed it on his head. Then he resumed his chair, tipped the snow globe on its head and righted it again, looking for his own future in it. He saw nothing in the lonely little cabin near the woods. And maybe that was prophetic, he thought unhappily.

He spotted a smudge on the glass, and as he rubbed it off with the sleeve of his robe, he heard the quiet clearing of a throat. He looked up to see Ashley standing just inside the door. She wore blue cotton pants and a white shirt with three little blue hearts on the pocket. A little white purse dangled from her shoulder. Her blond hair was pulled into one neat French braid. He wondered if Mariah had done it.

"Can you tell my fortune?" she asked eagerly.

He remembered what Mariah had mentioned about her, and felt a sudden sense of panic. He couldn't deny her, but he would have to handle this carefully. After the disaster with Mariah, he doubted his ability to do so.

"Yes, I can," he said. "Come in and sit down."

She opened her purse with distinctly feminine movements, then handed him a five-dollar bill. He gave her four dollars change.

"The sign says five dollars," she pointed out.

He nodded. "But we have a special rate for children because…ah…because they're smaller."

Her brow wrinkled. "It should cost more for children because there's more of a future for you to see."

After that astute observation, he doubted his ability to put anything over on her.

"I'm at kind of a crossroads," she said seriously, like one adult to another.

He listened intently. "I see."

"I've had a guardian since my parents died," she said, "and I don't see him very often. Everyone's trying to keep it a secret, but he's sick. He's going to die."

Cam did his best to remain in character. "I'm sorry."

"Yes, I am, too. Not that I ever got to spend much time with him. He couldn't really decide what to do with me."

Cam felt sorry for the unknown guardian. What was there to know about dealing with such a beautiful, precocious little girl? She sounded as though she'd have been grateful for any attention.

"What I was wondering about," she continued, leaning toward him conversationally, "is if you can see me getting new parents."

The question rendered him momentarily speechless.

"The Manor isn't taking boarding students next year, so when I leave at the end of next week, I won't be coming back. So…" She shrugged bony little shoulders in an artless acceptance of fate. "I wondered if I was going to get real parents, since I can't pretend to be Mariah's daughter anymore." She leaned forward to peer into the ball and asked, "How does that work, anyway? Can I see things, or just you?"

"Well…" He forced himself to try to analyze how best to reply. He could promise nothing, but there had to be a way he could give her hope. "Sometimes I see things," he said, tipping the ball, then righting it again. "And sometimes I don't. The ball usually only works for the one who owns it." That was probably Gypsy fortune-telling heresy—he wasn't sure.

"It's not a crystal ball." She expressed that as an observation rather than an accusation. "It's a snow globe."

"I read things in the snow," he replied, wondering if his crystal ball was the only thing she could see through.

But she seemed to accept that and settled down to listen.

"I see…" He thought frantically. "I see success in your future," he said. "You have a briefcase."

She frowned again. "I want to be a ballerina."

"Well…a successful ballerina will have a stock portfolio, appointments, fan mail to reply to." He looked up to smile at her. "And she might keep her ballet slippers in her briefcase."

Ashley giggled, liking that notion. "What else?" she asked, sitting forward.

"I see audiences applauding," he said, "and ballet companies fighting over you. And do you know why?"

Her blue eyes were wide with curiosity. "Why?"

"Because you've studied and worked so hard to learn

to dance and to conduct your own business that you're the best dancer in the world. You're a self-made woman."

"What does that mean?"

"That you did it on your own. That it wasn't because you had all kinds of people working for you. It was because you knew what you had to do to be good, and you did it."

She thought about that a moment, seemed undecided about whether it was good or bad, then asked with a disappointed wince, "So I'm not getting the parents?"

He looked her in the eye. "I can't see whether you do or not. It doesn't mean you won't, just that I can't see it. All I can tell you for sure is that you're going to grow up to be a woman who makes her own future."

"By studying hard."

"Yes. By figuring out what has to be done and doing it."

She considered that, then nodded. "By taking responsibility. Mariah always talks to us about that."

"She's right. And taking responsibility for your own life is the smartest thing you can do."

She agreed, yet appeared to remain somewhat dissatisfied. She reached for the globe, turned it over, shook it, then put it back on the table. "Would you look one more time?" she asked hopefully. "Just in case? Even parents with another kid would be good 'cause then I'd have a sister. Or a brother. A sister would be better, though. Do you see it?"

He looked closely until the snow settled, a pain in his heart for the wish he couldn't promise, the right every child should be able to count on.

He steeled himself and met her longing gaze. "I'm sorry," he said. "I can't see it. Remember that it doesn't mean you won't have it, just that I can't see it."

"How come," she asked politely, "you can see some things and not others?"

Good question. He sought frantically for an answer. "That's a mystery to me, too," he said finally. "It could be that the energy in the air today just isn't letting it come through." That sounded lame, even to him.

But the trusting little girl believed him. His heart ached even more.

She stood and pushed her chair up to the table as Mariah had taught the children to do in the kitchen at the carriage house. "Thank you very much," she said. "At least I know I'll be a ballerina because I'm going to work hard."

"That's right. Good luck, Ashley."

She turned on her way to the tent flap, her eyes wide. "You saw my name?"

"Yes, I did," he replied.

She took a step back toward him. "What's my last name?"

He couldn't remember if he'd ever heard it. He shook his head. "I didn't see that."

"Oh." She smiled. "That's okay. I thought if it was different from what it is now, I'd know if I was going to get parents. Bye."

"Bye." He watched the tent flap close as she disappeared, then collapsed into his chair. That interview had taken every nerve he possessed and tied it in a knot. How could a child like that not have everything she wanted? What kind of a world was it, anyway? He wanted answers.

The thought had no sooner formed than the tent flap opened again and Father Chabot, pastor of St. Anthony's, walked in with a five-dollar bill, which he slapped on the table in front of Cam.

"Do the Sox have a chance at the pennant this year or not?" The priest, a rotund, habitually cheerful man, sat across from him in everyday garb of slacks and plaid shirt.

Cam was sure the priest knew his identity. He had helped him with church projects and had dinner in the rectory on several occasions.

Cam worked his hands over the globe. "I can see it wouldn't be wise to put money on it, Father."

The priest laughed. "Your salvation's in jeopardy, son," he said.

Cam didn't have to look into the ball to know that was true.

CHAPTER NINE

MARIAH NOTICED THAT Ashley was pensive at dinner. While the other children happily devoured the cake Mariah had won, Ashley played with her piece, decorating the frosting with the tines of her fork.

"Don't like butter brickle?" Mariah asked.

Ashley sighed. "I guess I'm full."

Mariah put a hand diagnostically to the child's cheek. "Do you feel all right?"

"Yeah." Ashley pushed her plate away and took a long pull on her milk. She daintily wiped away the resultant milk mustache with her napkin. "Did you know," she asked, leaning back in her chair, "that you can make your life turn out any way you want it to?"

Mariah ignored the instinct to answer with a qualifier, deciding that life would do that soon enough without any help from her. The best thing she could do was strengthen Ashley's belief in that premise.

"Yes, I did."

"Do you know how to do it?"

Mariah smiled. Talking with children was always full of booby traps. "Um, I think you do it by studying hard so that you understand how things work, then by working hard so that you can get things done."

Ashley smiled, clearly delighted that she grasped the concept. "And by never giving up. Because if things get bad, you might be able to fix it if you're trying, but if you're not, then nothing good can happen."

Mariah nodded her approval, wondering where this philosophical thought had come from.

"Did you come to understand this all by yourself?" she asked.

Ashley shook her head. "The fortune-teller told me."

Mariah's heart punched her in the ribs. "He did?"

Ashley nodded, her right leg swinging as she reached for her milk again. She took a sip, then put the glass back, running her index finger along the stem of a flower decorating the side. "He couldn't tell me if I'm going to get parents, though."

Before Mariah could recover from her surprise at that statement, Ashley added with a very adult acceptance, "I know Mr. Kerwin is sick, and pretty soon he'll have to give me to someone else."

Mariah opened her mouth, wanting to offer all kinds of assurances that the man had her best interests at heart and would find her a wonderful family. But she knew she couldn't promise that. She was sure he cared about Ashley, but he also seemed to have little clue about what she needed.

"He also couldn't see whether I'm going to get a brother or a sister if I get a family."

"No. I imagine that would be hard to predict." Mariah tried to revive the anger she'd felt after her "reading" with Cam; however, the good advice he'd given Ashley made it impossible. "But you understand that the fortune-teller was just pretending. I mean, he wasn't really able to predict the future. He was just one of the men from St. Anthony's in a robe and a turban, trying to make money for the school. Just like all the other games at the fair."

Ashley sat up and leaned earnestly toward her. "No, I believed him. And he didn't tell me any lies. He said sometimes he can see stuff and sometimes he can't."

Mariah didn't want to do anything to diminish the good message Ashley had gotten out of the experience, but she felt called upon to repeat, "That was probably because he can't really do it. He was just pretending to help the school make money."

Ashley shook her head. "It's because sometimes the energy can't come through the air, or something."

"Really."

"It doesn't mean I won't get them," Ashley said, sounding hopeful. "Just that he can't see it. But he could tell that I'll get all the other stuff I want—like be a ballerina—if I take responsibility for my life. Just like you always say."

"Right," Mariah had to agree. "How much did he charge you?" she asked, wanting something to use against Cam for his using her dreams against her.

"Just a dollar," Ashley replied. "I told him I thought kids should be more expensive 'cause they have a bigger future to look into, but he said no. They get a deal 'cause they're kids."

"He did."

"Yeah." Ashley pulled her cake toward her and picked up her fork to attack it with new vigor.

"So, I'm going to believe that I'm gonna get parents, and maybe a sister, and when I grow up, I'm gonna be a ballerina." Ashley popped a forkful of cake into her mouth and chewed, nodding to herself as though everything she'd just explained to Mariah was settling inside her like a truth.

So. Cameron Trent had given Ashley hope—a valuable gift. Mariah gathered up the dishes, trying not to think about him. All he'd tried to do was give her hope, just as he'd done for Ashley, so it was hard to stay angry. But she'd been around long enough to know that even the most stalwart determination to achieve a particular goal could be thwarted by insurmountable facts. She'd given up on her dreams. It had been painful to discover they apparently hadn't given up on her.

She put a Disney movie in the DVD player and the children sprawled on the floor to watch.

Only Brian held back, lingering at the table over a second glass of milk.

"Tired?" Mariah asked, filling the dishwasher. "I hear you and the twins sank so many baskets at the free-throw booth that all the girls were after you for the stuffed animals you won."

He nodded, a wistful smile on his lips. "I'm gonna miss this kind of stuff. At home, everything's…" He shrugged, having difficulty expressing himself. "I don't know. Big. Fancy. They do a lot of stuff and it's for charity, too, but if we go, we always have to get dressed up and smile for the cameras and my mom talks to reporters or other actors. I usually walk around by myself and wish I was here, instead, where it's small and friendly."

Mariah's heart ached for him. She went to sit beside him and gave him the last piece of cake. "I know what you mean. Sometimes I feel out of place at parties."

Baby showers, particularly. Or children's birthday parties. "But it doesn't usually last very long. And chances are your mom will look for another small private school like this one, where they'll do a lot of the small-town things we do here."

He gave her a skeptical look, then leaned back in his chair and studied the cupboards. "These cabinets aren't that old. I wonder if the gold's behind them."

THE SECOND DAY OF THE spring fair dawned sunny and warm, and the children were up early, looking forward to another day of playing games and eating junk food. Mariah had to admit that she wouldn't mind a second plate of curly fries herself.

She divided the cash earned from the signs they'd helped with and distributed it among them.

The Lightfoot sisters again took the children for the day so that Mariah could man her booth. She restocked her display, delighted by the number of signs she'd sold. She'd even dug out her Christmas stock, knowing that for some shoppers, it was never too early.

Parker leaned around the corner of her booth to hand her a paper cup with a lid. "Mocha," she said. "Figured I owe you for the iced tea yesterday. Want a muffin? I've got those sour cream-blueberry ones from Perk Avenue."

"Yum." Mariah left her booth to step into Parker's. It was time for the fair to open, but the real crowd wouldn't arrive until after the ten-thirty mass—another five minutes.

Parker handed Mariah a muffin in a little white box, a golf-ball-size dollop of whipped butter included. Her sister appeared a bit flushed this morning, Mariah thought as she dug into a paper bag for napkins and plastic forks. They sat on two folding chairs Parker had placed against the side of her booth.

"You look a little…" Mariah tried to analyze her sister's expression.

Parker glanced at her, then away, obviously embarrassed. Mariah watched her in surprise, thinking that Parker was usually so open about her thoughts and behavior that nothing gave her pause.

Then Parker stared her right in the eye and seemed unable to stop smiling. Mariah remembered she'd had a date.

"He was Mel Gibson in disguise?" Mariah guessed playfully.

Parker giggled. "Better than that. He was just Gary Warren."

"Ah." Mariah found herself smiling, too. "It went well?"

Parker took a bite of muffin and chewed slowly, clearly buying time. Mariah waited patiently.

Parker looked into Mariah's eyes again and this time flushed bright red. "He is the nicest, dearest, sexiest man I have ever met. I'm in love."

Mariah felt obliged to ask, "Park, does he have his own money?"

"He does landscaping and gardening for Whitcomb's Wonders—I told you that."

Mariah nodded. "Why doesn't he go out on his own?"

"Because he has two teenagers, and Hank's willing to schedule him so that he can be around for them. But they'll both be in Europe for the month of June—one of those school-exchange things." She smiled again, then just as quickly frowned. "They were very polite, but it was hard to tell if they liked me or not."

Mariah made a face at her. "How could anyone not like you? Where's their mother?"

"Died five years ago of a heart attack. She'd always been frail. Mariah." Parker's eyes grew wide with the intensity of her feelings. "I know my track record is questionable, but he's so…special! And—miracle of miracles—he thinks I am, too."

Mariah wrapped her left arm around her, careful of the mocha she held in that hand. "Only because you are. I'm excited for you, sis, but…you know. Be careful. It's a little early yet, and two teenagers—I mean, that's major lifestyle adjustment."

Mariah sighed. "Uh-huh. I'm trying to keep a cool head. But you know how I am about love. It just fills me up and spills over and I want to give everyone everything." Before Mariah could suggest caution again, Parker cut her off with a vigorous nod. "I've managed to be interested but calm. Even when he told me he loved me, I kept my feelings to myself. I told him we'd only dated once, even though we've known each other for months and talk about important things all the time."

"He told you he loved you?"

Parker blushed anew. "He was very firm about it. He said he's watched me for months and was sure someone younger and richer would snap me up." She wrinkled her nose. "Isn't that cute?"

Mariah had to nod, unable to cast a shadow on her delight. "Very cute. When are you seeing him again?"

"Tonight," Parker replied. "He and the kids are coming here this afternoon, then we're going to the fried chicken dinner in the parish hall."

"Oh!" Mariah was meeting Letitia, Lavinia and the children there. "Then you can introduce me." She had to see this paragon for herself. Parker was simply not trustworthy where men were concerned. By her own admission, she fell in love quickly and hard, only to wake up a year or two later alone and disillusioned—and broke!

The church bell rang, and within minutes the crowd began to thicken. Mariah closed the box on the half muffin remaining, swallowed her last sip of mocha and gave Parker a supportive hug. "Good luck today," she said.

Mariah went back to her booth, where she did a brisk business, even selling more of her Christmas signs. It was midafternoon before things slowed down.

Parker peered around the corner, her expression pleading. "If you watch my booth for a few minutes, I'll go find us something for lunch."

Parker had taught her the basics of massage, but her sister had a rare touch. "You brought breakfast. I should buy lunch."

"No, no. The choir mothers are selling German dogs. Doesn't that sound good?"

"Yes. And you want to share a plate of curly fries?"

"Absolutely."

Mariah reached for her purse, but Parker was gone before she could dig out her wallet. She pinned the curtains back between their booths with a large clothespin so that she could move easily from one to the other.

There was no action in her booth, so she occupied herself by straightening her display. She had only half a dozen signs left—two longer, and therefore more expensive, ones; two Christmas signs encouraging snow; and two signs the children had helped with.

She heard a throat clear behind her and turned, a welcoming smile on her face—to see Cam standing next to Parker's massage chair.

CAM HAD NEVER MET a woman who could kill a smile as quickly as Mariah could. He ignored her sudden frown and said politely, "I have a two-thirty appointment."

"Parker hasn't been making appointments here," she said.

"She did for me," he insisted.

"Well, she's gone for about fifteen minutes," she replied, equally polite, if a little stiff.

He glanced at his watch. "I'm supposed to be at city hall in half an hour. Some problem in a bathroom on the second floor."

Her eyes went to the ten-dollar bill in his hand and devotion to her sister apparently overtook her unwillingness to help him. He had to give himself credit for that. From across the midway, he'd seen her watching both booths and guessed waving cash around—cash her sister could use—might earn him a little one-on-one with her. She made him nuts when he wasn't with her; he might as well go for stark-raving mad when he was.

She took the ten from him, spread a clean towel on the top of a chair that looked like some exotic bicycle without wheels and beckoned him to it.

He knelt astride it, waiting for it to collapse under him. Mercifully, it didn't.

She patted the little shelf where she'd placed the towel. "Rest your head here."

He made a production of looking up and around. "Is there a blade that's going to come down from somewhere and behead me?"

He could see that she wanted to smile but wouldn't give him the satisfaction.

"If you have an appointment, we really don't have time for comedy, do we?"

"There's always time for comedy," he said, placing his right cheek on the towel. "Some of us have just forgotten how to laugh. Stay off my ribs. I'm ticklish."

Something changed inside him the moment her fingertips touched him. He'd tried to be hopeful and positive despite his childhood and the Allison experience, but he knew old grudges had hidden in corners, gotten lost inside with old memories.

Mariah's hands in the middle of his back, between his shoulder blades, seemed to touch those places. He knew it was probably wishful thinking on his part. Old injuries didn't simply disappear under the hands of a woman who didn't even like him—even though he wanted to think she did. But as her hands worked over him in firm but gentle circles, he swore he felt edges soften inside him, barbs being smoothed away.

"Why didn't you go into massage, too?" he asked. His mind was trying to put another spin on this experience, and he had to keep talking to distract himself. He could remember her in the middle of his bed, and the long strokes of her hands down his sides now made him wonder how they'd feel without the barrier of a shirt. "Wouldn't it be easier than taking care of children?"

"Life's not supposed to be about doing the easy thing," she said, leaning into the massage. Her touch was now almost punitive. "You made that pretty clear to Ashley, Gypsy prince, son of Othar."

"She's a beautiful little girl," he said, preparing to defend himself for his "reading" to her. "And I didn't promise her anything. I just—"

"She told me all about it," she interrupted. He felt her knuckles under his shoulder blades. "You told her she was in control of her own life and that she'd get what she wanted if she worked hard for it. That was very good advice."

He sat up with a hand to his heart and she stood back worriedly. "What? Oh, God, did I hurt something? A rib? I know how to do this, but I push too—"

He caught her wrist to stop her. "Did you just compliment me?" he asked.

She expelled a breath and rolled her eyes, clearly relieved that he wasn't injured. He allowed himself to be flattered by that.

"I believe I did," she admitted, pushing on his shoulders until his cheek was on the towel. "But that doesn't mean anything. I'm sure I'll be completely annoyed with you again any time now."

"I'm sorry about your reading," he said quietly as she worked down his spinal column with gentle pressure. "I didn't mean to embarrass you, just to...give you your dreams."

A sturdy blow struck his right shoulder. He guessed

it was more therapeutic for her than for him. "That isn't within your power to do," she said.

"Maybe it is."

A similar blow struck his left shoulder. "I'm telling you it's not. There. Finished."

He sat up, rubbing a hand where that last blow had landed. Now he was annoyed. Her touch was so delicious. How could her brain be so out of sync with it?

"You know, just because you spend your days telling little children what they can and can't do," he said, "you shouldn't delude yourself into thinking it works with me."

She blinked at him in mild surprise, taking a step backward when he stood.

He stepped toward her. "You're not the only one who's had your dreams ripped out of you, you know. But they're plans for tomorrow, and if you let them go or let them die, then you go backward. There's no standing still in life. Time keeps moving."

She stared at him, apparently trying to decide between anger at his presumption and acceptance of the truth of what he'd said. He should have known which she'd choose.

She put on a haughty expression and tapped the face of her watch. "Then you should be moving on to city hall."

Now really annoyed, he caught her wrist and hauled her with him into her booth.

"What do you think you're doing?" she demanded, trying to yank free of him. He held on.

"Buying a sign," he said, reaching for a long one he'd admired several times as he'd walked by unnoticed.

Live Well, Laugh Often, Love Much, it read. It had made him decide to buy Hank's house.

He finally freed her hand to reach for his wallet.

She wrapped the sign in tissue and thrust it at him.

He handed her several bills.

"Thank you," she said stiffly.

"You're welcome," he replied. "Will you have dinner with me tonight in the parish hall?"

He asked her simply to torture himself. When things were impossible, he loved to push them just a little further to show himself he could survive.

"I'm meeting the Lightfoot sisters and the children there." Her arms were folded belligerently, but there was a different message in her eyes. One she probably understood no better than he did. He was considering whether to accept her rejection or suggest another time and place, when she said with an almost defiant squaring of her shoulders, "You can sit with us."

It took him a second to get over the initial shock, then he nodded casually. "Good. I'll be by for you at closing."

"Fine."

He was afraid to think of this as progress, but he couldn't help it. God. He was turning into an optimist!

PARKER RUSHED INTO the booth holding two paper trays containing German dogs with sauerkraut and curly fries with ketchup. She stopped just inside the booth to frown at her sister. "What happened?" she demanded. "Your cheeks are purple."

"Nothing happened," Mariah replied calmly, taking one of the trays. "But if you're going to make appointments to give massages, you shouldn't walk away for fifteen minutes when one is due. Did you bring drinks?"

"I didn't make any appointments." Parker turned sideways so that Mariah could see the can of soda protruding from the pocket of her slacks. "What are you talking about?"

Mariah fell into one of the folding chairs, rested the tray in her lap and popped the top on her can of diet cola. She had to do something about that man. "Cam said he had a two-thirty appointment with you. I had to do the massage because he couldn't wait until you got back. He had a job."

Parker raised an eyebrow at her gullibility. "And you think I'm the one with no defenses." She grinned before taking a bite of curly fry. "I walked right past him when I went to find our lunch. He knew I was gone."

Mariah really wanted to be angry. But all she could remember was the warm, tight muscle under her hands, the sturdy structure of his back and shoulders, the impulse to lean against him and close her eyes that she'd almost succumbed to.

She didn't know why she had invited him to join their table tonight. Her mind, which had once been very organized and determined, was now muddled and wishy-washy. She hated that.

"He's joining me and the kids and Letitia and Lavinia tonight at the dinner. Why don't you and Gary Warren and his kids sit with us?" She felt the need for reinforcements. "I promise not to cramp your style. You can go off together as soon as dinner's over. I imagine his kids will be staying for the rock band in the gym."

Parker smiled widely, her expression one of longing.

"That'd be great. When things were crazy with Mom and Dad and we were stuck out on the farm, even though I loved the life, I was a young teenager and sure I'd never meet anybody."

Mariah tried to relate that information to their present conversation and couldn't quite do it.

Parker put her cold can of soda to her cheek as she stared ahead of her. "And I wanted so much to meet someone. I wanted to get married and have children so that when you got married, I'd already have a house with a big yard and we could all have Sunday dinner together, and our children could play together and have one another for support as they grew up." She turned to Mariah with a sigh. "Wouldn't that be just perfect?"

Mariah understood that Parker had no clue she was torturing her. So she simply nodded, finding it easy to buy into that dream. It was what she'd imagined when she'd gotten married—families reaching from the past to the future, an ongoing stream of love and support. It was hard to realize that that stopped with her.

A couple of boys ran by, shouting to each other, and Parker seemed to snap back to reality. She blinked at Mariah, as though just realizing what she'd said. "That didn't hurt you, did it? I mean, even though we're still childless, I want to believe that one day our kids will play together and we'll have those Sunday dinners."

Mariah smiled. "I'm sure you can have that, and I'd love to come as long as I can be the eccentric bachelor-girl aunt who brings back presents from exotic places."

Parker gave her an impatient look. "That isn't what you want and…" She raised a hand for silence before Mariah could interrupt with a denial. "It isn't, and you know it. You're beginning to want Cam. I can see it in your face."

Oh, God, Mariah thought. Could *he?*

"It may be what I want," she admitted in a whisper, making sure no one else could hear, "but I know I can't have it. He'll want his own children, and I don't want to deprive him of them."

"Maybe he wants you more."

Mariah rolled her eyes. "I don't think so. We barely tolerate each other."

"Because you can't find a way to deal with the attraction. It's there, but you don't like it when it hurts, so you keep trying to put it away. Love isn't that manageable."

"Yeah, well, love and attraction are not the same thing."

"Maybe, but when you're obviously experiencing both, you'd better find a way to deal with your desire for him before it chomps its way out of you like some extraplanetary monster."

Mariah turned to her sister at that dramatic metaphor, the tension easing. "That's a little theatrical even for you. Each of us will find our way. Just don't try to force on me what you want for yourself. I'll be fine. I've been wanting to go to Europe for so long."

"You're going to be lonely," Parker predicted.

Mariah shook her head. "I'm going to find myself."

Parker growled impatiently. "You're so lost the CIA wouldn't be able to find you."

CHAPTER TEN

ST. ANTHONY'S PARISH HALL, festooned with crepe paper streamers in blue and gold—the school's colors—was bursting with patrons for the chicken dinner. The laughter and conversation were so loud that Cam had to put his lips to Mariah's ear to be heard. He didn't mind that at all.

Earlier, he'd stopped by her booth, intending to help her and Parker take down their pavilions, only to find that Gary Warren and his kids were already there, pulling Parker's apart.

Gary had spotted him, and with a broad smile held a post in one hand as he reached out with the other to shake his hand. Cam had moved forward to help Parker, struggling with a large box of oils and ointments.

"How'd it go?" he'd asked, taking the box from her.

"Very well," she'd replied, her cheeks pink, her eyes alight. "I made a small fortune, and Mariah sold just about everything she brought with her."

Mariah had looked up from the screen she was folding. "Okay, how come she has all the help? Is my abs exercise tape finally working and I look as though I don't need any?"

Gary's kids had hurried to help her. Jeff was a senior at Maple Hill High, and Stacey, a junior. They were redheaded and tall—attributes stocky, dark-haired Gary said they'd acquired from their mother.

Cam had wondered what Gary was doing here, then saw a look pass between him and Parker that made it pretty clear. Romance was in bloom.

"I'll take that to the car for her," Gary had offered. Cam had handed it over and watched them walk away, exchanging some private remark that made them laugh.

He'd turned back to the tent and caught Mariah watching them, too, her expression difficult to read. He'd been unable to tell if she approved of the relationship or not.

He still couldn't tell, though they'd all come together to the parish hall. They'd met up with the Lightfoot sisters and the children, and were now part of a line of people waiting to be served that stretched out the door.

Gary and Parker were ahead of them, separated from them by Brian and the twins. Gary's kids had joined their friends, Letitia and Lavinia were sitting at a table with Mr. Groman and the girls were clustered around Cam and Mariah, giggling over some treasure they'd won at the coin toss.

"You don't like him?" Cam asked Mariah, having to get so close to make himself heard that he felt the fragrant silkiness of her hair against his cheek and his nose.

She turned in surprise. "Who?"

"Gary."

"Yes, I do like him," she corrected. "I just worry about her."

"She seems very capable to me. And isn't she older than you are?"

"Yes. But she's all heart and falls in love very quickly. I don't want her to be disappointed again." She stood on tiptoe to ask him, "Do you know him very well?" Her lips bumped his earlobe and he had to put an arm around her to steady her as the line moved forward. Pretending to remain unaffected took considerable effort.

"As well as co-workers do. I'm not familiar with gardening, but he appears to be very good at it. They've hired him to do summer flower baskets on the square, and to put flowers around the Minuteman and his lady."

She nodded. "His kids seem sweet and well adjusted."

"He does a lot with them. He's always trying to schedule work around their games and activities."

"Good fathers aren't always good husbands, though."

"I'm sure that's true. But Gary appears to be an all-around nice guy." He grinned. "Maybe you'll have to get him alone and interrogate him to find out the truth. You're pretty scary when you want to be."

He was surprised when she smiled. "That doesn't seem to have put you at a distance."

He shrugged. "If you survive a bad childhood, you grow up fearless. You've already stared into the face of stuff most people never have to deal with."

Their discussion was interrupted suddenly when Mariah, counting noses, realized Brian was missing. "Where did he go?" she asked Peter.

He shrugged. "I don't know. I was at the dessert table."

Mariah stepped out of line to peer down the length of it. There was no sign of the boy. She groaned.

"Maybe he went to the bathroom," Cam suggested. "I'll check."

"I'll look outside." She caught Parker's arm. "Will you and Gary keep an eye on the kids for me? Brian's missing."

Cam dodged the crowd to hurry to the men's room at the far end of the hall. He was instantly rewarded with Brian's reflection in the long mirror over a bank of sinks. The boy washed his hands halfheartedly, then yanked down a wad of paper towels.

"Brian," Cam said, walking into the room. It was lit by the harsh glare of overhead fluorescents and smelled of antiseptic. "Are you all right? We didn't know where you'd gone."

The boy wasn't wearing his usual irrepressible smile. He seemed grim. "I told Pete," he said.

"He was busy checking out the dessert table and didn't hear you. Mariah was afraid something had happened to you."

Brian shook his head. "I'm fine. But the fair's over and that's kind of…you know…the end."

Cam put an arm around his shoulders and led him toward the door. "The end?"

"Of the school year. We're not coming back, you know."

"Yes, I heard that."

Brian stopped in the doorway and gazed up at Cam. "Can we go outside for a minute?"

"Sure. Mariah's out there looking for you."

They stepped out into the twilight. The playground and parking area, which had been so lively just an hour ago, was now bare of the colorful tents and booths. But the stir of conversation remained where people were still putting things away in their cars, calling to one another and laughing.

"I like the trees here," Brian said, looking around him. "At home they're all palms. Some are pretty, but they don't move like these do. Kind of like somebody's dancing."

Cam drew the boy to a bench near the parish hall doorway and sat down. "You'll make friends at another school, Brian," he said, thinking that though the boy's situation was very different, he reminded him of himself. Lots of people moved around in Brian's life, but no one knew how to change his situation, so he was still isolated and alone. Cam caught the boy's neck in the crook of his arm and pretended to squeeze. "You're a nice kid when you're not making holes in the bathroom wall and falling out of the attic."

Brian grinned reluctantly. "The gold's gotta be in the carriage house somewhere."

"Maybe someone's found it and never told anybody, on the chance he'd have to give it back."

"If it was a kid, he'd be too excited not to tell. And the carriage house has been a kids' dorm since they started using cars instead of horses." He gazed up at Cam and asked seriously, "Do you remember that?"

Cam tightened his elbow. "No, I don't remember that. It had to be eighty years ago. Do I look that old?"

Brian laughed, the sound the first childlike thing Cam had heard out of him since he'd found him.

Cam released him, but his smile lingered. "I'm probably not gonna find it," Brian added, "but I like to think about it. So does Ashley. We're going to spend a whole week going on all the rides at Disneyland."

"Then what?"

"I want to live there, but Ashley says we can't. So we'll go to Disney World in Florida. Then there's a new place in Europe. Mariah said she might go there on her trip." Brian sighed. "If I find the gold, I'm going with her." He grinned knowingly at Cam. "You'd like to come, too, wouldn't ya? You like her a lot."

"Yes, I do. But she seems to think she'd enjoy the trip more all by herself."

That didn't upset Brian. "Then you and me'll go and we'll just follow her around. Maybe we'll bring Ashley. She's a girl, but she can walk the playground fence without falling off. And she pitches like a guy."

"Sounds like a plan." Cam made himself add, "But you should also have a plan if you *don't* find the gold."

Brian shrugged, looking out into the darkening parking lot. "Then I guess Mariah goes to Europe, you stay here and finish work on the Manor's plumbing and Ashley and I go back to where we always go. At least for the summer. Then we'll have to find new schools."

He sounded accepting of his situation. Cam remembered how awful he'd felt having to accept the unacceptable because there was no way out. He, at least, had had siblings in the same boat. Brian was an only child. Granted, he had more material things than Cam had had, but material things would not have eased his desperate longing for one kind word from either parent.

He gently put a hand to Brian's back. "This is going to sound like a long, long time to you," he said, "but one day you'll look around and realize that you're eighteen, and you can make your own decisions about what you want to do. So make sure you're prepared for when that day comes. Don't learn any bad habits, and be smart so you can take yourself wherever you want to go."

Brian nodded without enthusiasm. "Yeah."

Cam spotted Mariah wandering around the parking lot, scanning the people coming and going. He stood and waved in her direction. "Mariah!" he called. "Over here!"

She ran toward them, the folds of her long cotton skirt moving gracefully around her ankles. "Is he all right?" she demanded, leaning over Brian and lifting his chin in her hand. "Are you okay, sweetie?"

"I'm fine," Brian assured her. "I just went to the bathroom. I told Pete, but I guess he didn't hear me."

She put a hand to her heart and breathed a sigh of relief. Then she caught Brian's hand and pulled him to his feet. "Come on, we're missing dinner."

In a gesture she seemed completely unaware of, she caught Cam's arm and drew him along, too. He told himself to attach no importance to it, and while he accepted that intelligently, his heart couldn't help the cheerful suspicion that he was wearing her down.

IT LOOKED TO MARIAH as though Cam, Gary, Jeff and the children had eaten enough chicken to nullify the intent of the fund-raiser. They all went back several times for more meat, more beans, more corn bread.

Hank, Jackie and their children were seated with the Megraths at the table behind them.

"We're clearing up in a little while for dancing," Hank said to Cam. "We need volunteers."

"I thought the dance was in the gym?" Cam replied.

"That's for the teenagers. This one's for us mature types."

Cam laughed. "Mature? I've seen you push Evan Braga into the lake while on a run rather than let him pass you."

Hank dismissed the incident with a shake of his head. "We had a bet on who could do the fastest lap. There was money at stake. And I meant mature in age. Are you staying to dance?"

Cam turned to Mariah. "Are we staying to dance?"

She searched her brain for an excuse. She'd love to stay and dance with him, and that convinced her that she shouldn't. "I have the children—" she began.

But Hank interrupted. "So does almost everyone here. Some of the teenage girls have set up child care in a couple of the classrooms. We suggest generous tipping, since they're missing the teen dance to do this for us."

Her excuse demolished, Mariah finally nodded. "Sure." She smiled blandly at Cam. "But *you* have to tip the girls. I'm saving my money to go to Europe, remember?" She wanted to remind him—and herself—that despite the cozy weekend of community effort and tonight's camaraderie, she was moving on.

"How could I forget? You find a way to insert it in every conversation."

"Just want you to bear it in mind."

He nailed her with a glance. Hank and Gary were talking now, and everyone else around them was engaged in other conversations.

"Or maybe you have to keep telling yourself you're planning to go," he said softly, "because you no longer want to leave as badly as you used to."

She was shocked that he'd picked up on her vacillation. She'd done everything she could to pretend it wasn't there.

"Maple Hill was always only a temporary stop for me," she said, her voice less firm than she'd intended. "And my job at the Manor is finished."

"You said Letitia wanted to give you another position."

"It's the ideal time to leave. If I'm going to go, I should go now."

He nodded in amiable agreement. "As long as you're going for the right reasons."

Suddenly, there was a great commotion as Father Chabot stood in the outside doorway and invited the teens to move to the gym, where the band could be heard warming up.

As they streamed out, six girls organized at the other end of the hall and asked that all the children staying for child care gather around them.

Mariah collected her group and took them to the girls as the men began moving tables.

"I didn't know you were staying to dance," Ashley said. "Are you gonna dance with Cam?"

"Probably cheek to cheek," Brian said, catching Julia's hand when she lagged behind. Erica and Rachel Whitcomb followed, each carrying one of their twin brothers. Sister Mary Alice and Sister Theresa from the school were watching infants in the convent.

"No speculating on my love life," Mariah scolded him with a smile. "You guys are all going to be charming and cooperative for the girls, right?"

"Right," they replied in unison.

Mariah turned to Brian, needing extra assurance. "Please, Brian. Promise me you won't look for gold."

He rolled his eyes at her. "I won't. Besides, Debbie Bonatello is one of the girls watching us. Her little brother's in my class. She's a babe. I've wanted to get to know her for a long time."

"Okay, but remember to be polite. I wouldn't call her a babe to her face."

"I know that!"

"Good. That's the sign of a gentleman."

As the girls and the nuns left the room with the children, the atmosphere in the hall changed dramatically. The noise level quieted, tables were folded, and while the men whisked them away to be stored in the basement, the women lined the chairs and benches up along the side of the room. A group of four of Maple Hill's senior citizens, two men and two women who called themselves Golden Oldies, gathered on the stage.

Someone brought them chairs, turned on the stage lights, put a table nearby with a water pitcher and glasses.

The hall lights were dimmed and the Oldies leaned into a circle to tune their instruments. As Hank appeared to wrap his arms around Jackie, and Parker and Gary wandered away, completely unaware of Mariah's presence, Mariah found herself feeling alone. And it wasn't simply the loneliness of solitude, but the loneliness of not being part of a couple.

One moment she was startled, even horrified that she recognized the feeling for what it was, then Cam appeared and she forgot everything except how gorgeous he was in jeans and an Amherst sweatshirt, and how happy she was that he was back.

The music started, a sweet rendition of "Embraceable You," and he opened his arms. She walked into them without hesitation, realizing this as a rare moment that should be enjoyed without too much analysis.

Cam intended to find a topic of conversation that would relax her, help her feel they'd put aside their customary antagonism, but there wasn't time. The instant she walked into his arms he felt her lean into him. There was none of the stiffness he'd expected, no resistance to the intimacy of dancing together. She wrapped her arms around his neck, rested her forehead against his chin and seemed to dissolve into his embrace.

He couldn't think, simply gave himself over to the romantic Gershwin music, the unexpected pleasure of the moment, and danced away with her.

He recognized the evening as a turning point. Up to now, he'd been attracted to Mariah, challenged by her, intrigued, even excited by her physically and emotionally. He'd thought he *might* be falling in love.

Tonight, he knew it with a certainty that changed his perception of everything. As she relaxed in his arms for reasons known only to her, he realized with the sudden brightness of an epiphany that she *was* his.

All he had to do now was make sure she understood that he was hers.

Throughout the evening, their friends changed partners, changed back again, sat on the sidelines to talk, then danced once more. But Cam and Mariah remained wrapped in each other's arms in a small shadowy corner of the floor, moving slowly to the nostalgic tunes the Golden Oldies preferred, not noticing when they played the occasional up-tempo number.

Cam saw things in Mariah's eyes he hadn't seen before. He saw her as she could be with her defenses lowered, sweet and trusting and open.

She made him feel refreshed and renewed, as though this second chance at his life in Maple Hill might really be a new lease on happiness.

Just after ten, she drew away from him with obvious regret. "I have to get the children home," she said, her hands still linked with his.

He felt sixteen. He felt ageless.

Parting from her was the last thing he wanted, but he understood her responsibilities. He was about to tell her he'd take her and the children home, when Letitia appeared beside them.

"You two keep dancing," she said, waving plump hands at them. "Vinnie and I are going to take the children to the dorm and stay so you can enjoy your evening."

Mariah tried to protest. "But you've watched them all weekend. I can't…"

"And you've watched them day and night for months." Letitia patted her cheek. "Don't hurry home. We don't intend to wait up. You two have a wonderful time, stay up to watch the sunrise, whatever you want to do. Don't worry about the kids." Then she walked away.

"I feel so guilty," Mariah said to Cam.

He leaned down and kissed her soundly. "Don't waste time on that. She wants you to enjoy yourself. Come on." He swirled her away, then was forced to stop abruptly when the music changed to a rumba.

Everyone on the dance floor looked at everyone else, the style uncharacteristic for the Golden Oldies. But

Gary and Parker were getting into it, and Hank and Jackie made a brave attempt. Haley, apparently feeling too pregnant to try, led Bart off the floor.

"Can you rumba?" Mariah asked Cam with a grin.

"No," he replied honestly, noting the spark of laughter in her eyes and thinking this night was indeed a miracle. "Can you?"

She nodded. "I dated a boy from Cuba in college. It's simple. It's just a matter of step, close, step." She demonstrated. "Shifting your weight and moving your hips."

She demonstrated again, putting her hips into it this time as she turned. She held her arms out, feet and hands keeping the rhythm, her hips in the simple cotton skirt taking him to the edge of apoplexy.

She caught his hands, encouraging him to move with her. He had to struggle to concentrate.

The number was over before they were able to move in sync and she collapsed against him laughing when the Oldies picked up with a romantic rendition of "Cape Cod Bay."

"We'll have to work on that," she said, sounding a little breathless. "I'd forgotten how much fun the rumba can be. Or just how much fun dancing can be."

He had to agree. "I haven't had the opportunity to do that much since high school. Most of the functions my wife and I attended were more formal and serious."

Mariah nodded. "We did lots of things with Ben's family. They were very nice, but there were so many of them there wasn't time or room in our lives for friends. I think that's why he wanted his own children so desperately. He must have felt like a failure in his big family."

The thought seemed to eclipse her mood.

"Let's not talk about our exes," he said, hating to lose the wonder of this night. "Did I tell you I'm buying Hank's house on the lake?"

"No." She looked at him with interest. "Don't he and Jackie live near downtown?"

"They do. That's Jackie's place. In his bachelor days, Hank bought a great place on the far side of the lake. But the house in town works better for Jackie's job as mayor and for the children, so he's selling it to me and they're going to find something a little farther away for a weekend and holiday getaway. You have to come and see it. He's already given me the key, but we don't sign papers for a few more days, so I hate to go in until it's mine."

"Fred will like that," she predicted with a smile.

"I'm sure he will. It's a great place for children and pets."

She didn't tune out when he mentioned children. "Do you fish?" she asked.

"Not successfully, no. But I plan to improve my technique after I move in. I just bought a four-man rowboat from Jimmy Elliott."

"Just sunbathing on a boat would be nice."

"Then I'll have to get something in the yacht class. That might take a while. But you can sunbathe on the deck of the house."

He saw reality struggle to take control in her eyes. She sighed, possibly trying to fend it off. "Are you going to have a housewarming when you're finally in?"

"Good idea," he praised. "You can help me. Your children should all be on their way home by then."

She looked cautious and opened her mouth to reply, but he forestalled her with "Don't tell me you'll be on your way to Europe. I'm working on a fantasy here."

She smiled—the curve of her lips both sweet and sad. "Okay. We'll say I'll help you. I presume you're talking cooking and not housecleaning."

"Right. We've got someone at Whitcomb's who's already agreed to clean for me in exchange for the occasional barbecue."

"Now, there's an arrangement. Can I work the same bargain?"

He kissed her. "It's a deal."

"Aren't we supposed to seal it with a handshake?" she asked, laughing.

His hands rested lightly in the middle of her back and he pressed gently. He wouldn't have moved hers, wrapped around his neck, for all the gold in the treasury. "Not when our hands are otherwise occupied."

She looked into his eyes, the expression in hers changing from levity to seriousness without warning, then she tightened her grip on him, leaned her head against him and fell silent.

He held her tightly, feeling the night slip away from him and willing to do anything to hold on to it.

CHAPTER ELEVEN

THE GOLDEN OLDIES PLAYED "Good Night, Sweetheart" at 2:00 a.m. Cam and Mariah, the Megraths, the Whitcombs and Parker and Gary met at the sparsely occupied Breakfast Barn for coffee. Two young busboys pulled a couple of tables together and the group settled in, high on friendship and good cheer.

"I haven't been up this late on noncity business," Jackie said, "since before Rachel was born."

"Me, either." Gary seated Parker, then sat beside her. "The last time I was up after midnight was New Year's Eve, 1995. I remember because Jeff, who was nine at the time, had climbed onto the roof to blow my old bosun's pipe, fell off and broke his leg and mine."

While everyone else sympathized, Jackie laughed. "Kids do make dates memorable. I remember my thirtieth birthday because my girls gave me chicken pox."

A waitress appeared amid the laughter and groans and they were forced to concentrate on their menus instead of the conversation. But the moment she left it began again.

Mariah listened quietly to one story after another of how children made even usually ordinary occasions momentous. She glanced at Bart to see if he was af-

fected by the reminiscences. She knew he'd lost his unborn twins when his first wife had died.

But he was laughing, his pregnant wife apparently
blunting the pain and loss of the past. Even Haley had
a story about the baby giving her morning sickness
when she interviewed the governor of the state, who
was visiting Maple Hill.

Parker seemed to find Gary's stories endlessly amus-
ing. His children appeared to like her, and she claimed
to like them. If this relationship between Parker and
Gary worked out, the children wouldn't be a problem.

Cam, too, laughed at their stories.

That was a good thing, she thought, as she regained
emotional equilibrium after her fantasy evening. She'd
indulged herself with the pretense that she and Cam had
nothing to worry about but each other, and she'd found
it delicious. Now she had to remember the truth.

She couldn't have children. She wasn't whining or
engaging in self-pity; she was simply reminding herself
of the very real barrier to Cam's happiness—and her
own.

Should she develop a serious relationship with Cam
and they got married, he would be odd man out on
every occasion like this. Every time men pulled their
wallets out to show off photos of children stamped with
their features, he'd have to simply watch and listen
rather than participate. Whenever parents talked about
the fearless boy who took after his father, or the girl who
wanted to be president because she was just like her
brilliant mother, he would have to sit back quietly.

That had been so clear to her when Ben had left, but
in her loneliness recently, she'd forgotten how that in-

ability to reproduce struck at the heart of a man. It had once struck at her own heart, but she'd adjusted. It was harder for a man, though. He thought of himself as the link between past and future, and if he loved *her,* the chain would be broken.

Though she kept an outward appearance of cheer for the sake of their companions, she felt sadness settle inside her like a cold brick.

When they finally all said goodbye at 3:30 a.m., Cam took her back to the school parking lot to pick up her car. The place was dark and deserted now, with not even the sound of insects on the air. Everything was asleep.

He walked around his truck to open her door. She rose out of the vehicle and into his arms as naturally as if they were on their honeymoon. He felt the urgency in her as she clung to him.

"Don't go to the Manor," he whispered, kissing her cheek, her eyes, her lips. "Come home with me. I'll bring you back in time to get the kids ready for school. I promise."

She returned his kisses, held him one extra moment, then dropped her arms, her voice calm but firm. "I can't," she said. Then she looked into his eyes, her own filled with an unsettling resolve. "Cameron, you have to understand me when I tell you this isn't going to work. I'm going to be gone, and the best thing you can do for yourself is find someone who can be everything you need."

He knew this speech. He'd heard it several times in one form or another since the night he'd rescued her from Brian's flood.

It exasperated him, and it terrified him. He wanted to shake her for presuming to think she knew what he wanted, and he wished there were some way to make it clear to her that his future would be even colder than his past if she wasn't in it.

But she might already know that. That was probably why she insisted on pushing him away. She knew that what they shared was significant, and she didn't want to take the chance that it might hurt her.

"I don't need you to be anything for me except what you need to be for yourself." He realized there was little point in arguing with her, but he'd be damned if he'd let her blame him for this. "Maybe a little braver—a little more daring."

Tears welled in her eyes. "Do you have any idea how much courage it takes to get pregnant when you know there's a fifty-fifty chance the baby won't survive—again? And to somehow know you're always on the wrong side of the gamble?"

He regretted his remark immediately, and put a hand to her arm and rubbed gently. "I'm sorry. I'm not minimizing what you've been through. I'm just trying to make you understand that while it was traumatic for Ben, I don't care. Let's get married and adopt a whole passel of children if you want to. Your life isn't over because you can't give birth."

Her lips firmed. "I am not going to argue this with you again," she said. "My life is my business."

"Pardon me," he corrected her calmly, "but when it's tied to mine, 'your business' is a partnership. We *are* going to argue this."

In the yard of the residence behind the school, a

dog barked loudly. Across the street, another dog barked in reply.

"You're waking up the neighborhood!" she whispered harshly, trying to push him back toward his truck.

Intrepidly, he followed her to her car. "If you'd accepted my invitation," he reminded her quietly, "we'd be on our way to my place by now and we wouldn't be bothering anybody—except each other."

She stopped at her car door to jab his chest with her index finger. "Sex doesn't solve everything! You think you'll show me how wonderful it is to make love with you and I'll abandon my dreams of Europe so you can have what you want?"

He slapped her hand away and glowered down at her, now annoyed. "No. I thought I'd show you how wonderful it is for us to make love, and give you back your dreams of home and family. We can have that. You're just afraid of it!"

His voice had risen despite his efforts to keep it down, and the dogs now barked continuously.

"I'm afraid," she said, enunciating, her eyes sparking in the dark, "that if I stay here a moment longer I'm going to slug you!"

He took a step back and spread his arms. "Hey," he challenged. "Give me your best shot. I'm more than ready."

For an exciting instant, he thought she was going to take him up on the offer. Instead, she ripped open her door, got in her car and turned on the motor.

From the yard next door, someone shouted, "Go home and fight, for God's sake!"

She backed out of her parking spot with a squeal of

brakes and roared away, thinking, he guessed, that she'd won the argument.

She had a thing or two to learn about him.

MARIAH HAD NO IDEA what to do about Cam. It had been four days since their argument, and while she hadn't seen him, not gotten a call from him in that time, he'd done other, more insidious, things to completely distract her and—frankly—charm her. And she didn't want to be charmed. She didn't.

But the morning after their argument, she left the house with the children for the walk to school and there'd been a French bouquet spilling gloriously out of the mailbox. A tag with her name was attached and nothing else.

The following day she'd awakened to a mild thumping on her bedroom window. She'd turned groggily to find colorful orbs bumping against it. She'd sat up abruptly, rubbing her eyes, wondering what on earth they were.

A closer investigation revealed a bouquet of balloons tied to the temperature gauge outside her bedroom window—on the second floor!

A single red Mylar balloon in the shape of a heart bore her name.

The day after, when she'd arrived home from an errand on which Letitia had sent her, she found the kitchen table set for two with china, crystal and flowers. A white-jacketed waiter with a black bow tie served her a crab-and-shrimp Caesar salad with cheese bread and an iced mocha. That was her favorite meal at the Old Post Road Inn, where she and Parker sometimes met for lunch. She suspected collusion.

Taped to the chair pulled up to the second place setting was a note that read: "Imagine I'm here, then think about how much more fun this meal would be if you didn't have to imagine it."

"Arrogant!" she muttered.

"No, ma'am," the waiter countered as he offered her more cheese bread. "Honest."

On this, the fourth morning, Mariah was almost afraid to get out of bed. But the children were already collected in her doorway, enjoying her mysterious surprises as much as she was confounded by them. They knew as well as she did that Cam was at the bottom of the mysteries.

"There's nothing downstairs!" Brian reported.

"And nothing in the mailbox!" Ashley added. All the children ran to her window.

"And nothing on the thermometer!" Jessica said. "Maybe there's no surprise today."

"There has to be a surprise," Ashley said. "There's been one every day."

"Maybe Cam gave up," Brian suggested.

Ashley shook her head. "He'd never give up. You don't get to be successful if you give up. The Gypsy prince told me."

Brian rolled his eyes. "That was make-believe."

"Make-believe," she explained didactically, "can come true. I'm going to be a ballerina."

"Okay, okay." Mariah raised both hands to stop the argument. "If you'll all get breakfast on the table while I shower and dress, I'll take you out to the Barn tonight for dinner to celebrate tomorrow being the last day of school."

The twins and the Morris girls left her room in a gale of laughter and cheers. Ashley and Brian, however, looked at each other, their response to the end of school understandably less enthusiastic.

They finally followed the others, Ashley saying hopefully to Brian, "Maybe you'll find the money today."

Mariah fell back to the mattress with a groan. She'd have to remember to wear her boots and a hard hat if Brian was going to keep looking.

Breakfast was uneventful. She walked the children to school, checked the mailbox on her way back and found a Priority Mail package from the travel agent with whom she'd made arrangements for her trip. She ripped open the envelope to discover her tickets, an itinerary and several brochures she'd requested. She left in six days.

She stood there with everything she'd wanted this entire year spread out in the palms of her hands. Her pulse quickened; her hands shook just a little. At last. Escape.

She froze, wondering why she'd chosen that word. Escape? Why would she sum up the dream of a lifetime in a word that suggested bailing out? Because that wasn't what she was doing.

Okay, the trip wasn't the dream of a lifetime; it was a fairly recent passion. She'd always loved her art but had never believed she could pursue it before until…until she had nothing else to do.

But it was a noble goal. She was going to Europe to learn, to improve herself, to make a life that would be fulfilling now that husband and family were out of the question.

She was still analyzing when she heard the unmistakable note of a pitch pipe. She looked up to discover six young people ranged in a row, blocking the carriage house's front door. They were a mixed group of teens, boys and girls, and they were dressed in black pants, white shirts, red vests and straw hats. She recognized Gary Warren's children and Mike McGee, the young man Haley and Bart had taken under their wing.

She took all this in with a sense of disbelief. Had she stepped back in time to the movie set of *Meet Me in St. Louis?*

The group burst into song. With a sort of barbershop harmony in keeping with their costumes, they sang about two people being meant for each other, about how heaven must have sent one to the other, gathering all the qualities one had longed for and rolling them into one perfect package.

Mariah stared. After the first verse, they broke into a Busby Berkeley sort of tap dance, with broad smiles and big movements.

That finished, they sang another verse, then finished on a high note, arms extended to the sky. Then Stacey Warren came forward, handed Mariah a note that said they were the Maple Hill High School Madrigals and were available for weddings, parties and dances, and that the proceeds from their work would take them to the All Schools Competition in New York in January.

She gave Mariah a giant chocolate kiss wrapped in red cellophane with a silver bow and said perkily, "Our performance was compliments of Mr. Cameron Trent."

Mariah didn't know how to explain that she was shocked but not surprised. That wouldn't have made sense. But, then, nothing about Cam's insistence that they have a relationship did.

"Thank you," she said. "I enjoyed it very much."

The girl grinned. "Thank you. Please tell your friends about us. We have to make a small fortune by the holidays."

"I certainly will."

Stacey hurried off to the van all the others were piling into. Parked beside it was Cam's truck, Cam himself leaning against the front fender. When the van drove off, he walked across the lawn toward Mariah, Fred barking from the truck. She had to remember that his charming attitude today would not survive his eventual disappointment in her. He didn't realize it, but it wouldn't. She'd seen Ben change from the man who'd loved her to the man who resented her. She had to make Cam understand once and for all that what he wanted was not going to happen.

"They're pretty good, aren't they?" he asked, taking her mail from her as she fiddled with her key.

She gave him a glare over her shoulder, pushed the door open, yanked him inside with her, then pushed the door closed and confronted him with both hands on her hips.

"Cameron Trent," she said firmly, looking him right in the eye. "I don't love you. If I can make it any plainer, please tell me how. I am not going out with you again. We are not going to have a relationship. *It's over.* Do you hear me? Over!"

He shifted his weight and folded his arms, her mail caught against his chest. "Then you're admitting that it *was.*"

"I'm not admitting anything except that you're starting to annoy me beyond reason! Look!"

She snatched the mail from him, tossed everything but the package from the travel agent at a chair and waved the ticket in front of him. "I'm leaving next Wednesday and you will never see me again! Is that clear? I do not want to marry you, or love you, or whatever it is you want from me."

He caught her wrist and pulled it down so that he could see her face above the tickets. "But you do," he said, "love me. You may not want to, but you do."

She turned away on the pretense of gathering up the mail so he wouldn't see that that was true. "Cam, this is bordering on harassment. Go away!"

The sudden peal of the doorbell was a surprising sound in the middle of their argument. Cam, still standing just inside the door, reached an arm out and opened it.

Letitia stood there, her face pale. She looked at Mariah in relief, then at Cam in surprise. "Thank goodness you're here, too."

Mariah braced herself for bad news. "What is it?"

"Ashley's guardian passed away during the night." She looked from one to the other again. "I spoke to him on the phone just two days ago, and he expected to live until the holidays. He said he and Ashley had a long talk on the phone Sunday night and he'd promised to take her to see the Joffrey Ballet."

Mariah felt her heart lurch. Poor Ashley. Who would decide her future now? She prayed that Walter Kerwin had made sound arrangements for her. Tears burned her eyes and emotion clogged her throat. Ashley was such a game little girl, always trying to adjust, always eager to please. She dreaded having to tell her.

"Do you want me to get her out of class?" Mariah asked.

Letitia shook her head. "She's already in my office with Lavinia and Mr. Beresford."

"Mr. Beresford?"

"Mr. Kerwin's lawyer. He's here to…to conduct some business."

"Ashley business?"

Letitia waved her hands in the air. "It's complicated and a little…tricky. Come with me to my office." She caught Cam's arm and leaned on him. "You, too."

"But I don't know anything about Ashley's guardian," he said.

She nodded. "He seems to have known something about you."

He turned a questioning eye on Mariah, who shrugged and followed them out the door.

Lavinia, Ashley and Noel Beresford, a tall, young-ish man with dark hair and a designer suit, had pulled their chairs into a circle.

As Mariah, Letitia and Cam walked in, the lawyer stood and Lavinia excused herself to get more chairs. Cam went to help her.

The "tricky" business they were conducting did not seem to be going well. Lavinia looked wide-eyed with concern, and Ashley was pale, her expression forlorn. She ran to Mariah, and though she wasn't crying, her slender frame was trembling.

No surprise there, Mariah thought. Every child had a basic right to family and a sense of security—two things this child was continually deprived of. Mariah wrapped her arms around her and drew her back to the chair she'd occupied, sharing it with her.

"Honey, I'm so sorry," Mariah whispered. "But I'm sure Mr. Kerwin made good plans for you."

Ashley apparently found no comfort in that. She sat with her arms folded, staring at the Oriental carpet.

Three chairs from the library were fitted into the circle; Noel Beresford resumed his place and smiled. He appeared affable, Mariah noted, and not at all affected by whatever had upset the Lightfoot sisters and Ashley. Lawyers, she imagined, had to maintain a certain distance from their clients' problems.

Letitia made halfhearted introductions, no doubt eager to get down to business. "Mr. Beresford, Mariah and Cameron. Children, this is Mr. Beresford, Walter Kerwin's attorney."

He smiled around the circle. "So. You've explained why I'm here, Miss Lightfoot?"

Letitia frowned. "No," she said on a hesitant note, then added more firmly, "No. I thought it would be best coming from you."

"Well." He opened a file folder in his lap and squared up the papers inside on his knee. "I guess the best thing to do is come straight to the point." He smiled at Mariah, then, curiously, at Cam and said, "I imagine you'll both have questions afterward, but I'm sure I can answer all those. Let me just tell you that Walter has mentioned the two of you in his will. I'll read you the pertinent passages."

Mariah would have questioned that she rated a mention in Walter Kerwin's will, but she saw Cam, clearly as puzzled as she was, simply lean back and give the man his full attention. She decided that was a good idea. With an arm around Ashley, who continued to tremble, she listened.

Noel Beresford looked up from his notes to smile again. "He left a considerable endowment to the school, then he mentions the two of you. Now, where…oh, yes. Here it is." He cleared his throat:

> And to Cameron and Mariah Trent I leave custody of my ward, Ashley Weisfield. Having been aware of my condition for some time, I studied friends and acquaintances, searching for a good situation for Ashley, one that would provide her with the siblings and playmates I've been unable to supply. But most of my friends are of my own age, and therefore unsuitable. I did not want to leave her in the care of a guardian again, as I've realized over time how sadly I've failed her as a parent and would not wish to impose such a situation on her again.
>
>   So I went to the source. In a lengthy conversation with Ashley, which I have recorded, I asked her if she had her choice of the perfect family, with whom she would like to live. She answered without hesitation—"With Mr. and Mrs. Trent."

Beresford looked up to smile at them again, and continued.

> I include this in my will now because of the unpredictability of the course of my illness, and

will follow this up with a discussion with Mr. and Mrs. Trent.

Beresford lowered the sheet of paper, his expression now grave. "Unfortunately, he passed away before he had the opportunity to do so. So, Mr. and Mrs. Trent, I'm sure this comes as quite a surprise, but I also see that you seem very fond of Ashley and hope you can accommodate Mr. Kerwin's wishes."

Mariah couldn't think, couldn't imagine, how this mistake had been made. She opened her mouth to speak, but didn't know what to say. She didn't want to betray Ashley by telling Beresford that she and Cam weren't husband and wife, weren't even engaged, weren't even intending...well, *he* might be, but she wasn't!

Cam hadn't said anything, either. She glanced at him and saw that he was watching her, apparently preparing to follow her lead.

Mariah was desperately trying to decide on a course of action, when Ashley burst into tears. "I'm sorry!" she sobbed. "I'm sorry! I shouldn't have lied! But he asked if I could have anything I wanted, and...he never said that before. He always just told me where I had to go. And it was my chance. The Gypsy said so!"

Beresford, now not only puzzled but alarmed, asked with a wince, "The Gypsy?"

Ashley nodded. "He told my fortune at the fair. He said I had to make my own happiness! That I had to decide what I wanted and be responsible for getting it. So I did. I wanted to live with Mariah and Cam, so that's what I told Mr. Kerwin!"

She collapsed against Mariah, crying her heart out.

Beresford looked from Mariah to Cam. "You mean…you're not married?"

Mariah turned to Letitia, who'd also apparently kept that secret, probably unsure how Mariah and Cam would react and, in Ashley's interest, unwilling to betray them.

"No, we're not," Mariah said. Then she, who had never been a mother but always thought like one, instantly abandoned her plan of solitary travel and asked urgently, "Couldn't you just give her to me?" She looked down at Ashley, but the child was still pressed against her, weeping. "We get along well, I've taken care of her for—"

Beresford was shaking his head. "The will says Mr. and Mrs. Cameron Trent. If we do anything other than what's specified in the will, Children and Family Services will have to be informed. There'll be interviews, home studies, possibly other homes considered."

Hating that she had to do this but realizing that getting a well-meaning but beleaguered agency involved would mean bureaucracy and red tape, Mariah turned to Cam. Certainly he understood Ashley's desperate situation.

CAM READ THE LOOK in Mariah's eyes and knew that fate was handing him a golden opportunity. Self-preservation skills honed on years of rejection and neglect rose to point him in the direction that would serve his needs.

"Mr. Beresford," he said, leaning forward in his chair, "would you excuse Mariah and me for a few minutes, please?"

Letitia sprang out of her chair as though ejected. "Use the office. Vinnie and I will take Mr. Beresford for a cup of tea. Mr. Beresford, you'd like that, wouldn't you?"

Before the lawyer could express concern over the turn of events, Lavinia whisked him out into the hallway, while Letitia lingered to blow them a kiss, then caught Ashley's hand and followed her sister. Cam smiled to himself. Collaborators on all sides.

He had to play this cool.

The moment the door closed behind Letitia, Mariah stood in agitation and paced back and forth from the chair to the window, finally leaning against the front of Letty's desk.

"You're going to make me ask you, aren't you?" She met his gaze cautiously, aware her cause was too desperate for her to risk being belligerent.

He had to make this hard for her; otherwise, if things didn't have the positive outcome he hoped for, she might blame him down the road for the fact that she'd had to marry him after all. He wanted her to feel responsible for what they had to do.

"I don't know what to say, Mariah." He stretched out his legs and crossed them at the ankles. "Just fifteen minutes ago you were telling me you never wanted to see me again. You even threatened to have me arrested."

"Fifteen minutes ago," she reminded him, "we didn't know Walter Kerwin had died." She came toward him, her eyes sparking, her manner suggesting she was forgetting her underdog position. "And who told Ashley to take charge of her own destiny?" she demanded. "Huh? Who, O Mighty Stick-in-the-Works son of Othar?"

He returned her glare intrepidly. "That was good advice and you know it." He grinned. "Who expected her to follow through on it with such… style?"

Apparently unable to dispute that, Mariah turned away from him and went back to the desk; she sank onto the end of it with both hands to her face.

"What'll it take?" she finally asked quietly.

"For what?" he asked, pretending innocence. He couldn't say he was precisely enjoying this, but he did appreciate having the advantage for a change.

She huffed a long-suffering sigh and replied without looking at him, "For you to marry me. Something short-term. Something that'll allow us to get her, then when it's all legal, file for divorce so she can come with me. What'll it take?"

"Well," he answered, "a clarification of terms, for one thing."

She straightened off the desk, her expression cautious but hopeful. "What terms? What do you mean?"

"Tell me what you have in mind exactly," he said. "Then I'll tell you whether or not I agree with it."

She paced across the office and back. She was buying time, and he could understand that. This had all happened so quickly, so unexpectedly, that she was making things up as she went along.

"Okay." She stopped pacing finally and took the chair next to his. She sat sideways in it, both hands on the arm of his chair. He could feel her energy, her need for his cooperation. He forced himself to remain relaxed. "I *don't* want to be married."

He nodded once. "So you've made clear."

"But Ashley needs us."

"I agree."

"If we marry, we can claim her."

"Yes."

"But I don't want to stay married."

"Poor example to set for a child."

She growled impatiently. "It'll get her what she wants. She'll understand."

"She wants both of us, if you'll recall," he pointed out calmly.

She sighed. "Do you want to help her or not?"

"I'm listening." Though he knew he wasn't going to get terms he could be happy with, she might come up with something he could settle for in hope of better times.

"Two months," she said abruptly. "A marriage without sex, then I obtain a divorce and take her with me to Europe."

"No," he said.

She uttered a gasp of indignation. "No to what?"

"No to all of it," he replied. "Two months isn't long enough for her to get her bearings. I am not agreeing to a marriage without lovemaking, and I thought you were going to Europe to find yourself? You can't just haul her out of school and drag her around with you while you search for a meaning to your life."

"I can home-school her while we're touring. That's a very acceptable way for a child to be educated today. There are well-outlined programs. And what she'll see in Europe will contribute to, not detract from, her education."

He had to give her that. "But what about you?"

"I'm thinking of her."

Hmm. That was interesting, and possibly a step in his

favor. "Okay. Maybe Europe wouldn't hurt her. But two months together isn't long enough."

She folded her arms and faced him, sitting up stiffly. "How long do you want?"

"At least a year," he said.

"A year is too long."

"A year."

"You're being obstructive."

He smiled blandly. "I'm not surprised you recognize the tactic."

She sighed. "All right. A year."

"And we work at being married. Otherwise we aren't giving Ashley what she wants."

She said with disdain, "I suppose by that you mean we have sex."

"By that I mean," he corrected her, sitting up, drawing his legs in, "that we behave with each other as though we want to get along and create a home for this child."

She looked momentarily chastened. He added with more than a little enjoyment, "And we make love as regularly as we're inclined."

"I won't be inclined."

"You're wrong about that."

"I won't."

"When you are," he insisted, "you just have to say so."

She tried to stare him down on that point, but he didn't blink. She finally dropped her lashes, then told him with sudden briskness, "Then we're agreed. We get married for a year, make love when we're so inclined—" her tone clearly added, *Like that'll happen* "—and after a year we divorce, I get custody and take her to Europe."

The terms were bad, but they would give him his chance, and he was sure that was all he needed.

"And, of course," she added, "we make Beresford believe we've been planning to marry all along and we're eager to do this or he might decide this does not comply with his client's wishes at all."

She offered her hand.

He took it. "Agreed," he said.

CHAPTER TWELVE

THE OFFICE WAS CHAOS when the meeting reconvened and Cam and Mariah shared their decision.

"And when will you do this?" Beresford asked.

Mariah opened her mouth to say that it would take a little time for blood tests, to get a plan together, to…

"This weekend," Cam said.

The lawyer appeared pleased. "Good. I'll stay for the wedding and while I'm here I can get the information I need from you to file adoption proceedings." He drew a deep breath as he looked out the window at the tops of spring-green maple trees. "One could get addicted to this place."

"This weekend!" Letitia said, walking halfway to the door, then turning back. "There's so much to prepare! Do you have a preference of churches? And where should we have the reception?"

Lavinia said, her eyes wide, "The Franklins, Mrs. Morris and Brian's mother will be arriving tomorrow to take the children home. We mustn't forget that in all the excitement. Oh, dear. And you'll need things. Flowers and a photographer and someone to sing 'Oh, Promise Me'—oof!"

Letitia and Lavinia collided in a dramatic meeting of considerable bosoms.

"We'll take care of everything," Cam said. "You ladies don't have to fuss."

"Nonsense!" Letitia was firm. "Mariah's very dear to us, and you, Cameron, have bailed us out of so many plumbing crises that you've become dear to us, too. And since neither of you has parents, we're taking over. I'm sure Parker will understand and want to help us. Or want us to help her."

The group disbanded shortly after, but Ashley hung back in the hallway, her face still pale, confusion in her eyes.

Mariah put a hand to her face. "What is it, Ashley?"

"I don't understand what happened," the child admitted. She peered around Mariah at Cam, who'd been headed for the stairs and had turned back when he realized they'd stopped. "Miss Lightfoot was talking about a church and a reception."

Mariah nodded. "Because we're getting married."

Ashley met her eyes, as though waiting for more.

"So we can adopt you," Cam added.

Ashley glanced from one to the other, a tear sliding down her cheek. "And we're going to…live together?"

"Yes," Mariah confirmed.

"In a house I just bought on the lake," Cam explained. "The three of us and Fred."

"Isn't that what you want?" Mariah asked when the child continued to appear uncertain.

"Yes!" Ashley confirmed quickly. "It's just that…I never really get what I want. So I was just…wondering if I had it right."

"You have it right." Mariah hugged her. "Now, would

you like to go back to the dorm and rest? You can have the day off."

Ashley shook her head. "I feel sad about Mr. Kerwin, but…" She smiled for the first time since the strange meeting had begun. She came to Cam, wrapped her arms around his middle and held on.

He kissed the top of her head, determined to give her what she wanted—permanently.

"I want to go back to class," she said, "and tell everybody!"

She ran down the stairs with a squeal of delight, leaving Cam and Mariah to stare at each other in the hallway.

"This is all your fault, you know," she said, marching past him on the stairs.

"My *fault?*" he asked, following her. "I thought it was all *thanks* to me."

"We're tricking her," she said, pushing her way through the big double doors to the sunny morning outside.

"We're rescuing her from a life of loneliness," he corrected her. He caught Mariah's arm and yanked her to a stop. "And who proposed to whom, Miss Mercer?"

"All right, all right!" She shook off his arm and glared at him. "Now we have a little girl thinking she has a family for a lifetime when that isn't true."

"The deal," he reminded her in a stern tone, "was that we put everything into the marriage while we're together."

Her shoulders sagged, as though she knew she couldn't blame him but was having second thoughts about her solution. "We're not going to mar her forever, are we?"

"No," he replied.

She expelled a breath and seemed to acquire new resolve.

"Fine. Well, I have a lot to do." She started off again down the path toward the carriage house.

Again he followed. Fred barked at him as he approached the truck, the dog's head sticking out of the open window. "I'll come by in the morning, and we can move some of your things over."

"Can you make it afternoon?" she asked over her shoulder. "Parents will be picking up their children in the morning and I'd like to be there. All the kids are supposed to be gone by noon."

"Of course. In the afternoon, then."

Weird day, he thought as he climbed into his truck, Fred kissing his ear. He'd begun the morning by having Mariah serenaded with a romantic tune, in the hope of scaling the battlements she'd erected between them. Now, at just—he glanced at his watch; could it be only 11:00 a.m.?—he was scheduled to marry her in four short days. And the battlements remained.

Should make for an interesting marriage.

MARIAH CANCELED HER travel plans. The agent refunded her money, promised to keep her destinations on file and re-create the package if and when Mariah was ready.

She had her belongings packed in an hour, but instead of putting them into storage with what she'd brought with her after her divorce, she put them in a corner of the downstairs hall in preparation for tomorrow's move.

She tried to call Parker, knowing she was at her office in city hall, but her sister didn't pick up.

Mariah spent the rest of the afternoon making sure the children had all their things together—searching under beds, behind drawers and in the bottom of closets for treasures that might have escaped.

Escaped. The word brought to mind her canceled trip. But she had not been escaping, she comforted herself. She'd intended to live a dream.

Instead, she was probably now in for a lot of sleepless nights as she tried to figure out how to cope with Cameron Trent.

But she'd saved Ashley from foster care, and was giving her what she wanted and thought she'd never have.

In all fairness, Mariah had to admit that Cam had helped considerably, though he probably had his own goals in mind. How many men, she wondered, would have risen to an unorthodox proposal quickly enough to save a child from the system? Not many, she was sure. She had to remember that and do her best to comply with his terms. Even if she was never inclined to…

God! How did she get into this mess?

When the children came home, they carried with them armloads of artwork and crafts that they'd made in the classroom. She gave them each a large manila envelope for the flat things, and found some boxes left over from her sign venture for storing their three-dimensional creations.

As they worked, they talked excitedly about her impending marriage to Cam and Ashley's adoption. Amy compared it with a story they'd read in her class. "You might even find out you're a princess!" she said to Ashley.

Jalisa, wide-eyed, suggested she might be able to wear a crown and a frilly gown.

Ashley laughed that off. "No, I won't, but I'll be able to go fishing with Cam in his boat."

The boys seemed to think that was as good as getting to wear a crown. The Morris girls clearly thought she was crazy.

Once all the boxes of belongings were labeled, the children lined them up in the hallway for the morning. A moment of quiet followed as the children realized, probably for the first time, the finality of this move. They had become like a family, but in all probability they would not see one another again.

Before their mood could become maudlin, Mariah packed them all in her van and headed for the Breakfast Barn as she'd promised. They had burgers and fries, and pie for dessert, then she gave each of them a binder she'd prepared with one another's addresses and birth dates, so that they could keep in touch. She'd included photos of special events, as well as the name sign on their bedroom doors.

When they got back to the carriage house, she put in a movie, but they were too restless to watch it. They seemed to want to share fears on their last night together.

The Morris girls were still concerned about their mother's boyfriend.

"Your mom's a smart woman," Mariah reminded them. "And she loves you all very much. She'd never marry someone who'd be mean to you, or whom she thought you wouldn't like. So, give him a chance."

Peter and Philip had just learned that their parents were abandoning stunt work and moving to New York, where their mother had been cast in a small role on Broadway.

"There's gangs and weird people there," Peter said.

Philip agreed with a loud "Yeah!"

"There are also lots of wonderful things to see, and great people doing all kinds of important work. You'll have new opportunities. And your parents will be home more."

"Dad says we'll be able to go to school and live at home." Philip nudged Peter with his elbow. "That'll be cool."

Peter was the adventurer and Philip the homebody. The quiet twin who never did anything but back up his brother, Mariah realized with a private smile, might finally be coming into his own.

Brian had wandered into the kitchen and was sitting on the counter, his head tipped back against the cupboard as he stared upward. He'd been morose all evening, worried about going home, worried about missing his friends, worried about the next school. And she knew he'd miss Ashley; was probably a little resentful that she got to stay and he didn't.

"Think the gold might be up there?" Mariah asked.

"Yeah." Brian swung a stocking foot. "That part's blocked off in the attic, so I couldn't look."

Mariah patted his knee as she walked past him to the refrigerator. "Someday you'll be a brilliant businessman and make your own money to do whatever you want with it. Want some milk?"

"No, thank you. I wonder if my mom will be home this summer or if she'll be working."

Mariah tried to remember what news Lavinia's last conversation with the woman had yielded. "I think she's doing another movie, but it's in L.A. It's about a boys' baseball team. She's going to get you a part as an extra."

He made a face. "I've done that before. You wait around a long time in these dorky costumes, then all you do is walk by the camera or sit in a crowd. It's boring. When I grow up, I'm going to be a plumber."

Mariah bit her lip to withhold a smile. Did Cam know he was creating competition for himself by being the children's hero?

"That'd be an excellent career choice," she encouraged. "You're smart enough to make a good life for yourself, Brian."

He sighed. "Yeah, that's what Cam said. That I'll be eighteen before I know it and can decide things for myself."

"That's right."

He sighed. "Still seems to me that eight years is a really long time." With that, he slithered off the counter, hugged her good-night and went up to bed.

Her heart ached.

She went upstairs to do her final tuck-in, then was on her way back downstairs when the doorbell rang.

She pulled the door open to find Parker standing there, a frown pleating her forehead. "Married?" she said without preamble, storming past Mariah and into the house. "You're getting *married* and you didn't tell me?"

Mariah shushed her. "I just got the kids to bed. It's a complicated story. I tried to call you this morning, but you didn't answer your cell, and there's been so much going on since that I sort of…forgot."

Refusing to be placated, Parker stood her ground. Wearing a yellow sweatshirt over black leggings, with a giant fabric pouch made of quilt squares over her shoulder, she was hard to ignore. "You forgot. If Rita Robidoux hadn't waited on me at the Barn, I still wouldn't know!"

Mariah arched an eyebrow. "Rita knew? It just happened this—"

"Rita works for Perk Avenue's catering service on the side. They called her about a wedding reception Tuesday night—the Trent-Mercer wedding. Talk fast. Massage correctly applied can be lethal, you realize."

Mariah gestured her to a corner of the sofa and microwaved the last two cups of coffee in the pot. Then she added Irish Cream to them.

Sitting beside Parker with a cushion between them, she explained about Ashley's guardian, Ashley's creative fib and her and Cam's decision to make the untruth a reality in order to save the child from foster care.

Parker looked worried. "But if you split up in a year, how is that going to help Ashley?"

Mariah didn't have an answer. "We're taking it day by day."

"But…"

"Park, please. Just let it be as it is, okay?"

Parker smiled. "I rather like it as it is, I just wondered how you're going to cope. I presume you and Cam will be sleeping together?"

"If and when we feel ready."

"How can you look at him and not feel ready?"

Mariah pursed her lips at her sister. "Because that's not what I want."

"Now, that's an outright lie. You look at him as though he's *everything* you want."

"If I'd met him before Ben, he'd have been everything I wanted then. Now I know better, so I want different things. Haven't we had this discussion?"

Parker dropped her head against the back of the sofa. "Probably. You're very repetitious. You think you can't want him because you can't be what he wants, or some such idiocy. Frankly, I'm tired of discussing it. You can redeem yourself by telling me I'm your maid of honor."

"You're my maid of honor."

"All right, then."

MRS. MORRIS ARRIVED at 9:00 a.m. with a portly middle-aged man in an Italian suit and glasses. He was only slighter taller than she, and not at all who Mariah would have expected to interest the beautiful woman whose first husband had been a model.

He worked on Wall Street Monday through Friday, he explained to the girls, but had a farm in upstate New York, where they would all spend weekends.

They went from cautiously suspicious of him to excitedly hopeful when he told them about the horse on the farm and Missy, the golden retriever, who'd just given birth to thirteen puppies.

Mariah hugged the girls goodbye, delighted to see that the sadness of leaving was practically forgotten as they piled into the station wagon. Letitia and Lavinia were on hand to wave them off.

Brian and Ashley ran after them all the way to the road, still waving.

The Franklins pulled in shortly after.

Their mother was tall and California blond; their father, handsome and thickly built, looking precisely the way Mariah expected a stuntman to look.

"I can't believe Mom's really gonna act," Philip said, "instead of fall off stuff and wreck cars."

"Now that you two are getting older—" she wrapped an arm around each boy as her husband went into the house to get their things "—we thought it'd be nice if we were all in the same place at the same time."

Brian and the twins shook hands manfully, Mariah hugged them, the Lightfoot sisters embraced them and wished them well.

Silence seemed to fall when the car drove out of sight. Ashley and Brian stood together a little bit ahead of Mariah, staring at the spot where the car had disappeared from view.

"The Game Boy's still connected," Ashley said to Brian. "You want to play until your mom comes?"

"I beat you all the time," he said dispiritedly as they turned to walk back to the house.

"That's 'cause I let you," Ashley said.

He made a scornful sound. "You do not."

"Come on," she said. "I'll show you."

"We're going back to my office," Letitia said, heading for the old Packard they'd driven from the school building. "Call me when Brian's mother arrives. We'd like to say goodbye."

"Of course."

Mariah went back into the house, made cocoa for Ashley and Brian, then busied herself cleaning out the refrigerator and straightening up the cupboards.

Shortly after two o'clock, she heard a car in the

driveway and looked out the window, expecting to see a rental vehicle, which would mean Brian's mother had gotten there. Instead, she saw Cam's truck.

In a moment she heard him talking to Ashley and Brian. When she went out to greet him, the living room was empty. She peered around in surprise, then turned to a commotion at the top of the stairs. Ashley had a lamp from Mariah's room, Brian had a light wicker chair and Cam and a man she didn't recognize had a wooden chest she'd filled with clothes and linen.

"Mariah," Cam said as he and the other man moved carefully down the stairs, "Evan Braga. Evan, Mariah Mercer."

Evan was about Cam's height, with dark-blond hair and dark-brown eyes. He was attractive in jeans and a paint-smeared sweatshirt, but there was a world-weary mien about him that touched her.

He smiled and inclined his head politely. "Hello," he said. Then he blew her first impression of him by adding, "I can't believe you're marrying this guy. Do you know about his fanatical devotion to baseball and his fascination with the old Chandler Mill building?"

That caught her interest. She met them at the bottom of the stairs. "I love the old Chandler Mill building. Cam said you two might buy it. Did you?"

"We did," Cam said. He and Evan picked up their pace as they crossed to the door. "The owner was so eager to get out from under that Evan got us a real deal. He put up the money."

Evan grinned. "Well, I'm counting on your smarts to make us a fortune."

She followed them out to the truck. "You're not

going to tear it down, right? I mean, you said you'd fix it up."

Cam gave her an impatient glance as they placed her trunk on a padded tarp in the truck bed. "Of course we're not going to tear it down. We have a few tenants. We want to convert it to office space downstairs but use the upstairs for apartments."

She thought about that. "I'll bet the view of the lake from the upstairs rooms is wonderful."

He nodded. "And the construction's solid. It just needs remodeling inside to outfit it for residential spaces, and a time-appropriate face-lift outside."

Evan grinned. "I think this makes us entrepreneurs, or slum landlords. I'm not sure which."

Mariah noticed the empty cab of the truck. "Where's Fred?" she asked.

"I left him home," he replied. "Having him run around our feet while we're trying to move you wouldn't be a good thing. And he has a fenced yard on the side of the house, and a dog door for getting in and out. He's in heaven after the apartment." He caught her hand and pulled her with him toward the house. "Now, could we have more moving and less chatter?"

She frowned teasingly at Evan. "I can't believe you want to be in partnership with this man."

Evan blinked at her. "You're entering into the ultimate partnership with him. At least I don't have to look at his ugly mug at night."

Night. She felt a frisson of anxiety.

Or was it anticipation?

When the truck was loaded, the children pleaded to go with Cam.

"What if your mother arrives while you're gone?" she asked Brian.

He saw her point but looked bitterly disappointed. He was clearly enjoying the male companionship.

"I'll have him back in half an hour," Cam bargained. "The house is only five minutes away. We'll just unload and come right back."

"Okay," she conceded, then cautioned the children, "but you two be careful. And please do as you're told."

They raced each other toward the truck—an action she took optimistically as consent.

"Don't worry," Cam said. "We'll be right back."

"I'll have coffee and brownies ready."

"All *right!*" Cam gave her a quick kiss and a grin. "This relationship is looking hopeful already."

IT WAS DINNERTIME. Cam and Evan and the children had been back for brownies, left again and made yet another trip, and there was still no sign of Brian's mother.

Letitia and Lavinia had come to the carriage house to wait, and they all now sat around the dining room table eating pizza Cam had ordered.

Brian had adopted a nonchalance Mariah found difficult to watch.

The scenario was all so familiar to Cam from his own childhood. How many times had he waited to be picked up from a school function or some other outing, only to be left sitting on his sports bag or leaning against a public telephone because no one came and no one answered the phone?

Brian was doing the same thing he always did—pretending it didn't matter. The way Cam used to pretend that he wasn't so tired of his life he'd do anything to get out of it. Suicide had crossed his mind once, but he'd immediately rejected it, certain that when he was in control of his own life, things would be different. Besides, a permanent solution to a temporary problem was stupid.

But at ten, eighteen seemed like a lifetime away.

Letitia went into the living room to call Brian's mother to find out why she was delayed.

Mariah looked ready to blow up. She got up to refill everyone's glasses and to give the children more napkins.

Ashley was uncharacteristically quiet, obviously unsure what to do for Brian.

Cam glanced at the clock. He'd promised Evan he'd have him at his place by seven for a poker game.

He pushed his chair away from the table. "If you'll excuse us," he said, "I have to get Evan home. But I'll be back in fifteen minutes."

There was a desperate look in the boy's eyes as he pleaded with Mariah, "Can I go, too?" She prepared to reply, her expression reluctant, and he interrupted with "You know she's not coming. You'll have to put me on a plane tonight, and Bianca—that's her personal assistant," he added for Cam's benefit, "will pick me up at the airport."

Mariah turned to Cam.

"Fine with me. Let's go."

Mariah shook Evan's hand and thanked him for his help with a bag of brownies.

Cam pretended hurt feelings. "None for me?"

"Now that you're going to be my husband," she said

heartlessly, walking them out to the porch, Ashley beside her, "you're required to help me without expecting payment."

"Really. Well, that's a misconception we'll have to straighten out when I return."

Evan lived in a cottage in the woods on the other side of town. He had a big family somewhere in the Midwest, and had come East to escape their well-intentioned hovering after an automobile accident that killed his brother and left him in the hospital for months.

He ran Lake Road with Hank regularly, and Cam found it hard to see that he'd ever had a physical problem. He played basketball on the team most of the Wonders belonged to, and pickup games at the gym. There was a determination about him, despite his easygoing manner, that spoke of a hard fight back to health and fitness.

He never volunteered much and Cam didn't ask. He understood a man's right to privacy.

"Thanks for the help," he said as Evan leaped out of the truck.

"Sure." Evan reached in to shake hands with Brian. "Good luck, Brian."

"Thanks." Brian slid onto the far edge of the seat as Evan closed the door and gave them a final wave.

"Nice guy," Brian said.

"Yeah," Cam agreed. He turned around in the small gravel drive, then headed down the narrow road through the woods to the main road.

They drove in silence halfway back to the Manor, then Brian said with a sigh, "My mom forgot me."

"It's hard to tell what happened," Cam said diplomatically. "We'll just have to wait and see if Miss Light-foot can find out why she isn't here."

The boy sighed again. "She probably got high and just forgot me. It's happened before."

Cam thought the responsible, adult thing would be to discourage this kind of thinking. But caseworkers had done that to him his entire life, and it had never altered the underlying truth. Some people could be reha-bilitated and some people couldn't.

Maybe it would be more responsible to help Brian see that he could survive his childhood. "My parents did that to me all the time, too."

Brian turned slightly toward him. "What did you do?"

"I made sure I survived to get out of there. And I was lucky. I got in with a great foster family."

Brian was silent a moment. "I never get taken away when my mom goes into rehab," he said finally. "'Cause Bianca's there. And it'd be bad publicity if my mom lost me. But once Bianca gets me back home, she doesn't show up again until Mom's out. Usually, it's just me and the housekeeper. She's very nice, but she's old and she can't do much fun stuff."

"Stinks, doesn't it?"

"Big time."

Darkness had fallen by the time they reached the carriage house. Letitia was on the porch to meet them.

"Oh-oh," Brian said.

"Don't borrow trouble," Cam advised.

Brian gave him a grim look. "I don't have to. I own a whole bunch of it."

"What happened, Miss Letty?" Brian asked as they approached the house.

Letitia said with her usual positive approach, "Well, you were right, Brian. Your mother isn't coming. Let's go inside and I'll explain. Cam?" She pointed him around the side of the house. "Mariah's in the garden."

It didn't occur to him to question why she was in the garden in the dark. This was Mariah, after all.

He heard her before he found her under a giant maple. It took an instant to adjust to the knowledge that she was crying; she was always so tough, so determined. Except where the children were involved. And he was sure that was what was prompting her tears now.

He went to her.

She turned at the sound of his footsteps and walked into his arms, just as she'd done Sunday night on the dance floor. But this was grief, not romance.

"What happened?" he asked, wrapping his arms around her.

"She did it again!" she said angrily, sobbing. "I can't believe it! How can you have a child and care so little about what…"

"Mariah. Did what again?"

She swallowed. "She had an accident on her way to the airport. Hit another car. Multiple injuries, but no deaths, thank God. Cocaine in her blood. This time it's not just rehab. She's facing criminal charges."

"Oh, God."

"Yeah. Bianca called." Mariah stood back, swiped a hand across her eyes, spread her arms and dropped them in complete exasperation. "And in the crush of things, everybody forgot about Brian. Do you believe it?"

He nodded. "I do."

She sighed, turned away, turned back, her fingers

linked and twisting with a nervousness he'd never seen in her.

He waited.

"Bianca wanted to know if the school could keep Brian over the summer," she finally blurted, "until she learns what'll happen to his mother."

He saw where this was going and thought God seemed to be coming out on his side in this relationship.

"What did you tell her?"

"Letitia talked to her. She said the school was closed for the summer." More tears slid down her cheeks. She wiped them away impatiently. "That we could send someone home with Brian, but then she'd have to make arrangements for him. And if his mother goes to jail, they'll have to be long-term."

He nodded, remembering his conversation with Brian on the way home. "So even the kind but elderly housekeeper won't do this time."

"No."

The good thing about having few options, he'd always thought, was the time saved in deliberation.

"Okay," he said. "You call her back and I'll put Brian's stuff in the truck."

He turned away to do just that, but she caught his arm and turned him back to her.

She leaped onto him, her cheek wet against his as she wrapped her legs around him. "Thank you," she whispered tearfully in his ear. "Thank you, Cam."

He started toward the house with her. "Just remember, I'm doing this without having received any extra brownies."

"I'll make you brownies every day for a year."

A year. There was that deadline.

He pushed it from his mind, preferring to think that by the time it came around, it would be forgotten.

Letitia met them at the door, took one look at Mariah's unorthodox position and said with a smile at Cam, "I'll call Bianca."

Brian needed more convincing than Bianca.

"Where am I going?" he wanted to know, as Cam carried a stack of his boxes to the truck.

"Home with us," he replied, not sure how he'd receive the news, uncertain what Letitia had told him about his mother and the accident.

"For how long?"

"Until things are decided." That was ambiguous enough. "Probably most of the summer, anyway."

The boy made a sound that was difficult to interpret in the dark. "You mean…at *your* house?"

"Yeah."

"With Mariah and Ashley. And Fred."

"Yeah."

That sound again. "My mom hurt some people in an accident."

"So I heard." Cam put the boxes in the bed of the truck, then headed back to the house. Brian kept pace with him. "But that doesn't have anything to do with you."

"She screws up all the time, but it's like she can't do anything about it."

"I know. Same kind of parents, remember?"

"I'm not going to be like that."

"I know."

They'd reached the house and Brian stopped in his tracks. Cam stopped with him.

"And I really get to live with you?" the boy asked. His amazement was flattering. Cam wished that Mariah was infected with the same enthusiasm.

"For now. We'll have to see what happens when your mother's case is decided."

"Man. This is like Amy's princess book."

With a weird sense of life being in control of him instead of the other way around, Cam drove home half an hour later to his new house on the lake with his fiancée at his side and two kids in the jump seat.

CHAPTER THIRTEEN

CAM'S HOUSE WAS BEAUTIFUL, but Mariah had to view it while contending with Fred trying to kiss her face. Until he noticed the children, trailing behind with their sleeping bags. He pounced on them and they dissolved into laughter in the middle of the living room floor. She looked up, the dramatic vaulted ceiling snagging her attention. Then she caught sight of the sign Cam had bought from her hanging over the doorway to the kitchen. Live Well, Laugh Often, Love Much.

Cam led Mariah through a living room so large it had two conversation areas and two sets of furniture, one with deeply upholstered green-and-beige check sofa and chairs, another with chairs in a coordinating fabric. He pointed toward the kitchen, then beckoned her to follow him upstairs.

"My room's downstairs," he said, and motioned to the right side of the hallway. "Rooms for the kids." He indicated the two rooms side by side, flipping on lights.

"Everything's furnished," she said in amazement. "I mean, considering you just bought it…"

"Hank left a lot of the furniture because Jackie's place is full of her family's antiques."

"That's lucky, since none of the bedroom furniture at

the Manor was ours. I thought the kids would have to use their sleeping bags until we could buy them furniture."

"Your room." He crossed to the large room on the left side of the hall and turned on the light. "Bathroom off each room. You have a fireplace, but just a shower, no tub. There's one in my bathroom, though. You can use it anytime."

Mariah walked into a spacious bedroom with soft yellow walls, large oak furniture, lace curtains and a pastel bedspread. A small escritoire stood in a corner, with a ladder-back chair pulled up to it, and next to it, a small, marble-framed fireplace.

"Overlooks the garden and the lake," he said, as she held a hand up to shield her eyes and peer out the window. "Not very much of a garden, but we can work on that over the summer if you want to."

"All I've ever done is plant a window box," she laughed.

"I haven't even done that. We can always call Gary Warren if we get desperate. Maybe we'll even get a deal since he's seeing your sister."

Mariah crossed the room to examine the wardrobe closet and found one that you could wander into, with hanging rods at different heights, built-in cubbyholes, a shoe rack. She stood back and gasped.

"What?" he asked, coming to check the closet, thinking something was wrong.

"My closet is bigger than the room I slept in as a child." She smiled in sheer feminine delight. "How fabulous is this?"

"If all your clothes are in that trunk, you'll have to do a lot of shopping to fill it up."

She shrugged blissfully. "I don't even have to fill it up. I just have to know everything won't get crushed when I hang it up. Hooks for hats, shelves for boxes, racks for shoes. I can't believe it!"

"I can go you one better," he taunted, catching her hand and taking her with him downstairs. "My room has a special fireplace."

"Special?"

"Yes." He led her into the huge blue-green-and-gold room done in Black Watch wallpaper, dark-blue wood-work and pine furniture. He pointed to the fireplace outlined with green tile and topped with a large slab of pine.

"I thought mine was wonderful, but this is gorgeous!" She put a hand to her heart. "I'll bet that's wonderful on a February night."

The image that sprang to mind as she spoke featured him beside her under the covers.

"But the best part," he said, tugging her around the corner and into the large bathroom, "is that it can be used in both rooms."

"Oh!" She sank onto the wide edge of the tub opposite the fireplace. In this room it had a country styling to match the decor. "I love to soak in a tub, but since I've been at the Manor, the best I could manage was a quick shower in the morning before I woke everybody up."

"Well, feel free to use this one anytime."

There was uproarious giggling and loud barking coming from the living room. Mariah got to her feet. "I'd better make sure they're not wreaking havoc. They're great kids, but they get a little careless when they're excited."

Fred had pinned Ashley to the carpet and she was beside herself with laughter while he licked her cheeks. Brian sat nearby, urging the dog on.

"Come and see your bedrooms," Mariah said, having to fend off the dog, who ran to her the moment he saw her.

She fussed over him, then followed with him as Cam led the way upstairs and showed the children the two rooms. "Can you come to a peaceful agreement over who gets which?"

Together, Ashley and Brian peered into the first one, done in paneled walls, with large blue-and-white plaid bedspread and drapes. Then they checked the second one, done in large pink-and-blue flowers and white furniture. This room definitely had a feminine twist. Cam must have thought so, too, Mariah noted, spotting Ashley's boxes in a corner.

"The other one's for me," Brian said, going back to it immediately, the dog still following him.

Ashley walked into the flowered room and stared out the long window. "What's out there?" she asked.

"The lake," Cam answered. "You can see it from Brian's window, too. It has a deck outside that runs the whole length of this side of the house."

Her eyes were huge. "We can have picnics out there!"

He nodded. "That's the plan. I made up the beds this morning, so you can jump in whenever you're ready. I'm going to get the rest of Brian's stuff."

"I'll help you." Mariah prepared to go, too, but Brian stood in Ashley's doorway, Fred at his side.

"I'll help," he said. "It's my stuff."

While heavy male footsteps and laughter traveled from the room next door to the garage and back again, Fred barking in tune with them, Mariah helped Ashley put her things away.

"I can't believe Brian and I got here," Ashley said, shaking her head. "And he didn't even have to find the gold."

"Sometimes," Mariah said, putting shorts and shirts in a drawer, "we get lucky and life gives us good things."

Ashley bristled at the suggestion that she'd gotten lucky. "It's because I took charge. I knew how I wanted it, and I made it happen, just like the Gypsy said. You're getting married! I have parents again and I'm going to be a really good daughter. When you're old, I'm going to buy you expensive presents from my travels with the ballet company."

Mariah couldn't take issue with the young girl. The simple truth was, Ashley was right. The complicated truth—a conflicted woman, a generous man—was too daunting to think about right now.

Mariah laughed and handed her a towel. "Don't wait until I'm too old."

While Ashley showered, Mariah turned her bed down, then went to check on Brian. He had put his clothes away and was placing a collection of race car models on his windowsill.

"Everything okay?" she asked. He hadn't said much about his mother when Letitia had told him about the accident, except to ask if she was going to be all right. When Letitia assured him that she would, but that she might have to go to jail, he'd nodded. "The housekeeper used to talk to Bianca about it. She said someday my mother was going to kill herself or somebody else. I'm glad nobody died."

It was a generous thought, yet a pathetic reason for a child to be grateful.

He turned to smile at her, looking weary. "I'm good. This is a cool room. My one at my mom's is really big and has a bunch of stuff in it, but this one feels just right.

"And he's pretty cool," Brian said. There was no need to explain who he was talking about.

She had to agree with that. "Where is he?"

"He said he had to make a few calls. He's got this desk in the kitchen, where he does his stuff for graduate school." He looked amazed. "Imagine *wanting* to go to school that long."

"He has plans he thinks he could better accomplish with a degree. His life was pretty rough when he was a kid."

"Yeah, he told me. It's funny that he'd finally get rid of all of his problems and still want to have kids around with sort of the same problems he just got rid of."

Mariah hugged Brian, giving him credit for powers of observation beyond his years. "Shower before you go to bed, okay? It'll help you sleep better."

"Okay."

"I'll be back to tuck you in."

He rolled his eyes. "We're not at the school anymore. And I'm ten. You don't have to tuck me in."

"What if I just look in and say good-night?"

"That'd be okay."

Mariah went downstairs to make something hot to drink and Fred stayed with Brian.

Cam, seated on an overstuffed sofa across the room, waved at her as he spoke on a cordless phone.

"Yeah, that'd be great," he said as she found a kettle on the stove and searched the cupboards for tea. "No, I don't expect you to be here for the wedding, I just thought I should let you know. I'll send you pictures. Yeah, there's plenty of room. If you guys can come later in the summer, we'd love to have you. The boys would like it here. And I've got an old boat for fishing on the lake."

Mariah found a box of chamomile tea and winced—she'd almost rather go without, but not quite. She took down the box, then prayed she could locate some honey to blunt the taste. She held the jar of it to her chest in gratitude when she did. "Thank you!" she whispered prayerfully.

"You're welcome," Cam said as he appeared beside her. "What did I do?"

She took the kettle to the sink and filled it. "Actually, I was thanking the fates for honey, but you're probably the one who bought it."

"I am. What are you putting it on?"

"In," she corrected him, then held up the box. "My tea."

"Hank left that." He made a face. "He didn't like it and I pretty much agree."

She placed the kettle on the burner and turned it on. "I do, too, but it's better than nothing. Tomorrow I'll buy some black tea."

"Make a list of what you and the kids need and I'll take you shopping. Unless there's a plumbing crisis somewhere, then you're on your own. My brother's thinking of visiting at the end of the summer. You'll like him. His wife had four little boys when he married her."

She smiled. "Another knight in shining armor?"

He laughed lightly. "Yeah. Runs in the family." He asked as an afterthought, "Do you cook?"

"Yes," she was happy to reply. "I'm not brilliant, but I'm not bad. And I did promise you brownies."

He nodded, the air changing subtly between them. She felt her skin prickle, her pulse quicken.

"Every day for the whole year," he reminded her, leaning against the counter with both disbelief and amusement in his eyes. "I suppose I should have gotten that in writing."

"I'm true to my word. But I have some other treats you might want to sample."

By the time she heard the words come out of her mouth, it was too late to edit them. And in the change of atmosphere in the corner of the kitchen, they sounded particularly suggestive.

"I make a mean lemon meringue," she added quickly, feeling the color creep up from her neckline. She didn't understand it. She'd been married for four years. There was no reason to be embarrassed by sexual innuendo. "Strawberry shortcake, peanut butter pie, chocolate chip cake with cooked..." She'd have listed the entire contents of the dessert section of her cookbook if he hadn't stopped her abruptly by taking her chin in the vee of his thumb and forefinger.

He concentrated on her with languid hazel eyes, then lowered his mouth to take hers. He was fairly quick, though that kiss reached right into her soul.

"What was that for?" she asked breathlessly when he released her.

He smiled in self-deprecation. "Because you're cute

when you're embarrassed. I apologize if that sounds sexist, but it's honest. You're always so controlled that it was fun to see you in a fluster."

"Ready, Mariah!" Ashley shouted from beyond the hallway before Mariah could react or reply.

"Ready for what?" Cam asked.

"For tucking in."

"You still do that at this age?"

She shrugged, trying to reestablish equilibrium. "I always did because they were away from home and I wanted them to feel safe and cherished. But Brian told me just a few minutes ago that he's too old for it. Maybe you should tell him good-night. He won't resent it coming from you."

"Sure," he said, following her up as she went toward Ashley's room. He stopped at Brian's.

Brian sat up in bed, holding in his hands the globe that normally stood on a built-in shelf. Fred, who'd been lying across Brian's feet, ran to Cam.

"Going somewhere?" Cam asked, indicating the globe.

"No." Brian gave the globe a spin, his expression thoughtful. Fred barked at the suspicious movement and went closer to sniff.

"I was just thinking how cool it is that there are all these faraway places full of interesting stuff that I just don't care about. No, I don't mean I don't *care* about them—I just mean I don't care if I *see* them. 'Cause I like it right here."

He scrambled out of bed to put the globe away, then climbed back under the covers.

The kid, Cam thought, was remarkable.

"You warm enough?"

"Yeah, thanks."

"Found the towels okay?"

"Yeah."

"We're making a list to go shopping tomorrow. Anything you need?"

He reflected, then asked, "Is model car glue a need?"

"Absolutely. I always need anchovies."

Brian crossed his eyes and made a horrible face.

Cam laughed and resisted a surprising impulse to straighten his blankets. It didn't take long, he realized, for children to take over your mind.

He turned out the light. "Sleep well. Holler if you want anything."

As Cam backed out of the room, he collided with Mariah, peeking in. She caught his arm to steady herself.

"Good night, Brian," she called.

He replied, already sounding sleepy.

"'Night, Cam," Ashley shouted.

"Good night, Ashley."

Fred couldn't decide whether to stay or go, but then he followed Cam.

Mariah maintained her hold on Cam's arm as they walked together back down to the kitchen. The kettle was whistling.

She took it off the burner and made her tea. "Can I fix you anything?" she asked.

He knew he couldn't be around her tonight and maintain his sanity. She was wearing pink cotton sweats, and since they'd gotten home, she'd brushed her hair out. She was smiling and relaxed. He could only guess that it was because she finally had what she wanted, though not in the way she'd intended to get it.

Instead of babies, she had two ten-year-olds, and though they had no idea what would happen to Brian eventually, for now she had her two children.

Whatever the reason, she appeared ripe and seductive. Her baggy clothes hid nothing, clinging to her probably bare breasts and her sweet round backside. She was small and perfect, and if he succumbed to impulse, he'd make love to her until he'd wiped Europe from her mind.

He shook his head and moved over to the sofa. Fred sank onto the carpet in front of it. "Thanks. But I'm taking a computer course over the summer and I've got some reading to do."

She came toward him, determination in her eyes. The air changed as it had before. Electricity made his heart stutter and almost fail.

She put a hand to his arm. "I am so grateful for your willingness to help the children."

"I don't think anyone could have turned away," he said. He felt weak. Wanted to take a step back, out of her reach, but there was something wonderful about the torture of her touch.

"Nine men out of ten would have," she said, her voice softening. "Probably 99 out of 100."

He saw it in her eyes—affection born out of gratitude. He wasn't sure he was strong enough to do what he had to.

He crossed his arms in an unconscious attempt to ward her off, but she put a hand to his wrist, her index finger rubbing gently, silkily, over the bone there.

"What if I told you," she asked, her voice a whisper, "that I was so *inclined?*"

In his fantasy, he caught a fistful of her hair, kissed her senseless, swept her up in his arms and took her to bed.

In reality, he knew he had to fight for a better foundation for this marriage. He drew a breath, hating himself, and replied quietly, "I'd say that as desperately as I've longed to hear that from you, I'd prefer it under different conditions."

She blinked at him, momentarily more shocked than embarrassed.

"I want this marriage to be about us, not about them. I'm happy to have them—don't misunderstand me—but I'd have done my damnedest for them without you, and I'd have moved heaven and earth to get you to marry me whether or not they'd been in the picture."

She closed her eyes for a moment, then opened them and faced him squarely. "Let me get this straight," she began in a strangled voice. "You said when I asked you to marry me that you weren't going to have a marriage without sex. Or did I imagine that?"

Fred sat up, unhappy about the change of atmosphere.

His arms still crossed so that he wouldn't abandon his lofty position and grab her, anyway, Cam said, "Well, Mariah, you're missing a subtle difference here."

She put her hands on her hips, growing angry. "Do tell. What am I missing?"

"I said I didn't want a marriage without lovemaking."

She shook her head in exasperation. "You think I don't know the difference?"

He drew a breath, hoping the oxygen would help him reason clearly. "No, but I think you think *I* don't know the difference."

While she took a moment to ponder that, he went on. "This would have been thank-you sex, rather than love-from-the-bottom-of-your-heart sex."

She stared at him, absorbing that, then spread her arms and said, "Cameron, I don't believe you!"

He ran a hand over his face, feeling as though every system in his body was working backward because rejecting her was contrary to his every inclination. "Neither do I," he sighed.

"You're actually turning me down."

"No, I'm not. I'm holding out for better terms."

Fred whined. Cam felt like whining, too.

She reached to the counter for her cup of tea. "Well, I hope you have patience and endurance, because it'll be spring in Outer Mongolia before I feel so inclined again. Good night."

She walked away.

He reminded himself that putting off immediate gratification in the hope of working toward a more permanent fulfillment later was really a noble thing.

It didn't help.

CHAPTER FOURTEEN

CAM AND MARIAH'S WEDDING was supposed to be a simple affair, but the Lightfoot sisters got carried away. Cam guessed that only the time constraint prevented them from booking New York's Plaza Hotel and asking Luciano Pavarotti to sing.

As it was, they were married at the Maple Hill Methodist Church, with Mariah in an ice-blue gown Jackie lent her and with a veil Addy made.

Parker and Ashley were dressed in dark blue, their hair done up with small white flowers. Cam, Hank and Brian wore suits they'd bought in Springfield the day before.

Jackie and Hank hosted the reception at the Yankee Inn.

Mariah couldn't believe how many people attended.

"They're all friends of Cam's," Jackie said, "or clients he's done work for. When word got out that you two took the kids in—well, Maple Hill's devoted to its children."

"But they don't even know me and look at that table of gifts!"

"Don't question. Just be grateful."

Grateful.

That word was beginning to have a worse effect on

her than *escape* did. She stopped in her tracks every time she thought it, and she'd thought it a lot as Parker, the Lightfoot sisters, Jackie, Haley and all the Wonders had rallied the last few days to put this wedding together.

She had intended the lovemaking she'd proposed to Cam to be about gratitude. As she thought about it in hindsight, she decided it would have put her in a superior position. She'd have taught him that giving her what she wanted would be beneficial to him.

Instead, he'd taught her that he welcomed the children for himself and not for her, and that if she thought offering him sex would bend him to her will, she was mistaken.

Coming to that conclusion had taken her three days. And during that time, they'd seen very little of each other. He'd been working day and night on the kitchen at the Manor to make sure it was ready for the crew putting up wallboard on Wednesday.

She'd spent the days finding things for the children to do, signing them up with the Parks and Recreation Department's various sports and craft projects, learning about the house, preparing meals.

Cam usually grabbed dinner on the run, but he never failed to thank her for it or tell her it was delicious. The children were all over him for the brief time he was home, but he dealt with them patiently, laughing with them over reports of Fred's antics.

The dog was a devoted companion and personal comedy act all in one. He chased the children, then ran from them to encourage their pursuit. He mooched treats in a style Cam insisted wasn't begging but highway robbery.

Whenever Mariah sat, Fred sat beside her with his head in her lap or on her feet.

It had been only three days, she mused as she watched Cam with their guests, and she was in love with their life. And, God help her, she was in love with him. She didn't want to be, had fought it with everything in her, but his determination to love her was stronger than her ability to resist him.

This felt very different from the love she'd had for Ben. That had been warm and sweet and hopeful—but turned out to be cold and unforgiving, with every hope dashed.

What she felt for Cam was hot and had no sweetness about it. It felt bigger than she was, louder than her thoughts, stronger than her own life force.

She could barely contain it and had to admit—if only to herself—that she was almost afraid of it.

Jackie came to her with Ashley and Brian and two of her four children. "The kids and I have talked it over," she said, "and your two are spending the night with us."

"But you have four of your own!"

"That'll only make it more fun. Ashley can sleep with the girls, and Brian can bunk on the couch. The twins are too loud for anyone to sleep with."

"Well…are you sure?" Mariah felt a sense of panic. Jackie was trying to give her a wedding night. "Maybe we should check with Cam."

"We already have," Ashley said, looking excited. She was flanked by Jackie's girls, who were giggling. "He says it's okay if it's okay with you."

"Good." Without waiting for an answer, Jackie

shooed the children toward the cake table. She sniffed the small nosegay Mariah carried. "You can throw your bouquet and take off any time you want. Try to aim this at Parker. She and Gary are looking pretty serious."

Mariah looked across the room where Cam had been and found him wending his way through the crowd toward her.

"Are you ready to go?" she asked.

"Any time you are," he replied.

Jackie clapped for everyone's attention, then beckoned all the single women forward. There was laughter and jostling as some took positions in the back, hiding behind while others took offensive positions in front.

Jackie offered her hand to help Mariah stand on one of the dining room chairs.

Mariah spotted Parker in the crowd, playfully fighting Glory Anselmo, Jackie's nanny and Jimmy Elliott's girlfriend, for a front spot. Mariah turned and tossed the small bouquet over her shoulder in Parker's direction. There were screams and squeals and when she turned back round, Glory and Parker each had a piece of it, both women laughingly refusing to let go.

Until Gary appeared to kiss Parker, who suddenly seemed to forget her need for the bouquet.

Glory screamed and leaped in the air with it, waving it triumphantly over her head. Jimmy caught her to him, laughing.

Mariah looked for Jackie to help her down, but found Cam, instead. Rather than offer his hand, he bracketed her waist and swept her to the floor.

"Where's everybody going?" she asked. A general

exodus was under way. At the door, they all flanked the long walkway from the church to the street.

"This must be the rice gauntlet," Cam speculated.

"Not rice. Birdseed," Mariah corrected him, remembering that Jackie had had everyone at city hall making the little bags on their lunch hours.

Cam looked puzzled. "I didn't know birdseed promised fertility."

"It doesn't," she explained. "But the birds eat it, so rice doesn't litter the street."

"So the significance of the ritual's just lost?"

"Relax," she said. "It wouldn't have worked with me, anyway. You ready?"

He caught her hand and started forward. "Am I ready!"

CAM TOOK OFF HIS TIE as he drove them home in Mariah's van—a more reputable vehicle for a special occasion than his truck. It was now dark and cool, the fragrance from the open window a mixture of woods and wildflowers.

She leaned her head back against her seat, her veil in her lap. Jackie and Haley had helped her wind her hair into a knot, and she now shifted uncomfortably on it. Finally, she pulled out the pins and combed out the dark, glossy mass with her fingers.

Her hair was magnificent, he acknowledged for the umpteenth time since he'd met her. He had to make himself concentrate on the road.

She seemed different today, more mellow and relaxed despite the festive ceremony, but it didn't mean anything would change tonight. He accepted that.

At least he'd dealt with it philosophically most of the day. But now, with her resting languidly in her seat beside him and the perfume of fecund summer all around them, to continue deluding himself was hard. He wanted her desperately.

The house, when they arrived, was dark and filled with that same fragrance of promise. They'd left the windows open on the lake side and the sound of lapping water greeted their arrival.

He locked the door behind him, intercepted Fred's assault of ecstatic welcome while Mariah sidestepped the dog to save Jackie's dress.

"Be right back!" she called as she ran for the hallway. "Evan left a bottle of champagne when he dropped off his gift!"

That suggested she intended for him to open it. Hmm. He tossed his jacket on a chair and his tie after it, and undid the top two buttons of his shirt. Fred settled under the table.

The bottle opened with a satisfying pop. Lacking champagne flutes, he was pouring the wine into two water glasses when Mariah came up beside him in a long white slip. No, it was a negligee.

He forgot to stop pouring.

With a soft squeal of laughter, Mariah righted his hand and moved it and the overflowing glass to the sink. She sopped up the mess with a paper towel and glanced at him with unmistakable affection. He'd caught that glance a few times today while they'd been separated by well-wishing friends at their reception. He'd been sure he was imagining things.

She held the fluid silk of the negligee's skirt out and

did a turn. It highlighted the curve of her hips and thighs, and through the openwork of the lace, he caught a glimpse of the rosy tips of her breasts. He couldn't speak.

"It was a gift from Letitia and Lavinia," she said, her fingertips running up the vee neckline to her white shoulder. "They're convinced we're going to fall madly in love."

A note in her tone suggested they were wrong. Now he was even more off balance.

"You're sure they're mistaken," he said.

"I know they're mistaken," she replied, holding up her glass. Then she added in a whisper he knew he'd remember until the day he died, possibly even after, "I've already fallen."

His heart stalled. Had she said that, or was he hallucinating?

She answered that by clinking her glass against his and toasting, "To us."

He drank to the toast. Then lifted her in his arms and carried her to his bedroom. Fred followed, watching with confused surprise as he was left on the wrong side of the door.

MARIAH COULDN'T BREATHE. For so long in her marriage to Ben, lovemaking had meant reproduction. The simple wonder of making love, the soul-stirring, mind-boggling impact of it, had been lost in the rigorous details and timing called for in the interest of conception. It had ceased to be about him or her.

Now Cam's every movement revered her. He set her gently on her feet by the side of his bed, removed the negligee carefully and draped it over the foot of the bed. Then he held her away from him and studied her with flattering seriousness.

His eyes finally met hers with admiration in them, and a possessiveness she felt all the way to her heart.

"You're very beautiful," he said softly.

She dismissed that with a shift of her shoulders and was about to deny it verbally, when he put a hand to her waist and sensation ricocheted up her body and then down. She lost the power of speech.

He used that hand to draw her to him and then he simply held her. She wrapped her arms around him, knowing instinctively how critical the moment was, that making love would change everything.

"I love you," he said, hugging her to him.

She felt the buttons of his shirt embossing her skin, the fabric of his slacks rubbing the soft flesh on the inside of her thigh.

There'd been a time when she'd thought she'd never want to make love again. Now she couldn't wait to fill herself with him.

"I love you, too," she whispered against his collarbone. "Oh, Cam, I love you, too."

He lifted her to place her on the bed, then sat down to pull off his shoes and socks. She scrambled onto her knees to help him, lifting his shirt out of his slacks, unbuttoning buttons, tugging off his clothes. They finally lay together in the middle of the bed and settled into each other's arms.

Cam's hand traced the length of her body, trailing sparks over her shoulder, down her side, across her tummy.

She explored his back, finding the jut of his shoulder blades, the crenellated line of his spine, the muscled curve of his buttocks.

He pressed her close and turned so that she lay atop him. His hands explored every curve while she planted kisses across the dusting of hair on his chest, then down the middle of him to his navel.

With an intake of breath, he tipped her sideways into his arm and kissed the hollow of her throat. His hand swept along the inside of her thigh, then touched the now warm and pulsing heart of her.

She trembled.

He raised his head to look into her eyes, his turbulent with desire, yet somehow gentle. "You're shaking," he observed softly. "Is that good or bad?"

"It's good," she murmured.

"You have to tell me the truth."

"I am." She'd half expected to react negatively to the intimate touch. For so long her body had symbolized all her failures as a woman—all the babies she'd lost.

But this lovemaking was about her and him and the gift of this moment.

He cradled her in his arms and brushed the tumbled hair from her face. "Do you hate this part?" he asked, his thumb massaging her temple.

She was surprised by his perception. "I used to," she replied honestly. Then she smiled. "But I'm liking this very much. Please don't stop."

He whispered her name and touched her again, reaching inside her with an artistry that made looking backward a waste of time. She lost awareness of everything but the two of them; her world now the narrow space they occupied in the middle of the bed.

Even that seemed to dissolve as pleasure approached her, eluded her, then came upon her with the impact of a punch. Sensation throbbed inside her, so strong that she felt as though she'd gone headfirst off a cliff, only to land miraculously on a feather pillow as pleasure echoed and echoed again before drifting away.

She didn't want to think about gratitude, but that was what she felt. Not because Cam had given her pleasure, but because he'd restored her sense of the woman she'd felt sure had died with the last baby.

CAM WAS HAPPY, RELIEVED, that she was as invested in this effort to communicate as he was. She was so focused on him, made the softest, most desperate little sounds, then said his name on a gasp before pressing her face into his shoulder and dissolving into a long series of tremors.

He'd known they'd be good together. Later, he'd have to remind her that if she'd listened to him in the first place…

He lost the idea when she touched him.

He'd thought it would be nice to take her through it again so that she couldn't forget how right he'd been, but she had her own plan. And he wasn't man enough to resist.

Actually, he was, but her uses for his masculinity were more positive. Her soft touch ran over and over him until he had the intellect of an idiot but the sensitivity of an empath.

By the time he pushed her back against the pillows and rose over her, he felt he could see into her soul. Touch translated all the things there were no words for into feeling.

When he entered her and she welcomed him, it was as though a star had opened up and enveloped them. Brightness filled the space inside him and out and every bad thing that had ever happened to him faded into insignificance.

Mariah shuddered under him and he held her tightly as they fell back to reality together. But it was reality with a new truth to it. Love prevailed.

CHAPTER FIFTEEN

MARIAH HAD NEVER BEEN so happy. The month of June was like a fairy tale for adults.

Cam started work on the homeless shelter, a project that had been stalled for months but was now finally under way. She sent him off every morning with a bag lunch and a kiss after having lain in his arms all night.

On alternate mornings, she and Fred took the children to the park for their scheduled activities, stopped at the bakery, then hurried home to work on a painting she'd begun of a family on the beach.

She picked up the children midafternoon, then listened to their laughing and bickering and Fred's barking as they shot hoops outside, or heard the teenybopper voices on afternoon television when they stayed in. Either way, she found the cacophony a happy background as she prepared dinner. On weekends, they went for drives or barbecued at home, and Cam often took the kids and the dog fishing in the small boat tied up to their dock.

She couldn't quite believe how she and Ben had pursued this life and it had always been out of reach. Then, when she'd been sure all hope of family life was lost to her, it had practically fallen on her from the sky. Well, Brian had, anyway.

Addy Whitcomb, who lived on the other side of the lake, hosted a Fourth of July picnic. The Megraths and Mike, Hank and Jackie and their children, Parker and Gary and his teenagers and Evan Braga sat on lawn chairs or on blankets on the rich grass that sloped down to the lake. Fred was beside himself with so much attention.

They ate and laughed all afternoon while the children and the dog chased one another until they were exhausted.

At dusk they had a last round of strawberry shortcake and settled down to listen to Gary's kids and Mike McGee, who were practicing several new numbers for the high school choir and tried them out on their willing audience.

Addy joined in, familiar with many of the old romantic ballads, then soon everyone else did, the music mellowing their moods. Families moved together into little knots, a part of the group yet separate, songs of love reminding them of their bond.

As Mariah leaned into Cam, with Ashley, Brian and Fred sprawled against them, she let herself be swallowed in the moment. Love and contentment closed over her head and she said a prayer of gratitude for the gift of her family.

It occurred to her that this *could* last forever.

Weary from their busy day's misadventures, the children were asleep shortly after nine, Fred on his back on the foot of Brian's bed. The house was filled with the nighttime glow of a contented household.

Mariah found Cam in a tub filled with bubbles at nine-thirty, his arms beckoning her to him. There were candles on the windowsill and the wide rim of the tub.

She ripped off shorts, shirt and underwear, toed out of her shoes and climbed in to fit between his knees and lie back against him with an "Aah!" of bliss.

After a few moments of soaking, they soaped each other, scrubbed shoulders and backs with a loofah, then somehow lost the purpose of the bath…or found it.

Bubbles flew and floated on the candlelit air as they made love, lost in their continuing discovery of each other.

THE MIDDLE OF THE FOLLOWING week, the children were at classes at the swimming pool, and Cam was enjoying a day off. Mariah had just warmed blueberry muffins and made coffee, Fred glued to her heels, hoping for a handout. Bart Megrath had just stopped by and Mariah invited him to stay.

"I'd love to, but I can't." He glanced at his watch. "I have court in half an hour. I know all Ashley's clothes and toys were shipped to you, but this box of legal paperwork was sent to my office." He handed it to Cam. "I thought you should have it first, then if there's anything you want me to look over, let me know."

Cam walked him out to his car while Mariah opened the box and pulled out several file folders. The tab on one of them read "Ashley Weisfield's Adoption."

Cam returned and read over her shoulder. "Anything interesting?"

They sat at a right angle to each other and shared the pages in the file. Mariah gave Fred a muffin to move him out from between them.

She was trying to make sense of Walter Kerwin's notes in a mostly illegible hand, when Cam, looking at a long, legal document, said, a startling note in his voice, "Oh, my God!"

Mariah glanced up with a sense of foreboding. "What?"

Cam stared at the document, sure he must have misread it. This couldn't be? What were the odds? Astronomical at best.

"What?" Mariah demanded for a second time. She put her hand to his wrist. "Cam, what's the matter? You're gray!"

He tried to think clearly. He held up a finger for silence so that he could reread the document. He had to be sure he wasn't misunderstanding this.

"Adoptive father," it read, "James Weisfield. Adoptive mother, Eleanor Simms Weisfield." Okay, that was a surprise, but he understood it. Ashley had been adopted by the Weisfields, not born to them.

He looked at the bottom of the form, where Ashley's natural parents were listed. The name of the father was blank. He stared at the name of the mother again and felt the shock run through him and settle in the pit of his stomach.

He handed the form to Mariah.

She studied him worriedly as she took it. "What's wrong?"

"Ashley was adopted by the Weisfields," he said.

She nodded. "I know that. When she was a baby."

"Read the name of the natural mother," he said.

Mariah's eyes scanned the sheet. "Barbara Elizabeth Tr—" She stopped, her eyes widening, her mouth open in astonishment as she gazed up at him. "Barbara *Trent*." She swallowed. "Ashley is… yours?"

It hadn't occurred to him that she might think that. "No," he corrected her, riffling through the file for something that might offer an explanation. "Barbara was my sister. Ashley is my niece."

Mariah gasped. "But I can't believe…I mean, how could this have happened? The coincidence is…"

"We used to come here as children," he said, flipping through a sheaf of papers torn from a yellow pad. The handwriting was more legible and seemed to be a case-worker's notes. "Maybe Barbara came back here. We lost track of her for more than two years before she died."

"But the Weisfields were from New York."

He caught Barbara's name in some notes and laid the papers flat on the table. He went backward a page to find the beginning of the reference.

"'The Weisfields hired Barbara while summering in Maple Hill,'" he read aloud. "'She kept house for them and prepared meals, and they liked her so much they brought her back to New York with them in the winter. Their relationship was closer than that of employer-employee, and when she revealed that she was pregnant, they were already providing insurance but helped her with prenatal classes. Barbara and her child lived with them and Barbara continued working for them until her death in a motorcycle accident when Ashley was three months old.

"'I believe their bid to adopt Ashley is motivated by a genuine affection for the child and the child's mother. I support it wholeheartedly.'"

Cam leaned back in his chair, a storm of emotion inside him. He hated to think Barbara had stayed away because she'd been embarrassed that the modeling agency chose not to represent her or because she'd gotten pregnant.

But even as a little girl she'd been so sure of herself, so certain she was going to escape their lives and do big things.

He was comforted by the knowledge that before she died, Barbara had found people who cared for her and a place where she was happy. He was glad she'd had a child, if only for such a short time, so that she'd known the familial love they'd all longed for as children and never found—except in one another.

A gasp escaped him and Mariah came around the table to wrap her arms around him. "Oh, Cam!" she said, kissing his cheek. "Over all these years and across all the miles and the convoluted paths you and she have taken, you and Barbara are reconnected in…Ashley."

He heard an odd, new sound in Mariah's voice, but he didn't dwell on it because he was consumed with himself at the moment and his connection to the child living under his roof.

Unaware of the blow he was dealing his marriage, he said with the sincere wonder he felt, "I can't believe it! Ashley is my own flesh and blood."

Mariah felt as if she'd been hit in the head with a tire iron. Flesh and blood. You could deny its importance, convince yourself it really didn't matter, but you couldn't fight instinct. Blood is thicker than water. Blood calls to blood. Scores of aphorisms about blood connections had survived the generations because their truth could not be disputed.

She was pleased for him, thrilled for Ashley because

there wasn't a man the child loved more in the world. But Mariah saw problems ahead for herself. Cam's joy at the discovery was genuine and touching. He was ecstatic to have found his flesh and blood.

How happy would Mariah be able to make him in this marriage, she wondered anew, if he was just beginning to realize how important blood ties were?

The doorbell pealed urgently. Mariah went to answer it, happy to have an excuse to leave the room, misery moving in where only moments ago she'd felt so contented and secure.

Parker flew at her the moment she opened the door. She wrapped her in an herbal embrace, then stood back, beaming. Then she held up her left hand, the third finger bearing a silver band with a beautiful round-cut diamond in the center.

"We're getting married!" Parker stated the obvious, wrapping her arms around Mariah again. "Can you believe it? And the kids are happy about it, too! I don't know how I got this lucky, but I'm not going to question it."

Mariah didn't have to force a smile, despite her own suddenly precarious happiness. She wanted very much for her sister to be happy. "That's so wonderful! We all love Gary and his kids. You got this lucky because he's a smart man and knows you're a wonderful woman. Have you set a date?"

"Two weeks from Saturday."

Mariah blinked. "That's pretty fast."

Parker rolled her eyes. "This from the woman who was married in four days." When Mariah conceded that with a nod, trying not to think about all that hung in the balance, Parker added, "You and Ashley and Stacey are wearing lavender. The three of us'll go shopping next week, okay? And we'll need Cam and Brian for groomsmen. I'll call you." She was already backing out the door. "I've got a million things to do. Kisses to Cam and the kids."

"Bye!" Mariah called after her as Parker ran out to her car. "Congratulations!"

"Congratulations to whom?" Cam asked. "For what?" He came up behind Mariah, tossing car keys on a ring on his index finger. He'd said earlier that he was going to stop by Hank's office to check next week's schedule, so he would pick up the children. He still looked a little stunned. Fred pranced, eager to accompany him.

"Parker," she replied. "She's getting married." Now she had to force the smile. She felt stiff and awkward, all the easy camaraderie of the past six weeks lost in her concern over an issue she'd thought settled.

She saw his eyes run over her face, as though he noted something wrong and was trying to figure out what it was.

"You're not happy about that?"

"I'm delighted," she replied, smiling wider, sure her pleasure must appear fake. "I love Gary. They'll be wonderful together."

"Then what's the matter?"

"Nothing," she said. She sounded convincing to her ear, but he now knew every inch of her body and every subtle change in her emotions. He wasn't fooled. So she kept talking as she backed toward the kitchen, hoping he'd go out the door as he'd intended and she could collapse on a kitchen chair and have the breakdown she felt sure would be upon her any moment. "If you don't mind, while you're out, we need milk, eggs, bread and that juice stuff the kids like so much. You remember. We put vodka in it the other night when we ran out of tonic."

He was following her back to the kitchen and she was sure he hadn't heard a word of her impromptu grocery list. He was trying to read her eyes. At their heels, Fred looked anxiously from one to the other.

"You'll be late if you don't go now," she chattered, still backing away. "And you know Brian. If you aren't there on time, he'll find something outrageous to do, like drive a tractor home or…"

"They won't be out for half an hour."

"You were going to stop by the office first."

"I can do that after. Mariah." He drew her toward him as she tried to pull away. "What's the matter with you? You're not upset that Ashley's my…oh, God."

He understood; she saw it in his face.

His expression hardened, he dropped his hand and turned away from her, walking halfway toward the door, then turning back, temper igniting like kindling under a match.

"What is wrong with you, woman?" he asked.

"You know what's wrong with me!" she shot back, everything inside her churning into a ball of conflict and misery. "I'm not blaming you, Cam," she said, making an effort to remain calm, "but you just said it yourself. Ashley's your flesh and blood. That's why you're so happy you've found her. And you have every right to that."

"Damn it, Mariah!" he shouted. Fred whined and Cam ignored him. "I'm happy because she's Barbara's flesh and blood, not because she's mine! She reconnects me with the sister I lost! We had such a grueling childhood that we were everything to each other. This is a little like having Barbara back."

"I know," she insisted. "Blood connections are important. I'm happy for you."

He shook his head at her. "Yeah. You look happy."

She tried to make him see reason. "Cam, I'll bet even you were surprised by how much it means to you that Ashley's your niece. We have fun together, and you generously agreed to shelter the kids—"

"Shelter them?" he questioned hotly. "I'm not sheltering them. We're adopting Ashley, and we're making a home for Brian until—"

"Cam, that's semantics! You agreed to marry me so I could adopt—"

"No." He cut her off quietly, but so abruptly that she felt it almost physically. "I agreed to marry you because I wanted to marry you. And it was a wonderful bonus that Ashley was part of the deal."

She tried one more time. "Cam, you can *have* children."

"I do have children," he said.

She sighed patiently. "One day they're going to make arrangements for Brian…"

"Maybe not. Maybe they'll let him stay here."

She'd harbored that hope, too, but it wouldn't help her argument at the moment.

"And when a year's up," she continued as though he hadn't spoken, "Ashley's coming to Europe with me. You should have children, Cam. Babies with your genes would be a wonderful addition to this world."

There. She'd cut him loose. She waited in anguish for him to take advantage of the opportunity.

CHAPTER SIXTEEN

CAM COULD NOT REMEMBER ever feeling so close to mayhem in his life. Even during his childhood years of neglect, then his wife's easy dismissal of him from her life, he'd never wanted to hurt anyone in return.

But to have the love he felt for Mariah and the children handed back to him was just about more than he could take.

He had to make contact. Much as he would have liked to throttle her, he settled for grabbing the collar of her shirt, instead. "Don't you dare pretend that you're nobly trying to give me my freedom, when we both know damn well what you're really doing."

Her wide eyes were blank. Was it possible she didn't really understand herself at all?

"I'm not the one who can't live without flesh-and-blood children," he said brutally, too hurt and angry to be diplomatic. "You are. So your infertility broke up your first marriage. That's sad. But instead of looking for someone who wouldn't care about it, you'd rather grieve for your lost babies by refusing to ever be happy with other children who need you even more. You'd rather be a martyr to the tragedy than be happy with me."

She went pale.

He was still too angry to feel guilty. He freed her and turned away, afraid to be too close.

"You're the one who went after what you wanted," she said, her voice loud but tight, "and was determined to hammer me into place where I didn't fit. You were ready to settle down, and you had to have me. I warned you—"

"Oh, stop it." He spun on her and went on without mercy. "If you're going to tell me you warned me I'd want my own children one day, I don't want to hear it again. You are the most single-minded woman I've ever met. Which would be a good trait if you applied some sense to your determination. Well, you know what?" He reached into his back pocket for his wallet, removed a credit card from it and slapped it into her hand. "You're the one who should go. Go to Europe. Go to Bora Bora. Go wherever the hell you want, because I'm not about to spend a lifetime with you questioning my love at every turn."

She was going to cry, but God forgive him, he had to get the rest of it out so that she knew he was as determined as she was.

"Bon voyage. If I'm still single when you return, look me up. Maybe the kids and I will take you back."

Sudden horror filled her eyes. "If I go, I'm taking the children with me."

"I thought going to Europe was a mission of self-discovery."

"I've discovered," she countered, "that I want them."

He shook his head. "The state won't let you take Brian out of the country. He'll have to stay with me. And if you're going to put so much stock in flesh and blood,

Ashley's mine, not yours. Our adoption is nowhere near final, so that's what the courts will have to go by."

"You wouldn't," she whispered.

He met her gaze and held it. "If you believe that, then you don't know me at all. I'm going to pick up the kids."

HE FELT AS THOUGH HE WAS dying. His heart was pounding, his head ached and he was having difficulty taking an even breath. Fighting down the need to scream bloody murder was taking its toll on him.

The kids were chattering away in the back seat. He glanced in the rearview mirror. Their faces were rosy from their strenuous morning of swimming. Brian's hair was spiky and wet; Ashley's was wound into precisely the same style of knot Mariah often wore. He couldn't live without those two kids. And he didn't know how he was going to live without Mariah. He could only pray she'd come to her senses. But every time he thought she had, this insanity about babies reared its head again.

He couldn't quite believe he'd told her to go. If she did, he'd have to be put on life support.

"We passed it!" the children whined in unison.

He pulled up at a red light, grateful that he'd even seen it in his state of mind. "Passed what?"

"Minuteman Ice Cream! You said we could stop."

"I did?"

Brian sounded puzzled. "We asked if we could get butterscotch sundaes and you said yes."

He turned his right blinker on. "Then we'll go back," he said.

When they got home, Mariah's van was still there, but there was no sign of her. He put the sundae the kids had insisted he buy her in the freezer and noticed that the credit card was gone. He was about to leave the children to finish their ice cream and wander through the house to see if he detected Mariah's presence, but Ashley noticed her name on the file folder on the table and sat down to look at the papers still spread there.

"What is all this stuff?" she asked, still working on her sundae. Brian had hiked up onto the counter to finish his.

Cam sat down opposite her. "It's some legal papers your guardian sent our lawyer. You know Mr. Megrath?"

"Yes. He's Rachel and Erica's uncle."

"Right. Well, he brought them over and I was looking through them. I found out something really interesting. And I thought it was neat."

She smiled across the table. "What is it?"

"You know that your parents adopted you when you were just a baby," he said.

She nodded. "Yes. They thought I was special."

"Do you know where you were born?"

She nodded. "In New York. The lady I was born to was a friend of my mom and dad's."

"Right." He considered that a sensitive way for the Weisfields to have put it to her. "There's something very special to me about that."

"What?"

"Your biological mother—the lady you were born to—was my sister."

For a moment, Ashley didn't react, then she asked tentatively. "So…you're my uncle?"

He was worried about her look of concern.

"Yes. Does that make you unhappy?"

"No." That appeared to be a lie. "But…does that mean you can't be my dad?"

So, that was it. Relieved, he drew a breath and reached across the table to touch her arm. "No. I'm still going to adopt you as we planned. But your natural mother was very special to me, and you've been very special to me all along, and now we're sort of connected through her. I like that."

She nodded, happy to believe him but seemingly unable to absorb what it meant to him. Her bottom line remained. "As long as you can still adopt me."

"Rachel and Erica's uncle is working on it right now."

"Okay." She gathered up her empty cup and plastic spoon to throw them away. "Come on, Brian," she beckoned. "Cartoons are on."

Brian sat on the counter, looking woeful as she skipped away.

Cam, understanding the boy's jealousy, went to hook an arm around him and sweep him off the counter. He turned him upside down until the boy laughed helplessly. He'd like to promise Brian the same future he'd promised Ashley, but he couldn't. The boy still had a mother, such as she was.

He carried him into the living room and dropped him on the sofa beside Ashley, who was already settled in with the remote.

Cam went in search of Mariah, his heart thumping uncomfortably. What if she'd believed that he was telling her to go, instead of understanding that he was simply frustrated by her unwillingness to trust his love for her, trust that it did not have to include biological children?

He concluded a few moments later that she was not in the house. He checked the garage, hoping to find her standing in front of her easel. No such luck.

For a moment, he was distracted by her painting. A boy and a girl Ashley's and Brian's ages ran along the beach, a big black dog in pursuit. A woman trailed after them, her dark hair flying out behind her. In the foreground, a man lying on the sand some distance back from them watched their antics. The tie that connected the four and the dog was somehow palpable.

It was them, he thought. He wished Mariah could have heard Ashley a few minutes ago. She hadn't given a rip about the fact that he and she were related by blood. She just wanted to be sure he could adopt her.

He walked around onto the deck and found it empty. He went the length of it, panic beginning to bubble in his chest, and then, around the far side of the house, he found her on her hands and knees, pulling weeds out of a bed of tomatoes.

Fred stood beside her, looking over her shoulder and occasionally licking her ear. He leaped at Cam when he saw him, tail wagging.

"Hey, Fred."

Mariah cast Cam a glance that said although she was still here, she wasn't happy about it.

"I promised Parker I'd be in her wedding," she explained, "a week from Saturday. And we'll have to see Bart about who takes the children. Just because you declare something to be true doesn't mean that I have to believe it is."

"Obviously," he said, pushing the old bucket she was tossing weeds into nearer to her as she moved down the row. The dog leaned closer to inspect the bucket, but Cam drew him away from it. "You don't believe me when I tell you I love you."

"I believe you," she corrected him. "I just know that feelings can change."

"I thought I was the fortune-teller."

"This isn't a vision. I've seen this phenomenon for myself."

"That wasn't me." He didn't know how to put it any more clearly. "My feelings for you will not change. Except that I don't consider you as smart as I once did."

She didn't answer, just kept weeding the tomatoes. Fred lay down beside her.

Cam went inside to call Hank, since he never had checked in at the office. He was happy to learn that his brief respite was over, and that he'd have to put in a lot of overtime for the rest of this week to keep on schedule.

He stayed away as much as possible for the next four days. When he and Mariah did cross paths, they treated each other with cool politeness in the knowledge that sharp words wouldn't be good for the children. They slept in the same room, but Mariah was usually fast asleep when he came in around midnight, and still asleep when he left before six.

He stayed on his side of the bed, careful not to touch her, unwilling to let her think he was signaling a truce and was willing to capitulate on anything he'd said.

Despite their efforts, he saw that the children were aware of the antagonism between them and seemed tense themselves. They spent a lot of time in Ashley's room on her computer, Fred at their feet. Cam hated that his argument with Mariah had split their little family into camps.

He slept in Saturday morning, the job finally completed in the wee hours. He was drawn to the kitchen midmorning by a wonderful aroma, and found Mariah serving coffee cake and cocoa to Ashley and Brian, Fred begging between them.

Mariah poured a cup of coffee, set it at his place, then dished up a piece of coffee cake for him. She also pushed the mail toward him.

He took a sip of coffee and looked through the catalogs, junk mail and bills. In the middle of the bills was a legal-size envelope with the seal of the Commonwealth of Massachusetts in the upper left-hand corner.

Assuming it had something to do with the adoption, he slit it open with his butter knife.

He unfolded the one-page letter and read silently.

Dear Mr. and Mrs. Trent,
It has come to the attention of Services to Children and Families that Ashley Weisfield, whom you have filed to adopt, was a twin, and that her brother was given up at birth to a family in Los Angeles. Because of circumstances involving lack of interest and prison time, his family would like to give him up for adoption and would like to place him with his sister. His name is Brian Barrow. Please contact your attorney and make the necessary arrangements.

Sincerely,
The Governor

Three things were instantly apparent about the letter. First, the paper on which it was printed had been created by copying another letter with the Commonwealth's letterhead and blanking out its contents by placing a clean sheet of paper over it. The line that marked the edge of the sheet was clearly visible.

Second, it had been signed in lavender ink. Ashley was the only one he knew who used lavender ink.

Third, the language had a nonprofessional sound.

Cam was torn between laughter at the effort and anguish that a child's life should come to this—a forged letter pleading for adoption.

He handed Mariah the letter. "You might be interested in this," he said. He looked at the children, one across from him, one on his left, their faces wide-eyed with innocent interest.

"What is it?" Ashley asked.

"You can read it when Mariah's finished," he said. "Would you pass the butter, please?"

Ashley obliged, a stolen glance at Brian the only clue that she was part of the scam.

Mariah turned to Cam, her eyes brimming with tears. For an instant they forgot their animosity in their love and concern for the clever, desperate children who would think up such a scheme. Brian wanted them for a family, and Ashley was lending her skills to help him acquire them.

On the pretext of rereading the letter, Mariah held it up, shielding her face, until she got herself under control.

Then she passed the letter to Ashley, who read it quickly, gasped, passed it on to Brian, then joined him in a well-orchestrated, grandly theatrical round of hugs and grins of surprised delight.

"This is really interesting," Mariah said finally after a deep sip of coffee. "Because I seem to remember that your birthday is in May, Brian, while Ashley's is in December. You've always made a point that you're half a year older than she is."

The children stared, momentarily at a loss. Then Brian said quickly, "That's probably just the date my adoptive mother gave me when she took me in."

"I don't think so." Mariah shook her head. "It was listed on the birth certificate in the office at the school."

"Well…" Cam could see the boy's brain at work in his eyes.

"And I don't think the governor gets involved in these kinds of cases."

Brian fell against the back of his chair, busted.

"I told you!" Ashley said, beside herself with exasperation. "I told you! In all my records, the governor's name wasn't mentioned once!"

"It was the purple ink!" Brian shot back at her. "Nobody in the government uses purple ink!"

"You were pretty clever, though," Cam felt obliged to praise. "It was a very artistic approach to the problem. Would have probably landed you in jail if you'd pulled it on anybody else, but, hey. I liked it."

"Cam, you have to find a way to keep me," Brian said, coming to stand beside his chair. "This is the absolute best my life has ever been. Don't let them take me back. Can't we see if your lawyer can work it out so I can stay?"

Cam saw the caution in Mariah's eyes, but he ignored

it. "I will," he replied, wrapping his arm around Brian. "I'll talk to him this afternoon."

"Cam," Mariah said under her breath.

A cool glance her way told her to stay out of it.

"What were you doing?" she demanded an hour later. They'd driven the children, showered and clothes changed, to a birthday party at Jackie's house. Now they were on their way home.

"I've been where he is," Cam said calmly. "I know what it's like. I'd have given everything for someone to rescue me."

"But…"

He knew what she was going to say. "I know. You're leaving. But that doesn't mean the court won't let me have him."

"You've been gone fifty hours out of the last sixty-two! How can you raise a child that way?"

"I was avoiding *you,* Mariah," he said with a scolding glance at her. "Hank will adjust my schedule."

"You want us to stay married," she challenged, hurt feelings visible in her eyes, "and you can't stand to be around me."

"I can't stand not to touch you," he corrected her. "Big difference."

She made a sound of exasperation. "Will you please pull over somewhere so we can talk about this?"

He kept driving. "What's to talk about? You've made up your mind."

"I want you to understand," she pleaded, her voice tight and high, "that I sincerely do have your best interest at heart!"

He pulled into a lay-by under the branches of several large maples at the edge of the woods. Once the motor was off, he tore off his seat belt and faced her, one hand on the steering wheel, the other on the back of his seat.

"You want to rip our family apart, leave me to have babies with someone else, and you consider that in my best interest? What is wrong with you?"

"You only want me to stay because you feel sorry for me!" she shouted. "Who wouldn't want to have their own babies if they could?"

"The man who's in love with a woman who *can't* have them!" he roared back at her. "Listen to yourself, Mariah. You're the one with the problem. It isn't…"

His cell phone rang, a weird noise amid the barrage of harsh words. He answered it in the same tone in which he'd been speaking to her. "Hello!"

Then he drew a breath for calm and said on a grim glance at Mariah, "Sorry, Addy. I didn't mean to bark at you. Who's Victorian shower fell in? Oh. Okay. Tell Haley I'll be right there."

He turned off the phone and pulled back out onto the road. "Let's just not talk about it anymore," he said. "You stay for Parker's wedding, and the kids and I'll find a way to get along without you afterward."

In his anger, he was pleased to hear that he sounded as though he could really do that.

CHAPTER SEVENTEEN

CAM WOULD BE JUST FINE without her. Mariah hated that, but reminded herself that whether he believed her or not, she was doing this for him.

He dropped her off at the house, reminded her that she'd have to pick up the children in the middle of the afternoon, then roared away again, headed for Haley and Bart's.

Needing physical activity, Mariah went into a cleaning frenzy, Fred watching but staying a safe distance away. She cleared up the kitchen, cleaned out the refrigerator, then washed the kitchen floor. She emptied the trash, put a new plastic bag in the can, then, with fresh soapy water in the bucket, headed for the bathrooms.

She'd scrubbed one and was about to start on the other one, when she heard the front door open, followed by what sounded like the entire roster of the Chicago Bulls headed her way. Fred ran out to investigate.

Mariah followed just as Ashley thumped past her and into her bedroom. "We're going in-line skating at the Armory!" she shouted from the floor of her closet. Fred wriggled in beside her, tail wagging. "Freddy!" she complained, giggling.

"I thought this was a swimming party."

"Yeah, but the pool's closed 'cause something cracked or something. So Erica's dad brought me home to get my Rollerblades. Where are they?"

Mariah went to help rummage through the rubble in the bottom of her closet. She had a shoe rack, but somehow her shoes never got into it.

Mariah swept everything out.

"There's one!" Ashley said gleefully.

Mariah crawled into the closet, certain the other must be stuck in a corner.

"Did you know that Cam's my uncle?" Ashley asked.

On her hands and knees, with pants and coats brushing her face, Fred kissing her and game or puzzle pieces digging into her hands, Mariah stopped her search, wondering why Cam hadn't mentioned that he'd told Ashley. Then she remembered that he couldn't have because they'd barely spoken, except to shout at each other.

She backed out of the closet to look into Ashley's face. The little girl had sounded concerned, but she was turning the wheels on her Rollerblade with childish distraction.

"You don't like that he's your uncle?" Mariah asked.

Still fiddling with her Rollerblade, Ashley shook her head. "At first I didn't."

"Why?"

"Because." She put the skate down beside her on the bed and lifted her thin shoulders. "Because I thought if he was my uncle, then they wouldn't let him be my dad. You know. The lawyer or the judge. Whoever decides this stuff."

Mariah wondered if Cam had sufficiently explained their connection.

"Cam is the brother of the woman who gave birth to you, Ashley," she explained gravely. "He's a blood relative."

She didn't seem to get it. "I know," she said, clearly unimpressed, "but he said it's okay 'cause he can still adopt me. I want him to be my dad more than I want him to be my uncle." She smiled, an artless twinkle in her eye. "I've been thinking about you as my mom all year. I still can't believe I made it happen!"

Mariah stared at her, unable to comprehend for a moment that to Ashley, the blood connection meant nothing. Only the fact that Cam still intended to adopt her did.

Ashley held up her Rollerblade. "I need my other one!" she reminded Mariah.

"Right." Mariah shifted mental gears in the interest of Hank, who was waiting in the driveway. On sudden inspiration, she looked under the bed. Mussed and flushed, she produced the missing skate. Fred barked triumphantly.

Mariah hugged her tightly, then ran for the front door. Mariah followed, catching Fred's collar and waving at Hank as he backed out of the driveway. She felt disoriented, as though she were standing on her head and the view was familiar but not quite right.

Hank stopped and she forced herself to come out of her absorption and display good manners.

Hank leaned out his window to call, "Hey! How's it going?" Then, his eyes narrowing on her face, he asked in concern. "Everything all right?"

"Um…yes. Just got a little frazzled. Ashley was

missing one Rollerblade and I didn't want to keep you waiting."

He shrugged that off. "I live with three women and two babies. I wait around a lot. Sorry we had to tear Cam away from you on a Saturday, but the old shower ring fell on Haley while she was shampooing her hair. That old colonial they bought is a disaster, but she loves it. I had a couple of guys buffing up the upstairs bedrooms just so there's a safe place for them and the baby."

"I hope she wasn't hurt when the shower fell."

He grinned. "No. Seems Bart was showering with her. Caught it as it came down." He waggled his eyebrows wickedly. "Now we have something to use against them. Lucky they didn't get stuck. She's pretty big these days."

Mariah shook her head. "Never a candid camera crew around when you need one."

Hank laughed and waved again as he backed out of the driveway.

Mariah returned to the house in a mild trance, her conversation with Ashley playing over in her mind. Fred, apparently worn out from the excitement, collapsed in the middle of the floor, coltish legs stretched out.

Once again, she remembered the child's complete lack of reaction to the knowledge that Cam was her uncle, but her obvious delight that the man she'd loved for some time now wanted to take her into his life on a permanent basis.

Blood relationships were important.

Love relationships were everything.

Mariah sat down before the impact of her new perception knocked her down. She felt dizzy, slightly nauseous, sad and happy all at the same time.

This acceptance of a truth she'd denied for so long meant that she had to make some changes in her life. She had to put her babies to rest.

Tears sprang to her eyes as she thought about them—Sarah, who'd survived less than three months in Mariah's womb; Chase, who'd made it to four months; Jane, who'd barely survived two; then Stephanie, who'd lived almost to birth. Mariah had held her lifeless little body, touching tiny fingers and toes, grieving over her with a pain she could still feel with all its hooks and barbs.

She wiped her tears away and drew a steadying breath. She no longer had room for pain, she told herself as she got to her feet and went to the kitchen table for her car keys. She had a child to raise—maybe two, if things could be made to work in her favor.

And she had a man to love—if it wasn't too late.

She left Fred behind, knowing he would only complicate what she had to do next, then she climbed into her van and drove across town to Maple Hill Mini-Storage, tucked behind an antiques barn. She went to space 27 and dug out her keys.

When she opened the door, she saw the old maple bedroom set that had been her parents and that she and Ben had shared while they were married, and wondered idly if Parker would want it for her new life with Gary.

As an avoidance tactic, she went from item to item, deliberately ignoring the things corralled in the rear corner of the room.

There was the hutch that had been her grandmother's; chairs she'd suspected might be Hepplewhite
but that she had yet to check on; a Victorian floor lamp
with a gorgeous dragon-shape stand, the shade for it lost
long ago. There were boxes of kitchen utensils, books,
belongings that had seemed important to save, though
there'd been no room for them in her life at the Manor.
She'd have to go through them, she thought, and see
what she should keep, what Parker might need.

Then, unable to avoid it any longer, reminding herself that this was the reason she'd come, she crossed the
empty floor in the middle of the storage space to the collection of baby furniture in the back.

There was everything a new mother might need—the
booty from two baby showers and gifts from relatives.
A complete nursery in oak decorated with hand-painted
ducklings. It had been a present from Ben's parents in
their ecstasy over Stephanie's impending arrival. There
was a crib, a cradle, a changing table and a bookshelf.

There was the lace-covered bassinet a friend had
given her, lavender ribbon woven through the eyelet that
covered the white wicker. Beside it were a high chair,
a two-speed swing, a car seat and a stroller with all the
bells and whistles, which had been a gift from Parker.

In boxes, there were bottles, rattles, toys, blankets
and clothing.

As she surveyed the mound now, a sob rose in her
throat that she had to swallow away. But she did it. She
had too much, she decided, to bemoan what was lost.
And the babies would always be with her. Always.

She walked back out to her van to assess space.

As she did, she saw that the spot beside hers was now

open and a spiffy white van was pulled up to it. She did a double take when she saw the name painted on the side of it. Evan Braga Painting, part of the Whitcomb's Wonders team.

She was still staring at it when Evan walked out of the dark interior.

He smiled a greeting. "You spring-cleaning, too?" he asked. Then he laughed. "I know it's July, but I'm always a little behind."

"Actually, I'm giving some things to a friend." She laughed. "I was just trying to get an idea of space so that I don't haul out anything that won't fit and have to drag it back in again."

"Can I lend you a hand?" he asked.

That was tempting, but she felt obliged to demur. "Certainly you have better things to do on a Saturday afternoon."

He nodded. "I realize it's pathetic, but I haven't. I'll be happy to help. If we fill both vans, maybe we can make it in one trip. Show me what's going."

She brought him inside and indicated the baby things.

Everyone knew she and Cam were adopting Ashley, and she wouldn't be surprised—given Rita Robidoux's informal information center and Addy Whitcomb's commitment to anyone who needed it—if everyone didn't also know about her divorce and the reason for it.

"All of it?" he asked, surveying the stack.

"All of it," she replied. "I…I have another life now."

He gave her a sympathetic smile. "Me, too. And to get it, I had to part with a lot of things that were grafted onto me. At least, that's how it seemed when I had to leave them."

She felt the comfort offered in his admission and thanked him with an answering smile.

"All right," he said briskly. "You have a seat in your van and I'll pack everything."

"I'll help with the smaller stuff," she insisted.

"Why not." He hefted the crib, still in its original box. "Cam says there's little point in arguing with you."

She followed him out to the van with a clown lamp in one hand and a giant teddy bear in the other, sure Cam hadn't meant that in a good way.

CAM STRADDLED THE EDGES of Haley and Bart's ball-and-claw tub while he reconnected the shower ring to the ceiling supports. He'd already repaired the faucet, which had ripped a few threads when the ring fell, and reconnected the back part of the ring, and was applying the last few turns of a wrench to the front.

Haley sat on the closed lid of the john, kibitzing. She'd taken one look at him when he'd arrived, given him a cup of coffee with something in it he wasn't supposed to have while on the job, then wheedled out of him the reason he looked like someone condemned to die.

He'd tried to explain briefly, only because she was feeling guilty, sure he appeared so grim because she'd dragged him away from his family on a Saturday. But she hadn't been satisfied with a brief explanation and had demanded details.

"So, she has been unreasonable and mistrustful," she said of Mariah. "But women aren't rational about their children. And I'm trying to imagine how I would feel if I woke up tomorrow and realized the baby I was carrying was no longer alive. I'd…I'd want to die myself! And if it had happened after three other miscarriages, well…" Her eyes welled with tears.

"Haley…" He wanted to sidetrack her. Bart had told him she'd been emotional and weepy.

But she was determined. "Cam, it's not an even playing field," she said urgently. "You have to try to understand her. If Bart left me because I couldn't give him a child after all I'd been through in the attempt—"

"What is going on?" Bart demanded. He walked into the bathroom, a cordless phone in his hand, a frown on his face as he glanced from Haley's tear-filled eyes to the weary misery in Cam's.

"We were talking about babies dying and husbands leaving," she said, giving the roll of toilet tissue a slap and ripping off a length to dry her eyes. "I'm trying to help him with Mariah."

"Maybe it would be a good idea to talk about more positive things," Bart proposed.

"Those are her problems," Haley insisted on a sniffle. "We've dealt with our dragons and want the world to be sunny and bright, but she's still dealing with hers. And the death of babies…my God. It isn't fair to expect her to see things from our positive points of view."

Cam held on to the shower ring as he viewed Mariah's attitude from a new perspective. Because he hadn't had much in the way of love and security from the beginning of his life, he'd been able to take most of his disappointments—including his marriage—with a certain philosophical steadiness.

Mariah, however, had loved Ben, thought she had the perfect situation, then lost everything. That had to be worse.

He heard himself tell her to leave, that he'd cope without her, and wished desperately that he could take back the words. He felt morose—and mean.

"If anyone says one more thing to me about death or divorce, I will leave the two of you to your miseries and eat my jambalaya all by myself," Bart threatened.

Haley grabbed his arm and used it to lever herself to her feet. "There's no need to get nasty," she said, wrapping her arms around him. Because of her bulky tummy, she made it only halfway. "I was just trying to do a little marriage counseling. Poor Cam looks like death." At the sound of the word, she quickly put a hand over her mouth. "That was involuntary," she said.

Bart pointed her out of the room. "Go sit with your feet up and think cheerful thoughts. Think about the baby shower your mom can finally give you now that we have space to put things."

She smiled at Cam as she backed out of the room. "It never hurts to try one more time. If Bart hadn't been patient with me, I'd be someone else's problem now."

Bart shook his head wryly. "If only I'd known then…"

"You'd have loved me anyway!" she shouted after she disappeared.

Cam tested the ring for steadiness. The back wobbled slightly. He turned and walked gingerly back toward it to tighten the connection.

"About Brian," Bart said, leaning against the pedestal sink.

Cam stopped, wrench to the joint. "Yeah?"

"I just spoke to his mother."

Cam was shocked. He'd mentioned to Bart when he'd first arrived today that he'd like to talk to him about obtaining temporary custody of Brian, but he hadn't expected Bart to get right on it. And he hadn't expected him to be able to reach Anjanette Barrow.

"And?" he asked.

"One of the people she hit is paralyzed. She's going to jail for a while. She's open to the idea. She wants to speak to her lawyer about it."

Cam tried to remember that he was straddling a small chasm. "You're kidding!"

"I'm not. I'm sure we can make it work. He'll want to have a look at you, of course, but what's not to like? And it'll be easy to get testimonials from the Lightfoot sisters."

"I can't believe it."

Bart grinned. "Brian will be thrilled. Seems to think the world of you, no matter how hard I try to straighten him out."

Haley appeared in the doorway again. "Mariah's here with Evan," she announced, looking surprised.

"Evan?" Cam asked. Had Mariah replaced him already?

"Yeah. He pulled up right behind her."

The doorbell pealed as they spoke.

"You'd better hurry out there, mister," Haley said to Cam. "Evan's a cutie. Don't want to let her develop any ideas."

Cam got off the tub and followed Haley and Bart to the living room. Haley opened the door and Evan walked in carrying a large box with Crib stenciled on it. "Where do you want this?" he asked.

"I didn't order…" Haley began, but Mariah led the way around her, pushing a stroller bearing a lamp with a clown base.

"I have all this…stuff," Mariah said, her voice a little choked despite her sincere, if fragile smile. "I can't use it, and I thought of you."

She steered the stroller around the corner and almost collided with Cam. She stopped. The look in her eyes was clear—clearer than he'd ever seen it—except for a peripheral pain she appeared determined to ignore. She seemed curiously unburdened.

"Hi," she said with a hesitant but affectionate smile. "How's the shower ring going?"

He wondered if he was delusional. "Almost finished," he replied. "What's all this?"

She expelled a breath. "The contents of my storage locker. We're not going to need it. There's lots more stuff, if you wouldn't mind helping. Poor Evan put most of it in the vans."

The contents of her storage locker. It seemed to symbolize the babies she'd never quite been able to give up. She must have found a way to deal with them. What had happened while he'd been gone?

And…*we're* not going to need it?

"Here." Evan handed him the large box. "We'll form a brigade. I'll carry in and hand off to Bart, who'll carry to you. While we're working, the women will make us refreshments."

Bart appeared with a rocking chair. "Haley's in no condition to be trusted with fire. She's running around like an insane person, looking into the van windows and weeping."

"Evan, you push the stroller," Mariah advised, skinnying by them in the hallway. "I'll get coffee going and see what I can find for refreshments."

Evan scratched his head. "I had such a good plan and already we have a bottleneck."

The things were moved in and carried upstairs in half an hour. One bedroom, smelling of fresh paint and floor wax, was set up with the baby furniture, and another was filled with toys and other paraphernalia.

Haley couldn't stop crying.

Bart finally wrapped his arms around her and rubbed her back. "Honey, you have to calm down," he advised gently. "You're going to make yourself sick."

Haley shook her head. "I'm fine, and I'm thrilled. But it touches me to know that this represents all Mariah's hopes and dreams and…she's given it to us!"

Needing desperately to touch Mariah, to hold her, Cam smiled at Bart over the top of Haley's head. "Excuse Mariah and me if we don't stay. We've got to…"

"Go," Bart said, apparently not requiring an explanation.

Evan caught Cam's arm as he walked past him. "Lots of people start over," he said quietly, "but not all of them have to do it by ripping out the old life. That hurts. You gotta respect those who can do that."

Cam nodded. "I know." He hadn't a clue how that nugget of wisdom related to Evan's life, but he understood what it meant in Mariah's.

He ran down the stairs and into the kitchen, where Mariah stood on a step stool, rooting through a cupboard for something.

MARIAH'S HANDS WERE TREMBLING as she searched through the cupboards for sugar for the coffee and some small treat to go with it.

Cam hadn't looked entirely pleased to see her. Not that she'd expected him to be—except in her wildest dreams involving forgiveness or, at least, loss of memory.

She turned at the sound of footsteps in the kitchen and saw him walking toward her. Her perch gave her a slight height advantage over him.

"I want to talk to you," he said, as a demand rather than a suggestion. He was apparently unaware of *any* advantage on her part. Still, it was better than the "I never want to see you again!" she thought might be on his tongue.

"Let me just finish…" she began, pointing to the coffee dripping into the steamy carafe.

"Sorry." He wrapped an arm around her hips and scooped her off the stool. "Can't wait that long."

"Cam!" she squealed, holding on with both arms around his neck as he strode toward the door, tipped her sideways as he went through it, then put her on her feet beside his truck, which was parked on the street.

Neighbors working on their lawns paused to stare.

"Where are we going?" she asked.

"Home," he replied, opening the passenger door and leaning on it as he looked into her eyes. His were dark and purposeful. "If you have a problem with that, speak now."

Her answer was to climb into the truck.

He locked and closed the door, then drove home. He didn't say a word while he pulled into the driveway, parked and came around to open her door.

He was trying to find a diplomatic way to tell her it was over, she thought, feeling panicky. Her epiphany had come too late. He'd probably brought her home to get her things.

He led her around the house onto the deck, to the pair of wicker chairs they'd bought at a rummage sale. She'd made bright flowered cushions for them— She had a sudden, overwhelming realization of all she was about to lose.

From inside the house, Fred barked a question. No one ever returned from a trip to town and went out onto the deck without first releasing him to join them.

Cam put her into one of the chairs, then turned his back to the lake and leaned against the railing.

"You gave away all your baby things," he observed quietly.

She nodded, her throat tightening. "I finally realized that I have to act on what I have now, rather than what I lost then." She hitched a shoulder, the pain persisting despite her new understanding. "Hank brought Ashley home to pick up her Rollerblades and she told me you explained about being her uncle. I thought she was upset about it, but it was only because she thought that meant you couldn't be her dad." A tear slid down her cheek. "I finally got it. A year ago, I'd have been happy to die with Stephanie. Today, I really want to be Ashley's mother." She held Cam's gaze, emotion burning her throat. "I want to stay here with you and be your wife for a long, long time."

That was everything he wanted to hear. He caught her hand to pull her out of the chair and wrapped her in his arms. He held her close as she kissed his neck.

"I love you," she said tearfully. "I do. But to admit that to myself, I had to put my babies away and that was hard." She kissed his cheeks. "Can you understand that?"

"Of course. I don't expect you to forget them—just to make room for me and Ashley." He looked into her eyes. "And while you're doing that, you'd better make room for Brian, because Bart seems to think we're going to get him."

He explained about the jail sentence and Brian's mother's willingness to give them temporary custody of the boy. He grinned. "So, according to your message from the future," he said, assuming his son of Othar accent, his arms looped around her, his hands joined at her back, "we have to get a swing set, paint Fred yellow and visit the capitals of Europe."

Her expression was almost rapturous. And he felt everything reflected in her eyes and her smile. He could hardly believe this was his life.

The sound of a motor in the driveway was followed almost instantly by childish shouts of "Cam! Mariah!" There was pounding on the front door.

"We're out here!" Cam shouted.

Fred, standing at the living room window, barked furiously.

The children thundered toward them, Hank following more slowly.

"Guess what?" Ashley asked breathlessly, her eyes enormous.

Before Cam or Mariah could try, Brian said, beside himself with excitement, "They found the gold!"

For a minute, Cam didn't know what he was talking

about. Then he remembered. "The gold the Confederate stole?"

"Yeah! Some of my men were working on the ceiling in Mariah's old room—"

"They had to take off all the plaster and wood and when they got to the…you know…the wood stuff—"

"The beams! They found an old bank bag tied to the beam with a belt!"

The children talked over each other, almost levitating in their excitement.

Cam looked up at Hank, unable to believe they had the facts straight.

Hank confirmed it with a nod. "My guys called me. Do you believe it? I dropped by with the kids to see it on our way home. Brian's going to get his picture taken with it, too, since he looked so hard for it, according to Letitia. Got to go. Just wanted to make sure you were here."

"Thanks, Hank!" Mariah called as he walked away. He waved as he rounded the corner.

Cam put a hand to Brian's shoulder. "I'll bet you're pretty disappointed you're not the one who found it."

Brian smiled. It didn't seem to be the case. "That was just so me and Ashley could go to Disneyland. But who cares about that."

Now that the children had joined them, Fred was apoplectic. But Cam wanted to make sure Mariah caught the full import of this.

"You don't want to go to Disneyland anymore?" Cam asked.

"Well, yeah," Brian replied. "Someday when we can all go. But so far, this summer's been the *best* right here."

"How come Fred's inside?" Ashley asked, frowning at the dog, who was all but standing on his head for attention. "Can I go get him?"

"Sure," Mariah replied. "Bring a couple of colas and the tin of brownies."

The children pushed each other toward the back door and exploded into the house, the dog barking and leaping at them.

"Did you hear that?" Cam asked Mariah, leaning down to kiss her gently.

"Means we have to go to Disneyland before we go to Europe," she said.

She squeezed him with surprising strength in someone so small. Love, he knew, was empowering.

Everything you love about romance...
and more!

*Please turn the page for Signature Select™
Bonus Features.*

Bonus Features:

BONUS FEATURES

THE MEN OF MAPLE HILL

A conversation with
MURIEL JENSEN

Muriel Jensen has written over seventy books and novellas. This prolific author has given us some wonderful and warm stories to cherish. Read on to learn more about Muriel.

4

Tell us a bit about how you began your writing career.

I've always loved to write and created teen romances on notebook paper for my friends in school. But I got married, we adopted children and there never seemed to be time to hide myself away and write—until I went to work for a friend managing her bookstore. I worked alone one long winter—the loneliest time in the retail business. To keep myself busy, I wrote a book about an infertile young woman, a man who wanted children and the marriage they embarked upon to save a little girl from foster care. I finished it at the same time that Harlequin Books opened its New York office and was looking for manuscripts about American women. That was *Winter's Bounty*, published in October of 1983.

Do you have a writing routine?
I write ten pages a day, six days a week, and just sit at the computer until I have them. On a good day, I can be finished in three hours. Sometimes I labor all day for half a page I throw out the next day.

When you're not writing, what do you love to do?
I live in Astoria, the most beautiful town in the breathtaking Northwest. I love walking on the River Walk with Ron and Fred (husband and dog). I love meeting friends for tea or lunch and shopping, even if I don't buy anything. I love seeing what's new.

What or who inspires you?
The beauty of my city and my friends and neighbors inspire me. At the risk of being repetitious, Astoria is remarkably beautiful. It's impossible to feel neutral or even depressed when ships sail by, eagles fly and trees are green all winter. The Columbia River meets the Pacific Ocean at Astoria, and the Native Americans have long held that the mouth of the river is a source

of creativity. It must be true. The most wonderful people live here.

Is there one book that you've read that changed your life somehow?
Hawaii by James Michener made me a writer. I love his picky attention to detail. I don't write in that same way (who could?), but his descriptions painted such a clear picture that I "lived" in Hawaii for three months while I rode the bus back and forth to work in Los Angeles and read the book. When I was finished, I felt changed—not by the story, which was wonderful, but by the man who'd allowed me the experience. I wanted to give someone else the stories that lived in me.

What are your top five favorite books?
This is a curious collection—

Hawaii by James Michener

The Snow Goose by Paul Gallico

The Fur Person by May Sarton

Hot Ice by Nora Roberts

Dream a Little Dream by Susan Elizabeth Phillips

What matters most in life?
The three Fs—Family (first, foremost and always,) Friends and Good Food! And if you can have them all together, life doesn't get any better.

If you weren't a writer what would you be doing?
I've always said I'd love being an actress for the
adventure of discovering character. But now that
memory fails me more often than not, I know I'd
never remember my lines. I'd have to be the
script girl.

Marsha Zinberg, Executive Editor, Signature Select
spoke with Muriel in the Winter of 2004.

8

LUCKY IN LOVE
by Muriel Jensen

≈

THIS WASN'T QUITE the career in fine art she'd imagined, Rosie Sutton thought as she painted hearts with dollar signs in them all over the shop windows in Jester, Montana. But it paid the rent, allowed her to live in the town she'd fallen in love with on her last vacation with Steve and placed her right in the middle of a warm and wonderful town at the very moment of its great good fortune. Twelve of Jester's merchants, who pitched in to play the lottery every week, had recently won forty million dollars.

There were reporters everywhere, television trucks, visitors from near and far, and—thanks to Rosie— painted hearts everywhere you turned. There was also an undercurrent of excitement, a magical disbelief, a grin on the face of everyone walking into the savings and loan, whose window she now worked on while standing on a kitchen stool. Since this was Jester's only savings institution and the place where all the winning locals would be banking, the manager had suggested one giant heart with dollar signs flowing into it. What-

the notion lacked in subtlety it gained in humor—
and humor abounded in Jester.

"Good job, Rosie!" Shelly Dupree praised as she
pulled open the door of the savings and loan. She was
average in height, wore jeans and a gray sweater pulled
on over a blue sweatshirt for the quick trip from her restaurant. She owned The Brimming Cup across the street,
where news and gossip countywide was exchanged over
breakfast and lunch. She was a warm and practical
woman with short dark hair and lively hazel eyes, one
of the first people Rosie had met when she'd moved here
three months ago. Rosie had already covered the Cup's
windows with heart-shaped steam coming out of a
lineup of coffee cups. "Brisk morning, isn't it? How're
your fingers holding up?"

10 Rosie flexed the red-smeared fingertips protruding
from her fingerless gloves. Her shortish, slender body
was bundled into an old brown parka she'd bought at the
thrift shop in neighboring Pine Run when she realized
she'd be working outdoors for several weeks in the middle of a Montana winter. Her long, dark blond hair was
piled into a dark blue woolen watch cap that she'd pulled
down over her ears. "Still working, but I can't feel them.
Found a valentine for the dance yet?"

Shelly waved away that possibility with a mittened
hand. "That's a good three weeks away." She grinned.
"If I don't have a significant other by then, my winnings
will have arrived and I can pay some handsome bon vi-
vant to escort me. Shall I make sure he has a friend?"

A cloud settled on Rosie's sunny morning. The issue
was complicated. Technically, she was married, but

when a husband was gone by choice eight months out of the year, she felt that probably negated the contract. But Steve, the most respected foreign correspondent in the print media, had apparently not even returned to L.A. yet to realize that she was gone. She refused to acknowledge the pain that caused her. She hadn't expected him to track her down and reclaim her. Not when she was thinking clearly, anyway. Realizing Shelly still waited for an answer, she smiled and replied lightly, "No, thank you. The only man I'm interested in is Art."

Shelly laughed and disappeared inside the building. Rosie tried to revive her enthusiasm for painting hearts. Several more customers came and went throughout the morning. Rosie was standing on tiptoe on a ladder, following a sudden inspiration to alternate hearts and dollar signs in a border across the top of the window, when a male voice asked right behind her, "How is it possible that a woman without a heart can paint so many of them so well?"

The question was followed instantly by the touch of a possessive hand to her backside. It pulled her sideways off the ladder and into Stephen Chancellor Sutton's arms. Those dark brown eyes that could spot a global crisis thousands of miles away but never seemed to notice what was happening in his own home were just inches from hers. There was a vertical frown line between them she didn't remember being there. As her left arm automatically hooked itself around his neck for stability, she stared into the planes and angles of her husband's very handsome face and realized grimly that she didn't hate him after all. She wouldn't mind if a piano fell on him, but she didn't hate him. That was a horrible truth to face after two months of convincing herself that she could face her life alone. But he didn't have to know that.

"Steve," she said with a smile she hoped looked unaffected by his sudden appearance, "what are you doing back in the States? I can't believe there are no more wars anywhere."

He raised an eyebrow, sharpening that frown line. "There's about to be one here," he replied.

When Steve had returned home to L.A. after months of traveling with the Special Forces through Afghanistan, Pakistan, then Yemen, yearning, burning, for an armful of his wife, he'd been disappointed to find that she was probably out shopping or off to the little Wilshire gallery that showed her work. Then he'd noticed that her favorite wicker chair was gone, that the hook where the Boston fern she babied usually hung now dangled emptily and her entire half of the closet was empty. It felt as though a giant fist had come down and smacked him on top of the head. She'd left him! He'd been risking life and sanity to bring the world the important details of war and strife, and she'd left him?

"How could you just walk away like that?" he demanded.

"I drove," she corrected, kicking until he placed her on her feet. She made a production of wriggling herself back into order, tugging on the hem of her coat. "I'd pleaded with you not to go in the first place, then it was weeks before I heard anything from you, and that was a fax from your mother's office telling me she'd gotten a report from you out of Afghanistan and you *hadn't* been killed on the raid on that mountain as the entire news community had feared."

He was confused by her anger. "And you weren't happy to hear that?"

She looked at him as though he were simple. "Yes, I was, but for the three weeks before that, when I thought you were with the unit that disappeared and were found dead deep inside a cave, I was…" She finally growled, apparently unable to describe in words what she'd felt.

He thought this was a good sign until she made a fist and smacked him in the chest with it.

"You will never make me feel like that again! You go to the farthest corners of the world and take the biggest chances because you have to prove to the whole world and to your own family that you're the world's best print reporter because you *are* and not because your parents own the newspaper chain. You were infected with that need to prove something when I married you, but I, in my innocence, thought, Well, surely the day will come when he feels he has something to prove to *me,* so I can be happy until the day comes when I'm as important to him as reporting the news." She got right into his face and shouted at full volume, "But that didn't happen! And after four years, I got tired of waiting."

Her voice cracked and she had to stop to clear her throat. He noticed in the time it took that her cheeks were flushed and her eyes looked a little soupy. She was still the beautiful woman who'd lived in his mind during all those awful months, but she looked a little piqued. He almost smiled at the realization that it hadn't reduced her volume at all, but he was sure that wouldn't be wise. And he wasn't quite ready to be amused with her anyway.

"You have your own stuff to prove," he accused. "Because your father wasn't interested enough in you to stick around, you intend to show the world that you don't need any man, even me. So you just pack your bags and go. Really adult behavior, Rosie."

"You can just turn around and go home," Rosie said, hurt feelings visible in her eyes, "because there's nothing…" She was making her point with the tip of a heart-red index finger when a FedEx driver, trying to maneuver a cart through the door of the savings and loan, slipped on the snow and hit the side of the building instead.

A large block of snow from atop the overhead sign dislodged and fell squarely on Steve and Rosie. He swore. She screamed. When the snow settled, she gasped while hopping up and down and trying to reach a hand down her back.

He pulled off his glove, turned her around and reached his right hand into familiar territory. Her back was warm and silky and he caught a whiff of her fragrance from the moist interior of the sweater under her jacket. He faltered for a moment, dizzy with desire, then his thumb connected with the icy chunk of snow that had fallen inside her coat and moved quickly to sweep it up and out. She seemed frozen to the spot, the look in her eyes completely confusing to him. She looked as though she wanted him desperately and hated him unconditionally. Confusion was bad news to a reporter.

He spotted the sign of The Brimming Cup across the street and caught her arm. "I'll buy you a cup of coffee," he said, starting to pull her toward the crosswalk.

She stopped stubbornly. "I want a divorce," she said firmly.

Steve took another look into Rosie's eyes and the ambivalence was still there. But he was suddenly tired of dealing with it. "No, you don't," he argued, pulling her a little more forcefully toward the Cup. "Come on."

"What can I get you?" Shelly asked cheerfully as they settled into their seats.

Even though Rosie had let Steve bring her here to talk, she found it difficult to concentrate. For a woman who'd made the brave decision to leave a life that was less than she wanted for herself, who'd driven a thousand miles alone, started over alone and had slept alone for all the months he'd been gone, she knew she should show more backbone than she was feeling right now. She should be filled with the resolve that had taken her this far.

But Steve Sutton had always been powerful stuff. The same sharp wit, coupled with the charm that showed even in his news reports, had been difficult to resist when she'd been twenty-two, and nothing had changed in the interim. In fact, she was even at more of a disadvantage now that she knew what it was like to live with his lively sense of humor, his delight in and curiosity for absolutely everything and his ability to make love as though it was the ultimate moment and there would never be another chance.

Rosie felt as though she was going to implode. "Lemon chamomile tea, please," she said to Shelly. "And sourdough toast."

Steve frowned at her over his menu. "What? What happened to the usual triple-shot mocha grande and a raspberry croissant to keep your blood sugar up?"

She sat up straighter and pulled herself together. He was gorgeous and sexy, but she was his last priority. She had to remember that. She smiled sweetly. "It's stabilized since I left you."

"Left you?" Shelly asked in surprise, looking from one to the other. Then realizing she was intruding into personal territory, she added quickly, "I'm sorry. I was...I mean, I didn't know you were...you had..." She waggled her pen from one to the other.

Steve offered Shelly his hand. "Steve Sutton," he said with a smile, shaking her hand, then giving her back the menu. "I'm Rosie's husband. She may have been acting as though she was single since she's been here, but she's not."

"Shelly Dupree," Shelly replied, clearly falling for his charm. "No, she hasn't acted single. She just never said she was married. And she did turn down my offer to get her a date for the Sweetheart Dance. Not that I really had one in mind. I mean, we were fantasizing about hiring an escort, and I offered..." At Rosie's frown and Steve's raised eyebrow, Shelly stopped midsentence. "Never mind," she said quickly. "What'll you have, Steve?"

He ordered coffee and a piece of coconut cream pie. As Shelly walked away, Rosie leaned across the table toward Steve and said firmly, "You should go, Steve. There's no point in staying. I'm not going back with you."

Shelly was already back with a cup, which she placed before him. He leaned back as she poured. "Actually, I'm here on business," he said when Shelly left again. "I'm covering the lottery story."

He didn't really think she was going to swallow that? "The print version of the great Walter Cronkite was sent to Jester, Montana, to cover a lottery win? I don't think so."

"The print version of the great Walter Cronkite gets to call the shots sometimes," he admitted with no evidence of shame. "I just got home from Yemen, and when I couldn't find you and nobody seemed to know where you were, I happened to spot your face in the background of a TV news story about Jester's merchants winning the lottery, and told my father I was coming to cover it."

"Isn't this going to put a big kink in your effort to prove your greatness? I mean, it's wonderful for Jester, but it's a pretty small story after all."

He looked her in the eye. "You never know what's inside a story until you delve. The simplest detail can turn into something big. You have to be willing to explore."

"I'll save you the effort." She sighed and settled into the corner of the booth, pulling off her coat and hat. She felt as though her temperature had gone up thirty degrees in the past fifteen minutes. It had to be the warm restaurant. "If your intention is to explore what's left of our relationship while filing a story on the lottery win, you'll come up empty. There's nothing left, Steve. We had a promising beginning, but you're more interested in proving you're the best than in proving that you care about us. And I'm tired of it. Spare us both a dramatic breakup and accept that it's over."

Rosie had serious hat hair, but somehow the tumbled, disheveled effect of all that autumn gold freed from her cap turned him on rather than put him off. It brought to mind lazy Sunday mornings in bed, midnight lovemaking followed by forays for food, wrestling for the remote, then forgetting why they wanted it in the passion that always ignited when their bodies touched.

He caught her hand as she played restlessly with her utensils. "What I feel for you will never be *over*. And you're lying through your teeth. Your eyes lit up when they first looked into mine across the street. You were glad to see me. Admit it."

She tried to yank her hand away, but he held fast. "Of course I was glad to see you," she whispered harshly. "I haven't seen you in four months, and for three weeks of that time, I thought you were dead! I'm happy you're safe. But I no longer love you. You put yourself first every time there's a choice, and I'm not going to live that way anymore."

Shelly arrived with their food. Steve freed Rosie's hand, because she looked as though she needed that tea. "I put the news first," he said reasonably, passing her the jam caddy for her toast. "Not myself. You're always first in my heart, Rosie, but I have to go where things are happening. You knew that when we got married. You said you'd use the time alone to do your art."

"Art has to be fed!" she retorted. "An artist needs emotion and experience. You're never around to provide either, Steve. We're working at cross-purposes here. I'm never going to get anywhere as an artist if I'm continually fearing your death. And I'm sure you're tired of my complaining about it."

"You're a brilliant artist," he disputed, "and I always thought our relationship was a masterpiece. I can't believe you'd just throw it away."

She sighed dispiritedly. For an instant he saw a glimpse of the old Rosie, who loved and understood him and found his work exciting. Then she shook her head as though certain that whatever she'd remembered in that moment couldn't be recaptured. "You'd have to spend some time in Jester to see how love really works. People are there for each other, do for each other, support each other. They don't just claim to care then take off."

He looked out the window at the hopping little town, remembering that he had been gone a lot, that much of his work was fueled by a desperate need to share what he knew. But now that he was forced to stop and think, he wondered if what he'd always thought of as a professional thirst for fact was in some part the prideful need to prove himself to his family and to the world in general.

His eyes rested on Rosie's half-painted heart on the window of the savings and loan across the street, and he thought with wry amusement that it could be considered a metaphor for their marriage. Half brilliantly executed, half simply…not there. He turned to Rosie, looking pale and cornered across the table, and knew he had to do something about that. And suddenly realized she'd unwittingly provided him with his next step.

"You know," he said genially, taking a slow sip of his coffee, "you're probably right about that."

She looked wary, suspicious, as she bit the point off a piece of toast. "About…the divorce?"

He liked the note of disappointment in her voice when she asked the question. "No," he denied quickly. "About my staying for a while." He nodded to reinforce his willingness. "It does seem like a nice little town." Then he added with an innocent smile, "Where do we live?"

Mercy! Rosie thought, staring at his smiling face. She was sure the innocence she saw there was false. Steve Sutton was too savvy to ever be innocent. What have I done?

"I've left you," she said firmly, striving for severity in voice and demeanor. It didn't seem to be affecting him. "You cannot move in with me."

He nodded as though he understood completely, then said, "I understand that it's not the ideal solution, but there's not a room to rent in this town. I tried when I arrived this morning. Jester is so full of reporters, photographers and cameramen that they're sleeping in their cars." He grinned. "I got here from the airport in a rented subcompact. I'd have to fold myself in three to lie down."

She felt a range of emotions—interest, fear, excitement, exasperation. He always seemed to know where she was vulnerable. He pushed while she was still unsure what to feel. "It was your suggestion," he said with that same questionable innocence. "If you're right and Jester is a lesson in love, how do you expect me to put what I observe into practice if we're not together? Wasn't that your complaint about me in the first place?"

She struggled against his logic. "I was speaking in general about love," she said, "not about you and me. It's too late for us, Steve."

The innocence in his expression vanished and she saw determination take its place. This was the man, after all, who got an interview with Fidel Castro when the Cuban dictator wasn't speaking to anyone. "This relationship has two of us involved," he said quietly. "You can't decide all by yourself that it's over. You ran away from me, you'll recall, and I followed you here. So, if you file for divorce, which one of us is going to look like the party who tried?" Then he added with a subtle suggestion of self-satisfaction, "Particularly if the judge is a news junkie and knows my work?"

He had her there. She hated his ability to manipulate a story. As she thought about it, she felt a little fire building in the center of her being. She fought against it, but it had started the moment he swooped her off the ladder, and was rapidly building strength. She didn't want him to stay with her. But she didn't want him to go.

The tea was making her feel a little stronger, and she was suddenly, curiously nervy in a way she hadn't been for months. She could deal with this without reconciling. If anything, spending time with him would probably convince him as well as her that it was over and he'd stop making it so difficult for her to move on.

"You can stay with me while you research your story," she bargained. "There's only one bed, but you can use the sofa."

He nodded without looking triumphant or even particularly pleased. "Fair enough. I'll bet you haven't had anyone to rub your feet while I've been gone."

That was true. That *was* a perk of life with him that she'd missed. "No, I haven't."

"I'll repay your hospitality with a foot massage," he promised, "and maybe even a cranberry-white-chocolate cheesecake."

She smiled. Cranberry-white-chocolate cheesecake, she thought longingly. For a man with adventure on his mind, he had a wonderful way with desserts. Just the thought of his cheesecake made her willing to take this risk.

But she had no doubts about it. She was making a terrible mistake.

Her home was a very small house located between the town hall and fire station. It was white with green shutters and had a surprisingly big front porch, considering the dimensions of the house. The paint was peeling, but there was a welcome sign on the front door decorated with a painted sunflower and cat. Steve couldn't explain why it seemed inviting—unless it was that he knew she lived there.

The kitchen, with yellow daisies on the wallpaper,

22

was immediately on their left, and had a small, round table in the window. The appliances were probably from the sixties—yellow stove, olive-green fridge. "No dishwasher?" he asked in surprise. She hated to do dishes.

She smiled wryly. "No. I eat on paper plates a lot. This is the living room."

It was probably no more than ten-by-ten with mismatched furniture and the wicker chair she'd bought at a flea market two years ago and painted Chinese-red. A big, gray cat with a notch in one ear was curled into a tight bundle atop an ugly black woodstove that stood right in the middle of everything. His wide head came up when they approached. It had to be a male; he looked mean and world-weary. But when Rosie stroked his head, he purred loudly and pushed into her hand.

"This is Bill Matisse," she said, leaning down to rub her cheek against the cat. His purr rose in volume.

"*Bill* Matisse?" Steve asked, coming forward to stroke the cat. Steve bet he was a twenty-pounder.

"He came with the house," she explained. "The previous renter was moving into an apartment in Pine Run and couldn't take him. He'd named him Bill. But I talk over my paintings with him, so I thought he should have a last name appropriate to his position as art consultant."

"He seems happy with the situation," Steve noted.

She turned to him with a significant smile. "We both are." She led the way into a sort of parlor with beige walls and dark green curtains. Her paintings hung all over. Some he remembered from their condo; others must have been created here. Her style was a sort of Impressionist approach to landscapes, but painted in bright, primary colors. He recognized the rolling hills and angular bluffs of the area.

He'd always been proud of her ability and felt a strange disconnection at the knowledge that she'd created work he didn't even know about. And that she claimed to be happy with the situation. He looked into her eyes, trying to determine if that was really true. But all he could see there was that slightly bleary, red-nosed quality he'd noticed before.

"Are you all right?" he asked as she led the way upstairs. "You don't seem to have quite your old…sparkle."

She gave him a wry grin as she led him into the middle of a loftlike room that took up the entire second floor. "Is that you trying to win me back?"

24

He laughed lightly, then sobered and caught her chin in his hand to study her face. "It's me, concerned about you."

She caught his wrist to pull his hand away. He resisted and for an instant they were eye-to-eye, caught together in the voltage that always ran between them. She finally pulled away with a yank. "I've had a cold for weeks," she said, pointing to a bathroom in the far corner of the room. "And working outside hasn't helped me get over it in a hurry. But I'm fine. That's the only bathroom."

A wrought-iron bed stood against one wall with a two-drawer file cabinet on one side of it for a bedside table. Her easel stood in the middle of the room with all her familiarly messy drawers and tables around it. Everything near the easel was spattered with drips and daubs of bright color, and a pottery jar stood tall with a bouquet of brushes. A window in the ceiling probably intended for thermal heat lent the room a Parisian-sky-lit-attic sort of quality.

On the easel was a half-finished painting he thought he recognized as downtown Jester. The neon sign of The Brimming Cup tipped him off. He went forward to study it.

"Something's wrong with it," she said, following him. She was in artist mode now, a state he never entirely understood. He was pragmatic, uncomplicated. "I'm not sure what it is, but I don't seem to be able to move ahead."

The underpainting was done and she'd painted a bright blue sky and the snow-topped bluff against it. She'd once explained to him that she always worked forward when painting—started with what was most distant and came to the foreground. "How can you tell something's wrong if you haven't finished it?" he asked practically, moving around it to study it. "It looks fine to me."

She followed him as he moved, colliding with him when he stopped. He felt her breast against the back of his arm and he forced himself to remain still and withhold reaction while the air left his lungs. Now that he was here, he didn't want to do anything to panic her.

"I don't know," she said, apparently unaware of the tension. She was focused on the painting. "The process has to feel right, you know? I mean, painting's more than inspiration. Sometimes it's the tedious and mechanical re-creation of detail rather than the free expression of feeling you wish it was. But I always get lost in it." She sighed and looped her arm in his unconsciously. It was an old habit she'd probably fallen into because she'd always talked over her paintings with him, even when he had no clue what she was talking about. And he always loved listening to her. He had to fight himself not to take her in his arms. "Something's holding me away this time, and I can't figure out what it is. I love Jester. I thought it would just flow through my fingers." She tipped her head sideways as she studied the canvas with a thoughtful frown. "Maybe I've put something in it that isn't supposed to be there. Or left out something important."

He was considering the possibility of suggesting that what she'd left out was him, when she suddenly became aware that she'd taken his arm and even leaned into him as she contemplated her painting. She dropped it as though he were toxic and took several steps back. She glared at him as though it was all his fault. "I have to go," she said finally. "I don't cook, so you'll have to get something at the Cup."

"I do cook," he reminded her. "Dinner at six."

"I work later than that," she argued.

"After dark?"

She met his challenge with a reluctant softening of her glower and a sigh—as though she was very, very tired. "I'll see you at six o'clock." And she hurried down the stairs and slammed the door on her way out.

He approached the painting, saw that she'd sketched in herself in the underpainting, working on the window of The Brimming Cup. She'd captured a charming mo-

26

ment of small-town life. He was going to spend his time here believing that what she didn't like about her painting was that she knew the woman painting the window was without the man she loved.

Rosie had never considered herself the kind of woman who could die of sexual deprivation. She'd never needed the amorous adventures most of her friends talked about in high school and college. She'd been convinced she was less of a sexual being than most of her peers—until she met Steve Sutton at Queen of the Angels High School on career day five years ago.

He'd pep-talked her out of her terror of discussing her artist's life in front of a gymnasium filled with teenagers, then he'd taken her to dinner afterward. She'd sat across a table filled with all her favorite Chinese dishes and fallen in love while he talked about his life as a foreign correspondent. He had such a love of the world and its people that she'd been enraptured by his stories. And she'd wanted him. All of him. It was a curiously all-pervading greed that seemed to be more than lust. She wanted to rip his clothes off, but she wanted him to keep talking while she did it.

And now, over four years later, after a marriage's ups and downs and an attempt to separate herself from him, he was sharing her house with her and all she could think about was what it used to be like to make love with him. He had a way of holding her that made her feel as though a bubble enclosed them, separating them from the world. He touched her with a tenderness she so revered, yet with an unmistakable possession that both humbled her and made her walk taller. He looked into her eyes with adoration, and made her feel as though she alone occupied his world and they had an eternity to love each other in it.

But not anymore. Now he occupied the sofa downstairs while she stared at the ceiling upstairs and wondered how they'd come to this sorry pass.

Still, she missed him with that same greed. It didn't make sense. Nothing had changed. But her body didn't seem to know that. It was embarrassing to admit that her nipples beaded when he was near, that her breath caught when he called her name, that she felt a warm liquidity at the heart of her femininity when he looked into her eyes.

Fortunately, he didn't seem to notice. He respected her unwillingness to eat breakfast, but met her for lunch at The Brimming Cup, brought her a cup of tea in the middle of the afternoon while she continued to work and had dinner ready when she came home. His repertoire was simple but delicious. He helped with laundry, with dishes, ran errands and fed the cat. And despite his earlier claims that their relationship wasn't over, that it had been a masterpiece, there was nothing romantic about his approach to her. He was warm, friendly, helpful— and just a little distant. She didn't know what to make of it. And she was grumpy to find herself disappointed.

Steve was convinced he was going insane. Rosie's proximity after almost five months without her was fraying his libido and making mush of his brain. In a constant state of sexual arousal, he had to keep his emotional distance at least or he was going to take her right in front of the Heartbreaker Saloon, where she was now working. He decided he had to simply get control of himself or risk losing her. And he hadn't followed her to Jester to go home without her.

In the interest of his story, and in the hope of scoring points with her, he immersed himself in Jester history and the busy society of newly rich merchants and their faithful if still-just-surviving friends. The winners were a motley lot, including a barber, a hairdresser, a veterinarian, the owner of the saloon and Shelly Dupree, whom he got to see every day. He wanted to focus his story on her plans, since she'd inherited the restaurant from her parents and had been just getting along until the big win. But a few of the other reporters had the same idea and she was keeping all of them at bay, insisting that the other winners were more interesting.

They might be, but she was pretty and she worked hard, and the average reader loved a pretty underdog. There was the added bonus that interviewing her kept him close enough to Rosie that all he had to do was look out the Cup's window to see her. And many of the other winners wandered through the Cup's doors at one time or another, so it was a great place for his base of operations.

He noticed that a good-looking doctor seemed to find Shelly as interesting as Steve did. "They're living together," a blowsy blonde with a formidable bosom half-exposed in a green knit blouse told him when she helped herself to the other side of his booth. "They're using the excuse that there's no place else to stay in town. And somebody left her a baby."

He'd heard about that. Shelly had returned to the

restaurant after a trip to the bank to deposit her winnings and found that someone had abandoned a baby.

"Yeah. In a carrier on the counter," the woman went on. "And the doc's a pediatrician, so he's been staying with her to help her out until they can find the mama." She rolled her eyes. "Good story, huh?"

"There *is* no place to stay in town," he said with a polite smile, feeling obliged to defend Shelly from gossip. "I know. I've tried."

She blinked, new interest apparently replacing her fascination with Shelly and the doc. "*You* need a place to stay?"

"No, I…"

"I've got two spare bedrooms and down comforters in both of them!" She was leaning toward him. He pulled his coffee closer. "You're a reporter. I've seen you in here a lot. I'm Paula Pratt, the mayor's secretary."

"It's nice to meet you, but I've…"

"One of the rooms has a TV—with cable—and the other has a new CD player and a buckwheat pillow."

"Pardon me?"

"A buckwheat pillow. You know, ergonomic shape and natural filler to help you sleep."

Life was filled with revelations. He'd traveled the world, listened to brilliant minds discuss important issues and never heard that buckwheat helped you sleep. But he could identify a predator when he saw one. "I'm married," he said.

She blinked again. "To who?"

"Rosie Sutton," he replied. When she looked blank, he pointed out the window toward the direction where he'd last seen Rosie's bundled-up form kneeling on a foam pad in front of the Heartbreaker—but she wasn't there. He turned away from the window to find her standing beside the booth, her nose and cheeks cherry-red, her eyes turbulent. "Rosie," he said, noting the icy glance she shot at his companion. "You know Paula Pratt?"

She smiled stiffly. "Paula."

Paula seemed to lose all interest in him. She tried to get out of the booth, but Rosie put her hand on her shoulder and pushed her back again. "No need to get up. I just came to tell you—" she turned that turbulent expression on Steve "—that I'm putting a cup of tea on your tab. I left without money this morning."

Steve smiled. "You did dress in rather a hurry," he said suggestively.

Rosie frowned questioningly, but Paula took the remark as he'd intended and backed away. "Nice meeting you," she said to Steve.

"You, too," he called after her retreating figure. He slid into the corner of the booth and patted the empty space to encourage Rosie to join him. "Thanks!" he said with relief. "You got here just in time."

Rosie sat and pulled her hat off, her hair falling to her shoulders in that ripple of light that stopped the breath in his throat. "She's ragingly single," Rosie explained, tipping her head back and closing her eyes. "The rumor is that she and the mayor have something going, but he has a long-suffering wife he's probably unwilling to part with, so Paula's looking out for number one."

Shelly brought a cup of tea and whole-wheat toast to the table. She grinned wickedly at Steve. "You're lucky you came out of that alive," she said. "Grown men scatter and hide from her."

Steve patted Rosie's hand. "Good thing I have a wife."

Rosie caught his fingers, then pinched them when Shelly walked away. "You don't have a wife. You have a landlady."

"Ow. And does the landlady always hit up her tenant for food money?"

"I left my purse on the bathroom counter," she explained, "and you were in the shower when I had to leave."

"Next time," he challenged, "come in and get it."

She sighed wearily and took a sip of her tea. "Steve," she said, turning slightly toward him, "I've enjoyed your cooking and you've been fairly pleasant company this week, but you have to understand that I'm staying in Jester and I'm going to paint my heart out and one day I'm going to save enough money to buy my house and turn it into a studio/gallery. You're no longer part of my plans."

She looked and sounded sufficiently serious that he felt a moment's panic. But he'd been in enough tight spots in his time to recover quickly and take the offensive.

"Well, that's too bad," he said coolly. "Because you remain part of my plans, and it isn't just about what you want, is it, though it seems to be the way we've conducted this marriage."

32

"Wanting us to be together," she said hotly, "isn't exactly a selfish demand, is it?"

"No, it isn't," he replied, "but the world is filled with men whose jobs require them to be away for long periods."

Her eyes brimmed with tears, making him feel like an ogre. "I thought you were dead!" she accused in a whisper. Then she snatched up one piece of toast and her cup and stormed off. From behind the counter, Shelly watched her walk away with her crockery and turned to frown at Steve. Okay. Not exactly a successful argument, but a look into those eyes brimming with tears convinced him that despite all her claims that it was over, she still loved him. There had to be a way to help her realize it.

Rosie found it difficult to paint hearts when she really wanted to paint daggers. Her argument with Steve that morning had upset her out of all proportion to the few words exchanged. Just to amuse herself, she painted a dagger in the corner of the window where she worked. She stepped back to look at it in concern. It wasn't really a dagger—it was more of an...arrow. Even as she resisted the impulse, her brush painted a heart around it and added initials: *R.* and *S.*

She dropped her brush in the jar of paint, folded her arms and paced back and forth in front of the Heartbreaker's window. Steve had been right when he'd said that many men had work that kept them away from their families, and she'd known what he did when she'd married him, but not knowing for three weeks if he was dead or alive was asking a lot of any woman. She had a right to be angry. She had a right to end it. Even though his nearness reminded her of everything that had been good about their relationship. Even though she felt as though she was about to explode with all the conflicting emotions inside her. Was it so wrong to want a husband who came home every night?

Amanda Bradley, who ran Ex Libris, the bookstore that shared the building with the Heartbreaker Saloon, hurried out of the shop, holding tightly to a teal-green wool shawl she'd wrapped around a long, oyster-colored dress. She had long, light brown hair and bright brown eyes. "Here they are!" she said, holding something out to Rosie. "Hot off the press. At the end of the evening we're drawing for a weekend getaway, all expenses paid, and a couple of gourmet baskets, so don't lose them."

Rosie accepted what appeared to be a pair of tickets. "What are these for?" she asked. "I don't remember buying tickets."

"Your husband bought them," Amanda replied. "He said I could just give them to you. He told me he was going out to explore Shelly's list today so he could make his choices like everyone else in town."

With a portion of her lottery winnings, Shelly Dupree wanted to give something back to the town that had supported her parents and now herself in The Brimming Cup. So she'd polled everyone in town about what they'd like to see restored or repaired and made a chart so that everyone could vote on what they'd like to see done first. As Rosie recalled, the church roof and the bleachers at the school were among them. The town hall

34

was in disrepair, as was the statue of Catherine Peterson and her horse on the lawn of the town hall. Once a proud tribute to the young woman who'd tamed the horse that had given the town its name, it was now green with age and the neglect of meager city funds.

Rosie had thought Shelly's plan magnanimous, and had admired the way the whole town got involved in the project. She was sure that for Steve it was good story material—the heart factor he insisted every story needed, even hard news.

"I like your husband," Amanda went on, huddling deeper into her shawl. "A lot of reporters don't really listen to you. They have an angle already in mind, or some agenda that doesn't necessarily relate to the truth. But you get the feeling he hears every word you're saying and understands how it relates. His stuff from Afghanistan was remarkable."

Rosie turned to her in surprise. There probably weren't many people in Jester who read the L.A. *Daily Observer.*

"Both sides of the issue," Amanda went on, "the abuses, the pain suffered, the hatreds, the losses and the longing for peace. On one level it was hard to read because it was so evenly presented that it was hard to see a solution. Then he made it clear that under all the politics, it's still a person-to-person world, and we'll still reach for each other, no matter what." She shook her head. "That he can see that after all those years in the trenches is amazing. He must be very special. Oops, there's the phone. You look tired. You should take a break."

Rosie stood rooted to the spot, surprised by Amanda's observations on Steve's talents, when all his excellent work had done was make Rosie feel put upon. She drew a breath and tried to think about his contributions to journalism as they related to the world, rather than to her. She felt her stance soften, her shoulders relax.

Steve was good. She remembered with sudden sharpness how impressed she'd been with his writing when she'd first met him—how insightful it was, how clearly written, how he related what he saw and learned to the pulse of the world and connected it to each individual reading his byline. In a time when people learned everything from broadcast news or on the Internet, he'd made them readers again. How could she fight that? she wondered, picking up her brush with a desultory gesture. Whether or not he was trying to prove something to himself or anyone else, the process had made him a brilliant reporter. She had no right to ask him to do something else. She just couldn't live with the pressure and loneliness of the past four months—particularly the horror of those three weeks. Even if she did still love him.

STEVE COULD SEE Jester's appeal for Rosie. It was very small and very charming, with beautiful vistas everywhere you turned. Everything was covered with snow, which lent a certain purity to landscapes that might be parched or muddy at other times of the year but were postcard perfect now. Downtown was a sort of mismatch of Old West storefronts and early-century buildings. No glamorous lines, but lots of nostalgic charm.

As he took a self-conducted tour to assess the points of interest in Jester that needed Shelly's help, he did his best to resist its appeal. The church roof had the most votes so far for the project to tackle first. The church was small and white with a steeple, stained-glass windows and a room in the basement that was used for community events. The dance, he knew, would be held there. He borrowed a ladder from the pastor to examine the roof. He had to sweep inches of snow from it to do so, then guessed by the condition of what was underneath that only the frozen snow was preventing it from leaking.

The bleachers were pathetic, as well, worm-eaten and broken in some places, and the statue of Catherine Peterson was a sorry sight, for sure. Though the woman's beautiful face magically translated into bronze retained its beauty despite the green and mildew. The horse was magnificent. He thought the statue was a sort of metaphor for the people of Jester—hearts of sturdy alloy defaced by time and hardship but somehow still beautiful.

He checked out the town hall, the site suggested for a public bathroom, the possibility of flower baskets hanging from the streetlights—all on the suggestion list. But he had to agree with the townspeople that the church was the neediest. It would be satisfying to see the statue tackled first, but the church served more people—harbored children and old people who should be protected from the rain.

When he got back to the house later than usual, Rosie was already home fixing dinner. He went into the kitchen, sniffing the aromatic garlic and onion. She stirred spaghetti sauce and looked up at him with a half smile. "Last I heard from Shelly, you were gone to the school to check out the bleachers, so I thought I'd get dinner started. So, do the bleachers get your vote?"

He washed his hands under the kitchen faucet and reached into the fridge for salad makings. "No, I'm with everyone else. The church is the worst. I climbed up for a look and it's a miracle the roof is still attached to the rest of the building."

She raised both eyebrows in surprise. "You climbed up to the roof?"

"Of course. A good story needs detail." He broke a head of romaine apart and began to wash it.

38

She watched him and thought, Of course. A good story needs detail. Climb a ladder to get it, brave the weather, weapons-fire, whatever it takes. Aloud, she said, "Amanda gave me the tickets to the dance."

"Good," he replied. "We need to get out. You don't do anything but paint, eat and sleep. And you don't eat very much or sleep very well."

She was surprised that he'd noticed that.

"I hear you tossing and turning, walking around. Your cold keeping you up?" He grinned suddenly. "Or are you lusting after my body, knowing it's just a stairway away?"

She made a scornful sound, but covered it quickly with a laugh when a swift, hot, unexpected blush rushed up through her cheeks. He didn't know how close to the truth he was. Or maybe he did. He glanced her way while slicing a tomato, and she was sure he'd noticed her reaction and drawn his own conclusion.

"It's all right," he said with a knowing smile in her direction. "I lust after you, too. It's hard not to remember how good it used to be, even when you're sure it just can't be anymore."

Well, thank goodness he was finally getting the message. But what had happened to his claim that loving her was still part of his plan? Not that she *wanted* him to pursue a reconciliation, but she'd just like to know.

"I suppose I have to buy a suit for the dance," he said, chopping green onions.

"I don't know. Ask Shelly. Angel-hair or shells?"

"Angel-hair."

"I thought you preferred shells."

"I do. But you like angel-hair."

She rested the spoon on the side of the pan and said with mild impatience, "Just tell me what you want."

He turned away from the counter to face her, his expression suddenly serious. "I want you to have what you want. Even if it isn't the same thing I want."

Well…good. She heard that answer and knew it applied on more than one level. And she understood that it was sweet even while it filled her with a weird new terror. Was he beginning to see that it just wasn't going to work? Was he finally accepting that sometimes love wasn't everything? Sometimes the practical, day-to-day adjustments were bigger than the emotion?

A pointed lump took form in her throat as she tried to swallow, seeing the long, lonely road ahead of her. A whole lifetime of the past four months. Great. Just when she was close to seeing things his way, he was changing his mind.

Steve hadn't danced since his wedding, but with the pastor serving as disc jockey, the music was classic and mellow, and it wasn't hard to simply take Rosie into his arms, close his eyes and let the voice of Frank Sinatra move them around the church hall floor. "It Had to Be You," "You Were Meant for Me," "Embraceable You" followed one another, making moody velvet of the atmosphere.

Shelly waltzed by with the doctor. Word had it they were engaged. She leaned out of the doc's arms to say, "We noticed you two sitting alone in the corner. We'd like you to join our table."

Rosie, who'd been doubtful about spending an entire evening in Steve's company, tried to demur. "We're not planning to stay all evening, and I've got to…"

Shelly ignored her protests and pointed to a table littered with punch glasses. A pretty woman sat at the table with Dr. Perkins, who ran the clinic. She was on a cell phone. "We're sitting over there. Vickie had to check on the kids. They have a passel, you know. We've got two vacant chairs, and you can't sit on the fringe by yourselves. Nobody's allowed privacy in Jester."

He expected Rosie to take the opportunity to say that he wasn't staying, that he'd be going home soon and therefore was exempt from whatever was required of people in Jester, but she simply accepted defeat and thanked her.

Steve twirled Rosie away. "Hard to fight her," he noted.

To his surprise, she smiled. She'd seemed so preoccupied since he'd arrived, so determined that their relationship was over, yet he could still feel the spark in her that had ignited their attraction all those years ago. It was as though her confusion over what to do about them had kept her relatively quiet and sometimes grim. Once she'd agreed to come with him, though, she was more like the old Rosie than she'd been in a year or more. She seemed more lighthearted, and she hadn't flinched at all from having to spend most of the night in his arms. He was afraid to think too positively about this, but didn't seem able to stop himself. Maybe he was going to be able to win her over after all.

During a brief intermission, the ladies' club poured coffee and served cookies, and Steve and Rosie moved their things to Shelly's table. Shelly introduced them to her fiancé, Connor O'Rourke, and the Perkinses. "Connor is Nathan's partner in the clinic," she explained. She turned her attention to Vickie. "Was everything okay at home?"

Vickie nodded. "There's been an attempt to flush a doll down the toilet, but the babysitter stopped it." She rolled her eyes and sipped her coffee. "I swear that child's going to be a submariner or an oceanographer. He's fascinated with water. We just recovered from the plumbing bill to reconnect the elbow pipe under the sink after Nathan had to take it apart to retrieve his watch."

Nathan grinned. "Have girls when you decide to

have babies," he advised Steve and Rosie. "In our experience, they're not as fascinated with flushing. Or does it make me sexist and oppressive to suggest that?"

Connor laughed. "Let's not even wonder about that. Sinatra's voice brings back a time when political correctness wasn't such an issue. Steve, I understand you're just back from the Middle East."

Vickie regaled Shelly and Rosie with more stories about her children. Rosie listened with one ear while watching the men in eager conversation. They seemed to be enjoying one another's company and, in the middle of what appeared to be a serious discussion, laughter erupted. Connor gave Steve's shoulder a fraternal slap and Rosie enjoyed the moment. She knew that one of Steve's complaints on the road was that friendships were hard to maintain. While it was true they all shared the difficulties and hardships together, when it came to getting the story, their jobs depended on reporting it first. While everyone understood that on principle, it was sometimes difficult to remember it when they were scooped. It sometimes made for hard feelings.

"Nice-looking man, your husband," Vickie said, leaning across the table toward Rosie to get her attention.

Rosie started guiltily. "Ah…yes, he is."

"He seems to like Jester. I ran into him at the town hall. I'm on Shelly's committee to count votes and implement the townspeople's decision. Steve and I talked a little. He's a sweetie as well as easy to look at."

Rosie was having difficulty remembering she'd been reluctant to come. In Los Angeles, she was so accustomed to attending events by herself, because Steve was away so much, that she dreaded being alone and, usually, bored at a fund-raiser or night at the theater where everyone was paired up. Everyone always asked about him, but understandably paid little attention to her, wrapped up in their own plans for the evening. It was wonderful to be here with Steve. And not simply because she didn't stand out as the woman alone, but because he was so attentive. She'd forgotten how soothing, how ego boosting that could be. He was always touching her, holding her, getting something for her. He listened with rapt attention when she spoke, and shared his observations on the evening with an insightful sense of humor. *This,* she thought, was the way she wanted to live the rest of her life. The women who fought for every woman's right to pursue a career and live life on her own terms might be horrified, but for her that meant a studio at home, a houseful of children and a husband who came home for dinner at six o'clock.

There was a cheer as the pastor returned and music began again. The men put aside their political discussion, and all three couples returned to the dance floor.

"You're smiling," Steve observed with his own smile. "Feather in your undies?"

She had to laugh at that image. "No. I'm having a good time. Shelly and Connor and the Perkinses are fun to be with." She'd intended to let it go at that, but saw in his eyes the conclusion that she was enjoying their company more than his. He'd been in Jester almost two weeks now and she'd resisted betraying any hope that their relationship could be restored. But he seemed to be so sincere in his efforts that she was beginning to re-think her position. It wasn't his fault that she'd thought him dead for three weeks, and if she loved him—and despite all her best efforts to convince herself that she didn't, she did—she was going to have to accept that he was what he was and she had no right to try to change that. "And," she added with a gusty sigh, "I've enjoyed being with you."

He stopped moving and stared at her. They stood, wrapped in each other's arms, as couples danced around them. "Did I hear you correctly?" he asked.

She tightened her grip on him. "Yes. In fact...I'm...I'm really glad you came to Jester."

She heard his intake of breath, felt his hand at her back turn to iron. "Can you...back that up with action?"

44   Her body slid against his as she rose on tiptoe to kiss him. He returned her kiss, lips, tongue striving to con-nect. Then they remembered where they were. She looked up to see that everyone around them had stopped to watch though the music played on.

He laughed lightly, muttered a swift "Excuse us," to Shelly and the others nearby, caught Rosie's hands and led her to the table to get her purse, then to the coatrack at the back of the church for her jacket.

They ran the block home in two minutes. Upstairs in the loft, her hair caught on the hook at the back of her black lace top and they wasted a precious few min-utes as he helped her disentangle it. Or maybe it wasn't wasted, she decided as she kissed his cheek as he tried to work with her fine hair and the delicate fabric. He groaned and she felt a certain satisfaction in torturing him as he'd tortured her since he'd arrived. When she was finally free, he helped her pull off the top, yank down the long skirt and slip, then stared with a sort of melting awe as she stood in black lace bikini and bra. She expected him to reach for her, but when his eyes went from her round bosom erupting from the top of her bra to her eyes, there was a reverence in them she remembered from the old days. She melted, too.

"I've dreamed of you like this for months," he said, holding a hand out to bring her to him.

She took it and flew into his arms. "Oh, Steve," she breathed, absorbing the blissful rediscovery of his hands sweeping down her back, tracing her backside and lingering there, reaching inside her leg. Even as his touch threatened to paralyze her, to take her where she hadn't been in months, she pulled at his shirt, needing the touch of his body against hers.

He stopped long enough to pull off his shirt and T-shirt while she unbuckled his belt. He almost lost all semblance of control when she lowered his zipper, but he struggled manfully to rid himself of the rest of his clothing as she threw the covers back. She fell backward, taking him with her, and they rolled into the middle, uncovered, unaware of the room's chill as heat filled them, fused them, exploded inside them.

Her life made sense again. Her art fulfilled her, the friends she'd made in Jester sustained her and the simple thrill of being part of the world was a blessing she recognized and was grateful for every moment. But Steve was her beating heart. He made her blood move, her breath flow. Her life, like her art, couldn't find its color without him.

They made love twice, and when they finally lay side by side, still wrapped in each other's arms, the only sad thought on her horizon was that she would have to leave Jester. But he was the backbone of his parents' operation, and it would be difficult for him to cover international news from the backwoods of Montana.

"What would you think," he asked, pushing her back against her pillow and leaning over her, "if I stayed in Jester?"

"What?" Rosie asked in disbelief. She pushed on his bare chest to break her body's contact with his so that she could concentrate on his shocking suggestion. "You'd be willing to move to Jester?"

46

Steve propped his elbow on the pillow beside her. "I would. It's a nice town. And with all the modern electronic amenities, I can still do my job. It's a little farther to the airport, but that's not a deal breaker."

Sun seemed to ooze out of her pores. She laughed. "I can't believe it!" She turned toward him to hug him fiercely. "That was the *only* hitch! I want us back together so badly, I was ready to go back to L.A., but dreading it." She leaned away from him, suddenly grave. "You're sure this will work for you? I mean, as much as I love it here, you can't give up everything. Please don't do this just to get me back, because in the end you'll be resentful and I..."

He put a fingertip to her lips to silence her. "It'll work. I'm not just doing it to get you back, because I really do like it here. And I won't be resentful." He, too, grew suddenly serious. "I hate it without you, Rosie."

She climbed atop him, half crying, half laughing. "I hate it without you, too. Oh, Steve, if we could stay here I'd be so happy."

"Then be happy," he said, pulling her down and entering her in one swift move that made her gasp then arch backward as pleasure raced toward her again. "Be happy," he whispered.

It was a miracle. It was the dead of winter with Christmas long past, but it was a miracle! After the bitterness of the past few months, Steve still loved her and wanted her back. And after the terrible fear of those three weeks and her decision never to put herself in the position of having to experience that again, she was putting herself on the line once more. She loved him too much to live without him, whatever it cost her.

And she could do it here, in Jester!

LATER THAT MORNING, Rosie painted large hearts with a book in each on the window of Ex Libris. Lettering wasn't her strong suit, but Amanda had given her a list of classics to fit as titles on the book covers. She'd expected it to be a tense and laborious project, but her soul was so full, her heart so light, that she stood back to examine her progress and decided that she was doing very well. Who knew, she asked herself with a smile, that love could improve one's ability to letter?

STEVE SAT CROSS-LEGGED in the middle of Rosie's bed and typed his story into his laptop. After all his research, his interviews and his personal investment in the town and its people, the words tripped off his fingers. Briefly, he profiled all the winners and talked about the long Jester ancestry enjoyed by almost everyone here. Because he'd finally talked Shelly into letting him focus his story on her, he wrote about how she'd grown up in the restaurant, found her own gift for cooking and hospitality even while she lost a part of her childhood to the demands of a growing business.

He talked about the efforts she'd made to turn her coffee shop into an upscale eating establishment and the disappointment she'd felt when her customers pleaded for a return to the basic menu her parents had made popular. Knowledge of her clientele and her sincere affection for them had convinced her to concede to their wishes. The Brimming Cup was, after all, the cradle of Jester events, the clearinghouse of news and gossip, the daytime social center of the community.

He'd gotten lost, he explained in his article, in the tempo and politics of the world. It was easy to forget, he wrote, that the world is made up of neighborhoods like downtown Jester. When politicians are in charge, people starve and go to war. When people are in charge, they reach out to one another, help one another, love one another.

He spell-checked, made one more pass through, then filed the story. He was surprised when he went downstairs to make himself a well-deserved cup of coffee, to find that snow was falling. It drifted down in silent grace and made him wish that Rosie was here so that they could make love while watching it.

But she was working. He had gained a new appreciation for her abilities, however commercial the window painting was, when he saw shoppers stop to watch her and kibitz, shop owners walk out of their stores to spur her on and praise her for the beautifully made hearts that now filled downtown Jester.

Well, he thought philosophically as he shrugged into his jacket, he could get her a cup of tea from Shelly and maybe earn a kiss and a promise for later. This was the last place in the world he'd expected to end up, he thought as old snow crunched underfoot as he made his way to the Cup. The new stuff was big and fluffy and the sky dark with more of it, though it was only midafternoon. He expected that by nightfall it would be a full-blown blizzard.

He stopped in front of the Cup, stomped his feet on the mat to leave the snow outside and walked in.

ROSIE'S FINGERS TREMBLED while she painted hearts, and it wasn't the sudden drop in temperature. After several hours of euphoria at her reconciliation with Steve, she was coming down to earth. There were urgent matters she had to take care of. Having her husband back in her life was something so wonderful, something she hadn't expected to happen at this point in time, that she felt like a furnace pipe rattling with the power of the ignited firebox. But the trembling was more than that. She hadn't been completely honest with him. At first, she hadn't thought it necessary because she knew he was angry with her and thought he'd followed her simply to berate her, and that, bored by the small town he'd simply threaten to countersue for divorce and be gone.

But he'd liked it here. And he'd wanted her back with a determination that was a part of that rattling force inside her. Then she'd kept the secret to herself because she was falling in love all over again, and knowing love to be a fragile and tenuous thing, she waited for the right moment, the natural opening to the subject. But it hadn't come. And now she had to make the moment.

When he suddenly appeared beside her as though she'd conjured him up herself, she stared at him in worried surprise. He raised an eyebrow and held up the paper cup with its heat-protective cuff. "You remember me?" he teased. "Purveyor of tea, or whatever else I can interest you in in the middle of Main Street at two-thirty in the afternoon." He lowered his voice and waggled his eyebrows as he added that last, and she found herself distracted by the velvet darkness of his eyes and the seductive quality of his voice, even though the theatrical tone was teasing. She forgot where she was and remembered only that last night that voice hadn't been teasing, and guessed that if she did lean into his arms he might kiss her even though every merchant in every shop up and down the street was probably peering through her hearts right now to see what she and Steve were doing.

Then Amanda's voice interrupted them with a teasing "Oh, for heaven's sake, get a room!" Then she laughed and said cheerfully, "Will you look at this snow? Everyone in town is going to be worried about staying warm tonight, but I'll bet you two won't. Love's a miracle of thermal units gone wild."

Steve laughed and Rosie was about to join them when Amanda raised the book she'd held at her side and swept it out, title uppermost, to offer it to Rosie.

Time stopped. Rosie's air left her as though a giant hand had slapped her silly and collapsed her lungs. Oh, no! Oh, no! she thought in urgent desperation even as she saw Steve's eyes follow the arc of Amanda's hand as she offered Rosie the book she'd ordered three weeks ago. It was upside down for him, and she saw him tilt his head to read the title. How could her heart keep beating, she wondered absently, when she wasn't getting any air?

"Your book's arrived," Amanda said to Rosie, completely unaware that she was about to cut the ground out from under Rosie's feet. "I'm sorry it took so long. This sells so well that my distributor is always out of it, and of course, because we're out in the boonies, the big chains and the shops with a lot of volume get the good stuff first."

"What To Expect," Steve read the title aloud, his laughing expression of a moment ago now changed to questioning confusion, *"When You're Expecting."*

But he was a smart man. It took just a moment for it to sink in. Then his expression grew darker than the storm-filled sky overhead. Rosie had a horrible, intuitive feeling that all her claims since he'd arrived had been prophetic. It *was* over. He caught a glimpse of Amanda's horrified expression as she realized that Steve hadn't known, and gave her a pat on the arm that absolved her of all responsibility.

Rosie closed her eyes and waited for the thunder.

"You're pregnant?" Steve demanded, snatching the book from Amanda's hand.

"Rosie, I'm so sorry!" Amanda whispered.

Steve turned to her and asked with strained civility, "Would you excuse us, please?"

At Rosie's nod, she went back inside the shop.

More than anything, Steve hated being stupid. Remembering Rosie's pallor, her soupy eyes, her unwillingness to eat much of anything, he couldn't imagine why he'd swallowed the story that she had a cold. She hadn't coughed or sneezed; there'd just been a pervading look of discomfort about her, that he'd sometimes wondered if his presence here was partially responsible for. Hating to admit that to himself, he'd happily believed she was ill with something simple like a cold. But it wasn't a cold. Rosie, who'd left him for doing his job, scared him to death with her absence until he found her in Jester, had lied to him for months.

"Well?" he prompted angrily. "Are you far enough along that the baby is mine?"

Asking Rosie if the baby was his had been low and cruel, Steve knew as he watched anger and hurt feelings war for supremacy in her eyes. But he was in no mood to be civil, much less polite. And he wasn't sure what he feared most—that she'd known for four months that she was pregnant and hadn't bothered to tell him because she'd intended to leave him, or that the pregnancy was more recent than that and the baby was another man's.

He got his answer to that when she doubled her fist and punched him right in the gut. It might have rocked him had he not still been rooted to the spot with righteous indignation.

"Of course it's yours, you idiot!" she screamed at him. She gestured widely with the hot tea in her left hand and it flew in a wide arc and fell to the snow, melting it in a half-moon pattern. Furiously she threw the cup. "You take off like…like Captain Adventure and do your important work and never stop to think what it's like for me! You were gone a long time! I didn't even know I was pregnant when you left. Then, I'd hear from you through your mom and I didn't want to tell her before you knew. Then you were in one hot spot after another, and I was afraid the news would…would distract you." Her voice cracked and her lips trembled as she raged on. "Then I thought you were dead! I thought our life together was over!"

He made himself calm down in the face of her formidable anger. "But you learned I wasn't dead. Why didn't you tell me then?"

"Because I was still hearing from you through your mother!" she screamed at him. He realized absently that they were collecting a small crowd of onlookers. "And while I was happy you were alive, I was beginning to realize I couldn't live with you anymore. And I was mad enough to run away so I could decide privately what I wanted to do."

"But I came to find you!" he reminded her, forgetting his efforts to quiet down. "I've been with you for two weeks! We made plans to get back together, but you still didn't tell me."

"Because I wanted us to reconcile because you wanted me, not because you knew I was pregnant."

"I have always loved you!" he roared at her. "Wherever the hell I am, I love you!"

She folded her arms and studied him warily, large tears standing in her eyes. "I know that. I also know how devoted you are to what you do, and that loving me has never stopped you from doing it, no matter how hard it is on our marriage. I was torn between wanting to be with you because I love you and wanting a different life for our baby. I wanted to be able to tell you with great joy, and…I just wasn't sure how things were going to go."

That made a sort of perverted sense, but there was a significant flaw in her argument. "But last night I told you I wanted to stay. And you still didn't tell me."

She nodded feebly. "Because we were in each other's arms, and I wasn't sure you'd still mean it in the light of day."

That was when he lost it. He'd had a tenuous grip on his temper at best, but he'd wanted to hear her out. Now he didn't trust himself to remain within reach of her. "I wasn't sure you'd still mean it in the light of day," she'd said. That was like calling him a liar. Him, a reporter respected for his attention to detail in the interest of presenting the most honest story possible. What was left of their relationship, he wondered, if she didn't trust him enough, didn't believe enough in his declaration of love, to tell him she was carrying his baby?

Rosie watched him storm away through the thickening snow and opened her mouth to call him back, but the rising wind tore his name from her lips. She packed up her paints and went home, half expecting to find him stuffing his things into his suitcase. But he wasn't there.

By seven o'clock that evening, she was convinced that he'd flown back to L.A. without his things. The house was deathly quiet and the snow drifting past the windows contributed to her sense of isolation. Bill Matisse sat curled up in the middle of her bed while she worked on the painting. At least she'd finally figured out what was wrong with it. Curious that pain was often more enlightening than joy. The telephone rang and Rosie put her brush down. She was shocked to hear Steve's mother's voice.

"Rosie!" Ellie Sutton was a tall, elegant woman with a lively intelligence and a despotic approach in the newsroom. She'd always been warm and kind to Rosie, though they had very little in common. "Hi! Can I talk to Steve, please?"

"Hi, Ellie," Rosie replied, forcing her voice to rise to a note of cheer. "He's…not here." He's probably on his way back to L.A., she thought, but didn't say it aloud.

"Would you have him call me?" Ellie asked, and before Rosie could decide whether or not to be honest with her and tell her he probably wouldn't be coming back, Steve's mother said, "I can't tell you how happy his father and I are that you're getting back together. I know you're two very different people, but you've always been so good for him, and he adores you."

Rosie could only presume that Ellie's last conversation with her son had taken place before today. But Ellie destroyed that notion by adding, "And congratulations on the baby! We're very excited at the prospect of being grandparents."

As far as Rosie could tell, there was no suggestion in her voice that Steve had been unhappy when he'd reported that news. "When did you speak to him?" Rosie couldn't help asking.

"This afternoon," Ellie replied. "And tell him that I've cashed in his profit-sharing and transferred it electronically to his bank account. But I forgot to ask if he wants some of the stock liquidated or just left alone."

Rosie was sure when she mentioned stock, she wasn't talking cattle. Why was Steve liquidating stock and cashing in his profit-sharing? Then it occurred to her with chilling certainty. Of course. He'd always fantasized about buying a place in London and writing a novel.

"I'll have him call you," she promised, having to clear her throat.

"You sound awful, Rosie," Ellie said candidly. "If it's any comfort, you should be feeling much better any day now. I was the soda-cracker queen until my fifth month, then I was invincible. Give Steve a hug for me, will you?"

"Yeah," she whispered, and hung up the phone. And the reality of what she'd done to Steve and their marriage closed in on her. Thanks to her selfishness and cowardice, she was facing a future alone with her baby's father across an ocean.

Feeling light-headed, she remembered that she hadn't eaten lunch, and while she wasn't particularly hungry, she knew she had to eat for the baby's sake. She went down to the kitchen, put on the kettle and stared desultorily at the contents of the refrigerator. Since Steve had been cooking, there was more there than there had been before, but nothing appealed to her. She opened the refrigerator, found several leftover pieces of the promised cheesecake and dug in the utensil drawer for a fork. She was carrying it to the table when the kitchen door burst open and Steve walked in, arms filled with grocery bags.

For a moment, she could only stare at him. He kicked the door closed with his foot and took the groceries to the counter, trailing ice and snow as he went. He took an envelope out of the pocket of his jacket and handed it to her. She backed away from him, fresh tears filling her eyes. In true protective fashion, he was going to stock her shelves with provisions and pay her child support before taking off for Europe. "I don't want it," she whispered, then remembered to add, "Thank you, though."

Generally he was a peaceful man, Steve thought, but this woman could drive him crazy. He tried to remember that she was pregnant and therefore hormonally challenged. And that she always looked so anguished when she talked about that three-week period when he'd been stuck in the mountains of Afghanistan and she'd thought he was dead.

"How do you know you don't want it," he asked reasonably, "if you don't look inside to see what it is?"

She looked at the envelope he held out as though it

could bite her. Then she looked at him, her eyes miserable. "It's a check." She sounded so sure.

"It's not a check," he assured her.

"Then what is it?"

He expelled a breath and prayed for patience. "What do you want most in all the world?" he asked.

"You," she replied, surprising him. He knew she loved him despite all the junk that had gone on between them, but he hadn't expected her to admit it, and without even stopping to think about it. She burst into sobs. "I don't want groceries or child support. I just want you here for me and for the baby!"

He went to wrap her in his arms and hold her close. "It's the deed to this house," he said, kissing the top of her head. "Shelly put me on to your landlord, who met me at his lawyer's, and it's done. It's ours. I figured while you're painting upstairs, I'm going to work on a novel down here. I'll have mornings and you can have afternoons, or the other way around, while the other's with the baby."

Rosie swallowed, joy so strong it was a pain in the center of her chest. "But...you were so angry with me."

He nodded, his expression firm. "I still am." He admitted with a shrug of self-deprecation, "But I know you're also justified in being angry with me. I'm sorry I've been out there doing what I do, taking risks to try to stay on top, when you're right—I do have a few things to prove to you. Primarily that I love you very much, that I'm really happy about the baby and I want to be here for both of you."

Rosie kissed him soundly and clung to him. She may

not have been one of the purchasers of the winning lottery ticket, but she felt very much like one of the Main Street Millionaires.

Steve swept her up in his arms and carried her upstairs. He was placing her in the middle of the bed when he noticed that she'd been working on the painting. He ignored her playful protest as he abandoned her for a closer look at the canvas on the easel. As he saw what she'd done, his hand went to his heart where a little fire was building. She'd figured it out. Added to the underpainting was…him! Standing on the corner, talking to Shelly. And on Rosie's back as she worked across the street was a baby in a backpack.

THE END

Originally published as an online read for
www.eHarlequin.com

Here's a sneak peek...

60

Season of Shadows
by
Muriel Jensen

She was getting close to the truth...maybe too close.

CHAPTER 1

At first, Kay Florio thought the smudge of red on Maple Hill Lake was the bobber on a fishing line. Then she realized there was no boat, no fisherman patiently waiting for a bite. She put the camera to her eye and let the auto-focus do its thing. The zoom lens she was using to get pictures of the community Labor Day celebration going on at the head of the lake brought in a clear image of the calm water.

She scanned back and forth, up and down, looking for that spot of red. It appeared suddenly in the center of the frame, a shock of sopping red hair atop the head of a small child whose little face was screwed up as she screamed soundlessly for help. Then the small head disappeared into the water.

"Oh, my God!" Kay's exclamation also carried no sound as the high school band struck up a Sousa tune. She tried anyway, shouting, "Help! Somebody!" and pointing to where she'd last seen the child.

But everyone gathered for the annual Maple Hill, Massachusetts, celebration was focused in the other

direction on the music being played in the newly installed bandstand. She noticed absently that the bright
sunlight flared off the polished instruments, off the
chrome and windshields on all the cars parked in the
lot and on Lake Road, off soda cans, sunglasses and
watchbands.

She experienced one instant of denial. She saw
Betsy's face superimposed on the little redhead's,
and felt all the old terror, guilt and inexplicable misery rise up to clog her throat and start that thumping
in her head that would take days to quiet.

Then the need to help *this* little girl forced that
aside. Kay held the camera against her chest as she
ran up the paved road until she was parallel to the
child. She whipped off her camera, put it down in the
grass and cursed the extra minute required to pull off
her hiking boots.

As she did that, a figure burst out of the trees
nearby and leapt into the water. Kay caught a quick
glimpse of a man in khaki shorts, a white T-shirt, big,
bare feet. And a slight limp. He sliced neatly through
the water at considerable speed, diving under like a
cormorant near the spot where the little redhead had
disappeared.

Her heart and her head thumping, Kay yanked up
her camera and focused on the spot, waiting, pray-
ing. Her whole body trembled in anticipation, and in
renewal of the old memories she always thought
she'd accepted—until something brought them up

again and made her wish she'd died instead of her little sister.

The man shot up out of the lake, water spewed in all directions, the little girl in one arm. Kay snapped the shutter.

One boot on, one boot off, she steadied herself for another shot as the man turned onto his back, clutching the seemingly lifeless child to his chest and began to swim to the shore, his free arm pumping strongly.

Kay was knocked off balance as a veritable wave of humanity raced past her, crowded around her. Someone at the celebration must have seen the man go into the water and alerted everyone else.

Her view of the drama completely obstructed, she tried to elbow her way through the crowd. It was impossible. She heard a woman's voice raised in fear, shouting, "Misty! Misty! Oh, my God! Oh, please!"

Looping the camera around her neck, she got a foothold at the base of a sturdy maple, reached up for a low-hanging branch and pulled herself into the tree. As she climbed, thanking heaven for her aerobics class and good muscle tone, she heard the crowd directing the man.

"Here! Over here! Lift her up!"

Holding tightly to the tree with one arm, Kay leaned through the leaves, her camera held as steadily as possible, and waited for a shot.

The man appeared suddenly in the viewfinder, wet hair plastered to his head, face set in anguished lines. He raised the limp little body in long, strong arms. Kay shot again as another man dangled over the bank, supported by bystanders, and took the child from him. She snapped the shutter on the dangling man, wondering if his grim expression identified him as the little girl's father.

That question was answered for her when a young blond woman, still crying out, "Misty!" knelt beside him on the bank as he leaned over the little body. "She's dead!" she shrieked. "Yale, she's dead!"

"Watch out. Let me have a look." Randy Stanton gently pushed the mother aside. Kay recognized him as an EMT with the Maple Hill Fire Department, though today he'd been a civilian manning the barbecue for the community picnic.

64 Randy put his ear to the child's lips, then to her heart. He tipped her head back slightly, held her nose closed and breathed twice into her mouth. One long-fingered hand applied compressions high on the small body, then he breathed into her mouth again.

The world fell silent while he worked, three pumps on the tiny chest to one breath. There wasn't a murmur in the crowd, just the sound of a breeze in the trees, the distant whoosh of traffic on the highway, the flat sound of a duck somewhere on the other end of the lake.

Then out of the relative quiet came a little gasp, a cough, the screech of a child now fully awake and screaming to the world her indignation at its treatment of her.

The mother held her close, sobbing hysterically.

The father wrapped his arms around Randy. Kay kept shooting.

She scanned right, looking for the rescuer, her journalist's brain already making up the front page, placing photos. She had to have the rescuer, but he wasn't there.

She dropped the camera to her chest and pushed a branch aside for a better view of the water, certain she hadn't seen him climb onto the bank. Nothing.

People were now following the parents and the weeping child back toward the parking lot. There was the distant wail of a siren. Kay watched the crowd go, searching it for the man's wet head, for square shoulders in a sopping white T-shirt, but she saw none.

Cursing the undeniable truth that climbing out of a tree was much more difficult than climbing into it, she finally swung from a bottom branch and landed with a bone-rattling thump on her unevenly shod feet.

Was Misty's rescuer a shy hero? she wondered. The little girl's parents hadn't noticed him in their concern for their daughter, but Kay was sure once a doctor declared the little girl healthy, they'd want to thank him. And his identity was critical to Kay's story.

All right. This could be good. She had a mystery, something else to think about so that all her memories of her little sister didn't come crowding in and make her hate herself all over again. Once a day for the past eighteen years was certainly enough.

"Kay!" Haley Megrath, the publisher of the *Maple Hill Mirror* and Kay's boss, came running toward her through the retreating crowd. She wore a blue-and-white Hawaiian print top over white cropped pants, her long, dark hair caught up in a knot. Except for the bright little girl bouncing up and down in her arms as she ran, Haley looked more like a surfer than the publisher of the local paper. But she'd proven time and again that looks were deceiving. "Did you get a shot?" she asked hopefully, stopping a foot from Kay. Henrietta, her little girl, gave Kay a big baby-toothed grin. "Tell me you got a shot."

66

Kay held up her camera. "Got it." She capped her lens, then patted it. "That was front-page stuff, Haley." She smiled at the toddler, who spent a lot of time in a playpen in the *Mirror*'s office. "From the man jumping into the water, to him handing her to her father. At least, I think that was her father."

"That was her father." Haley swept one hand in a gesture of helplessness and hoisted Henri a little higher onto her hip. "I missed everything. I'm trying desperately to make some headway in Henri's potty training, and took her to the ladies' room. By the time we heard the commotion and found the crowd, the ambulance arrived and everyone was heading for the parking lot."

"So, you know the little girl?" Kay asked, taking

a small notebook out of the large leather tote that served as purse and camera bag.

"Misty O'Neil. Her father worked for Hank for a while, but I think he's employed by the city now. Jackie would know."

Hank was Haley's brother, Hank Whitcomb, former NASA engineer turned local entrepreneur. Four years ago, he came home to start Whitcomb's Wonders, a unique collection of men who provided various skills required to maintain a home or business—plumbing, wiring, painting and papering, gardening, janitorial services. Most of the men he employed worked part-time because they were finishing an education, raising a family or fulfilling other pursuits and obligations.

As Kay recalled from a story she'd recently done about the service, Hank had also added a security team just two years ago.

He was not only a business success, but a personal one, as well. After returning home, he married Jackie Fortin, his high school sweetheart, and was raising her four children—a big job considering Jackie was also mayor of Maple Hill.

"The big mystery," Kay went on as they started back toward the group at the head of the lake, "is who jumped in after Misty. I've never seen him before, and he just disappeared."

"That was Jack Keaton," Haley said.

"How do you know that?" Kay asked, "if you weren't even here?"

"Because as I was running this way, I overheard one of Hank's guys say that Jack Keaton jumped in to save Misty."

"Jack Keaton." Kay repeated the unfamiliar name. "What's he do?"

"He works for Hank. Painting."

"Okay. I'm going to pay a call on him and see if he'll let me get a picture, give me some personal information."

"Good. I'm up to my ears with the back-to-school feature. This is great front-page stuff, especially since it all turned out well. Can't beat a hero story."

"Yeah. I got some good shots of Randy at work, too." At Haley's blank look, Kay explained, "Randy Stanton did CPR on Misty, brought her back. You really did miss everything."

"That's what motherhood does to you."

Kay was grateful motherhood wasn't in her future.

...NOT THE END...

Look for Season of Shadows *in bookstores June 2005 from Signature Select™.*

SPOTLIGHT

National bestselling author

JOANNA WAYNE

The Gentlemen's Club

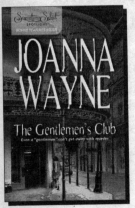

A homicide in the French Quarter of New Orleans has attorney Rachel Powers obsessed with finding the killer. As she investigates, she is shocked to discover that some of the Big Easy's most respected gentlemen will go to any lengths to satisfy their darkest sexual desires. Even murder.

A gripping new novel... coming in June.

Bonus Features, including:

Author Interview, Romance— New Orleans Style, and Bonus Read!

HARLEQUIN®
® *Live the emotion™*

COLLECTION

Nothing is what it seems...

SMOKESCREEN

An exciting NEW anthology featuring talented Silhouette Bombshell® authors...

Doranna Durgin
Meredith Fletcher
Vicki Hinze

Three women with remarkable abilities...

Three explosive situations that
only they can defuse...

Three riveting new stories that you will love!

> **Bonus Features,
> including:**
>
> **Author Interview**
>
> **Sneak Peek
> and Fearless Females**

Where love comes alive™

SCSR

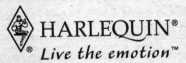

THE F**O**RTUNES OF TEXAS:™
Reunion

The price of privilege. The power of family.

**Your favorite family returns
in a twelve-book collection with a
new story every month starting this June.**

$1.⁰⁰ OFF

the purchase of *Cowboy at Midnight*
by *USA TODAY*
bestselling author Ann Major.

5 65373 00076 2 (8100) 0 11159

Visit Silhouette Books at
www.eHarlequin.com

Silhouette®

Where love comes alive™

THE FORTUNES OF TEXAS: Reunion

The price of privilege. The power of family.

Your favorite family returns in a twelve-book collection with a new story every month starting this June.

$1.⁰⁰ OFF

the purchase of *Cowboy at Midnight*
by *USA TODAY*
bestselling author Ann Major.

```
52605954
```

Visit Silhouette Books
at www.eHarlequin.com

Where love comes alive™

©2005 Harlequin Enterprises Ltd